D1715400

Hard-Luck Diggings

The Early Jack Vance

Edited by Terry Dowling and Jonathan Strahan

SUBTERRANEAN PRESS • 2010

First Edition

ISBN
978-1-59606-301-3

Acknowledgments

"Hard-Luck Diggings" first appeared in *Startling Stories* for July 1948; "The Temple of Han" originally appeared in *Planet Stories* for July 1951; "The Masquerade on Dicantropus" was first published in *Startling Stories* for September 1951; "Abercrombie Station" first appeared in *Thrilling Wonder Stories* for February 1952; "Three-Legged Joe" first saw publication in *Startling Stories* for January 1953; "DP!" originally appeared in *Avon Science Fiction and Fantasy Reader*, Vol 2, edited by Donald A. Wollheim, Avon Books, April 1953; "Sjambak" first appeared in *Worlds of If* for July 1953; "Shape-Up" was first published in *Cosmos Science Fiction and Fantasy* for November 1953; "The Absent-Minded Professor" originally appeared as "First Star I See Tonight" in *Malcolm's Mystery Magazine* for March 1954 (under the pseudonym John Van See); "When the Five Moons Rise" first appeared in *Cosmos Science Fiction and Fantasy* for March 1954; "The Devil on Salvation Bluff" originally appeared in *Star Science Fiction Stories, No 3*, edited by Frederik Pohl, Ballantine Books 1955; "The Phantom Milkman" was originally published in *Other Worlds Science Fiction* for February 1956; "Where Hesperus Falls" first appeared in *Fantastic Universe* for October 1956; "Dodkin's Job" originally appeared in *Astounding Science Fiction* for October 1959.

Quoted material from Jack Vance comes from *This Is Me, Jack Vance!*, Subterranean Press, 2009, the Introduction to *The Dark Side of the Moon*, Underwood Miller, 1992, and from conversations between Jack Vance and Terry Dowling, December 1995.

Subterranean Press
PO Box 190106
Burton, MI 48519

www.subterraneanpress.com

Table of Contents

Introduction

"I plead youth, inexperience and good intentions."

—Jack Vance

In the opening pages of his 2009 autobiography, *This Is Me, Jack Vance!*, the author reminds us that "Like any craft, writing is mastered by practice and patience, and if one has any 'knack' for it at all, that very knack—paradoxically—can explicate everything under the sun but itself."

That said, when you assemble a collection of stories from the first dozen years of any writer's career, you cannot help but find the author learning his or her craft, refining process, improving techniques for delivering narrative, creating characters, mastering dialog and motivation, invariably locking in favorite themes and preoccupations as well; in short, revealing the basic shape, form and direction of what that career will most likely become.

As well as delivering fine vintage entertainment from one of the true Grand Masters of science fiction and fantasy, that's the other thing you'll find in this collection. In a real sense, these stories show Vance working to become a "million-word-a-year-man" so he could pay the mortgage, buy the groceries, travel the world, eventually build his own private "dream castle" and start a family with his wife Norma.

In doing this, like any writer serious about staying in the game, he targeted the available venues of the day, doing what was required to cater to the tastes of the various editors and their readerships, while at the same time bringing his own special way of doing things to the table so that his name, in modern marketing parlance, stood a chance of becoming a viable "brand."

Fans of Vance's work know only too well how he succeeded at this task, and how, for reasons both practical and artistic, he quickly made the novel, often novels in series, his preferred form. The shorter, always interesting but far less lucrative work received less and less attention and was soon set aside altogether.

But as so many writers have said, it is in the shorter and mid-length work that the craft is best learned: the practicalities of economy, pacing and narrative style, the versatility and adaptability, how to manage the hook, the tease, everything from mastering point of view to self-editing for greatest effect. When reading (or re-reading) the stories featured here, all of these things are on show.

To take it further, the following selection illustrates the useful writing workshop corollary that you write short stories for the reputation and longer work to pay the mortgage. Novels take skill, ideas and time. Short stories take skill, ideas and *much less time*. You can afford to try different things, take risks, make mistakes, get feedback sooner. These stories, with their range and variety, show how Vance's shorter tales were first the mainstay then, with the "brand" sufficiently in place, became the other thing he did because there were often quick dollars to be made, invitations from editors, ideas that didn't require amplification beyond a certain point. Inevitably, those smaller notions and nifty ideas were incorporated into the plots of the longer work, and the shorter form became first a rarity, then a thing of the past.

This becomes even more evident when we put the stories in *Hard-Luck Diggings* in context and remember the other storytelling projects Vance was engaged in around the time of their writing, so that the nature of the output and the sheer "coal-face" experimentation going on can be seen as part of a definite rising curve of commitment, skill and confidence.

Our title story, for instance, was produced several years after Jack had already completed the suite of stories that would be published by Hillman in 1950 as *The Dying Earth*, and do so much to establish the Vance "brand." With its action adventure approach and spare delivery, "Hard-Luck Diggings" sits in striking contrast to those wry, lyrical, bittersweet pieces.

"Abercrombie Station", with its feisty female lead off to make her fortune among the Solar System's elite, appeared the same year that *Thrilling Wonder Stories* published "Big Planet", detailing the adventures of a handful of stranded space-travellers trekking across that enormous world. So, too, "Where Hesperus Falls" delivered its minor riff on the less salutary aspects of immortality in 1956, the same year that the rich and memorable immortality novel, *To Live Forever*, saw print. "Dodkin's Job" was published the year following "The Miracle Workers" and *The Languages of Pao*, and so on.

With this in mind, let's return now to the first twelve years of Vance's writing career to when the adventure was just beginning, to when the shorter works weren't the rarity, and any success at all was very likely counted success enough.

"Hard-Luck Diggings" originally appeared in *Startling Stories* for July 1948 when the author was in his early thirties, and is a no-nonsense who (or what) done it that was the initial outing for the author's earliest interstellar sleuth, Magnus Ridolph, complete with a wholly appropriate tip of the hat to Arthur Conan Doyle's Sherlock Holmes in its opening lines. Written soon after his time in the merchant marine, it was Jack's fifth story sale, an exotic puzzle story that, in the best pulp traditions of *Weird Tales* and *Blue Book*, might as easily have been set in the Amazon or darkest Africa as outer space. Ridolph's arrival at the site of his first investigation might be in humanity's interstellar future, but this is very much the space age with slide-rules, where a spaceship smells of "hot oil, men, carbolic acid, paint", giving us a taste of life aboard the more conventional freighters of the author's recent first-hand experience.

"The Temple of Han" was first published in *Planet Stories* for July 1951. It features another of Vance's competent, resourceful heroes in a rather dazzling trans-galactic adventure originally titled "The God and the Temple Robber", and was written in 1946 when Jack was 30 as part of an early, subsequently discarded novel. As well as being a quick-sketch tale tailored to the demands of the magazine market, the pacing, narrative economy and author confidence here are quite impressive, techniques well in advance of the rather conventional adventure storyline to which they are applied.

"The Masquerade on Dicantropus" originally appeared in *Startling Stories* for September 1951 and is a modest xenological mystery with a simple setting-up and, for modern readers, a simple enough resolution. Once again it's Vance writing according to perceived structures and expectations, though, again, we see that his economy of delivery, his sure-handedness with quick-sketch characters and dialog were there from the first, however slight, even perfunctory, the tale being told. "Masquerade" is of additional interest because of how the story's final reveal was used eleven years later in the author's Hugo-winning short novel *The Dragon Masters*.

While many of the earlier Vance stories show the lean, "steam and rivets" quality suited to the markets of the day, we can see how quickly the author hits his stride by comparing, say, "Hard-Luck Diggings" with "Abercrombie Station" when it appeared four years later in *Thrilling Wonder Stories* for February 1952. Given the additional length, and the fact that the story (and/or the author, to make that crucial distinction) was judged a sufficient draw-card to warrant the extra space, "Abercrombie Station" is a different order of achievement entirely, filled with assured characterization, an easy wit and an authorial voice comfortable with the added room to move. A second Jean Parlier adventure, "Cholwell's Chickens", appeared later the same year.

"Three-Legged Joe" first appeared in *Startling Stories* for January 1953 and is in many ways the classic "gadget story", to use Vance's own term for much of his early work. If "Hard-Luck Diggings" might as easily have been set in the Amazon, then "Three-Legged Joe" is a backwoods tall story, very much the "fairy-tale stuff" Milke describes it as to his partner Paskell on the lonely, supposedly dead world Odfars. Given Vance's flair for humor and witty dialog, it is easy to find similar "tall story" variations in his subsequent work, as with, say, the Bugardoig episode in *The Book of Dreams* nearly thirty years later.

"DP!" originally appeared in *Avon Science Fiction and Fantasy Reader*, Vol 2, in April 1953. Addressing subject matter that is as topical now as the day it was written, it was completed while the Vances were staying in the village of Fulpmes in the Austrian Tyrol in 1951, turned out in the same spate of writing that produced Jack's young adult novel, *Vandals of the Void*. As an interesting side-note, this particular tale remains one of Harlan Ellison's all-time favorite Vance stories.

"Sjambak" was first published in *Worlds of If* for July 1953. Despite a somewhat perfunctory ending (if ever a Vance story cried out for an extra thousand words, this is it), we have a beguiling, transplanted terrestrial culture and an intriguing example of the close cultural observation that would remain such an important trademark feature throughout the author's long career.

"Shape-Up" first appeared in *Cosmos Science Fiction and Fantasy* for November 1953. While the plot relies on a point of astral physics that seems all too obvious in hindsight, its staging is intriguing to the point of being compelling, even disturbing, a reminder too that many of Jack's stories were designed along the lines of classic mysteries because of his own great love for the form.

"The Absent-Minded Professor" (the author's preferred title) originally appeared as "First Star I See Tonight" in *Malcolm's Mystery Magazine* for March 1954 under the pseudonym John Van See. Again, it shows a true mystery writer's delight in creating situations where the schemer is caught out by his own schemes, both something his all-time favorite creation Cugel the Clever would specialize in eleven years later, and a reminder that the author's mystery novels, *The Fox Valley Murders* and *A Room to Die In* (under the Ellery Queen byline) among them, would turn upon situations where characters sought to carry out perfect crimes, only to be brought undone. This modest but elegant sampling of the form is one of the author's personal favorites, and lets Vance revel in his lifelong love of astronomy.

"When the Five Moons Rise" was first published in the March 1954 issue of *Cosmos Science Fiction and Fantasy*, and possesses the sort of eerie, unsettling quality Vance brings to so many of his tales set on alien worlds. This account of the fortunes of the occupants of a lonely lighthouse charged with safeguarding mariners sailing an alien ocean has much of the force and suspense of Wilfrid Wilson Gibson's haunting 1912 poem "Flannan Isle." Here, too, it is the mood and staging as much as plot that accounts for its effectiveness.

"The Devil on Salvation Bluff" first appeared in *Star Science Fiction Stories, No 3* in 1955 and showcases a key axiom demonstrated in almost all of the author's science fiction at novel length: alien worlds will invariably lead to alien ways and, in time, an alien humanity. This story enacts the process in a potent miniature form.

"The Phantom Milkman" originally appeared in *Other Worlds Science Fiction* for February 1956. Simple, linear and effective, it is based on a rather odd event in Vance's own life while on his way to Mexico with wife Norma and Frank and Beverly Herbert, and was published the same year as *To Live Forever*.

"Where Hesperus Falls" first appeared in *Fantastic Universe* for October 1956, and is, on the one hand, a thoughtful, bitter tale of disillusionment and personal obsession; on the other, a relaxed, confident if curious return to the "gadget" angle of the earlier work.

Completing our line-up is another of Jack's favorites, written when the author was in his early forties. "Dodkin's Job" originally saw print in *Astounding Science Fiction* for October 1959, and in a world where an unspecified "they" are still held accountable for so much—"Look what *they* did!" "*They* don't know what *they*'re doing!"—it holds as much irony now as when it was published half a century ago.

And a healthy sense of irony, a delight in wonder, a regard for craft, and a wholly allowable forbearance, are appropriate for approaching this sprightly, rag-tag bunch, this motley crew to push an entirely allowable seafaring, starfaring metaphor.

And to borrow one or two more, *Hard-Luck Diggings* becomes a kind of fireside archaeology, an agreeable armchair tour of how the Jack Vance enterprise came to be. It may be a "warts and all" tour at times, but it's also full of zest and life, the thrill of the upward climb, of so much more to be done. As such, this is a book to be approached and savored with a twinkle in the eye, a knowing smile, but most of all, with an appropriate love of adventure and high romance firmly in place.

Terry Dowling & Jonathan Strahan
Sydney and Perth, September 2009

Hard-Luck Diggings

In solving a problem, I form and consider every conceivable premise. If each of these results in an impossible set of implications, except one, whose consequence is merely improbable: then that lone hypothesis, no matter how unprecedented, is necessarily the correct solution of the problem.

—*Magnus Ridolph*

Superintendent James Rogge's office occupied the top of a low knoll at Diggings A, and his office, through a semi-circular window, overlooked both diggings, A and B, all the way down to the beach and the strange-colored ocean beyond.

Rogge sat within, chair turned to the window, drumming his fingers in quick irregular tempo. Suddenly he jumped to his feet and strode across the room. He was tall and thin, and his black eyes sparkled in a face parched and bony, while his chin dished out below his mouth like a shovel-blade.

He punched a button at the telescreen, waited, leaning slightly forward, his finger still holding down the button. There was no response. The screen hummed quietly, but remained ash-gray, dead.

Rogge clenched his fists. "What a demoralized outfit! Won't even answer the screen."

As he turned his back, the screen came alive. Rogge swung around, clasped his hands behind his back. "Well?"

"Sorry, Mr. Rogge, but they've just found another," panted the cadet engineer. Rogge stiffened. "Where, this time?"

"In the shower room. He'd just been cleaning up."

Rogge flung his arms out from his sides. "How many times have I told them not to shower alone? By Deneb, I can't be everywhere! Haven't they brains enough—" A knock at the door interrupted him. A time-keeper pushed his head in.

"The mail ship's in sight, Mr. Rogge."

Rogge took a step toward the door, looked back over his shoulder.

"You attend to that, Kelly. I'm holding you responsible!"

The cadet blinked. "I can't help it if—" he began querulously, but he was speaking to the retreating back of his superior, and then the empty office. He muttered, dialed off.

Rogge strode out on the beach. He was early, for the ship was still a black spot in the purple-blue sky. When it finally settled, fuming and hissing, on the glinting gray sand, Rogge hardly waited for the steam to billow away before stepping forward to the port.

There was a few minutes' delay while the crew released themselves from their shock-belts. Rogge shuffled his feet, fidgeting like a nervous race-horse. Metallic sounds came from within. The dogs twisted, the port opened with a sigh, and Rogge moved irritably back from the smell of hot oil, men, carbolic acid, paint.

A round, red face looked out the port.

"Hello, doc," called Rogge. "All cleared for landing?"

"Germ-free," said the red face. "Safe as Sunday school."

"Well, open 'er up!"

The flushed medico eyed Rogge with a detached bird-like curiosity. "You in a hurry?"

Rogge tilted his head, stared at the doctor, eye to eye. The red face disappeared, the port opened wider, a short plump man in blue shorts swung out on the stage, descended the ladder. He flipped a hand to Rogge.

"Hello, Julic," said Rogge, peering up past him to the open port. "Any passengers?"

"Thirteen replacements for you. Cat-skinners, a couple plumbers—space-sick all the way."

Rogge snorted, jerked his head. "Thirteen? Do you know I've lost thirty-three men this last month? Didn't you pick up a T.C.I. man in Starport?"

The captain looked at him sidewise. "Yes, he's aboard. Looks like you're anxious."

"Anxious!" Rogge grinned wickedly, humorlessly. "You'd be anxious yourself with two, three men strangled every day."

Captain Julic narrowed his eyes. "It's true, is it?" He looked up to the two tall cliffs that marked Diggings A and B, the raw clutter of barracks and machine-shops below. "We heard rumors in Starport, but I didn't—" His voice dwindled away. Then: "Any idea at all who's doing it?"

"Not one in the world. It's a homicidal maniac, no doubt as to that, but every time I think I've got him spotted, there's another killing. The whole camp's demoralized. I can't get an honest day's work out of any man on the place. I'm a month behind schedule. I radioed the T.C.I. two weeks ago."

Captain Julic nodded toward the port. "There he is."

Rogge took a half-step forward, halted, blinked. The man descending the ladder was of medium height, medium weight, and something past middle-age. He had white hair, a small white beard, a fine straight nose.

Rogge darted a glance at Captain Julic who returned him a humorous shrug. Rogge turned back to the old man, now gazing leisurely up and down the glistening gray beach, out over the lambent white ocean.

Rogge pulled his head between his bony shoulders, stepped forward. "Ah—I'm James Rogge, Superintendent," he rasped. The old man turned, and Rogge found himself looking into wide, blue eyes, clear and guileless.

"My name is Magnus Ridolph," said the old man. "I understand that you're having difficulty?"

"Yes," said Rogge. He stood back, looking Magnus Ridolph up and down. "I was expecting a man from the Intelligence Corps."

Magnus Ridolph nodded. "I happened to be passing through Starport and the Commander asked me to visit you. At the moment I'm not officially connected with the Corps, but I'll do all I can to help you."

Rogge clamped his teeth, glared out to sea. At last he turned back to Ridolph. "Here's the situation. Men are being murdered, I don't know by whom. The whole camp is demoralized. I've ordered the entire personnel to go everywhere in couples—and still they're killed!"

Magnus Ridolph looked across the beach to the hills, low rounded masses covered with glistening vegetation in all shades of black, gray and white.

"Suppose you show me around the camp."

Rogge hesitated. "Are you ready—right now? Sure you don't want to rest first?"

"I'm ready."

Rogge turned to the captain. "See you at dinner, Julic—unless you want to come around with us?"

Captain Julic hesitated. "Just a minute, till I tell the mate I'm ashore." He clambered up the ladder.

Magnus Ridolph was gazing out at the slow-heaving, milk-white ocean that glowed as if illuminated from beneath.

"Plankton?"

Rogge nodded. "Intensely luminescent. At night the ocean shines like molten metal."

Magnus Ridolph nodded. "This is a very beautiful planet. So Earthlike and yet so strangely different in its coloring."

"That's right," said Rogge. "Whenever I look up on the hill I think of an extremely complicated steel engraving…the different tones of gray in the leaves."

"What, if any, is the fauna of the planet?"

"So far we've found creatures that resemble panthers, quite a few four-armed apes, and any number of rodents," Rogge said.

"No intelligent aborigines?"

Rogge shook his head. "So far as we know—no. And we've surveyed a good deal of the planet."

"How many men in the camp?"

"Eleven hundred, thereabouts," said Rogge. "Eight hundred at Diggings A, three hundred at B. It's at B where the murders occur. I'm thinking of closing down the diggings for a while."

Magnus Ridolph tugged at his beard. "Murders only at Diggings B? Have you shifted the personnel?"

Rogge nodded, glared at the massive column of ore that was Diggings B. "I've changed every man-jack in the camp. And still the killings go on—in locked rooms, in the showers, the toilets, anywhere a man happens to be alone for a minute or two."

"It sounds almost as if you've disturbed an invisible *genius loci*," said Magnus Ridolph.

Rogge snorted. "If that means 'ghost', I'll agree with you. 'Ghost' is about the only explanation I got left. Four times, now, a man has been killed in a locked room with no opening larger than a barred four-inch ventilator. We've slipped into the room with nets, screened every cubic foot. Nothing."

Captain Julic came down the ladder, joined Rogge and Magnus Ridolph. They turned up the hard-packed gray beach toward Diggings A, a jut of rock breaking sharply out of the gently rolling hills.

"The ore," Rogge explained, "lies in a layer at about ground level. We're bull-dozing the top-surface off onto the beach. When we're all done, that big crag will be leveled flat to the ground, and the little bay will be entirely filled."

"And Diggings B is the same proposition?" asked Magnus Ridolph. "It looks about the same formation from here."

"Yes, it's about the same. They're old volcanic necks, both of them. At B, we're pushing the fill into a low canyon in back. When we're done at B—if we ever get done—the canyon will be level full a mile back, and we'll use it for a town-site."

They climbed up from the beach on a sloping shoulder of rock. Rogge guided them toward the edge of the forest, fifty feet distant.

"I'll show you something," Rogge said. "Fruit like you've never seen before in your life." He stopped at a shiny black trunk, plucked one of the red globes that hung within easy reach. "Try one of these." And Rogge bit into one of the soft skins himself.

Magnus Ridolph and the captain gravely followed suit.

"They are indeed very good," said the old man.

"They don't grow at B," said Rogge bitterly. "Just along this stretch here. Diggings B is the hard-luck spot of the entire project. The leopards and apes killed men at B until we put up a charged steel fence. Here at A there's some underbrush that keeps them out. Full of thorns."

A sound in the foliage attracted his attention. He craned his neck. "Look! There's one right now—an ape!" And Magnus Ridolph and the captain, looking where he pointed, glimpsed a monstrous black barrel, a hideous face with red eyes and a fanged mouth. The brute observed them, hissed softly, took a challenging step forward. Magnus Ridolph and the captain jerked back. Rogge laughed.

"You're safe. Watch him."

The ape lunged nearer, then suddenly halted, with a roar. He struck out a great arm at the air, roared again. He charged forward, stopped short, howling, retreated.

Rogge threw the core of the fruit at him. "If this were at B, he'd have killed the three of us." He peered through the foliage. "Gah! Get away from here, you ugly devil!" And Rogge ducked in alarm as a length of stick hurtled past his head.

"The creature apparently has a comparatively high order of intelligence," suggested Magnus Ridolph.

"Mmph," snapped Rogge. "Well—perhaps so. We killed one at Diggings B, and two others dug a grave for him under a tree, buried him while we were watching."

Magnus Ridolph looked soberly into the forest. "I can tell you how to stop these murders."

Rogge jerked his head around. "How?"

"Survey off an area of land, in such a way that both diggings, A and B, are a mile inside the perimeter. Around the boundary erect a charged steel fence, and clear the land inside of all vegetation."

Rogge stared. "But how—" His belt radio buzzed. He flipped the switch.

"Superintendent Rogge!" came a voice.

"Yes!" barked Rogge.

"Foundry-foreman Jelson's got it!"

Rogge turned to Captain Julic and Magnus Ridolph. "Come along. I'll show you."

Ten minutes later they stood staring down at the naked body of Foreman Jelson. He had been taking a shower and his body still glistened with the wet.

A red and blue bruise ringed his neck, his eyes popped, and his tongue lolled from the side of his mouth.

"We was right here, sittin' in the dressin' room," babbled a red-headed mechanic. "We didn't see a thing. Jelson went in to shower. The next thing, we heard him flop—and there he was!"

Rogge turned to Magnus Ridolph. "You see? That's what's been going on. Do you still think that building a fence will stop the murders?"

Ridolph mused, a hand at his white beard. "Tonight, if I am not mistaken, there will be a murder attempted at Diggings A."

Rogge's mouth opened slackly, then snapped shut. From behind came the sobbing breath of the red-headed mechanic.

"Diggings A? How? Why do you say that?"

"No one will be killed, I hope," said Magnus Ridolph. "Indeed, if I'm wrong my theory has been founded on a non-comprehensive survey of the possibilities, and there may be no attempt upon my life." He stared thoughtfully at the corpse. "Perhaps I overestimate the understanding and ability of the murderer."

Rogge turned away. "Call the medics," he snapped to the mechanic.

They rode back to Diggings A in a jeep, and Rogge took Captain Julic and Magnus Ridolph to his apartment for the evening meal.

"I could easily clear the land," he told Ridolph, "but I can't understand what you have in mind."

Magnus Ridolph smiled slowly. "I have an alternate proposal."

"And what's that?"

"Armor the necks of your personnel in steel bands."

Rogge snorted. "Then the murderer would go to smashing skulls or poisoning."

"Bashing heads, no—poisoning, possibly," said Magnus Ridolph. He reached for an enormous purple grape. "For instance, it would be an easy matter to poison the fruit."

"But why—*why!*" cried Rogge. "I've pounded my brain night after night, and all I can get is 'homicidal maniac'."

Magnus Ridolph shook his head, smiled. "I think not. I believe that these killings have a clear, very simple purpose behind them. So simple perhaps that you overlook it."

Rogge grunted, glared at the benign countenance. "Suppose you *are* murdered tonight—then what?"

"Then you'll know that my recommendation was founded on a correct analysis of the problem, and you'll do as I suggested."

Rogge grunted again, and for a moment there was silence.

"How long a job do you have here, Superintendent?" Magnus Ridolph asked mildly.

Rogge stared sourly out the window past the gray, black, white foliage, out to where a knife-edge horizon divided the bright white sea from the dark-blue sky. "About five years if I can keep men working. Another week of these killings, they'll break their contract."

Captain Julic chuckled. Rogge turned snapping black eyes on him.

"Already," said Captain Julic, "I've refused twenty men passage back to Starport."

"Contract-jumpers, eh?" snorted Rogge. "Just point them out to me, and I'll make them toe the mark!"

Captain Julic laughed, shook his head.

At last Magnus Ridolph rose to his feet. "If you'll show me to my quarters, I think I'll take a little rest."

Rogge pushed a button to summon the steward, quizzically eying the white-bearded sage. "You still think your life is in danger?"

"Not if I'm careful," said Magnus Ridolph coolly.

"So far there's been no killings at Diggings A."

"For an excellent reason—if my hypothesis is correct. A very manifest reason, if I may say so."

Rogge leaned back in his chair, curled his lip. "So far it has not been manifest to me, and I have been intimately concerned with the matter since we broke ground at Diggings B."

"Perhaps," said Magnus Ridolph, "you are too close to the problem. You must remember that this is not Planet Earth, and conditions—the psychological, the biological, and," he turned a vastly impassive stare at Rogge, "the essentially logical circumstances—are different from what you have been accustomed to."

He left the room. Rogge arose, paced up and down, kneading the palm of one hand with the fist of the other.

"What a pompous old goat!" he said between clenched teeth. He darted a burning glance at Captain Julic, who sat quietly smiling across a glass of liqueur. "Have you ever seen anything like it? Here I've been on the job seven months now, fighting this problem night and day—and he arrives, and in one hour delivers his opinion. Have you ever heard the like? Why, I believe I'll beam Starport this very minute! I asked for an Intelligence operative, not a tourist!" He started for the door.

Captain Julic arose from his seat. "I advise you, Superintendent—" But Rogge was gone. Captain Julic followed the tall wide-pacing figure to the Communications room. He knocked at the door, and as his signal was disregarded, quietly entered.

He found Rogge barking at the screen, where the space-blurred image of the chief of the Terrestrial Intelligence Corps showed.

"—and he's gone off to bed now," Rogge was bellowing. "And all he tells me is to build a fence!"

There was a short pause, while the message raced at near-instantaneous speed to Starport and back. Rogge stood like a great snapping-turtle temporarily without its shell, frozen, glaring at the image. The loudspeaker buzzed, crackled.

"Superintendent Rogge," came the words of the Corps chief, "I earnestly advise you to follow the advice of Magnus Ridolph. In my opinion you are fortunate to have him at hand to help you."

The image faded. Rogge turned slowly, looked unseeingly past Julic.

Julic approached, tapped the rigid arm. "If you'd asked me, I could have told you the same."

Rogge wheeled. "What about this Magnus Ridolph? Who is he?"

Captain Julic made an easy gesture. "Magnus Ridolph is an eminent mathematician."

"What's that got to do with the T.C.I.?" demanded Rogge bitterly. "Or the present case? He won't stop the killings with a slide-rule."

Captain Julic smiled. "I think he carries a slide-rule in his brain."

Rogge turned, stalked slowly from the Communications room. "How is it that the Corps commander sent him—a mathematician?"

Julic shrugged. "I imagine that he's an unofficial consultant, something of the sort."

Rogge jerked his long white fingers. "Suppose he's right? Suppose he's killed tonight?"

A steward approached, whispered in his ear. Rogge straightened up, clamped his thin lips together. "Sure. Get him anything he wants."

He and Captain Julic returned to the apartment.

After leaving Rogge, Magnus Ridolph had gone to his room, locked the door, and made a thoughtful survey of his surroundings. One wall was glass, framed on either side by the sharp gray and black foliage of two tall trees. Visible beyond was the curve of a hill down to the beach, the luminescence of the pallid ocean.

Darkness was falling, the sky deepened to a starless black, and the ocean, by contrast, shone softly bright as lamp-lit parchment.

Magnus Ridolph turned, inspected the remainder of the room. Empty, beyond all question. To the right was his couch, ahead the tiles of the bathroom glistened through an open door.

Ridolph closed the bathroom door, polarized the glass panels behind him, and pressed the call button for the steward.

"Bring me, quickly, please, a small power-pack, about twenty feet of glochrome wire, and three rolls of heavy insul."

The steward stared, then said, "Yes, sir," turned and closed the door.

Magnus Ridolph waited with his back to the door, looking ruminatively at the walls.

The steward presently returned. Magnus Ridolph removed his tunic, then on sudden thought, closely inspected the walls.

He donned his tunic once more, rang for the steward.

"Is there anywhere in the building a room with metal walls and a metal door?"

The steward blinked. "The refrigerator room, sir."

Magnus Ridolph nodded. "Take me there."

A short while later he returned to his room, walking stiffly, for his arms and legs were now wrapped with insul tape. He depolarized the glass wall, and in the wan light from the ocean, selected a chair, lowered himself into it, waited.

An hour passed, and Magnus Ridolph's eyelids grew heavy. He slept.

He awoke with a slight start, a sense of dissatisfaction. Were his deductions at fault? Why had not—

He stiffened, strained his ears, twisted slowly in his seat, glanced toward the bathroom. Nothing was visible. He relaxed in his chair.

Cable-like thongs snapped home—around his ankles, his chest, his throat, constricting with terrible angry strength.

Magnus Ridolph reacted instantly, fighting with primitive fright. Then the discipline of his brain took control. His big toe pressed a switch inside his shoe. Instantly up and down his arms and legs glochrome wires under his tunic burnt blue-hot, cutting the cloth like a razor, lighting the walls in the brilliance of their heat.

The bands around his arms and legs severed, Magnus Ridolph snatched a knife from his belt, slashed at the band around his neck. With the strength ebbing from his body, he hacked and hewed until he felt a pulsing along the knife, a doubt, a reluctance.

The knife cut through, and the garrote relaxed. Magnus Ridolph gave a great gasp. Tottering, he leaned his back against the wall, staring at the reality of the murdering agency, plain before his eyes.

He rang for the steward.

"Fetch Rogge at once."

Rogge, gaunt and ungraceful, came on the lope.

"Yes, what is it?"

Magnus Ridolph pointed. "Look."

Rogge stared, then reached to the floor, lifted a length of the severed thong.

"I don't understand," he said in a husky voice.

"It is very clear," said Magnus Ridolph. "In fact, it is a logical necessity. You yourself would have arrived at the solution if you had manipulated your thoughts with any degree of order."

Rogge stared at him, anger smouldering in his eyes. "I would be obliged," he said stiffly, "if you would explain what you know of this business."

"With pleasure," said Magnus Ridolph. "In the first place, it was clear that the killings were calculated to obstruct development of Diggings B. It was not the work of a homicidal maniac for you had changed the entire personnel, and still the killings continued. I asked myself, who profited from the abandonment of Diggings B? Clearly the agency cared nothing about Diggings A, for the work progressed smoothly. Then what was the distinction between the diggings?

"At first glance, there seemed little. Both were volcanic necks, barren juts of rock, and approximately equal. About the only difference was in your projected disposition of the waste. The rubble from Diggings A was to fill in the bay, that from Diggings B was to fill a wooded canyon. Now," and Magnus Ridolph surveyed the glowering Rogge, "do the facts presented in this light clarify the problem?"

Rogge chewed at his lips.

"I asked myself," Magnus Ridolph continued softly, "who or what suffers at Diggings B who does not suffer, or profits, at Diggings A? And the answer to my question came instantly—the trees."

"*Trees!*" barked Rogge.

Magnus Ridolph nodded. "I examined the situation in that light. At Diggings A the trees provided fruit and also erected for you a barrier against the beasts. There was neither fruit nor protection at Diggings B. The trees encouraged Diggings A because removing the volcanic neck and filling the bay would provide at once an added area for the growth and also removal of an obstacle to sunlight. The trees approved."

"But you are assuming intelligence in the trees?" gasped Rogge.

"Of course," said Magnus Ridolph. "What other alternative is there? I warned you not to expect on this planet the same conditions existent on Earth. You saw how the apes buried their comrade under a tree? Undoubtedly they were led to do so by the trees—persuaded, enticed, forced: that is a matter for speculation—in order that the trees might benefit by the enrichment of the soil. In any event, I reasoned that if the trees were intelligent, after seven months they very likely would comprehend human speech. In the presence of a tree I recommended that a large area of vegetation be cleared away—a wholesale murder of trees. Naturally I was marked as a threat, an individual to be removed. The attempt was made this evening."

"But how?" said Rogge. "A tree can't walk into a building and throw a rope around a man's neck!"

"No," said Magnus Ridolph. "But a tree has roots, and every room in the diggings has a drain or a ventilator, some sort of minute crevice. And I strongly suspect the presence of spy cells in the wood panels of every room—small eyes and ears. Not an action escapes the surrounding intelligences. And at this minute I suspect they are preparing to kill us both, by poison gas, possibly, or—"

A splintering crash sounded. A section of the floor broke open, and from the dark gap uncoiled a dull-brown hawser-like object. It threshed, wove, swung toward Rogge and Magnus Ridolph.

"Wait," said Magnus Ridolph calmly. "Wait. You are intelligent beings. Wait, listen to what I have to say to you."

The great root swung toward them with no pause.

"Wait," said Magnus Ridolph calmly. "There will be no clearing and all rubble will be dumped into the bay."

The root hesitated, wavered in mid-air.

"What malignant creatures!" breathed Rogge.

"Not at all," said Magnus Ridolph. "They are merely the denizens of a world defending their lives. Cooperation can be to our mutual benefit." He addressed himself to the root.

"In the future, if the trees will bar the animals from Diggings B and provide fruit at that location, men will in no way harm the trees. All waste will be transported to the ocean. In addition other men will come, discover your needs, make known our own desires. We will form a partnership beneficial to both our species. Men can irrigate and enrich sparse soils, curb insect parasites. Trees can locate minerals for man, synthesize complex organic compounds, grow him fruit." He paused for a moment. The root lay flaccid on the broken floor.

"If the trees understand and approve, let the root withdraw."

The root shivered, twisted, writhed—pulled itself to the gap in the floor. It was gone.

Magnus Ridolph turned to the frozen superintendent.

"There will be no more trouble."

Rogge seemed to come awake. He glanced at the splintered floor. "But the killings? Is there to be no punishment? The torment I've gone through—"

Magnus Ridolph surveyed him with cool contempt. "Have not your men cut down many trees?"

Rogge shook his head. "There'll be an added expense taking that fill to the bay. I doubt if the diggings will pay. Why, man, with a couple incinerator tubes and a few bulldozers we could clear off the whole area—" He caught Ridolph's eye.

"In my opinion," said Magnus Ridolph, "you are short-sighted and ruthless. You also flout the law. In fact you are not a fit administrator for this project."

Rogge knitted his brow. "What law am I flouting?"

"The statute created over thirty years ago for the protection and encouragement of friendly autochthones."

Rogge said nothing.

"You will either cooperate completely, or I will request your removal."

Rogge looked away. "Perhaps you are right," he muttered.

A faint sound came to their ears. Turning, they looked to the gap in the floor. It was fast disappearing. Even as they watched, the splinters, strangely pliant, turned themselves down, knitted to a smooth gleaming surface. Where the gap had been now shone a small gleaming object.

Magnus Ridolph strode forward, lifted it, displayed it wordlessly to Rogge. It was a complex crystal—blood-colored fire—perfectly formed except on one side, where it had been torn away from its matrix.

"A ruby, I believe," said Magnus Ridolph. He looked at the staring superintendent, then coolly returned to his inspection of the jewel.

Afterword to "Hard-Luck Diggings"

Norma's parents lived in Colton in southern California, and whenever opportunity offered we would drive down and spend time with them. On one occasion I had an experiment in mind. I was selling stories on a more or less regular basis, but the returns were not astronomical, and I thought to improve the situation by becoming a "million-word-a-year man". I knocked out two stories in two days, the first of the Magnus Ridolph set. I sent the first drafts, without revision, to my agent Scott Meredith in New York. He sold them at once with no apparent difficulty. So much for the experiment. I was moderately pleased with this sudden gush of productivity, but I realized that in the long haul my temperament was not suited to this method of writing. I returned to my old system, which meant first draft, second draft; and if I were lucky I would find this second draft acceptable.

Just then, I received startling news from my agent. 20th Century Fox had picked up one of these stories, "Hard Luck Diggings", for compensation which at the time seemed phenomenal. Furthermore they invited me to write a treatment and possibly a screenplay at an inordinate weekly salary, if I would report to Hollywood at once.

Norma and I jumped in the Packard and drove south. We presented ourselves to 20th Century Fox, where we were introduced to Julian Blaustein, the producer. I was installed in an office with my name on the door in gold, a secretary, and told to get to work.

We rented a spacious house with a swimming pool in Coldwater Canyon. Every morning I drove to my office at Fox and tried to produce the kind of material which Blaustein expected of me. In truth I found this sort of work unfamiliar and not particularly agreeable. For one thing, the money, while gratifying at first, frightened me a little: I did not want to become dependent upon sucking at this golden tit.

Luckily, my fears came to naught. Julian Blaustein was promoted to become an executive producer, and all his projects were shelved. I was told, "Don't call us, we'll call you." The golden letters of my name were scraped from the door, my secretary bade me farewell, and everything else was restored to as before I had arrived. Without overmuch regret I took my leave of Fox Studios.

—Jack Vance

The Temple of Han

In the nip-and-tuck business of keeping himself alive, Briar Kelly had not yet been able to shed his disguise. The adventure had turned out rather more ruggedly than it had started. He had not bargained for so much hell.

Up to the moment he had entered the queer dark temple at North City, the disguise had served him well. He had been one with the Han; no one had looked at him twice. Once inside the temple he was alone and disguise was unnecessary.

It was an oddly impressive place. A Gothic web of trusses supported the ceiling; alcoves along the walls were crammed with bric-a-brac. Red and green lamps cast an illumination which was stifled and absorbed by black drapes.

Walking slowly down the central nave, every nerve tingling, Kelly had approached the tall black mirror at the far end, watching his looming reflection with hypnotic fascination. There were limpid depths beyond, and Kelly would have looked more closely had he not seen the jewel: a ball of cool green fire resting on a black velvet cushion.

With marvelling fingers Kelly had lifted it, turned it over and over—and then tumult had broken loose. The red and green lights flickered; an alarm horn brayed like a crazy bull. Vengeful priests appeared in the alcoves as if by magic, and the disguise had become a liability. The tubular black cloak constricted his legs as he ran—back along the aisle, down the shabby steps, through the foul back alleys to his air-boat. Now as he crouched low over the controls sweat beaded up under the white grease-paint and his skin itched and crawled.

Ten feet below, the salt-crusted mud-flats fleeted astern. Dirty yellow rushes whipped the hull. Pressing an elbow to his hip Kelly felt the hard shape of the jewel. The sensation aroused mixed feelings, apprehension predominating. He dropped the boat even closer to the ground. "Five minutes of this, I'll be out of radar range," thought Kelly. "Back at Bucktown, I'm just one among fifty thousand. They can't very well locate me, unless Herli talks, or Mapes…"

He hazarded a glance at the rear-vision plate. North City could still be seen, an exaggerated Mont St. Michel jutting up from the dreary salt marsh. Misty exhalations blurred the detail; it faded into the sky, finally dropped below the horizon. Kelly eased up the nose of the boat, rose tangentially from the surface, aiming into Magra Taratempos, the hot white sun.

The atmosphere thinned, the sky deepened to black, stars came out. There was old Sol, a yellow star hanging between Sadal Suud and Sadal Melik in Aquarius—only thirty light years to home—

Kelly heard a faint swishing sound. The light changed, shifting white to red. He blinked, looked around in bewilderment.

Magra Taratempos had disappeared. Low to the left a giant red sun hulked above the horizon; below, the salt marshes swam in a new claret light.

In amazement Kelly gazed from red sun to planet, back up across the heavens where Magra Taratempos had hung only a moment before.

"I've gone crazy," said Kelly. "Unless…"

Two or three months before, a peculiar rumor had circulated Bucktown. For lack of better entertainment, the sophisticates of the city had made a joke of the story, until it finally grew stale and was no more heard.

Kelly, who worked as computer switchman at the astrogation station, was well-acquainted with the rumor. It went to the effect that a Han priest, dour and intense under his black cloak, had been tripped into the marsh by a drunken pollen-collector. Like a turtle the priest had shoved his white face out from under the hood of his cloak, and rasped in the pidgin of the planet: "You abuse the priest of Han; you mock us and the name of the Great God. Time is short. The Seventh Year is at hand, and you godless Earth-things will seek to flee, but there will be nowhere for you to go."

Such had been the tale. Kelly remembered the pleased excitement which had fluttered from tongue to tongue. He grimaced, examined the sky in new apprehension.

The facts were before his eyes, undeniable. Magra Taratempos had vanished. In a different quarter of the sky a new sun had appeared.

Careless of radar tracing, he nosed up and broke entirely clear of the atmosphere. The stellar patterns had changed. Blackness curtained half the sky, with here and there a lone spark of a star or the wisp of a far galaxy. To the other quarter a vast blot of light stretched across the sky, a narrow elongated luminosity with a central swelling, the whole peppered with a million tiny points of light.

Kelly cut the power from his engine; the air-boat drifted. Unquestionably the luminous blot was a galaxy seen from one of its outer fringes. In ever-growing bewilderment, Kelly looked back at the planet below. To the south he could see the triangular plateau shouldering up from the swamp, and Lake Lenore near Bucktown. Below was the salt marsh, and far to the north, the rugged pile where the Han had their city.

"Let's face it," said Kelly. "Unless I'm out of my mind—and I don't think I am—the entire planet has been picked up and taken to a new sun...I've heard of strange things here and there, but this is it..."

He felt the weight of the jewel in his pocket, and with it a new thrill of apprehension. To the best of his knowledge the Han priests could not identify him. At Bucktown it had been Herli and Mapes who had urged him into the escapade, but they would hold their tongues. Ostensibly he had flown to his cabin along the lakeshore, and there was no one to know of his comings and goings...He turned the boat down toward Bucktown, and a half hour later landed at his cabin beside Lake Lenore. He had scraped the grease-paint from his face; the cloak he had jettisoned over the swamp; and the jewel still weighed heavy in his pocket.

The cabin, a low flat-roofed building with aluminum walls and a glass front, appeared strange and unfamiliar in the new light. Kelly walked warily to the door. He looked right and left. No one, nothing was visible. He put his ear to the panel of the door. No sound.

He slid back the panel, stepped inside, swept the interior with a swift glance. Everything appeared as he had left it.

He started toward the visiphone, then halted.

The jewel.

He took it from his pocket, examined it for the first time. It was a sphere the size of a golf-ball. The center shone with a sharp green fire, decreasing toward the outer surface. He hefted it. It was unnaturally heavy. Strangely fascinating, altogether lovely. Think of it around the neck of Lynette Mason...

Not now. Kelly wrapped it in paper, tucked it into an empty pint jar. Behind the cabin, an old shag-bark slanted up out of the black humus and overhung the roof like a gray and tattered beach-umbrella. Kelly dug a hole under one of the arched roots, buried the jewel.

Returning to the cabin, he walked to the visiphone, reached out to call the station. While his hand was yet a foot from the buttons, the buzzer sounded... Kelly drew his hand back.

Better not to answer.

The buzzer sounded again—again. Kelly stood holding his breath, looking at the blank face of the screen.

Silence.

He washed the last of the grease-paint from his face, changed his clothes, ran outside, jumped into his air-boat and took off for Bucktown.

He landed on the roof of the station, noting that Herli's car was parked in its wonted slot. Suddenly he felt less puzzled and forlorn. The station with its machinery and solid Earth-style regulations projected reassurance, a sense of normality. Somehow the ingenuity and aggressive attack which had taken men to the stars would solve the present enigma.

Or would it? Ingenuity could take men through space, but ingenuity would find itself strained locating a speck of a planet a hundred thousand light-years in an unknown direction. And Kelly still had his own problem: the jewel. Into his mind's-eye came a picture: the cabin by the lake, the dilapidated gray parasol of the shag-bark, and glowing under the root, the green eye of the sacred jewel. In the vision he saw the black-robed figure of a Han priest moving across the open space before the cabin, and he saw the flash of the dough-white face...

Kelly turned a troubled glance up at the big red sun, entered the station.

The administration section was vacant; Kelly climbed the stair to the operations department.

He stopped in the doorway, surveyed the room. It covered the entire square of the upper floor. Work-benches made a circuit of the room, with windows above. A polished cylinder, the cosmoscope, came down through the ceiling, and below was the screen to catch the projection.

Four men stood by the star-index, running a tape. Herli glanced up briefly, turned back to the clicking mechanism.

Strange. Herli should have been interested, should at least have said hello.

Kelly self-consciously crossed the room. He cleared his throat. "Well— I made it. I'm back."

"So I see," said Herli.

Kelly fell silent. He glanced up through the window at the red sun. "What do you make of it?"

"Not the least idea. We're running the star-tapes on the off chance it's been registered—a last-gasp kind of hope."

There was more silence. They had been talking before he had entered the room; Kelly sensed this from their posture.

At last Mapes said with a forced casualness, "Seen the news?"

"No," said Kelly. "No, I haven't." There was more in Mapes' voice, something more personal than the shift of the planet. After a moment's hesitation he went to the visiphone, pushed the code for news.

The screen lit, showed a view of the swamp. Kelly leaned forward. Buried up to their necks were a dozen boys and girls from the Bucktown High-school. Crawling eagerly over them were the small three-legged salt-crabs; others popped up out of the slime, or tunnelled under toward the squirming bodies.

Kelly could not stand the screams. He reached forward—

Herli said sharply, "Leave it on!"—harder than Kelly had ever heard him speak. "The announcement is due pretty soon."

The announcement came, in the rasping toneless pidgin of the Han priests.

"Among the outsiders is a wicked thief. He has despoiled us of the Seven-year Eye. Let him come forward for his due. Until the thief has brought the Seven-year Eye in his own hand to the sacred temple of Han, every hour one of the outsiders will be buried in the crab-warren. If the thief hangs back, all will be so dealt with, and there will be an end to the Earth-things."

Mapes said in a tight voice, "Did you take their Seven-year Eye?"

Kelly nodded numbly. "Yes."

Herli made a sharp sound in his throat, turned away.

Kelly said miserably, "I don't know what came over me. There it was—glowing like a little green moon...I took it."

Herli said gutturally, "Don't just stand there."

Kelly reached out to the visiphone, pushed buttons. The screen changed, a Han priest stared forth into Kelly's face.

Kelly said, "I stole your jewel...Don't kill any more people. I'll bring it back to you."

The priest said, "Every hour until you arrive one of the Earth-things dies a wicked death."

Kelly leaned forward, slammed off the screen with a sudden furious sweep of his hand. He turned in anger.

"Don't stand there glaring at me! You, Herli, you told me I wouldn't even make it into the temple! And if any of you guys had been where I was and saw that jewel like I saw it, you'd have taken it too."

Mapes growled under his breath. Herli's shoulders seemed to sag; he looked away. "Maybe you're right, Briar."

Kelly said, "Are we helpless? Why didn't we fight when they took those twelve kids? There's maybe a million Han, but there's fifty thousand of us— and they have no weapons that I know of."

"They've seized the power station," said Herli. "Without power we can't distill water, we can't radiate our hydroponics. We're in a cleft stick."

Kelly turned away. "So long, fellows."

No one answered him. He walked down the stairs, across the parking strip to his air-car. He was conscious of their eyes looking down from the window.

In, up, away. First to his cabin by the lake, under the shag-bark for the Seven-year Eye, then the arc over the planet, south to north. Then the gray fortress of North Settlement, and the dark temple in the center.

Kelly dropped the air-car directly in front of the temple. No reason now for stealth.

He climbed to the ground, looked about through the strange purple twilight which had come to the ramshackle city. A few Han moved past, and Kelly saw the flash of their faces.

He walked slowly up the steps to the temple, paused indecisively in the doorway. There was no point in adding further provocation to his offenses. No doubt they planned to kill him; he might as well make it as easy as possible.

"Hello," he called into the dark interior, in a voice he tried to keep firm. "Any priests in there? I've brought back the jewel…"

There was no response. Listening intently, he could hear a distant murmur. He took a few steps into the temple, peered up the nave. The muffled red and green illumination confused rather than aided his vision. He noticed a curious irregularity to the floor. He took a step forward—another—another—he stepped on something soft. There was the flash of white below him. The floor was covered by the black-robed priests, lying flat on their faces.

The priest he had trod on made no sound. Kelly hesitated. Time was passing…He crammed all his doubts, fears, vacillations into a corner of his mind, strode forward, careless of where he stepped.

Down the center of the nave he walked, holding the green jewel in his hand. Ahead he saw the sheen of the tall black mirror, and there on the black cushion was a second jewel identical to the one he carried. A Han priest stood like a ghost in a black robe; he watched Kelly approach without movement. Kelly laid the jewel on the cushion beside its twin.

"There it is. I've brought it back. I'm sorry I took it. I—well, I acted on a wild impulse."

The priest picked up the jewel, held it under his chin as if feeling the warmth from the green fire.

"Your impulse has cost fifteen Earth lives."

"Fifteen?" faltered Kelly. "There were but twelve—"

"Two hours delay has sent two to the crab warren," said the Han. "And yourself. Fifteen."

Kelly said with a shaky bravado, "You're taking a lot on yourself—these murders—"

"I am not acquainted with your idiom," said the priest, "but it seems as if you convey a foolish note of menace. What can you few Earth-things do against Great God Han, who has just now taken our planet across the galaxy?"

Kelly said stupidly, "Your god Han—moved the planet?"

"Certainly. He has taken us far and forever distant from Earth to this mellow sun; such is his gratitude for our prayers and for the tribute of the Eye."

Kelly said with studied carelessness, "You have your jewel back; I don't see why you're so indignant—"

The priest said, "Look here." Kelly followed his gesture, saw a square black hole edged with a coping of polished stone. "This shaft is eighteen miles deep. Every priest of Han descends to the coomb once a week and carries back to the surface a basket of crystallized stellite. On rare occasions the matrix of the Eye is found, and then there is gratification in the city...Such a jewel did you steal."

Kelly took his eyes away from the shaft. Eighteen miles..."I naturally wasn't aware of the—"

"No matter; the deed is done. And now the planet has been moved, and Earth power is unable to prevent such punishments as we wish to visit upon you."

Kelly tried to keep his voice firm. "Punish? What do you mean?"

Behind him he heard a rustling, the shuffle of movement. He looked over his shoulder. The black cloaks merged with the drapes of the temple, and the Han faces floated in mid-air.

"You will be killed," said the priest. Kelly stared into the white face. "If the manner of your going is of any interest to you—" The priest conveyed details which froze Kelly's flesh, clabbered the moisture in his mouth. "Your death will thereby deter other Earth-things from like crimes."

Kelly protested in spite of himself. "You have your jewel; there it is...If you insist on killing me—kill me, but—"

"Strange," said the Han priest. "You Earth-things fear pain more than anything else you can conceive. This fear is your deadliest enemy. We Han now, we fear nothing—" he looked up at the tall black mirror, bowed slightly "—nothing but our Great God Han."

Kelly stared at the shimmering black surface. "What's that mirror to do with your god Han?"

"That is no mirror; that is the portal to the place of the gods, and every seven years a priest goes through to convey the consecrated Eye to Han."

Kelly tried to plumb the dark depths of the mirror. "What lies beyond? What kind of land?"

The priest made no answer.

Kelly laughed in a shrill voice he did not recognize. He lurched forward, threw up his fist in a blow which carried every ounce of his strength and weight. He struck the priest at a point where a man's jaw would be, felt a brittle crunch. The priest spun around, fell in the tangle of his cloak.

Kelly turned on the priests in the nave, and they sighed in fury. Kelly was desperate, fearless now. He laughed again, reached down, scooped both jewels from the cushion. "Great God Han lives behind the mirror, and moves planets for jewels. I have two jewels; maybe Han will move a planet for me..."

He jumped close to the black mirror. He put out his hand and felt a soft surface like a curtain of air. He paused in sudden trepidation. Beyond was the unknown...

Pushing at him came the first rank of the Han priests. Here was the known.

Kelly could not delay. Death was death. If he died passing through the black curtain, if he suffocated in airless space—it was clean fast death.

He leaned forward, closed his eyes, held his breath, stepped through the curtain.

Kelly had come a tremendous distance. It was a distance not to be reckoned in miles or hours, but in quantities like abstract, irrational ideas.

He opened his eyes. They functioned; he could see. He was not dead... Or was he?...He took a step forward, sensed solidity under his feet. He looked down, saw a glassy black floor where small sparks burst, flickered, died. Constellations? Universes? Or merely—sparks?

He took another step. It might have been a yard, a mile, a light-year; he moved with the floating ease of a man walking in a dream.

He stood on the lip of an amphitheater, a bowl like a lunar crater. He took another step; he stood in the center of the bowl. He halted, fought to convince himself of his consciousness. Blood made a rushing sound as it flowed through his veins. He swayed, might have fallen if gravity had existed to pull him down. But there was no gravity. His feet clung to the surface by some mysterious adhesion beyond his experience. The blood-sound rose and fell in his ears. Blood meant life. He was alive.

He looked in back of him, and in the blurring of his eyes could not distinguish what he saw. He turned, took a step forward—

He was intruding. He felt the sudden irritated attention of gigantic personalities.

He gazed about the glassy floor, and the faintest of watery gray lights seeping down from above collected in the concavity where he stood. Space was vast, interminable, without perspective.

Kelly saw the beings he had disturbed—felt rather than saw them: a dozen giant shapes looming above.

One of these shapes formed a thought, and a surge of meaning permeated space, impinged on Kelly's mind, willy-nilly translating itself into words:

"What is this thing? From whose world did it come?"

"From mine." This must be Han. Kelly looked from shape to shape, to determine which the god might be.

"Remove it quickly—" and to Kelly's mind came a jumble of impressions he had no words to express. "We must deal with the matter of…" Again a quick listing of ideas which refused to translate in Kelly's mind. He felt Han's attention focussing on him. He stood transfixed, waiting for the obliteration he knew to be imminent.

But he held the jewels, and their green glow shone up through his fingers. He cried out, "Wait, I came here for a purpose; I want a planet put back where it belongs, and I have jewels to pay—"

He felt the baleful pressure of Han's will on his mind—increasing, increasing; he groaned in helpless anguish.

"Wait," came a calm thought, transcendently clear and serene.

"I must destroy it," Han protested. "It is the enemy of my jewel-senders."

"Wait," came from yet another of the shades, and Kelly caught a nuance of antagonism to Han. "We must act judicially."

"Why are you here?" came the query of the Leader.

Kelly said, "The Han priests are murdering people of my race, ever since the planet we live on was moved. It's not right."

"Ah!" came a thought like an exclamation from the Antagonist. "Han's jewel-senders do evil and unnatural deeds."

"A minor matter, a minor matter," came the restless thought of still another shape. "Han must protect his jewel-senders."

And Kelly caught the implication that the jewel-sending was of cardinal importance; that the jewels were vital to the gods.

The Antagonist chose to make an issue of the matter. "The condition of injustice which Han has effected must be abated."

The Leader meditated. And now came a sly thought to Kelly, which he sensed had been channelled to his mind alone. It came from the Antagonist. "Challenge Han to a…" The thought could only be translated as 'duel'. "I will aid you. Relax your mind." Kelly, grasping at any straw, loosened his mental fibers, and felt something like a damp shadow entering his brain, absorbing, recording…All in an instant. The contact vanished.

Kelly felt the Leader's mind wavering over in favor of Han. He said hurriedly, improvising as best he could: "Leader, in one of the legends of Earth, a man journeyed to the land of the giants. As they came to kill him, he challenged the foremost to a duel with his life at stake." "*Of three trials*," came a thought. "Of three trials," added Kelly. "In the story, the man won and was permitted to return to his native land. After this fashion let me duel in three trials with Han."

The surge of thoughts thickened the air—rancorous contempt from Han, sly encouragement from the Antagonist, amusement from the Leader.

"You invoke a barbaric principle," said the Leader. "But by a simple yet rigorous logic, it is a just device, and shall be honored. You shall duel Han in three trials."

"Why waste time?" inquired Han. "I can powder him to less than the atoms of atoms."

"No," said the Leader. "The trial may not be on a basis of sheer potential. You and this man are at odds over an issue which has no fundamental right or wrong. It is the welfare of his people opposed to the welfare of your jewel-senders. Since the issues are equal, there would be no justice in an unequal duel. The trial must be on a basis which will not unwontedly handicap either party."

"Let a problem be stated," suggested the Antagonist. "He who first arrives at a solution wins the trial."

Han was scornfully silent. So the Leader formulated a problem—a terrific statement whose terms were dimensions and quasi-time and a dozen concepts which Kelly's brain could in no wise grasp. But the Antagonist intervened.

"That is hardly a fair problem, lying as it does entirely out of the man's experience. Let me formulate a problem." And he stated a situation which at first startled Kelly, and then brought him hope.

The problem was one he had met a year previously at the station. A system to integrate twenty-five different communication bands into one channel was under consideration, and it was necessary to thrust a beam of protons past a bank of twenty-five mutually inter-acting magnets and hit a pin-point filter at the far end of the case. The solution was simple enough—a statement of the initial vector in terms of a coordinate equation and a voltage potential—yet the solution had occupied the station calculator for two months. Kelly knew this solution as he knew his own name.

"Hurry!" came the Antagonist's secret thought.

Kelly blurted out the answer.

There was a wave of astonishment through the group, and he felt their suspicious inspection.

"You are quick indeed," said the Leader, non-plussed.

"Another problem," called the Antagonist. Once more he brought a question from Kelly's experience, this concerning the behavior of positrons in the secondary layer of a star in a cluster of six, all at specified temperatures and masses. And this time Kelly's mind worked faster. He immediately stated the answer. Still he anticipated Han by mere seconds.

Han protested, "How could this small pink brain move faster than my cosmic consciousness?"

"How is this?" asked the Leader. "How do you calculate so swiftly?"

Kelly fumbled for ideas, finally strung together a lame statement: "I do not calculate. In my brain is a mass of cells whose molecules form themselves into models of the problems. They move in an instant, the problem is solved, and the solution comes to me."

Anxiously he waited, but the reply seemed to satisfy the group. These creatures—or gods, if such they were—were they so naïve? Only the Antagonist suggested complex motives. Han, Kelly sensed, was old, of great force, of a hard and inflexible nature. The Leader was venerable beyond thought, calm and untroubled as space itself.

"What now?" came from the Antagonist. "Shall there be another problem? Or shall the man be declared the victor?"

Kelly would have been well pleased to let well enough alone, but this evidently did not suit the purposes of the Antagonist; hence his quiet jeer.

"No!" The thoughts of Han roared forth almost like sound. "Because of a ridiculous freak in this creature's brain, must I admit him my superior? I can fling him through a thousand dimensions with a thought, snap him out of existence, out of memory—"

"Perhaps because you are a god," came the Antagonist's taunt, "and of pure"—another confusing concept, a mixture of energy, divinity, force, intelligence. "The man is but a combination of atoms, and moves through the oxidation of carbon and hydrogen. Perhaps if you were as he, he might face you hand to hand and defeat you."

A curious tenseness stiffened the mental atmosphere. Han's thoughts came sluggishly, tinged for the first time with doubt.

"Let that be the third trial," said the Leader composedly. Han gave a mental shrug. One of the towering shadows shrunk, condensed, swirled to a man-like shape, solidified further, at last stood facing Kelly, a thing like a man, glowing with a green phosphorescence like the heart of the Seven-year Eye.

The Antagonist's secret thought came to Kelly: "Seize the jewel at the back of the neck."

Kelly scanned the slowly advancing figure. It was exactly his height and heft, naked, but radiating an inhuman confidence. The face was blurred, fuzzy, and Kelly could never afterward describe the countenance. He tore his gaze away.

"How do we fight?" he demanded, beads of sweat dripping from his body. "Do we set any rules—or no holds barred?"

"Tooth and nail," came the calm thoughts of the Leader. "Han now has organic sensibilities like yours. If you kill this body, or render it unconscious, you win. If you lose this trial, then we shall decide."

"Suppose he kills me?" objected Kelly, but no one seemed to heed his protest.

Han came glaring-eyed at him. Kelly took a step backward, jabbed tentatively with his left fist. Han rushed forward. Kelly punched furiously, kneed the onrushing body, heard it grunt and fall, to leap erect instantly. A tingle of joy ran down Kelly's spine, and more confidently he stepped forward, lashing out with rights and lefts. Han leapt close and clinched his arms around Kelly's body. Now he began to squeeze, and Kelly felt a power greater than any man's in those green-glowing arms.

"The jewel," came a sly thought. Sparks were exploding in Kelly's eyes; his ribs creaked. He swung a frenzied hand, clawing at Han's neck. He felt a hard protuberance, he dug his nails under, tore the jewel free.

A shrill cry of utmost pain and horror—and the god-man puffed away into black smoke which babbled in a frenzy back and forth through the darkness. It surged around Kelly, and little tendrils of the smoke seemed to pluck at the jewel clenched in his hand. But they had no great force, and Kelly found he could repel the wisps with the power of his own brain.

He suddenly understood the function of the jewel. It was the focus for the god. It centralized the myriad forces. The jewel gone, the god was a welter of conflicting volitions, vagrant impulses, insubstantial.

Kelly felt the Antagonist's triumphant thoughts. And he himself felt an elation he had never known before. The Leader's cool comment brought him back to himself:

"You seem to have won the contest." There was a pause. "In the absence of opposition we will render any requests you may make." There was no concern in his thoughts for the decentralized Han. The black smoke was dissipating, Han was no more than a memory. "Already you have delayed us long. We have the problem of"—the now familiar confusion of ideas, but this time Kelly understood vaguely. It seemed that there was a vortex of universes which possessed consciousness, as mighty or mightier than these gods, which was driving on a course that would be incommoding. There were qualifications, a host of contributory factors.

"Well," said Kelly, "I'd like you to move the planet I just came from back to its old orbit around Magra Taratempos. If you know what planet and what star I'm talking about."

"Yes." The Leader made a small exertion. "The world you mention moves in its previous orbit."

"Suppose the Han priests come through the portal and want it moved again?"

"The portal no longer exists. It was held open by Han; when Han dissolved, the portal closed...Is that the total of your desires?"

Kelly's mind raced, became a turmoil. This was his chance. Wealth, longevity, power, knowledge...Somehow thoughts would not form themselves—and there were curses attached to unnatural gifts—

"I'd like to get back to Bucktown safely…"

Kelly found himself in the glare of the outer world. He stood on the hill above Bucktown, and he breathed the salt air of the marshes. Above hung a hot white sun—Magra Taratempos.

He became aware of an object clenched in his hand. It was the jewel he had torn out of Han's neck. There were two others in his pocket.

Across the city he saw the light-blue and stainless-steel box of the station. What should he tell Herli and Mapes? Would they believe the truth? He looked at the three jewels. Two he could sell for a fortune on Earth. But one shone brilliantly in the bright sunlight and that was for Lynette Mason's tan and graceful neck.

Afterword to "The Temple of Han"

Talking shop has never appealed much to me, and I have spent most of my career trying to avoid it...

Early in my career I established a set of rather rigid rules as to how fiction should be written, but I find these rules difficult to formalize, or explain, or put into some sort of pattern which might instruct someone else. If I adhere to any fundamental axiom or principle in my writing, perhaps it is my belief that the function of fiction is essentially to amuse or entertain the reader. The mark of good writing, in my opinion, is that the reader is not aware that the story has been written; as he reads, the ideas and images flow into his mind as if he were living them. The utmost accolade a writer can receive is that the reader is incognizant of his presence.

In order to achieve this, the writer must put no obstacles in the reader's way. Therefore I try avoid words that he must puzzle over, or that he cannot gloss from context; and when I make up names, I shun the use of diacritical marks that he must sound out, thus halting the flow; and in general, I try to keep the sentences metrically pleasing, so that they do not obtrude upon the reader's mind. The sentences must swing...

Before my first sale: "The World-Thinker"...I wrote an epic novel in the style of E.E. Smith's cosmic chronicles. My own epic was rejected everywhere. I finally broke it into pieces and salvaged a few episodes for short stories. I think that "The Temple of Han" (originally "The God and Temple Robber") was one of these altered episodes.

—Jack Vance

The Masquerade on Dicantropus

Two puzzles dominated the life of Jim Root. The first, the pyramid out in the desert, tickled and prodded his curiosity, while the second, the problem of getting along with his wife, kept him keyed to a high pitch of anxiety and apprehension. At the moment the problem had crowded the mystery of the pyramid into a lost alley of his brain.

Eyeing his wife uneasily, Root decided that she was in for another of her fits. The symptoms were familiar—a jerking over of the pages of an old magazine, her tense back and bolt-upright posture, her pointed silence, the compression at the corners of her mouth.

With no preliminary motion she threw the magazine across the room, jumped to her feet. She walked to the doorway, stood looking out across the plain, fingers tapping on the sill. Root heard her voice, low, as if not meant for him to hear.

"Another day of this and I'll lose what little's left of my mind."

Root approached warily. If he could be compared to a Labrador retriever, then his wife was a black panther—a woman tall and well-covered with sumptuous flesh. She had black flowing hair and black flashing eyes. She lacquered her fingernails and wore black lounge pajamas even on desiccated deserted inhospitable Dicantropus.

"Now, dear," said Root, "take it easy. Certainly it's not as bad as all that."

She whirled and Root was surprised by the intensity in her eyes. "It's not bad, you say? Very well for you to talk—*you* don't care for anything human to begin with. I'm sick of it. Do you hear? I want to go back to Earth! I never want to see another planet in my whole life. I never want to hear the word archaeology, I never want to see a rock or a bone or a microscope—"

She flung a wild gesture around the room that included a number of rocks, bones, microscopes, as well as books, specimens in bottles, photographic equipment, a number of native artifacts.

Root tried to soothe her with logic. "Very few people are privileged to live on an outside planet, dear."

"They're not in their right minds. If I'd known what it was like, I'd never have come out here." Her voice dropped once more. "Same old dirt every day, same stinking natives, same vile canned food, nobody to talk to—"

Root uncertainly picked up and laid down his pipe. "Lie down, dear," he said with unconvincing confidence. "Take a nap! Things will look different when you wake up."

Stabbing him with a look, she turned and strode out into the blue-white glare of the sun. Root followed more slowly, bringing Barbara's sun-helmet and adjusting his own. Automatically he cocked an eye up the antenna, the reason for the station and his own presence, Dicantropus being a relay point for ULR messages between Clave II and Polaris. The antenna stood as usual, polished metal tubing four hundred feet high.

Barbara halted by the shore of the lake, a brackish pond in the neck of an old volcano, one of the few natural bodies of water on the planet. Root silently joined her, handed her her sun-helmet. She jammed it on her head, walked away.

Root shrugged, watched her as she circled the pond to a clump of feather-fronded cycads. She flung herself down, relaxed into a sulky lassitude, her back to a big gray-green trunk, and seemed intent on the antics of the natives—owlish leather-gray little creatures popping back and forth into holes in their mound.

This was a hillock a quarter-mile long, covered with spine-scrub and a rusty black creeper. With one exception it was the only eminence as far as the eye could reach, horizon to horizon, across the baked helpless expanse of the desert.

The exception was the stepped pyramid, the mystery of which irked Root. It was built of massive granite blocks, set without mortar but cut so carefully that hardly a crack could be seen. Early on his arrival Root had climbed all over the pyramid, unsuccessfully seeking entrance.

When finally he brought out his atomite torch to melt a hole in the granite a sudden swarm of natives pushed him back and in the pidgin of Dicantropus gave him to understand that entrance was forbidden. Root desisted with reluctance, and had been consumed by curiosity ever since...

Who had built the pyramid? In style it resembled the *ziggurats* of ancient Assyria. The granite had been set with a skill unknown, so far as Root could see, to the natives. But if not the natives—who? A thousand times Root had chased the question through his brain. Were the natives debased relics of a once-civilized race? If so, why were there no other ruins? And what was the purpose of the pyramid? A temple? A mausoleum? A treasure-house? Perhaps it was entered from below by a tunnel.

As Root stood on the shore of the lake, looking across the desert, the questions flicked automatically through his mind though without their usual pungency. At the moment the problem of soothing his wife lay heavy on his mind. He debated a few moments whether or not to join her; perhaps she had cooled off and might like some company. He circled the pond and stood looking down at her glossy black hair.

"I came over here to be alone," she said without accent and the indifference chilled him more than an insult.

"I thought—that maybe you might like to talk," said Root. "I'm very sorry, Barbara, that you're unhappy."

Still she said nothing, sitting with her head pressed back against the tree trunk.

"We'll go home on the next supply ship," Root said. "Let's see, there should be one—"

"Three months and three days," said Barbara flatly.

Root shifted his weight, watched her from the corner of his eye. This was a new manifestation. Tears, recriminations, anger—there had been plenty of these before.

"We'll try to keep amused till then," he said desperately. "Let's think up some games to play. Maybe badminton—or we could do more swimming."

Barbara snorted in sharp sarcastic laughter. "With things like that popping up around you?" She gestured to one of the Dicantrops who had lazily paddled close. She narrowed her eyes, leaned forward. "What's that he's got around his neck?"

Root peered. "Looks like a diamond necklace more than anything else."

"My Lord!" whispered Barbara.

Root walked down to the water's edge. "Hey, boy!" The Dicantrop turned his great velvety eyes in their sockets. "Come here!"

Barbara joined him as the native paddled close.

"Let's see what you've got there," said Root, leaning close to the necklace.

"Why, those are beautiful!" breathed his wife.

Root chewed his lip thoughtfully. "They certainly look like diamonds. The setting might be platinum or iridium. Hey, boy, where did you get these?"

The Dicantrop paddled backward. "We find."

"Where?"

The Dicantrop blew froth from his breath-holes but it seemed to Root as if his eyes had glanced momentarily toward the pyramid.

"You find in big pile of rock?"

"No," said the native and sank below the surface.

Barbara returned to her seat by the tree, frowned at the water. Root joined her. For a moment there was silence. Then Barbara said, "That pyramid must be full of things like that!"

Root made a deprecatory noise in his throat. "Oh—I suppose it's possible."

"Why don't you go out and see?"

"I'd like to—but you know it would make trouble."

"You could go out at night."

"No," said Root uncomfortably. "It's really not right. If they want to keep the thing closed up and secret it's their business. After all it belongs to them."

"How do you know it does?" his wife insisted, with a hard and sharp directness. "They didn't build it and probably never put those diamonds there." Scorn crept into her voice. "Are you afraid?"

"Yes," said Root. "I'm afraid. There's an awful lot of them and only two of us. That's one objection. But the other, most important—"

Barbara let herself slump back against the trunk. "I don't want to hear it."

Root, now angry himself, said nothing for a minute. Then, thinking of the three months and three days till the arrival of the supply ship, he said, "It's no use our being disagreeable. It just makes it harder on both of us. I made a mistake bringing you out here and I'm sorry. I thought you'd enjoy the experience, just the two of us alone on a strange planet—"

Barbara was not listening to him. Her mind was elsewhere.

"Barbara!"

"*Shh!*" she snapped. "Be still! Listen!"

He jerked his head up. The air vibrated with a far *thrum-m-m-m*. Root sprang out into the sunlight, scanned the sky. The sound grew louder. There was no question about it, a ship was dropping down from space.

Root ran into the station, flipped open the communicator—but there were no signals coming in. He returned to the door and watched as the ship sank down to a bumpy rough landing two hundred yards from the station.

It was a small ship, the type rich men sometimes used as private yachts, but old and battered. It sat in a quiver of hot air, its tubes creaking and hissing as they cooled. Root approached.

The dogs on the port began to turn, the port swung open. A man stood in the opening. For a moment he teetered on loose legs, then fell headlong.

Root, springing forward, caught him before he struck ground. "Barbara!" Root called. His wife approached. "Take his feet. We'll carry him inside. He's sick."

They laid him on the couch and his eyes opened halfway.

"What's the trouble?" asked Root. "Where do you feel sick?"

"My legs are like ice," husked the man. "My shoulders ache. I can't breathe."

"Wait till I look in the book," muttered Root. He pulled out the *Official Spaceman's Self-Help Guide*, traced down the symptoms. He looked across to the sick man. "You been anywhere near Alphard?"

"Just came from there," panted the man.

"Looks like you got a dose of Lyma's Virus. A shot of mycosetin should fix you up, according to the book."

He inserted an ampoule into the hypospray, pressed the tip to his patient's arm, pushed the plunger home. "That should do it—according to the Guide."

"Thanks," said his patient. "I feel better already." He closed his eyes. Root stood up, glanced at Barbara. She was scrutinizing the man with a peculiar calculation. Root looked down again, seeing the man for the first time. He was young, perhaps thirty, thin but strong with a tight nervous muscularity. His face was lean, almost gaunt, his skin very bronzed. He had short black hair, heavy black eyebrows, a long jaw, a thin high nose.

Root turned away. Glancing at his wife he foresaw the future with a sick certainty.

He washed out the hypospray, returned the Guide to the rack, all with a sudden self-conscious awkwardness. When he turned around, Barbara was staring at him with wide thoughtful eyes. Root slowly left the room.

A day later Marville Landry was on his feet and when he had shaved and changed his clothes there was no sign of the illness. He was by profession a mining engineer, so he revealed to Root, en route to a contract on Thuban XIV.

The virus had struck swiftly and only by luck had he noticed the proximity of Dicantropus on his charts. Rapidly weakening, he had been forced to decelerate so swiftly and land so uncertainly that he feared his fuel was low. And indeed, when they went out to check, they found only enough fuel to throw the ship a hundred feet into the air.

Landry shook his head ruefully. "And there's a ten-million-munit contract waiting for me on Thuban Fourteen."

Said Root dismally, "The supply packet's due in three months."

Landry winced. "Three months—in this hell-hole? That's murder." They returned to the station. "How do you stand it here?"

Barbara heard him. "We don't. I've been on the verge of hysterics every minute the last six months. Jim—" she made a wry grimace toward her husband "—he's got his bones and rocks and the antenna. He's not too much company."

"Maybe I can help out," Landry offered airily.

"Maybe," she said with a cool blank glance at Root. Presently she left the room, walking more gracefully now, with an air of mysterious gaiety.

Dinner that evening was a gala event. As soon as the sun took its blue glare past the horizon Barbara and Landry carried a table down to the lake and there they set it with all the splendor the station could afford. With no word to Root she pulled the cork on the gallon of brandy he had been nursing for a year and served generous highballs with canned lime-juice, Maraschino cherries and ice.

For a space, with the candles glowing and evoking lambent ghosts in the highballs, even Root was gay. The air was wonderfully cool and the sands of the desert spread white and clean as damask out into the dimness. So they feasted on canned fowl and mushrooms and frozen fruit and drank deep of Root's brandy, and across the pond the natives watched from the dark.

And presently, while Root grew sleepy and dull, Landry became gay, and Barbara sparkled—the complete hostess, charming, witty and the Dicantropus night tinkled and throbbed with her laughter. She and Landry toasted each other and exchanged laughing comments at Root's expense—who now sat slumping, stupid, half-asleep. Finally he lurched to his feet and stumbled off to the station.

On the table by the lake the candles burnt low. Barbara poured more brandy. Their voices became murmurs and at last the candles guttered.

In spite of any human will to hold time in blessed darkness, morning came and brought a day of silence and averted eyes. Then other days and nights succeeded each other and time proceeded as usual. And there was now little pretense at the station.

Barbara frankly avoided Root and when she had occasion to speak her voice was one of covert amusement. Landry, secure, confident, aquiline, had a trick of sitting back and looking from one to the other as if inwardly chuckling over the whole episode. Root preserved a studied calm and spoke in a subdued tone which conveyed no meaning other than the sense of his words.

There were a few minor clashes. Entering the bathroom one morning Root found Landry shaving with his razor. Without heat Root took the shaver out of Landry's hand.

For an instant Landry stared blankly, then wrenched his mouth into the beginnings of a snarl.

Root smiled almost sadly. "Don't get me wrong, Landry. There's a difference between a razor and a woman. The razor is mine. A human being can't be owned. Leave my personal property alone."

Landry's eyebrows rose. "Man, you're crazy." He turned away. "Heat's got you."

The days went past and now they were unchanging as before but unchanging with a new leaden tension. Words became even fewer and dislike hung like tattered tinsel. Every motion, every line of the body, became a detestable sight, an evil which the other flaunted deliberately.

Root burrowed almost desperately into his rocks and bones, peered through his microscope, made a thousand measurements, a thousand notes. Landry and Barbara fell into the habit of taking long walks in the evening, usually out to the pyramid, then slowly back across the quiet cool sand.

The mystery of the pyramid suddenly fascinated Landry and he even questioned Root.

"I've no idea," said Root. "Your guess is as good as mine. All I know is that the natives don't want anyone trying to get into it."

"Mph," said Landry, gazing across the desert. "No telling what's inside. Barbara said one of the natives was wearing a diamond necklace worth thousands."

"I suppose anything's possible," said Root. He had noticed the acquisitive twitch to Landry's mouth, the hook of the fingers. "You'd better not get any ideas. I don't want any trouble with the natives. Remember that, Landry."

Landry asked with seeming mildness, "Do you have any authority over that pyramid?"

"No," said Root shortly. "None whatever."

"It's not—yours?" Landry sardonically accented the word and Root remembered the incident of the shaver.

"No."

"Then," said Landry, rising, "mind your own business."

He left the room.

During the day Root noticed Landry and Barbara deep in conversation and he saw Landry rummaging through his ship. At dinner no single word was spoken.

As usual, when the afterglow had died to a cool blue glimmer, Barbara and Landry strolled off into the desert. But tonight Root watched after them and he noticed a pack on Landry's shoulders and Barbara seemed to be carrying a handbag.

He paced back and forth, puffing furiously at his pipe. Landry was right— it was none of his business. If there were profit, he wanted none of it. And if there were danger, it would strike only those who provoked it. Or would it? Would he, Root, be automatically involved because of his association with Landry and Barbara? To the Dicantrops, a man was a man, and if one man needed punishment, all men did likewise.

Would there be—killing? Root puffed at his pipe, chewed the stem, blew smoke out in gusts between his teeth. In a way he was responsible for Barbara's safety. He had taken her from a sheltered life on Earth. He shook his head, put down his pipe, went to the drawer where he kept his gun. It was gone.

Root looked vacantly across the room. Landry had it. No telling how long since he'd taken it. Root went to the kitchen, found a meat-axe, tucked it inside his jumper, set out across the desert.

He made a wide circle in order to approach the pyramid from behind. The air was quiet and dark and cool as water in an old well. The crisp sand sounded faintly under his feet. Above him spread the sky and the sprinkle of the thousand stars. Somewhere up there was the Sun and old Earth.

The pyramid loomed suddenly large and now he saw a glow, heard the muffled clinking of tools. He approached quietly, halted several hundred feet out in the darkness, stood watching, alert to all sounds.

Landry's atomite torch ate at the granite. As he cut, Barbara hooked the detached chunks out into the sand. From time to time Landry stood back, sweating and gasping from radiated heat.

A foot he cut into the granite, two feet, three feet, and Root heard the excited murmur of voices. They were through, into empty space. Careless of watching behind them they sidled through the hole they had cut. Root, more wary, listened, strove to pierce the darkness…Nothing.

He sprang forward, hastened to the hole, peered within. The yellow gleam of Landry's torch swept past his eyes. He crept into the hole, pushed his head out into emptiness. The air was cold, smelled of dust and damp rock.

Landry and Barbara stood fifty feet away. In the desultory flash of the lamp Root saw stone walls and a stone floor. The pyramid appeared to be an empty shell. Why then were the natives so particular? He heard Landry's voice, edged with bitterness.

"Not a damn thing, not even a mummy for your husband to gloat over."

Root could sense Barbara shuddering. "Let's go. It gives me the shivers. It's like a dungeon."

"Just a minute, we might as well make sure…Hm." He was playing the light on the walls. "That's peculiar."

"What's peculiar?"

"It looks like the stone was sliced with a torch. Notice how it's fused here on the inside…"

Root squinted, trying to see. "Strange," he heard Landry mutter. "Outside it's chipped, inside it's cut by a torch. It doesn't look so very old here inside, either."

"The air would preserve it," suggested Barbara dubiously.

"I suppose so—still, old places look old. There's dust and a kind of dullness. This looks raw."

"I don't understand how that could be."

"I don't either. There's something funny somewhere."

Root stiffened. Sound from without? Shuffle of splay feet in the sand—he started to back out. Something pushed him, he sprawled forward, fell. The bright eye of Landry's torch stared in his direction. "What's that?" came a hard voice. "Who's there?"

Root looked over his shoulder. The light passed over him, struck a dozen gray bony forms. They stood quietly just inside the hole, their eyes like balls of black plush.

Root gained his feet. "Hah!" cried Landry. "So *you're* here too."

"Not because I want to be," returned Root grimly.

Landry edged slowly forward, keeping his light on the Dicantrops. He asked Root sharply, "Are these lads dangerous?"

Root appraised the natives. "I don't know."

"Stay still," said one of these in the front rank. "Stay still." His voice was a deep croak.

"Stay still, hell!" exclaimed Landry. "We're leaving. There's nothing here I want. Get out of the way." He stepped forward.

"Stay still...We kill..."

Landry paused.

"What's the trouble now?" interposed Root anxiously. "Surely there's no harm in looking. There's nothing here."

"That is why we kill. Nothing here, now you know. Now you look other place. When you think this place important, then you not look other place. We kill, new man come, he think this place important."

Landry muttered, "Do you get what he's driving at?"

Root said slowly, "I don't know for sure." He addressed the Dicantrop. "We don't care about your secrets. You've no reason to hide things from us."

The native jerked his head. "Then why do you come here? You look for secrets."

Barbara's voice came from behind. "What *is* your secret? Diamonds?"

The native jerked his head again. Amusement? Anger? His emotions, unearthly, could be matched by no earthly words. "Diamonds are nothing—rocks."

"I'd like a carload," Landry muttered under his breath.

"Now look here," said Root persuasively. "You let us out and we won't pry into any of your secrets. It was wrong of us to break in and I'm sorry it happened. We'll repair the damage—"

The Dicantrop made a faint sputtering sound. "You do not understand. You tell other men—pyramid is nothing. Then other men look all around for other thing. They bother, look, look, look. All this no good. You die, everything go like before."

"There's too much talk," said Landry viciously, "and I don't like the sound of it. Let's get out of here." He pulled out Root's gun. "Come on," he snapped at Root, "let's move."

To the natives, "Get out of the way or I'll do some killing myself!"

A rustle of movement from the natives, a thin excited whimper.

"We've got to rush 'em," shouted Landry. "If they get outside they can knock us over as we leave. Let's go!"

He sprang forward and Root was close behind. Landry used the gun as a club and Root used his fists and the Dicantrops rattled like cornstalks against the walls. Landry erupted through the hole. Root pushed Barbara through and, kicking back at the natives behind him, struggled out into the air.

Landry's momentum had carried him away from the pyramid, out into a seething mob of Dicantrops. Root, following more slowly, pressed his back to the granite. He sensed the convulsive movement in the wide darkness. "The whole colony must be down here," he shouted into Barbara's ear. For a minute he was occupied with the swarming natives, keeping Barbara behind him as much as possible. The first ledge of granite was about shoulder height.

"Step on my hands," he panted. "I'll shove you up."

"But—Landry!" came Barbara's choked wail.

"Look at that crowd!" bit Root furiously. "We can't do anything." A sudden rush of small bony forms almost overwhelmed him. "Hurry up!"

Whimpering she stepped into his clasped hands. He thrust her up on the first ledge. Shaking off the clawing natives who had leapt on him, he jumped, scrambled up beside her. "Now run!" he shouted in her ear and she fled down the ledge.

From the darkness came a violent cry. "Root! *Root!* For God's sake—they've got me down—" Another hoarse yell, rising to a scream of agony. Then silence.

"Hurry!" said Root. They came to the far corner of the pyramid. "Jump down," panted Root. "Down to the ground."

"Landry!" moaned Barbara, teetering at the edge.

"Get down!" snarled Root. He thrust her down to the white sand and, seizing her hand, ran across the desert, back toward the station. A minute or so later, with pursuit left behind, he slowed to a trot.

"We should go back," cried Barbara. "Are you going to leave him to those devils?"

Root was silent a moment. Then, choosing his words, he said, "I told him to stay away from the place. Anything that happens to him is his own fault. And whatever it is, it's already happened. There's nothing we can do now."

A dark hulk shouldered against the sky—Landry's ship.

"Let's get in here," said Root. "We'll be safer than in the station."

He helped her into the ship, clamped tight the port. "*Phew!*" He shook his head. "Never thought it would come to this."

He climbed into the pilot's seat, looked out across the desert. Barbara huddled somewhere behind him, sobbing softly.

An hour passed, during which they said no word. Then, without warning, a fiery orange ball rose from the hill across the pond, drifted toward the station. Root blinked, jerked upright in his seat. He scrambled for the ship's machine gun, yanked at the trigger—without result.

When at last he found and threw off the safety the orange ball hung over the station and Root held his fire. The ball brushed against the antenna—a tremendous explosion spattered to every corner of vision. It seared Root's eyes, threw him to the deck, rocked the ship, left him dazed and half-conscious.

Barbara lay moaning. Root hauled himself to his feet. A seared pit, a tangle of metal, showed where the station had stood. Root dazedly slumped into the seat, started the fuel pump, plunged home the catalyzers. The boat quivered, bumped a few feet along the ground. The tubes sputtered, wheezed.

Root looked at the fuel gauge, looked again. The needle pointed to zero, a fact which Root had known but forgotten. He cursed his own stupidity. Their presence in the ship might have gone ignored if he had not called attention to it.

Up from the hill floated another orange ball. Root jumped for the machine gun, sent out a burst of explosive pellets. Again the roar and the blast and the whole top of the hill was blown off, revealing what appeared to be a smooth strata of black rock.

Root looked over his shoulder to Barbara. "This is it."

"Wha—what do you mean?"

"We can't get away. Sooner or later—" His voice trailed off. He reached up, twisted a dial labeled EMERGENCY. The ship's ULR unit hummed. Root said into the mesh, "Dicantropus station—we're being attacked by natives. Send help at once."

Root sank back into the seat. A tape would repeat his message endlessly until cut off.

Barbara staggered to the seat beside Root. "What were those orange balls?"

"That's what *I've* been wondering—some sort of bomb."

But there were no more of them. And presently the horizon began to glare, the hill became a silhouette on the electric sky. And over their heads the transmitter pulsed an endless message into space.

"How long before we get help?" whispered Barbara.

"Too long," said Root, staring off toward the hill. "They must be afraid of the machine gun—I can't understand what else they're waiting for. Maybe good light."

"They can—" Her voice stopped. She stared. Root stared, held by unbelief—amazement. The hill across the pond was breaking open, crumbling...

Root sat drinking brandy with the captain of the supply ship *Method,* which had come to their assistance, and the captain was shaking his head.

"I've seen lots of strange things around this cluster but this masquerade beats everything."

Root said, "It's strange in one way, in another it's as cold and straightforward as ABC. They played it as well as they could and it was pretty darned good. If it hadn't been for that scoundrel Landry they'd have fooled us forever."

The captain banged his glass on the desk, stared at Root. "But *why?*"

Root said slowly, "They liked Dicantropus. It's a hell-hole, a desert to us, but it was heaven to them. They liked the heat, the dryness. But they didn't want a lot of off-world creatures prying into their business—as we surely would have if we'd seen through the masquerade. It must have been an awful shock when the first Earth ship set down here."

"And that pyramid…"

"Now that's a strange thing. They were good psychologists, these Dicantrops, as good as you could expect an off-world race to be. If you'll read a report of the first landing, you'll find no mention of the pyramid. Why? Because it wasn't here. Landry thought it looked new. He was right. It *was* new. It was a fraud, a decoy—just strange enough to distract our attention.

"As long as that pyramid sat out there, with me focusing all my mental energy on it, they were safe—and how they must have laughed. As soon as Landry broke in and discovered the fraud, then it was all over…

"That might have been their miscalculation," mused Root. "Assume that they knew nothing of crime, of anti-social action. If everybody did what he was told to do their privacy was safe forever." Root laughed. "Maybe they didn't know human beings so well after all."

The captain refilled the glasses and they drank in silence. "Wonder where they came from," he said at last.

Root shrugged. "I suppose we'll never know. Some other hot dry planet, that's sure. Maybe they were refugees or some peculiar religious sect or maybe they were a colony."

"Hard to say," agreed the captain sagely. "Different race, different psychology. That's what we run into all the time."

"Thank God they weren't vindictive," said Root, half to himself. "No doubt they could have killed us any one of a dozen ways after I'd sent out that emergency call and they had to leave."

"It all ties in," admitted the captain.

Root sipped the brandy, nodded. "Once that ULR signal went out, their isolation was done for. No matter whether we were dead or not, there'd be Earthmen swarming around the station, pushing into their tunnels—and right there went their secret."

And he and the captain silently inspected the hole across the pond where the tremendous space-ship had lain buried under the spine-scrub and rusty black creeper.

"And once that space-ship was laid bare," Root continued, "there'd be a hullabaloo from here to Fomalhaut. A tremendous mass like that? We'd have to know everything—their space-drive, their history, everything about them.

If what they wanted was privacy that would be a thing of the past. If they were a colony from another star they had to protect their secrets the same way we protect ours."

Barbara was standing by the ruins of the station, poking at the tangle with a stick. She turned and Root saw that she held his pipe. It was charred and battered but still recognizable. She slowly handed it to him. "Well?" said Root.

She answered in a quiet withdrawn voice: "Now that I'm leaving I think I'll miss Dicantropus." She turned to him, "Jim…"

"What?"

"I'd stay on another year if you'd like."

"No," said Root. "I don't like it here myself."

She said, still in the low tone: "Then—you don't forgive me for being foolish…"

Root raised his eyebrows. "Certainly I do. I never blamed you in the first place. You're human. Indisputably human."

"Then—why are you acting—like Moses?"

Root shrugged.

"Whether you believe me or not," she said with an averted gaze, "I never—"

He interrupted with a gesture. "What does it matter? Suppose you did—you had plenty of reason to. I wouldn't hold it against you."

"You would—in your heart."

Root said nothing.

"I wanted to hurt you. I was slowly going crazy—and you didn't seem to care one way or another. Told—him I wasn't—your property."

Root smiled his sad smile. "I'm human too."

He made a casual gesture toward the hole where the Dicantrop spaceship had lain. "If you still want diamonds go down that hole with a bucket. There's diamonds big as grapefruit. It's an old volcanic neck, it's the grand-daddy of all diamond mines. I've got a claim staked out around it; we'll be using diamonds for billiard balls as soon as we get some machinery out here."

They turned slowly back to the *Method*.

"Three's quite a crowd on Dicantropus," said Root thoughtfully. "On Earth, where there's three billion, we can have a little privacy."

Afterword to
"The Masquerade of Dicantropus"

As a rule, seamen enjoy a great deal of spare time. I used this spare time to write, and much of what I wrote was subsequently published in one form or another...I did much of my writing in a deck chair where I could look off across the ocean. On a calm day in the tropics, the view across the ocean trivializes any attempts to describe it in words. There are endless miles of blue water, transparent at the swells, gently heaving all the way out to the horizon, where maybe a few cumulus clouds are mounting...I sold a set of fantasy stories to Hillman Publications, who issued the collection using the title *The Dying Earth*. I also wrote a mystery story, which was published as *The Flesh Mask*, and a frothy bit of foolishness to which the publisher attached a wildly misleading and inappropriate title, *Isle of Peril*.

—Jack Vance

Abercrombie Station

I

The doorkeeper was a big hard-looking man with an unwholesome horse-face, a skin like corroded zinc. Two girls spoke to him, asking arch questions.

Jean saw him grunt noncommittally. "Just stick around; I can't give out no dope."

He motioned to the girl sitting beside Jean, a blonde girl, very smartly turned out. She rose to her feet; the doorkeeper slid back the door. The blonde girl walked swiftly through into the inner room; the door closed behind her. She moved tentatively forward, stopped short. A man sat quietly on an old-fashioned leather couch, watching through half-closed eyes.

Nothing frightening here, was her initial impression. He was young—twenty-four or twenty-five. Mediocre, she thought, neither tall nor short, stocky nor lean. His hair was nondescript, his features without distinction, his clothes unobtrusive and neutral.

He shifted his position, opened his eyes a flicker. The blonde girl felt a quick pang. Perhaps she had been mistaken.

"How old are you?"

"I'm—twenty."

"Take off your clothes."

She stared, hands tight and white-knuckled on her purse. Intuition came suddenly; she drew a quick shallow breath. *Obey him once, give in once, he'll be your master as long as you live.*

"No...NO, I won't."

She turned quickly, reached for the door-slide. He said unemotionally, "You're too old anyway."

The door jerked aside; she walked quickly through the outer room, looking neither right nor left.

A hand touched her arm. She stopped, looked down into a face that was jet, pale rose, ivory. A young face with an expression of vitality and intelligence: black eyes, short black hair, a beautiful clear skin, mouth without make-up.

Jean asked, "What goes on? What kind of job is it?"

The blonde girl said in a tight voice, "I don't know. I didn't stay to find out. It's nothing nice." She turned, went through the outer door.

Jean sank back into the chair, pursed her lips speculatively. A minute passed. Another girl, nostrils flared wide, came from the inner room, crossed to the door, looking neither right nor left.

Jean smiled faintly. She had a wide mouth, expansive and flexible. Her teeth were small, white, very sharp.

The doorkeeper motioned to her. She jumped to her feet, entered the inner room.

The quiet man was smoking. A silvery plume rose past his face, melted into the air over his head. Jean thought, *there's something strange in his complete immobility. He's too tight, too compressed.*

She put her hands behind her back and waited, watching carefully.

"How old are you?"

This was a question she usually found wise to evade. She tilted her head sidewise, smiling, a mannerism which gave her a wild and reckless look. "How old do you think I am?"

"Sixteen or seventeen."

"That's close enough."

He nodded. "Close enough. What's your name?"

"Jean Parlier."

"Who do you live with?"

"No one. I live alone."

"Father? Mother?"

"Dead."

"Grandparents? Guardian?"

"I'm alone."

He nodded. "Any trouble with the law on that account?"

She considered him warily. "No."

He moved his head enough to send a kink running up the feather of smoke. "Take off your clothes."

"Why?"

"It's a quick way to check your qualifications."

"Well—yes. In a way I guess it is...Physical or moral?"

He made no reply, sat looking at her impassively, the gray skein of smoke rising past his face.

She shrugged, put her hands to her sides, to her neck, to her waist, to her back, to her legs, and stood without clothes.

He put the cigarette to his mouth, puffed, sat up, stubbed it out, rose to his feet, walked slowly forward.

He's trying to scare me, she thought, and smiled quietly to herself. He could try.

He stopped two feet away, stood looking down into her eyes. "You really want a million dollars?"

"That's why I'm here."

"You took the advertisement in the literal sense of the words?"

"Is there any other way?"

"You might have construed the language as—metaphor, hyperbole."

She grinned, showing her sharp white teeth. "I don't know what those words mean. Anyway I'm here. If the advertisement was only intended for you to look at me naked, I'll leave."

His expression did not change. Peculiar, thought Jean, how his body moved, his head turned, but his eyes always seemed fixed. He said as if he had not heard her, "Not too many girls have applied."

"That doesn't concern me. I want a million dollars. What is it? Blackmail? Impersonation?"

He passed over her question. "What would you do with a million if you had it?"

"I don't know…I'll worry about that when I get it. Have you checked my qualifications? I'm cold."

He turned quickly, strode to the couch, seated himself. She slipped into her clothes, came over to the couch, took a tentative seat facing him.

He said dryly, "You fill the qualifications almost too well!"

"How so?"

"It's unimportant."

Jean tilted her head, laughed. She looked like a healthy, very pretty high-school girl who might be the better for more sunshine. "Tell me what I'm to do to earn a million dollars."

"You're to marry a wealthy young man, who suffers from—let us call it, an incurable disease. When he dies, his property will be yours. You will sell his property to me for a million dollars."

"Evidently he's worth more than a million dollars."

He was conscious of the questions she did not ask. "There's somewhere near a billion involved."

"What kind of disease does he have? I might catch it myself."

"I'll take care of the disease end. You won't catch it if you keep your nose clean."

"Oh—oh, I see—tell me more about him. Is he handsome? Big? Strong? I might feel sorry if he died."

"He's eighteen years old. His main interest is collecting." Sardonically: "He likes zoology too. He's an eminent zoologist. His name is Earl Abercrombie. He owns—" he gestured up "—Abercrombie Station."

Jean stared, then laughed feebly. "That's a hard way to make a million dollars...Earl Abercrombie..."

"Squeamish?"

"Not when I'm awake. But I do have nightmares."

"Make up your mind."

She looked modestly to where she had folded her hands in her lap. "A million isn't a very large cut out of a billion."

He surveyed her with something like approval. "No. It isn't."

She rose to her feet, slim as a dancer. "All you do is sign a check. I have to marry him, get in bed with him."

"They don't use beds on Abercrombie Station."

"Since he lives on Abercrombie, he might not be interested in me."

"Earl is different," said the quiet man. "Earl likes gravity girls."

"You must realize that once he dies, you'd be forced to accept whatever I chose to give you. Or the property might be put in charge of a trustee."

"Not necessarily. The Abercrombie Civil Regulation allows property to be controlled by anyone sixteen or over. Earl is eighteen. He exercises complete control over the station, subject to a few unimportant restrictions. I'll take care of that end." He went to the door, slid it open. "Hammond."

The man with the long face came wordlessly to the door.

"I've got her. Send the others home."

He closed the door, turned to Jean. "I want you to have dinner with me."

"I'm not dressed for dinner."

He left the room. The door closed. Jean stretched, threw back her head, opened her mouth in a soundless exultant laugh. She raised her arms over her head, took a step forward, turned a supple cart-wheel across the rug, bounced to her feet beside the window.

She knelt, rested her head on her hands, looked across Metropolis. Dusk had come. The great gray-golden sky filled three-quarters of her vision. A thousand feet below was the wan gray, lavender and black crumble of surface buildings, the pallid roadways streaming with golden motes. To the right, aircraft slid silently along force-guides to the mountain suburbs—tired normal people bound to pleasant normal homes. What would they think if they knew that she, Jean Parlier, was watching? For instance, the man who drove that shiny Skyfarer with the pale green chevrets...She built a picture of him: pudgy, forehead creased with lines of worry. He'd be hurrying home to his wife, who would listen tolerantly while he boasted or grumbled. Cattle-women, cow-women, thought Jean without rancor. What man could subdue her? Where was the man who was wild and hard and bright enough?... Remembering her new job, she grimaced. Mrs. Earl Abercrombie. She looked up into the sky. The stars were not yet out and the lights of Abercrombie Station could not be seen.

A million dollars, think of it! "What will you do with a million dollars?" her new employer had asked her, and now that she returned to it, the idea was uncomfortable, like a lump in her throat.

How would she feel? How would she…Her mind moved away from the subject, recoiled with the faintest trace of anger, as if it were a subject not to be touched upon. "Rats," said Jean. "Time to worry about it after I get it…A million dollars. Not too large a cut out of a billion, actually. Two million would be better."

Her eyes followed a slim red airboat diving along a sharp curve into the parking area: a sparkling new Marshall Moon-chaser. Now there was something she wanted. It would be one of her first purchases.

The door slid open. Hammond the doorkeeper looked briefly in. Then the couturier entered, pushing his wheeled kit before him, a slender little blond man with rich topaz eyes. The door closed.

Jean turned away from the window. The couturier—André was the name stencilled on the enamel of the box—spoke for more light, walked around her, darting glances up and down her body.

"Yes," he muttered, pressing his lips in and out. "Ah, yes…Now what does the lady have in mind?"

"A dinner gown, I suppose."

He nodded. "Mr. Fotheringay mentioned formal evening wear."

So that was his name—Fotheringay.

André snapped up a screen. "Observe, if you will, a few of my effects; perhaps there is something to please you."

Jean said, "Something like that."

André made a gesture of approval, snapped his fingers. "Mademoiselle has good taste. And now we shall see…if mademoiselle will let me help her…"

He deftly unzipped her garments, laid them on the couch.

"First—we refresh ourselves." He selected a tool from his kit, and holding her wrist between delicate thumb and forefinger, sprayed her arms with cool mist, then warm, perfumed air. Her skin tingled, fresh, invigorated.

André tapped his chin. "Now, the foundation."

She stood, eyes half-closed, while he bustled around her, striding off, making whispered comments, quick gestures with significance only to himself.

He sprayed her with gray-green web, touched and pulled as the strands set. He adjusted knurled knobs at the ends of a flexible tube, pressed it around her waist, swept it away and it trailed shining black-green silk. He artfully twisted and wound his tube. He put the frame back in the kit, pulled, twisted, pinched, while the silk set.

He sprayed her with wan white, quickly jumped forward, folded, shaped, pinched, pulled, bunched and the stuff fell in twisted bands from her shoulders and into a full rustling skirt.

"Now—gauntlets." He covered her arms and hands with warm black-green pulp which set into spangled velvet, adroitly cut with scissors to bare the back of her hand.

"Slippers." Black satin, webbed with emerald-green phosphorescence.

"Now—the ornaments." He hung a red bauble from her right ear, slipped a cabochon ruby on her right hand.

"Scent—a trace. The Levailleur, indeed." He flicked her with an odor suggestive of a Central Asia flower patch. "And mademoiselle is dressed. And may I say—" he bowed with a flourish "—most exquisitely beautiful."

He manipulated his cart, one side fell away. A mirror uncoiled upward.

Jean inspected herself. Vivid naiad. When she acquired that million dollars—two million would be better—she'd put André on her permanent payroll.

André was still muttering compliments. "—Elan supreme. She is magic. Most striking. Eyes will turn…"

The door slid back. Fotheringay came into the room. André bowed low, clasped his hands.

Fotheringay glanced at her. "You're ready. Good. Come along."

Jean thought, *we might as well get this straight right now.*

"Where?"

He frowned slightly, stood aside while André pushed his cart out.

Jean said, "I came here of my own free will. I walked into this room under my own power. Both times I knew where I was going. Now you say 'Come along.' First I want to know where. Then I'll decide whether or not I'll come."

"You don't want a million dollars very badly."

"Two million. I want it badly enough to waste an afternoon investigating… But—if I don't get it today, I'll get it tomorrow. Or next week. Somehow I'll get it; a long time ago I made my mind up. So?" She performed an airy curtsey.

His pupils contracted. He said in an even voice, "Very well. Two million. I am now taking you to dinner on the roof, where I will give you your instructions."

II

They drifted under the dome, in a greenish plastic bubble. Below them spread the commercial fantasy of an out-world landscape: gray sward; gnarled red and green trees casting dramatic black shadows; a pond of fluorescent green liquid; panels of exotic blossoms; beds of fungus.

The bubble drifted easily, apparently at random, now high under the near-invisible dome, now low under the foliage. Successive courses appeared from the center of the table, along with chilled wine and frosted punch.

It was wonderful and lavish, thought Jean. But why should Fotheringay spend his money on her? Perhaps he entertained romantic notions…She dallied with the idea, inspected him covertly…The idea lacked conviction. He seemed to be engaging in none of the usual gambits. He neither tried to fascinate her with his charm, nor swamp her with synthetic masculinity. Much as it irritated Jean to admit it, he appeared—indifferent.

Jean compressed her lips. The idea was disconcerting. She essayed a slight smile, a side glance up under lowered lashes.

"Save it," said Fotheringay. "You'll need it all when you get up to Abercrombie."

Jean returned to her dinner. After a minute she said calmly, "I was—curious."

"Now you know."

Jean thought to tease him, draw him out. "Know what?"

"Whatever it was you were curious about."

"Pooh. Men are mostly alike. They all have the same button. Push it, they all jump in the same direction."

Fotheringay frowned, glanced at her under narrowed eyes. "Maybe you aren't so precocious after all."

Jean became tense. In a curious indefinable way, the subject was very important, as if survival were linked with confidence in her own sophistication and flexibility. "What do you mean?"

"You make the assumption most pretty girls make," he said with a trace of scorn. "I thought you were smarter than that."

Jean frowned. There had been little abstract thinking in her background. "Well, I've never had it work out differently. Although I'm willing to admit there are exceptions…It's a kind of game. I've never lost. If I'm kidding myself, it hasn't made much difference so far."

Fotheringay relaxed. "You've been lucky."

Jean stretched out her arms, arched her body, smiled as if at a secret. "Call it luck."

"Luck won't work with Earl Abercrombie."

"You're the one who used the word luck. I think it's, well—ability."

"You'll have to use your brains too." He hesitated, then said, "Actually, Earl likes—odd things."

Jean sat looking at him, frowning.

He said coolly, "You're making up your mind how best to ask the question, 'What's odd about me?'"

Fotheringay made no comment.

"I'm completely on my own," said Jean. "There's not a soul in all the human universe that I care two pins for. I do just exactly as I please." She watched him carefully. He nodded indifferently. Jean quelled her exasperation, leaned back in her chair, studied him as if he were in a glass case...A strange young man. Did he ever smile? She thought of the Capellan Fibrates who by popular superstition were able to fix themselves along a man's spinal column and control his intelligence. Fotheringay displayed a coldness strange enough to suggest such a possession...A Capellan could manipulate but one hand at a time. Fotheringay held a knife in one hand, a fork in the other and moved both hands together. So much for that.

He said quietly, "I watched your hands too."

Jean threw back her head and laughed—a healthy adolescent laugh. Fotheringay watched her without discernible expression.

She said, "Actually, you'd like to know about me, but you're too stiff-necked to ask."

"You were born at Angel City on Codiron," said Fotheringay. "Your mother abandoned you in a tavern, a gambler named Joe Parlier took care of you until you were ten, when you killed him and three other men and stowed away on the Gray Line Packet *Bucyrus*. You were taken to the Waif's Home at Paie on Bella's Pride. You ran away and the Superintendent was found dead...Shall I go on? There's five more years of it."

Jean sipped her wine, nowise abashed. "You've worked fast...But you've misrepresented. You said, 'There's five years more of it, shall I go on?' as if you were able to go on. You don't know anything about the next five years."

Fotheringay's face changed by not a flicker. He said as if she had not spoken, "Now listen carefully. This is what you'll have to look out for."

"Go ahead. I'm all ears." She leaned back in her chair. A clever technique, ignoring an unwelcome situation as if it never existed. Of course, to carry it off successfully, a certain temperament was required. A cold fish like Fotheringay managed very well.

"Tonight a man named Webbard meets us here. He is chief steward at Abercrombie Station. I happen to be able to influence certain of his actions. He will take you up with him to Abercrombie and install you as a servant in the Abercrombie private chambers."

Jean wrinkled her nose. "Servant? Why can't I go to Abercrombie as a paying guest?"

"It wouldn't be natural. A girl like you would go up to *Capricorn* or *Verge*. Earl Abercrombie is extremely suspicious. He'd be certain to fight shy of you. His mother, old Mrs. Clara, watches him pretty closely, and keeps drilling into his head the idea that all the Abercrombie girls are after his money. As a servant you will have opportunity to meet him in intimate circumstances. He rarely leaves his study; he's absorbed in his collecting."

"My word," murmured Jean. "What does he collect?"

"Everything you can think of," said Fotheringay, moving his lips upward in a quick grimace, almost a smile. "I understand from Webbard, however, that he is rather romantic, and has carried on a number of flirtations among the girls of the station."

Jean screwed up her mouth in fastidious scorn. Fotheringay watched her impassively.

"When do I—commence?"

"Webbard goes up on the supply barge tomorrow. You'll go with him."

A whisper of sound from the buzzer. Fotheringay touched the button. "Yes?"

"Mr. Webbard for you, sir."

Webbard was waiting, the fattest man Jean had ever seen.

The plaque on the door read, Richard Mycroft, Attorney-at-Law. Somewhere far back down the years, someone had said in Jean's hearing that Richard Mycroft was a good attorney.

The receptionist was a dark woman about thirty-five, with a direct penetrating eye. "Do you have an appointment?"

"No," said Jean. "I'm in rather a hurry."

The receptionist hesitated a moment, then bent over the communicator. "A young lady—Miss Jean Parlier—to see you. New business."

"Very well."

The receptionist nodded to the door. "You can go in," she said shortly.

She doesn't like me, thought Jean. *Because I'm what she was and what she wants to be again.*

Mycroft was a square man with a pleasant face. Jean constructed a wary defense against him. If you liked someone and they knew it, they felt obligated to advise and interfere. She wanted no advice, no interference. She wanted two million dollars.

"Well, young lady," said Mycroft. "What can I do for you?"

He's treating me like a child, thought Jean. *Maybe I look like a child to him.* She said, "It's a matter of advice. I don't know much about fees. I can afford to pay you a hundred dollars. When you advise me a hundred dollars' worth, let me know and I'll go away."

"A hundred dollars buys a lot of advice," said Mycroft. "Advice is cheap."

"Not from a lawyer."

Mycroft became practical. "What are your troubles?"

"It's understood that this is all confidential?"

"Certainly." Mycroft's smile froze into a polite grimace.

"It's nothing illegal—so far as I'm concerned—but I don't want you passing out any quiet hints to—people that might be interested."

Mycroft straightened himself behind his desk. "A lawyer is expected to respect the confidence of his client."

"Okay...Well, it's like this." She told him of Fotheringay, of Abercrombie Station and Earl Abercrombie. She said that Earl Abercrombie was sick with an incurable disease. She made no mention of Fotheringay's convictions on that subject. It was a matter she herself kept carefully brushing out of her mind. Fotheringay had hired her. He told her what to do, told her that Earl Abercrombie was sick. That was good enough for her. If she had asked too many questions, found that things were too nasty even for her stomach, Fotheringay would have found another girl less inquisitive...She skirted the exact nature of Earl's disease. She didn't actually know, herself. She didn't want to know.

Mycroft listened attentively, saying nothing.

"What I want to know is," said Jean, "is the wife sure to inherit on Abercrombie? I don't want to go to a lot of trouble for nothing. And after all Earl is under twenty-one; I thought that in the event of his death it was best to—well, make sure of everything first."

For a moment Mycroft made no move, but sat regarding her quietly. Then he tamped tobacco into a pipe.

"Jean," he said, "I'll give you some advice. It's free. No strings on it."

"Don't bother," said Jean. "I don't want the kind of advice that's free. I want the kind I have to pay for."

Mycroft grimaced. "You're a remarkably wise child."

"I've had to be...Call me a child, if you wish."

"Just what will you do with a million dollars? Or two million, I understand it to be?"

Jean stared. Surely the answer was obvious...or was it? When she tried to find an answer, nothing surfaced.

"Well," she said vaguely, "I'd like an airboat, some nice clothes, and maybe..." In her mind's eye she suddenly saw herself surrounded by friends. Nice people, like Mr. Mycroft.

"If I were a psychologist and not a lawyer," said Mycroft, "I'd say you wanted your mother and father more than you wanted two million dollars."

Jean became very heated. "No, no! I don't want them at all. They're dead." As far as she was concerned they were dead. They had died for her when they left her on Joe Parlier's pool-table in the old Aztec Tavern.

Jean said indignantly, "Mr. Mycroft, I know you mean well, but tell me what I want to know."

"I'll tell you," said Mycroft, "because if I didn't, someone else would. Abercrombie property, if I'm not mistaken, is regulated by its own civil code... Let's see—" he twisted in his chair, pushed buttons on his desk.

On the screen appeared the index to the Central Law Library. Mycroft made further selections, narrowing down selectively. A few seconds later he had the information. "Property control begins at sixteen. Widow inherits at minimum fifty percent; the entire estate unless specifically stated otherwise in the will."

"Good," said Jean. She jumped to her feet. "That's what I wanted to make sure of."

Mycroft asked, "When do you leave?"

"This afternoon."

"I don't need to tell you that the idea behind the scheme is—not moral."

"Mr. Mycroft, you're a dear. But I don't have any morals."

He tilted his head, shrugged, puffed on his pipe. "Are you sure?"

"Well—yes." Jean considered a moment. "I suppose so. Do you want me to go into details?"

"No. I think what I meant to say was, are you sure you know what you want out of life?"

"Certainly. Lots of money."

Mycroft grinned. "That's really not a good answer. What will you buy with your money?"

Jean felt irrational anger rising in her throat. "Oh—lots of things." She rose to her feet. "Just what do I owe you, Mr. Mycroft?"

"Oh—ten dollars. Give it to Ruth."

"Thank you, Mr. Mycroft." She stalked out of his office.

As she marched down the corridor she was surprised to find that she was angry with herself as well as irritated with Mr. Mycroft...He had no right making people wonder about themselves. It wouldn't be so bad if she weren't wondering a little already.

But this was all nonsense. Two million dollars was two million dollars. When she was rich, she'd call on Mr. Mycroft and ask him if honestly he didn't think it was worth a few little lapses.

And today—up to Abercrombie Station. She suddenly became excited.

III

The pilot of the Abercrombie supply barge was emphatic. "No sir, I think you're making a mistake, nice little girl like you."

He was a chunky man in his thirties, hard-bitten and positive. Sparse blond hair crusted his scalp, deep lines gave his mouth a cynical slant. Webbard, the Abercrombie chief steward, was billeted astern, in the special handling locker. The usual webbings were inadequate to protect his corpulence; he floated chin-deep in a tankful of emulsion the same specific gravity as his body.

There was no passenger cabin and Jean had slipped into the seat beside the pilot. She wore a modest white frock, a white toque, a gray and black striped jacket.

The pilot had few good words for Abercrombie Station. "Now it's what I call a shame, taking a kid like you to serve the likes of them...Why don't they get one of their own kind? Surely both sides would be the happier."

Jean said innocently, "I'm going up for only just a little bit."

"So you think. It's catching. In a year you'll be like the rest of them. The air alone is enough to sicken a person, rich and sweet like olive oil. Me, I never set foot outside the barge unless I can't help it."

"Do you think I'll be—safe?" She raised her lashes, turned him her reckless sidelong look.

He licked his lips, moved in his seat. "Oh, you'll be safe enough," he muttered. "At least from them that's been there a while. You might have to duck a few just fresh from Earth...After they've lived on the station a bit their ideas change, and they wouldn't spit on the best part of an Earth girl."

"Hmmph." Jean compressed her lips. Earl Abercrombie had been born on the station.

"But I wasn't thinking so much of that," said the pilot. It was hard, he thought, talking straight sense to a kid so young and inexperienced. "I meant in that atmosphere you'll be apt to let yourself go. Pretty soon you'll look like the rest of 'em—never want to leave. Some aren't *able* to leave—couldn't stand it back on Earth if they wanted to."

"Oh—I don't think so. Not in my case."

"It's catching," said the pilot vehemently. "Look, kid, I know. I've ferried out to all the stations, I've seen 'em come and go. Each station has its own kind of weirdness, and you can't keep away from it." He chuckled self-consciously. "Maybe that's why I'm so batty myself...Now take Madeira Station. Gay. Frou-frou." He made a mincing motion with his fingers. "That's Madeira. You wouldn't know much about that...But take Balchester Aerie, take Merlin Dell, take the Starhome—"

"Surely, some are just pleasure resorts?"

The pilot grudgingly admitted that of the twenty-two resort satellites, fully half were as ordinary as Miami Beach. "But the others—oh, Moses!" He rolled his eyes back. "And Abercrombie is the worst."

There was silence in the cabin. Earth was a monstrous, green, blue, white and black ball over Jean's shoulder. The sun made a furious hole in the sky below. Ahead were the stars—and a set of blinking blue and red lights.

"Is that Abercrombie?"

"No, that's the Masonic Temple. Abercrombie is on out a ways..." He looked diffidently at her from the corner of his eyes. "Now—look! I don't want you to think I'm fresh. Or maybe I do. But if you're hard up for a job—why don't you come back to Earth with me? I got a pretty nice shack in Long Beach—nothing fancy—but it's on the beach, and it'll be better than working for a bunch of side-show freaks."

Jean said absently, "No thanks." The pilot pulled in his chin, pulled his elbows close against his body, glowered.

An hour passed. From behind came a rattle, and a small panel slid back. Webbard's pursy face showed through. The barge was coasting on free momentum, gravity was negated. "How much longer to the station?"

"It's just ahead. Half an hour, more or less, and we'll be fished up tight and right." Webbard grunted, withdrew.

Yellow and green lights winked ahead. "That's Abercrombie," said the pilot. He reached out to a handle. "Brace yourself." He pulled. Pale blue check-jets streamed out ahead.

From behind came a thump and an angry cursing. The pilot grinned. "Got him good." The jets roared a minute, died. "Every trip it's the same way. Now in a minute he'll stick his head through the panel and bawl me out."

The portal slid back. Webbard showed his furious face. "Why in thunder don't you warn me before you check? I just now took a blow that might have hurt me! You're not much of a pilot, risking injuries of that sort!"

The pilot said in a droll voice, "Sorry sir, sorry indeed. Won't happen again."

"It had better not! If it does, I'll make it my business to see that you're discharged."

The portal snapped shut. "Sometimes I get him better than others," said the pilot. "This was a good one, I could tell by the thump."

He shifted in his seat, put his arm around Jean's shoulders, pulled her against him. "Let's have a little kiss, before we fish home."

Jean leaned forward, reached out her arm. He saw her face coming toward him—bright wonderful face, onyx, pale rose, ivory, smiling hot with life... She reached past him, thrust the check valve. Four jets thrashed forward. The barge jerked. The pilot fell into the instrument panel, comical surprise written on his face.

From behind came a heavy resonant thump.

The pilot pulled himself back into his seat, knocked back the check valve. Blood oozed from his chin, forming a little red wen. Behind them the portal snapped open. Webbard's face, black with rage, looked through.

When he had finally finished, and the portal had closed, the pilot looked at Jean, who was sitting quietly in her seat, the corners of her mouth drawn up dreamily.

He said from deep in his throat, "If I had you alone, I'd beat you half to death."

Jean drew her knees up under her chin, clasped her arms around, looked silently ahead.

Abercrombie Station had been built to the Fitch cylinder-design: a power and service core, a series of circular decks, a transparent sheath. To the original construction a number of modifications and annexes had been added. An outside deck circled the cylinder, sheet steel to hold the magnetic grapples of small boats, cargo binds, magnetic shoes, anything which was to be fixed in place for a greater or lesser time. At each end of the cylinder, tubes connected to dependent constructions. The first, a sphere, was the private residence of the Abercrombies. The second, a cylinder, rotated at sufficient speed to press the water it contained evenly over its inner surface to a depth of ten feet; this was the station swimming pool, a feature found on only three of the resort satellites.

The supply barge inched close to the deck, bumped. Four men attached constrictor tackle to rings in the hull, heaved the barge along to the supply port. The barge settled into its socket, grapples shot home, the ports sucked open.

Chief Steward Webbard was still smouldering, but now a display of anger was beneath his dignity. Disdaining magnetic shoes, he pulled himself to the entrance, motioned to Jean. "Bring your baggage."

Jean went to her neat little trunk, jerked it into the air, found herself floundering helpless in the middle of the cargo space. Webbard impatiently returned with magnetic clips for her shoes, and helped her float the trunk into the station.

She was breathing different, rich, air. The barge had smelled of ozone, grease, hemp sacking, but the station…Without consciously trying to identify the odor, Jean thought of waffles with butter and syrup mixed with talcum powder.

Webbard floated in front of her, an imposing spectacle. His fat no longer hung on him in folds; it ballooned out in an even perimeter. His face was smooth as a watermelon, and it seemed as if his features were incised, carved, rather than molded. He focused his eyes at a point above her dark head. "We had better come to an understanding, young lady."

"Certainly, Mr. Webbard."

"As a favor to my friend, Mr. Fotheringay, I have brought you here to work. Beyond this original and singular act, I am no longer responsible. I am not your sponsor. Mr. Fotheringay recommended you highly, so see that you give satisfaction. Your immediate superior will be Mrs. Blaiskell, and you must obey her implicitly. We have very strict rules here at Abercrombie—fair treatment and good pay—but you must earn it. Your work must speak for itself, and you can expect no special favors." He coughed. "Indeed, if I may say so, you are fortunate in finding employment here; usually we hire people more of our own sort, it makes for harmonious conditions."

Jean waited with demurely bowed head. Webbard spoke on. Jean nodded dutifully. There was no point antagonizing pompous old Webbard. And Webbard thought that here was a respectful young lady, thin and very young and with a peculiar frenetic gleam in her eye, but sufficiently impressed by his importance…Good coloring too. Pleasant features. If she only could manage two hundred more pounds of flesh on her bones, she might have appealed to his grosser nature.

"This way then," said Webbard.

He floated ahead, and by some magnificent innate power continued to radiate the impression of inexorable dignity even while plunging head-first along the corridor.

Jean came more sedately, walking on her magnetic clips, pushing the trunk ahead as easily as if it had been a paper bag.

They reached the central core, and Webbard, after looking back over his bulging shoulders, launched himself up the shaft.

Panes in the wall of the core permitted a view of the various halls, lounges, refectories, salons. Jean stopped by a room decorated with red plush drapes and marble statuary. She stared, first in wonder, then in amusement.

Webbard called impatiently, "Come along now, miss, come along."

Jean pulled herself away from the pane. "I was watching the guests. They looked like—" she broke into a sudden giggle.

Webbard frowned, pursed his lips. Jean thought he was about to demand the grounds for her merriment, but evidently he felt it beneath his dignity. He called, "Come along now, I can spare you only a moment."

She turned one last glance into the hall, and now she laughed aloud.

Fat women, like bladder-fish in an aquarium tank. Fat women, round and tender as yellow peaches. Fat women, miraculously easy and agile in the absence of gravity. The occasion seemed to be an afternoon musicale. The hall was crowded and heavy with balls of pink flesh draped in blouses and pantaloons of white, pale blue and yellow.

The current Abercrombie fashion seemed designed to accent the round bodies. Flat bands like Sam Browne belts molded the breasts down and out, under the arms. The hair was parted down the middle, skinned smoothly back to a small roll at the nape of the neck. Flesh, bulbs of tender flesh, smooth shiny balloons. Tiny twitching features, dancing fingers and toes, eyes and lips roguishly painted. On Earth any one of these women would have sat immobile, a pile of sagging sweating tissue. At Abercrombie Station—the so-called 'Adipose Alley'—they moved with the ease of dandelion puffs, and their faces and bodies were smooth as butter-balls.

"Come, come, come!" barked Webbard. "There's no loitering at Abercrombie!"

Jean restrained the impulse to slide her trunk up the core against Webbard's rotund buttocks, a tempting target.

He waited for her at the far end of the corridor.

"Mr. Webbard," she asked thoughtfully, "how much does Earl Abercrombie weigh?"

Webbard tilted his head back, glared reprovingly down his nose. "Such intimacies, miss, are not considered polite conversation here."

Jean said, "I merely wondered if he were as—well, imposing as you are."

Webbard sniffed. "I couldn't answer you. Mr. Abercrombie is a person of great competence. His—presence is a matter you must learn not to discuss. It's not proper, not done."

"Thank you, Mr. Webbard," said Jean meekly.

Webbard said, "You'll catch on. You'll make a good girl yet. Now, through the tube, and I'll take you to Mrs. Blaiskell."

Mrs. Blaiskell was short and squat as a kumquat. Her hair was steel-gray, and skinned back modishly to the roll behind her neck. She wore tight black rompers, the uniform of the Abercrombie servants, so Jean was to learn.

Jean suspected that she made a poor impression on Mrs. Blaiskell. She felt the snapping gray eyes search her from head to foot, and kept her own modestly down-cast.

Webbard explained that Jean was to be trained as a maid, and suggested that Mrs. Blaiskell use her in the Pleasaunce and the bedrooms.

Mrs. Blaiskell nodded. "Good idea. The young master is peculiar, as everyone knows, but he's been pestering the girls lately and interrupting their duties;

wise to have one in there such as her—no offense, miss, I just mean it's the gravity that does it—who won't be so apt to catch his eye."

Webbard signed to her, and they floated off a little distance, conversing in low whispers.

Jean's wide mouth quivered at the corners. Old fools!

Five minutes passed. Jean began to fidget. Why didn't they do something? Take her somewhere. She suppressed her restlessness. Life! How good, how zestful! She wondered, *will I feel this same joy when I'm twenty? When I'm thirty, forty?* She drew back the corners of her mouth. *Of course I will. I'll never let myself change…But life must be used to its best. Every flicker of ardor and excitement must be wrung free and tasted.* She grinned. Here she floated, breathing the over-ripe air of Abercrombie Station. In a way it was adventure. It paid well—two million dollars, and only for seducing an eighteen-year-old boy. Seducing him, marrying him—what difference? Of course he was Earl Abercrombie, and if he were as imposing as Mr. Webbard…She considered Webbard's great body in wry speculation. Oh well, two million was two million. If things got too bad, the price might go up. Ten million, perhaps. Not too large a cut out of a billion.

Webbard departed without a word, twitching himself easily back down the core.

"Come," said Mrs. Blaiskell. "I'll show you your room. You can rest and tomorrow I'll take you around."

IV

Mrs. Blaiskell stood by while Jean fitted herself into black rompers, frankly critical. "Lord have mercy, but you mustn't pinch in the waist so! You're rachity and thin to starvation now, poor child; you mustn't point it up so! Perhaps we can find a few air-floats to fill you out; not that it's essential, Lord knows, since you're but a dust-maid; still it always improves a household to have a staff of pretty women, and young Earl, I will say this for him and all his oddness, he does appreciate a handsome woman…Now then, your bosom, we must do something there; why you're nearly flat! You see, there's no scope to allow a fine drape down under the arms, see?" She pointed to her own voluminous rolls of adipose. "Suppose we just roll up a bit of cushion and—"

"No," said Jean tremulously. Was it possible that they thought her so ugly? "I won't wear padding."

Mrs. Blaiskell sniffed. "It's your own self that's to benefit, my dear. I'm sure it's not me that's the wizened one."

Jean bent over her black slippers. "No, you're very sleek."

Mrs. Blaiskell nodded proudly. "I keep myself well shaped out, and all the better for it. It wasn't so when I was your age, miss, I'll tell you; I was on Earth then—"

"Oh, you weren't born here?"

"No, miss, I was one of the poor souls pressed and ridden by gravity, and I burned up my body with the effort of mere conveyance. No, I was born in Sydney, Australia, of decent kind folk, but they were too poor to buy me a place on Abercrombie. I was lucky enough to secure just such a position as you have, and that was while Mr. Justus and old Mrs. Eva, his mother—that's Earl's grandmother—was still with us. I've never been down to Earth since. I'll never set foot on the surface again."

"Don't you miss the festivals and great buildings and all the lovely countryside?"

"Pah!" Mrs. Blaiskell spat the word. "And be pressed into hideous folds and wrinkles? And ride in a cart, and be stared at and snickered at by the home people? Thin as sticks they are with their constant worry and fight against the pull of the soil! No, miss, we have our own sceneries and fetes; there's a pavane for tomorrow night, a Grand Masque Pantomime, a Pageant of Beautiful Women, all in the month ahead. And best, I'm among my own people, the round ones, and I've never a wrinkle on my face. I'm fine and full-blown, and I wouldn't trade with any of them below."

Jean shrugged. "If you're happy, that's all that matters." She looked at herself in the mirror with satisfaction. Even if fat Mrs. Blaiskell thought otherwise, the black rompers looked well on her, now that she'd fitted them snug to her hips and waist. Her legs—slender, round and shining ivory—were good, this she knew. Even if weird Mr. Webbard and odd Mrs. Blaiskell thought otherwise. Wait till she tried them on young Earl. He preferred gravity girls; Fotheringay had told her so. And yet—Webbard and Mrs. Blaiskell had hinted otherwise. Maybe he liked both kinds?...Jean smiled, a little tremulously. If Earl liked both kinds, then he would like almost anything that was warm, moved and breathed. And that certainly included herself.

If she asked Mrs. Blaiskell outright, she'd be startled and shocked. Good proper Mrs. Blaiskell. A motherly soul, not like the matrons in the various asylums and waifs' homes of her experience. Strapping big women those had been—practical and quick with their hands...But Mrs. Blaiskell was nice; she would never have deserted her child on a pool table. Mrs. Blaiskell would have struggled and starved herself to keep her child and raise her nicely...Jean idly speculated how it would seem with Mrs. Blaiskell for a mother. And Mr. Mycroft for a father. It gave her a queer prickly feeling, and also somehow called up from deep inside a dark dull resentment tinged with anger.

Jean moved uneasily, fretfully. Never mind the nonsense! *You're playing a lone hand. What would you want with relatives? What an ungodly nuisance!* She would never have been allowed this adventure up to Abercrombie Station…On the other hand, with relatives there would be many fewer problems on how to spend two million dollars.

Jean sighed. Her own mother wasn't kind and comfortable like Mrs. Blaiskell. She couldn't have been, and the whole matter became an academic question. Forget it, put it clean out of your mind.

Mrs. Blaiskell brought forward service shoes, worn to some extent by everyone at the station: slippers with magnetic coils in the soles. Wires led to a power bank at the belt. By adjusting a rheostat, any degree of magnetism could be achieved.

"When a person works, she needs a footing," Mrs. Blaiskell explained. "Of course there's not much to do, once you get on to it. Cleaning is easy, with our good filters; still there's sometimes a stir of dust and always a little film of oil that settles from the air."

Jean straightened up. "Okay Mrs. B, I'm ready. Where do we start?"

Mrs. Blaiskell raised her eyebrows at the familiarity, but was not seriously displeased. In the main, the girl seemed to be respectful, willing and intelligent. And—significantly—not the sort to create a disturbance with Mr. Earl.

Twitching a toe against a wall, she propelled herself down the corridor, halted by a white door, slid back the panel.

They entered the room as if from the ceiling. Jean felt an instant of vertigo, pushing herself head-first at what appeared to be a floor.

Mrs. Blaiskell deftly seized a chair, swung her body around, put her feet to the nominal floor. Jean joined her. They stood in a large round room, apparently a section across the building. Windows opened on space, stars shone in from all sides; the entire zodiac was visible with a sweep of the eyes.

Sunlight came up from below, shining on the ceiling, and off to one quarter hung the half moon, hard and sharp as a new coin. The room was rather too opulent for Jean's taste. She was conscious of an overwhelming surfeit of mustard-saffron carpet, white panelling with gold arabesques, a round table clamped to the floor, surrounded by chairs footed with magnetic casters. A crystal chandelier thrust rigidly down; rotund cherubs peered at intervals from the angle between wall and ceiling.

"The Pleasaunce," said Mrs. Blaiskell. "You'll clean in here every morning first thing." She described Jean's duties in detail.

"Next we go to—" she nudged Jean. "Here's old Mrs. Clara, Earl's mother. Bow your head, just as I do."

A woman dressed in rose-purple floated into the room. She wore an expression of absent-minded arrogance, as if in all the universe there were no doubt, uncertainty or equivocation. She was almost perfectly globular, as wide as she was tall. Her hair was silver-white, her face a bubble of smooth flesh, daubed apparently at random with rouge. She wore stones spread six inches down over her bulging bosom and shoulders.

Mrs. Blaiskell bowed her head unctuously. "Mrs. Clara, dear, allow me to introduce the new parlor maid; she's new up from Earth and very handy."

Mrs. Clara Abercrombie darted Jean a quick look. "Emaciated creature."

"Oh, she'll healthen up," cooed Mrs. Blaiskell. "Plenty of good food and hard work will do wonders for her; after all, she's only a child."

"Mmmph. Hardly. It's blood, Blaiskell, and well you know it."

"Well, yes of course, Mrs. Clara."

Mrs. Clara continued in a brassy voice, darting glances around the room. "Either it's good blood you have or vinegar. This girl here, she'll never be really comfortable, I can see it. It's not in her blood."

"No, ma'am, you're correct in what you say."

"It's not in Earl's blood either. He's the one I'm worried for. Hugo was the rich one, but his brother Lionel after him, poor dear Lionel, and—"

"What about Lionel?" said a husky voice. Jean twisted. This was Earl. "Who's heard from Lionel?"

"No one, my dear. He's gone, he'll never be back. I was but commenting that neither one of you ever reached your growth, showing all bone as you do."

Earl scowled past his mother, past Mrs. Blaiskell, and his gaze fell on Jean. "What's this? Another servant? We don't need her. Send her away. Always ideas for more expense."

"She's for your rooms, Earl, my dear," said his mother.

"Where's Jessy? What was wrong with Jessy?"

Mrs. Clara and Mrs. Blaiskell exchanged indulgent glances. Jean turned Earl a slow arch look. He blinked, then frowned. Jean dropped her eyes, traced a pattern on the rug with her toe, an operation which she knew sent interesting movements along her leg. Earning the two million dollars wouldn't be as irksome as she had feared. Because Earl was not at all fat. He was stocky, solid, with bull shoulders and a bull neck. He had a close crop of tight blond curls, a florid complexion, a big waxy nose, a ponderous jaw. His mouth was good, drooping sullenly at the moment.

He was something less than attractive, thought Jean. On Earth she would have ignored him, or if he persisted, stung him to fury with a series of insults. But she had been expecting far worse: a bulbous creature like Webbard, a human balloon…Of course there was no real reason for Earl to be fat; the children of fat people were as likely as not to be of normal size.

Mrs. Clara was instructing Mrs. Blaiskell for the day, Mrs. Blaiskell nodding precisely on each sixth word and ticking off points on her stubby little fingers.

Mrs. Clara finished, Mrs. Blaiskell nodded to Jean. "Come, miss, there's work to be done."

Earl called after them, "Mind now, no one in my study!"

Jean asked curiously, "Why doesn't he want anyone in his study?"

"That's where he keeps all his collections. He won't have a thing disturbed. Very strange sometimes, Earl. You'll just have to make allowances, and be on your good behavior. In some ways he's harder to serve than Mrs. Clara."

"Earl was born here?"

Mrs. Blaiskell nodded. "He's never been down to Earth. Says it's a place of crazy people, and the Lord knows, he's more than half right."

"Who are Hugo and Lionel?"

"They're the two oldest. Hugo is dead, Lord rest him, and Lionel is off on his travels. Then under Earl there's Harper and Dauphin and Millicent and Clarice. That's all Mrs. Clara's children, all very proud and portly. Earl is the skinny lad of the lot, and very lucky too, because when Hugo died, Lionel was off gadding and so Earl inherited…Now here's his suite, and what a mess."

As they worked Mrs. Blaiskell commented on various aspects of the room. "That bed now! Earl wasn't satisfied with sleeping under a saddleband like the rest of us, no! He wears pajamas of magnetized cloth, and that weights him against the cushion almost as if he lived on Earth…And this reading and studying, my word, there's nothing the lad won't think of! And his telescope! He'll sit in the cupola and focus on Earth by the hour."

"Maybe he'd like to visit Earth?"

Mrs. Blaiskell nodded. "I wouldn't be surprised if you was close on it there. The place has a horrid fascination for him. But he can't leave Abercrombie, you know."

"That's strange. Why not?"

Mrs. Blaiskell darted her a wise look. "Because then he forfeits his inheritance; that's in the original charter, that the owner must remain on the premises." She pointed to a gray door. "That there's his study. And now I'm going to give you a peep in, so you won't be tormented by curiosity and perhaps make trouble for yourself when I'm not around to keep an eye open…Now don't be excited by what you see; there's nothing to hurt you."

With the air of a priestess unveiling mystery, Mrs. Blaiskell fumbled a moment with the door-slide, manipulating it in a manner which Jean was not able to observe.

The door swung aside. Mrs. Blaiskell smirked as Jean jumped back in alarm.

"Now, now, now, don't be alarmed; I told you there was nothing to harm you. That's one of Master Earl's zoological specimens and rare trouble and expense he's gone to—"

Jean sighed deeply, and gave closer inspection to the horned black creature which stood on two legs just inside the door, poised and leaning as if ready to embrace the intruder in leathery black arms.

"That's the most scary part," said Mrs. Blaiskell in quiet satisfaction. "He's got his insects and bugs there—" she pointed "—his gems there, his old music disks there, his stamps there, his books along that cabinet. Nasty things, I'm ashamed of him. Don't let me know of you peeking in them nasty books that Mr. Earl gloats over."

"No, Mrs. Blaiskell," said Jean meekly. "I'm not interested in that kind of thing. If it's what I think it is."

Mrs. Blaiskell nodded emphatically. "It's what you think it is, and worse." She did not expand on the background of her familiarity with the library, and Jean thought it inappropriate to inquire.

Earl stood behind them. "Well?" he asked in a heavy sarcastic voice. "Getting an eyeful?" He kicked himself across the room, slammed shut the door.

Mrs. Blaiskell said in a conciliatory voice, "Now Mr. Earl, I was just showing the new girl what to avoid, what not to look at, and I didn't want her swounding of heart stoppage if innocent-like she happened to peek inside."

Earl grunted. "If she peeps inside while I'm there, she'll be 'swounding' from something more than heart stoppage."

"I'm a good cook too," said Jean. She turned away. "Come, Mrs. Blaiskell, let's leave until Mr. Earl has recovered his temper. I won't have him hurting your feelings."

Mrs. Blaiskell stammered, "Now then! Surely there's no harm..." She stopped. Earl had gone into his study and slammed the door.

Mrs. Blaiskell's eyes glistened with thick tears. "Ah, my dear, I do so dislike harsh words..."

They worked in silence and finished the bedroom. At the door Mrs. Blaiskell said confidentially into Jean's ear, "Why do you think Earl is so gruff and grumpy?"

"I've no idea," breathed Jean. "None whatever."

"Well," said Mrs. Blaiskell warily, "it all boils down to this—his appearance. He's so self-conscious of his thinness that he's all eaten up inside. He can't bear to have anyone see him; he thinks they're sneering. I've heard him tell Mrs. Clara so. Of course they're not; they're just sorry. He eats like a horse, he takes gland-pellets, but still he's that spindly and all hard tense muscle." She inspected Jean thoughtfully. "I think we'll put you on the same kind of regimen, and see if we can't make a prettier woman out of you." Then she shook her head doubtfully, clicked her tongue. "It might not be in your blood, as Mrs. Clara says. I hardly can see that it's in your blood…"

V

There were tiny red ribbons on Jean's slippers, a red ribbon in her hair, a coquettish black beauty spot on her cheek. She had altered her rompers so that they clung unobtrusively to her waist and hips.

Before she left the room she examined herself in the mirror. *Maybe it's me that's out of step! How would I look with a couple hundred more pounds of grade? No. I suppose not. I'm the gamin type. I'll look like a wolverine when I'm sixty, but for the next forty years—watch out.*

She took herself along the corridor, past the Pleasaunce, the music rooms, the formal parlor, the refectory, up into the bedrooms. She stopped by Earl's door, flung it open, entered, pushing the electrostatic duster ahead of her.

The room was dark; the transpar walls were opaque under the action of the scrambling field.

Jean found the dial, turned up the light.

Earl was awake. He lay on his side, his yellow magnetic pajamas pressing him into the mattress. A pale blue quilt was pulled up to his shoulders, his arm lay across his face. Under the shadow of his arm his eye smouldered out at Jean.

He lay motionless, too outraged to move.

Jean put her hands on her hips, said in her clear young voice, "Get up, you sluggard! You'll get as fat as the rest of them lounging around till all hours…"

The silence was choked and ominous. Jean bent to peer under Earl's arm. "Are you alive?"

Without moving Earl said in a harsh low voice, "Exactly what do you think you're doing?"

"I'm about my regular duties. I've finished the Pleasaunce. Next comes your room."

His eyes went to a clock. "At seven o'clock in the morning?"

"Why not? The sooner I get done, the sooner I can get to my own business."

"Your own business be damned. Get out of here, before you get hurt."

"No, sir. I'm a self-determined individual. Once my work is done, there's nothing more important than self-expression."

"Get out!"

"I'm an artist, a painter. Or maybe I'll be a poet this year. Or a dancer. I'd make a wonderful ballerina. Watch." She essayed a pirouette, but the impulse took her up to the ceiling—not ungracefully, this she made sure.

She pushed herself back. "If I had magnetic slippers I could twirl an hour and a half. Grand jetés are easy…"

He raised himself on his elbow, blinking and glaring, as if on the verge of launching himself at her.

"You're either crazy—or so utterly impertinent as to amount to the same thing."

"Not at all," said Jean. "I'm very courteous. There might be a difference of opinion, but still it doesn't make you automatically right."

He slumped back on the bed. "Argue with old Webbard," he said thickly. "Now—for the last time—get out!"

"I'll go," said Jean, "but you'll be sorry."

"Sorry?" His voice had risen nearly an octave. "Why should I be sorry?"

"Suppose I took offense at your rudeness and told Mr. Webbard I wanted to quit?"

Earl said through tight lips, "I'm going to talk to Mr. Webbard today and maybe you'll be asked to quit…Miraculous!" he told himself bitterly. "Scarecrow maids breaking in at sunup…"

Jean stared in surprise. "Scarecrow! Me? On Earth I'm considered a very pretty girl. I can get away with things like this, disturbing people, because I'm pretty."

"This is Abercrombie Station," said Earl in a dry voice. "Thank God!"

"You're rather handsome yourself," said Jean tentatively.

Earl sat up, his face tinged with angry blood. "Get out of here!" he shouted. "You're discharged!"

"Pish," said Jean. "You wouldn't dare fire me."

"I wouldn't dare?" asked Earl in a dangerous voice. "Why wouldn't I dare?"

"Because I'm smarter than you are."

Earl made a husky sound in his throat. "And just what makes you think so?"

Jean laughed. "You'd be very nice, Earl, if you weren't so touchy."

"All right, we'll take that up first. Why am I so touchy?"

Jean shrugged. "I said you were nice-looking and you blew a skull-fuse." She blew an imaginary fluff from the back of her hand. "I call that touchiness."

Earl wore a grim smile that made Jean think of Fotheringay. Earl might be tough if pushed far enough. But not as tough as—well, say Ansel Clellan. Or Fiorenzo. Or Party MacClure. Or Fotheringay. Or herself, for that matter.

He was staring at her, as if he were seeing her for the first time. This is what she wanted. "Why do you think you're smarter, then?"

"Oh, I don't know…Are you smart?"

His glance darted off to the doors leading to his study; a momentary quiver of satisfaction crossed his face. "Yes, I'm smart."

"Can you play chess?"

"Of course I play chess," he said belligerently. "I'm one of the best chess players alive."

"I could beat you with one hand." Jean had played chess four times in her life.

"I wish you had something I wanted," he said slowly. "I'd take it away from you."

Jean gave him an arch look. "Let's play for forfeits."

"No!"

"Ha!" She laughed, eyes sparkling.

He flushed. "Very well."

Jean picked up her duster. "Not now, though." She had accomplished more than she had hoped for. She looked ostentatiously over her shoulder. "I've got to work. If Mrs. Blaiskell finds me here she'll accuse you of seducing me."

He snorted with twisted lips. He looked like an angry blond boar, thought Jean. But two million dollars was two million dollars. And it wasn't as bad as if he'd been fat. The idea had been planted in his mind. "You be thinking of the forfeit," said Jean. "I've got to work."

She left the room, turning him a final glance over her shoulder which she hoped was cryptic.

The servants' quarters were in the main cylinder, the Abercrombie Station proper. Jean sat quietly in a corner of the mess-hall, watching and listening while the other servants had their elevenses: cocoa gobbed heavy with whipped cream, pastries, ice cream. The talk was high-pitched, edgy. Jean wondered at the myth that fat people were languid and easygoing.

From the corner of her eye she saw Mr. Webbard float into the room, his face tight and gray with anger.

She lowered her head over her cocoa, watching him from under her lashes.

Webbard looked directly at her; his lips sucked in and his bulbous cheeks quivered. For a moment it seemed that he would drift at her, attracted by the force of his anger alone; somehow he restrained himself. He looked around the room until he spied Mrs. Blaiskell. A flick of his fingers sent him to where she sat at the end table, held by magnets appropriately fastened to her rompers.

He bent over her, muttered in her ear. Jean could not hear his words, but she saw Mrs. Blaiskell's face change and her eyes go seeking around the room.

Mr. Webbard completed his dramatization and felt better. He wiped the palms of his hands along the ample area of his dark blue corduroy trousers, twisted with a quick wriggle of his shoulders, and sent himself to the door with a flick of his toe.

Marvellous, thought Jean, the majesty, the orbital massiveness of Webbard's passage through the air. The full moon-face, heavy-lidded, placid; the rosy cheeks, the chins and jowls puffed round and tumescent, glazed and oily, without blemish, mar or wrinkle; the hemisphere of the chest, then the bifurcate lower half, in the rich dark blue corduroy: the whole marvel coasting along with the inexorable momentum of an ore barge...

Jean became aware that Mrs. Blaiskell was motioning to her from the doorway, making cryptic little signals with her fat fingers.

Mrs. Blaiskell was waiting in the little vestibule she called her office, her face scene to shifting emotions. "Mr. Webbard has given me some serious information," she said in a voice intended to be stern.

Jean displayed alarm. "About me?"

Mrs. Blaiskell nodded decisively. "Mr. Earl complained of some very strange behavior this morning. At seven o'clock or earlier..."

Jean gasped. "Is it possible, that Earl has had the audacity to—"

"*Mr.* Earl," Mrs. Blaiskell corrected primly.

"Why, Mrs. Blaiskell, it was as much as my life was worth to get away from him!"

Mrs. Blaiskell blinked uneasily. "That's not precisely the way Mr. Webbard put it. He said you—"

"Does that sound reasonable? Is that likely, Mrs. B?"

"Well—no," Mrs. Blaiskell admitted, putting her hand to her chin, and tapping her teeth with a fingernail. "Certainly it seems odd, come to consider a little more closely." She looked at Jean. "But how is it that—"

"He called me into his room, and then—" Jean had never been able to cry, but she hid her face in her hands.

"There, now," said Mrs. Blaiskell. "I never believed Mr. Webbard anyway. Did he—did he—" she found herself unable to phrase the question.

Jean shook her head. "It wasn't for want of trying."

"Just goes to show," muttered Mrs. Blaiskell. "And I thought he'd grown out of that nonsense."

"'Nonsense'?" The word had been invested with a certain overtone that set it out of context.

Mrs. Blaiskell was embarrassed. She shifted her eyes. "Earl has passed through several stages, and I'm not sure which has been the most troublesome...A year or two ago—two years, because this was while Hugo was still alive and the family was together—he saw so many Earth films that he began to admire Earth women, and it had us all worried. Thank Heaven, he's completely thrown off that unwholesomeness, but it's gone to make him all the more shy and self-conscious." She sighed. "If only one of the pretty girls of the station would love him for himself, for his brilliant mind...But no, they're all romantic and they're more taken by a rich round body and fine flesh, and poor gnarled Earl is sure that when one of them does smile his way she's after his money, and very likely true, so I say!" She looked at Jean speculatively. "It just occurred to me that Earl might be veering back to his old—well, strangeness. Not that you're not a nice well-meaning creature, because you are."

Well, well, thought Jean dispiritedly. Evidently she had achieved not so much this morning as she had hoped. But then, every campaign had its setbacks.

"In any event, Mr. Webbard has asked that I give you different duties, to keep you from Mr. Earl's sight, because he's evidently taken an antipathy to you...And after this morning I'm sure you'll not object."

"Of course not," said Jean absently. Earl, that bigoted, warped, wretch of a boy!

"For today, you'll just watch the Pleasaunce and service the periodicals and water the atrium plants. Tomorrow—well, we'll see."

Jean nodded, and turned to leave. "One more thing," said Mrs. Blaiskell in a hesitant voice. Jean paused. Mrs. Blaiskell could not seem to find the right words.

They came in a sudden surge, all strung together. "Be a little careful of yourself, especially when you're alone near Mr. Earl. This is Abercrombie Station, you know, and he's Earl Abercrombie, and the High Justice, and some very strange things happen..."

Jean said in a shocked whisper, "Physical violence, Mrs. Blaiskell?"

Mrs. Blaiskell stammered and blushed. "Yes, I suppose you'd call it that... Some very disgraceful things have come to light. Not nice, though I shouldn't be saying it to you, who's only been with us a day. But, be careful. I wouldn't want your soul on my conscience."

"I'll be careful," said Jean in a properly hushed voice.

Mrs. Blaiskell nodded her head, an indication that the interview was at an end.

Jean returned to the refectory. It was really very nice for Mrs. Blaiskell to worry about her. It was almost as if Mrs. Blaiskell were fond of her. Jean sneered automatically. That was too much to expect. Women always disliked her because their men were never safe when Jean was near. Not that Jean consciously flirted—at least, not always—but there was something about her that interested men, even the old ones. They paid lip-service to the idea that Jean was a child, but their eyes wandered up and down, the way a young man's eyes wandered.

But out here on Abercrombie Station it was different. Ruefully Jean admitted that no one was jealous of her, no one on the entire station. It was the other way around; she was regarded as an object for pity. But it was still nice of Mrs. Blaiskell to take her under her wing; it gave Jean a pleasant warm feeling. Maybe if and when she got hold of that two million dollars—and her thoughts went to Earl. The warm feeling drained from her mind.

Earl, hoity-toity Earl, was ruffled because she had disturbed his rest. So bristle-necked Earl thought she was gnarled and stunted! Jean pulled herself to the chair. Seating herself with a thump, she seized up her bulb of cocoa and sucked at the spout.

Earl! She pictured him: the sullen face, the kinky blond hair, the over-ripe mouth, the stocky body he so desperately yearned to fatten. This was the man she must inveigle into matrimony. On Earth, on almost any other planet in the human universe it would be child's play—

This was Abercrombie Station!

She sipped her cocoa, considering the problem. The odds that Earl would fall in love with her and come through with a legitimate proposal seemed slim. Could he be tricked into a position where in order to save face or reputation he would be forced to marry her? Probably not. At Abercrombie Station, she told herself, marriage with her represented almost the ultimate loss of face. Still, there were avenues to be explored. Suppose she beat Earl at chess, could she make marriage the forfeit? Hardly. Earl would be too sly and dishonorable to pay up. It was necessary to make him *want* to marry her, and that would entail making herself desirable in his eyes, which in turn made necessary a revision of Earl's whole outlook. To begin with, he'd have to feel that his own person was not entirely loathsome (although it was). Earl's morale must be built up to a point where he felt himself superior to the rest of Abercrombie Station, and where he would be proud to marry one of his own kind.

A possibility at the other pole: if Earl's self-respect were so utterly blasted and reduced, if he could be made to feel so despicable and impotent that he would be ashamed to show his face outside his room, he might marry her as the best bet in sight...And still another possibility: revenge. If Earl realized that the fat girls who flattered him were actually ridiculing him behind his back, he might marry her from sheer spite.

One last possibility. Duress. Marriage or death. She considered poisons and antidotes, diseases and cures, a straightforward gun in the ribs…

A bell chimed, a number dropped on a call-board and a voice said, "Pleasaunce."

Mrs. Blaiskell appeared. "That's you, miss. Now go in, nice as you please, and ask Mrs. Clara what it is that's wanted, and then you can go off duty till three."

VI

Mrs. Clara Abercrombie, however, was not present. The Pleasaunce was occupied by twenty or thirty young folk, talking and arguing with rather giddy enthusiasm. The girls wore pastel satins, velvets, gauzes, tight around their rotund pink bodies, with frothing little ruffles and anklets, while the young men affected elegant dark grays and blues and tawny beiges, with military trim of white and scarlet.

Ranged along a wall were a dozen stage settings in miniature. Above, a ribbon of paper bore the words *'Pandora in Elis*. Libretto by A. Percy Stevanic, music by Colleen O'Casey'.

Jean looked around the room to see who had summoned her. Earl raised his finger peremptorily. Jean walked on her magnetic shoes to where he floated near one of the miniature stage sets. He turned to a mess of cocoa and whipped cream, clinging like a tumor to the side of the set—evidently a broken bulb.

"Clean up that spill," said Earl in a flinty voice.

Jean thought, *he half-wants to rub it in, half-wants to act as if he doesn't recognize me.* She nodded dutifully. "I'll get a container and a sponge."

When she returned, Earl was across the room, talking earnestly to a girl whose globular body was encased in a gown of brilliant rose velvet. She wore rose-buds over each ear and played with a ridiculous little white dog while she listened to Earl with a half-hearted affectation of interest.

Jean worked as slowly as possible, watching from the corners of her eyes. Snatches of conversation reached her: "Lapwill's done simply a marvellous job on the editing, but I don't see that he's given Myras the same scope—" "If the pageant grosses ten thousand dollars, Mrs. Clara says she'll put another ten thousand toward the construction fund. Think of it! a Little Theater all our own!" Excited and conspiratorial whispers ran through the Pleasaunce, "—and for the water scene why not have the chorus float across the sky as moons?"

Jean watched Earl. He hung on the fat girl's words, and spoke with a pathetic attempt at intimate comradeship and jocularity. The girl nodded politely, twisted up her features into a smile. Jean noticed her eyes followed a hearty youth whose physique bulged out his plum-colored breeches like wind bellying a spinnaker. Earl perceived the girl's inattention. Jean saw him falter momentarily, then work even harder at his badinage. The fat girl licked her lips, swung her ridiculous little dog on its leash, and glanced over to where the purple-trousered youth bellowed with laughter.

A sudden idea caused Jean to hasten her work. Earl no doubt would be occupied here until lunch time—two hours away. And Mrs. Blaiskell had relieved her from duty till three.

She took herself from the hall, disposed of the cleaning equipment, dove up the corridor to Earl's private chambers. At Mrs. Clara's suite she paused, listening at the door. Snores!

Another fifty feet to Earl's chambers. She looked quickly up and down the corridor, slid back the door and slipped cautiously inside.

The room was silent as Jean made a quick survey. Closet, dressing room to one side, sun-flooded bathroom to the other. Across the room was the tall gray door into the study. A sign hung upon the door, apparently freshly made:

PRIVATE. DANGER. DO NOT ENTER.

Jean paused to consider. What kind of danger? Earl might have set devious safeguards over his private chamber.

She examined the door-slide button. It was overhung by an apparently innocent guard—which might or might not control an alarm circuit. She pressed her belt-buckle against the shutter in such a way as to maintain an electrical circuit, then moved the guard aside, pressed the button with her fingernail—gingerly. She knew of buttons which darted out hypodermics when pressed.

There was no whisper of machinery. The door remained in place.

Jean blew fretfully between her teeth. No keyhole, no buttons to play a combination on…Mrs. Blaiskell had found no trouble. Jean tried to reconstruct her motions. She moved to the slide, set her head to where she could see the reflection of the light from the wall…There was a smudge on the gloss. She looked closely and a tell-tale glint indicated a photo-electric eye.

She put her finger on the eye, pressed the slide-button. The door slipped open. In spite of having been fore-warned, Jean recoiled from the horrid black shape which hung forward as if to grapple her.

She waited. After a moment the door fell gently back into place.

Jean returned to the outer corridor, stationed herself where she could duck into Mrs. Clara's apartments if a suspicious shape came looming up the corridor. Earl might not have contented himself with the protection of a secret electric lock.

Five minutes passed. Mrs. Clara's personal maid passed by, a globular little Chinese, eyes like two shiny black beetles, but no one else.

Jean pushed herself back to Earl's room, crossed to the study door. Once more she read the sign:

PRIVATE. DANGER. DO NOT ENTER.

She hesitated. "I'm sixteen years old. Going on seventeen. Too young to die. It's just like that odd creature to furnish his study with evil tricks." She shrugged off the notion. "What a person won't do for money."

She opened the door, slipped through.

"There's a lot to see here," she muttered. "I hope Earl doesn't run out of sheep's-eyes for his fat girl, or decide he wants a particular newspaper clipping..."

She turned power into her slipper magnets, and wondered where to begin. The room was more like a warehouse or museum than a study, and gave the impression of wild confusion arranged, sorted, and filed by an extraordinary finicky mind.

After a fashion, it was a beautiful room, imbued with an atmosphere of erudition in its dark wood-tones. The far wall glowed molten with rich color—a rose window from the old Chartres cathedral, in full effulgence under the glare of free-space sunlight.

"Too bad Earl ran out of outside wall," said Jean. "A collection of stained glass windows runs into a lot of wall space, and one is hardly a collection... Perhaps there's another room..." For the study, large as it was, apparently occupied only half the space permitted by the dimensions of Earl's suite. "But—for the moment—I've got enough here to look at."

There were rock crystals from forty-two separate planets, all of which appeared identical to Jean's unpracticed eye.

There were papyrus scrolls, Mayan codices, medieval parchments illuminated with gold and Tyrian purple, Ogham runes on mouldering sheepskin, clay cylinders incised with cuneiform.

Intricate wood-carvings—fancy chains, cages within cages, amazing interlocking spheres, seven vested Brahmin temples.

Centimeter cubes containing samples of every known element. Thousands of postage stamps, mounted on leaves, swung out of a circular cabinet.

There were volumes of autographs of famous criminals, together with their photographs and Bertillon and Pevetsky measurements. From one corner came the rich aromas of perfumes—a thousand little flagons minutely described and coded, together with the index and code explanation, and these again had their origin on a multitude of worlds. There were specimens of fungus growths from all over the universe, and there were racks of miniature phonograph records, an inch across, micro-formed from the original pressings.

She found photographs of Earl's everyday life, together with his weight, height and girth measurement in crabbed handwriting, and each picture bore a colored star, a colored square, and either a red or blue disk. By this time Jean knew the flavor of Earl's personality. Near at hand there would be an index and explanation. She found it, near the camera which took the pictures. The disks referred to bodily functions; the stars, by a complicated system she could not quite comprehend, described Earl's morale, his frame of mind. The colored squares recorded his love life. Jean's mouth twisted in a wry grin. She wandered aimlessly on, fingering the physiographic globes of a hundred planets and examining maps and charts.

The cruder aspects of Earl's personality were represented in a collection of pornographic photographs, and near at hand an easel and canvas where Earl was composing a lewd study of his own. Jean pursed her mouth primly. The prospect of marrying Earl was becoming infinitely less enchanting.

She found an alcove filled with little chess-boards, each set up in a game. A numbered card and record of moves was attached to each board. Jean picked up the inevitable index book and glanced through. Earl played postcard chess with opponents all over the universe. She found his record of wins and losses. He was slightly but not markedly a winner. One man, William Angelo of Toronto, beat him consistently. Jean memorized the address, reflecting that if Earl ever took up her challenge to play chess, now she knew how to beat him. She would embroil Angelo in a game, and send Earl's moves to Angelo as her own and play Angelo's return moves against Earl. It would be somewhat circuitous and tedious, but fool-proof—almost.

She continued her tour of the study. Sea-shells, moths, dragon-flies, fossil trilobites, opals, torture implements, shrunken human heads. If the collection represented bona fide learning, thought Jean, it would have taxed the time and ability of any four Earth geniuses. But the hoard was essentially mindless and mechanical, nothing more than a boy's collection of college pennants or signs or match-box covers on a vaster scale.

One of the walls opened out into an ell, and here was communication via a freight hatch to outside space. Unopened boxes, crates, cases, bundles—apparently material as yet to be filed in Earl's rookery—filled the room. At the corner another grotesque and monumental creature hung poised, as if to clutch at her, and Jean felt strangely hesitant to wander within its reach. This one stood about eight feet tall. It wore the shaggy coat of a bear and vaguely resembled a gorilla, although the face was long and pointed, peering out from under the fur, like that of a French poodle.

Jean thought of Fotheringay's reference to Earl as an 'eminent zoologist'. She looked around the room. The stuffed animals, the tanks of eels, Earth tropical fish and Maniacan polywriggles were the only zoological specimens in sight. Hardly enough to qualify Earl as a zoologist. Of course, there was an annex to the room…She heard a sound. A click at the outer door.

Jean dove behind the stuffed animal, heart thudding in her throat. With exasperation she told herself, *He's an eighteen-year-old boy…If I can't face him down, out-argue, out-think, out-fight him, and come out on top generally, then it's time for me to start crocheting table-mats for a living.* Nevertheless, she remained hidden.

Earl stood quietly in the doorway. The door swung shut behind him. His face was flushed and damp, as if he had just recovered from anger or embarrassment. His delft-blue eyes gazed unseeingly down the roof, gradually came into focus.

He coiled up his legs, kicked against the wall, dove directly toward her. Under the creature's arm she saw him approaching, bigger, bigger, bigger, arms at his sides, head turned up like a diver. He thumped against the hairy chest, put his feet to the ground, stood not six feet distant.

He was muttering under his breath. She heard him plainly. "Damnable insult…If she only *knew! Hah!*" He laughed a loud scornful bark. "*Hah!*"

Jean relaxed with a near-audible sigh. Earl had not seen her, and did not suspect her presence.

He whistled aimlessly between his teeth, indecisively. At last he walked to the wall, reached behind a bit of ornate fretwork. A panel swung aside, a flood of bright sunlight poured through the opening into the study.

Earl was whistling a tuneless cadence. He entered the room but did not shut the door. Jean darted from behind her hiding place, looked in, swept the room with her eyes. Possibly she gasped.

Earl was standing six feet away, reading from a list. He looked up suddenly, and Jean felt the brush of his eyes.

For a moment he made no sound, no stir. Then he came to the door, stood staring up the study, and held this position for ten or fifteen seconds. From behind the stuffed gorilla-thing Jean saw his lips move, as if he were silently calculating.

He went out into the alcove, among the unopened boxes and bales. He pulled up several, floated them toward the open door, and they drifted into the flood of sunshine. He pushed other bundles aside, found what he was seeking, and sent another bundle after the rest.

He pushed himself back to the door, where he stood suddenly tense, nose dilated, eyes keen, sharp. He sniffed the air. His eyes swung to the stuffed monster. He approached it slowly, arms hanging loose from his shoulders.

He looked behind, expelled his breath in a long drawn hiss, grunted. From within the annex Jean thought, *he can either smell me, or it's telepathy!* She had darted into the room while Earl was fumbling among the crates, and ducked under a wide divan. Flat on her stomach she watched Earl's inspection of the stuffed animal, and her skin tingled. *He smells me, he feels me, he senses me.*

Earl stood in the doorway, looking up and down the study. Then he carefully, slowly, closed the door, threw a bolt home, turned to face into the inner room.

For five minutes he busied himself with his crates, unbundling, arranging the contents, which seemed to be bottles of white powder, on shelves.

Jean pushed herself clear of the floor, up against the under side of the divan, and moved to a position where she could see without being seen. Now she understood why Fotheringay had spoken of Earl as an 'eminent zoologist'.

There was another word which would fit him better, an unfamiliar word which Jean could not immediately dredge out of her memory. Her vocabulary was no more extensive than any girl of her own age, but the word had made an impression.

Like the objects in his other collections, the monsters were only such creatures as lent themselves to ready, almost haphazard collecting. They were displayed in glass cabinets. Panels at the back screened off the sunlight, and at absolute zero, the things would remain preserved indefinitely without taxidermy or embalming.

They were a motley, though monstrous group. There were true human monsters, macro- and micro-cephalics, hermaphrodites, creatures with multiple limbs and with none, creatures sprouting tissues like buds on a yeast cell, twisted hoop-men, faceless things, things green, blue and gray.

And then there were other specimens equally hideous, but possibly normal in their own environment: the miscellaneity of a hundred life-bearing planets.

To Jean's eyes, the ultimate travesty was a fat man, displayed in a place of prominence! Possibly he had gained the conspicuous position on his own merits. He was corpulent to a degree Jean had not considered possible. Beside him Webbard might show active and athletic. Take this creature to Earth, he would slump like a jelly-fish. Out here on Abercrombie he floated free, bloated and puffed like the throat of a singing frog! Jean looked at his face—looked again! Tight blond curls on his head...

Earl yawned, stretched. He proceeded to remove his clothes. Stark naked he stood in the middle of the room. He looked slowly, sleepily along the ranks of his collection.

He made a decision, moved languidly to one of the cubicles. He pulled a switch.

Jean heard a faint musical hum, a hissing, smelled heady ozone. A moment passed. She heard a sigh of air. The inner door of a glass cubicle opened. The creature within, moving feebly, drifted out into the room...

Jean pressed her lips tight together; after a moment looked away.

Marry Earl? She winced. *No, Mr. Fotheringay. You marry him yourself, you're as able as I am...Two million dollars?* She shuddered. Five million sounded better. For five million she might marry him. But that's as far as it would go. She'd put on her own ring, there'd be no kissing of the bride. She was Jean Parlier, no plaster saint. But enough was enough, and this was too much.

VII

Presently Earl left the room. Jean lay still, listened. No sound came from outside. She must be careful. Earl would surely kill her if he found her here. She waited five minutes. No sound, no motion reached her. Cautiously she edged herself out from under the divan.

The sunlight burnt her skin with a pleasant warmth, but she hardly felt it. Her skin seemed stained; the air seemed tainted and soiled her throat, her lungs. She wanted a bath...Five million dollars would buy lots of baths. Where was the index? Somewhere would be an index. There had to be an index...Yes. She found it, and quickly consulted the proper entry. It gave her much meat for thought.

There was also an entry describing the revitalizing mechanism. She glanced at it hurriedly, understanding little. Such things existed, she knew. Tremendous magnetic fields streamed through the protoplasm, gripping and binding tight each individual atom, and when the object was kept at absolute zero, energy expenditure dwindled to near-nothing. Switch off the clamping field, kick the particles back into motion with a penetrating vibration, and the creature returned to life.

She returned the index to its place, pushed herself to the door.

No sound came from outside. Earl might be writing or coding the events of the day on his phonogram...Well, so then? She was not helpless. She opened the door, pushed boldly through.

The study was empty!

She dove to the outer door, listened. A faint sound of running water reached her ears. Earl was in the shower. This would be a good time to leave.

She pressed the door-slide. The door snapped open. She stepped out into Earl's bedroom, pushed herself across to the outer door.

Earl came out of the bathroom, his stocky fresh-skinned torso damp with water.

He stood stock-still, then hastily draped a towel around his middle. His face suddenly went mottled red and pink. "What are you doing in here?"

Jean said sweetly, "I came to check on your linen, to see if you needed towels."

He made no answer, but stood watching her. He said harshly, "Where have you been this last hour?"

Jean made a flippant gesture. "Here, there. Were you looking for me?"

He took a stealthy step forward. "I've a good mind to—"

"To what?" Behind her she fumbled for the door-slide.

"To—"

The door opened.

"Wait," said Earl. He pushed himself forward.

Jean slipped out into the corridor, a foot ahead of Earl's hands.

"Come back in," said Earl, making a clutch for her.

From behind them Mrs. Blaiskell said in a horrified voice, "Well, I never! Mr. Earl!" She had appeared from Mrs. Clara's room.

Earl backed into his room hissing unvoiced curses. Jean looked in after him. "The next time you see me, you'll wish you'd played chess with me."

"Jean!" barked Mrs. Blaiskell.

Jean had no idea what she meant. Her mind raced. Better keep her ideas to herself. "I'll tell you tomorrow morning." She laughed mischievously. "About six or six-thirty."

"Miss Jean!" cried Mrs. Blaiskell angrily. "Come away from that door this instant!"

Jean calmed herself in the servants' refectory with a pot of tea.

Webbard came in, fat, pompous, and fussy as a hedgehog. He spied Jean and his voice rose to a reedy oboe tone. "Miss, miss!"

Jean had a trick she knew to be effective, thrusting out her firm young chin, squinting, charging her voice with metal. "Are you looking for me?"

Webbard said, "Yes, I certainly am. Where on earth—"

"Well, I've been looking for you. Do you want to hear what I'm going to tell you in private or not?"

Webbard blinked. "Your tone of voice is impudent, miss. If you please—"

"Okay," said Jean. "Right here, then. First of all, I'm quitting. I'm going back to Earth. I'm going to see—"

Webbard held up his hand in alarm, looked around the refectory. Conversation along the tables had come to a halt. A dozen curious eyes were watching.

The door slid shut behind her. Webbard pressed his rotundity into a chair; magnetic strands in his trousers held him in place. "Now what is all this? I'll have you know there've been serious complaints."

Jean said disgustedly, "Tie a can to it, Webbard. Talk sense."

Webbard was thunderstruck. "You're an impudent minx!"

"Look. Do you want me to tell Earl how I landed the job?"

Webbard's face quivered. His mouth fell open; he blinked four or five times rapidly. "You wouldn't dare to—"

Jean said patiently, "Forget the master-slave routine for five minutes, Webbard. This is man-to-man talk."

"What do you want?"

"I've a few questions I want to ask you."

"Well?"

"Tell me about old Mr. Abercrombie, Mrs. Clara's husband."

"There's nothing to tell. Mr. Justus was a very distinguished gentleman."

"He and Mrs. Clara had how many children?"

"Seven."

"And the oldest inherits the station?"

"The oldest, always the oldest. Mr. Justus believed in firm organization. Of course the other children were guaranteed a home here at the station, those who wished to stay."

"And Hugo was the oldest. How long after Mr. Justus did he die?"

Webbard found the conversation distasteful. "This is all footling nonsense," he growled in a deep voice. "Two years."

"And what happened to him?"

Webbard said briskly, "He had a stroke. Cardiac complaint. Now what's all this I hear about your quitting?"

"And then Earl inherited?"

Webbard pursed his lips. "Mr. Lionel unfortunately was off the station, and Mr. Earl became legal master."

"Rather nice timing, from Earl's viewpoint."

Webbard puffed out his cheeks. "Now then, young lady, we've had enough of that! If—"

"Mr. Webbard, let's have an understanding once and for all. Either you answer my questions and stop this blustering or I'll ask someone else. And when I'm done, that someone else will be asking you questions too."

Jean turned toward the door. Webbard grunted, thrashed himself forward. Jean gave her arm a shake; out of nowhere a blade of quivering glass appeared in her hand.

Webbard floundered in alarm, trying to halt his motion through the air. Jean put up her foot, pushed him in the belly, back toward his chair.

She said, "I want to see a picture of the entire family."

"I don't have any such pictures."

Jean shrugged. "I can go to any public library and dial the Who's-Who." She looked him over coolly, as she coiled her knife. Webbard shrank back in his chair. Perhaps he thought her a homicidal maniac. Well, she wasn't a maniac and she wasn't homicidal either, unless she was driven to it. She asked easily, "Is it a fact that Earl is worth a billion dollars?"

Webbard snorted. "A billion dollars? Ridiculous! The family owns nothing but the station and lives off the income. A hundred million dollars would build another twice as big and luxurious."

"Where did Fotheringay get that figure?" she asked wonderingly.

"I couldn't say," Webbard replied shortly.

"Where is Lionel now?"

Webbard pulled his lips in and out desperately. "He's—resting somewhere along the Riviera."

"Hm...You say you don't have any photographs?"

Webbard scratched his chin. "I believe that there's a shot of Lionel...Let me see...Yes, just a moment." He fumbled in his desk, pawed and peered, and at last came up with a snap-shot. "Mr. Lionel."

Jean examined the photograph with interest. "Well, well." The face in the photograph and the face of the fat man in Earl's zoological collection were the same. "Well, well." She looked up sharply. "And what's his address?"

"Quit dragging your feet, Webbard."

"Oh well—the Villa Passe-temps, Juan-les-Pins."

"I'll believe it when I see your address file. Where is it?"

Webbard began breathing hard. "Now see here, young lady, there's serious matters at stake!"

"Such as what?"

"Well—" Webbard lowered his voice, glanced conspiratorially at the walls of the room. "It's common knowledge at the station that Mr. Earl and Mr. Lionel are—well, not friendly. And there's a rumor—a rumor, mind you—that Mr. Earl has hired a well-known criminal to kill Mr. Lionel."

That would be Fotheringay, Jean surmised.

Webbard continued. "So you see, it's necessary that I exercise the utmost caution..."

Jean laughed. "Let's see that file."

The address was: Hotel Atlantide, Apartment 3001, French Colony, Metropolis, Earth.

Jean memorized the address, then stood irresolutely, trying to think of further questions. Webbard smiled slowly. Jean ignored him, stood nibbling her fingertips. Times like this she felt the inadequacy of her youth. When it came to action—fighting, laughing, spying, playing games, making love—she felt complete assurance. But the sorting out of possibilities and deciding which were probable and which irrational was when she felt less than sure. Such as now...Old Webbard, the fat blob, had calmed himself and was gloating. Well, let him enjoy himself...She had to get to Earth. She had to see Lionel Abercrombie. Possibly Fotheringay had been hired to kill him, possibly not. Possibly Fotheringay knew where to find him, possibly not. Webbard knew Fotheringay; probably he had served as Earl's intermediary. Or possibly Webbard was performing some intricate evolutions of his own. It was plain that, now, her interests were joined with Lionel's, rather than Fotheringay's, because marrying Earl was clearly out of the question. Lionel must stay alive. If this meant double-crossing Fotheringay, too bad for Fotheringay. He could have told her more about Earl's 'zoological collection' before he sent her up to marry Earl...Of course, she told herself, Fotheringay would have no means of knowing the peculiar use Earl made of his specimens.

"Well?" asked Webbard with an unpleasant grin.

"When does the next ship leave for Earth?"

"The supply barge is heading back tonight."

"That's fine. If I can fight off the pilot. You can pay me now."

"Pay you? You've only done a day's work. You owe the station for transportation, your uniform, your meals—"

"Oh, never mind." Jean turned, pulled herself into the corridor, went to her room, packed her belongings.

Mrs. Blaiskell pushed her head through the door. "Oh, there you are..." She sniffed. "Mr. Earl has been inquiring for you. He wants to see you at once." It was plain that she disapproved.

"Sure," said Jean. "Right away."

Mrs. Blaiskell departed.

Jean pushed herself along the corridor to the loading deck. The barge pilot was assisting in the loading of some empty metal drums. He saw Jean and his face changed. "You again?"

"I'm going back to Earth with you. You were right. I don't like it here."

The pilot nodded sourly. "This time you ride in the storage. That way neither of us gets hurt...I couldn't promise a thing if you're up forward."

"Suits me," said Jean. "I'm going aboard."

When Jean reached the Hotel Atlantide in Metropolis she wore a black dress and black pumps which she felt made her look older and more sophisticated. Crossing the lobby she kept wary look-out for the house detective. Sometimes they nursed unkind suspicions toward unaccompanied young girls. It was best to avoid the police, keep them at a distance. When they found that she had no father, no mother, no guardian, their minds were apt to turn to some dreary government institution. On several occasions rather extreme measures to ensure her independence had been necessary.

But the Hotel Atlantide detective took no heed of the black-haired girl quietly crossing the lobby, if he saw her at all. The lift attendant observed that she seemed restless, as with either a great deal of pent enthusiasm or nervousness. A porter on the thirtieth floor noticed her searching for an apartment number and mentally labelled her a person unfamiliar with the hotel. A chambermaid watched her press the bell at Apartment 3001, saw the door open, saw the girl jerk back in surprise, then slowly enter the apartment. Strange, thought the chambermaid, and speculated mildly for a few moments. Then she went to recharge the foam dispensers in the public bathrooms, and the incident passed from her mind.

The apartment was spacious, elegant, expensive. Windows overlooked Central Gardens and the Morison Hall of Equity behind. The furnishings were the work of a professional decorator, harmonious and sterile; a few incidental objects around the room, however, hinted of a woman's presence. But Jean saw no woman. There was only herself and Fotheringay.

After an instant of surprise he stood back. "Come in."

Jean darted glances around the room, half-expecting a fat crumpled body. But possibly Lionel had not been at home, and Fotheringay was waiting.

"Well," he asked, "what brings you here?" He was watching her covertly. "Take a seat."

Jean sank into a chair, chewed at her lip. Fotheringay watched her cat-like. Walk carefully. She prodded her mind. What legitimate excuse did she have for visiting Lionel? Perhaps Fotheringay had expected her to double-cross him... Where was Hammond? Her neck tingled. Eyes were on her neck. She looked around quickly.

Someone in the hall tried to dodge out of sight. Not quickly enough. Inside Jean's brain a film of ignorance broke to release a warm soothing flood of knowledge.

She smiled, her sharp white little teeth showing between her lips. It had been a fat woman whom she had seen in the hall, a very fat woman, rosy, flushed, quivering.

"What are you smiling at?" inquired Fotheringay.

She used his own technique. "Are you wondering who gave me your address?"

"Obviously Webbard."

Jean nodded. "Is the lady your wife?"

Fotheringay's chin raised a hair's-breadth. "Get to the point."

"Very well." She hitched herself forward. There was still a possibility that she was making a terrible mistake, but the risk must be taken. Questions would reveal her uncertainty, diminish her bargaining position. "How much money can you raise—right now? Cash."

"Ten or twenty thousand."

Her face must have showed disappointment.

"Not enough?"

"No. You sent me on a bum steer."

Fotheringay sat silently.

"Earl would no more make a pass at me than bite off his tongue. His taste in women is—like yours."

Fotheringay displayed no irritation. "But two years ago—"

"There's a reason for that." She raised her eyebrows ruefully. "Not a nice reason."

"Well, get on with it."

"He liked Earth girls because they were freaks. In his opinion, naturally. Earl likes freaks."

Fotheringay rubbed his chin, watching her with blank wide eyes. "I never thought of that."

"Your scheme might have worked out if Earl were half-way right-side up. But I just don't have what it takes."

Fotheringay smiled frostily. "You didn't come here to tell me that."

"No. I know how Lionel Abercrombie can get the station for himself...Of course your name is Fotheringay."

"If my name is Fotheringay, why did you come here looking for me?"

Jean laughed, a gay ringing laugh. "Why do you think I'm looking for you? I'm looking for Lionel Abercrombie. Fotheringay is no use to me unless I can marry Earl. I can't. I haven't got enough of that stuff. Now I'm looking for Lionel Abercrombie."

VIII

Fotheringay tapped a well-manicured finger on a well-flanneled knee, and said quietly, "I'm Lionel Abercrombie."

"How do I know you are?"

He tossed her a passport. She glanced at it, tossed it back.

"Okay. Now—you have twenty thousand. That's not enough. I want two million…If you haven't got it, you haven't got it. I'm not unreasonable. But I want to make sure I get it when you do have it…So—you'll write me a deed, a bill of sale, something legal that gives me your interest in Abercrombie Station. I'll agree to sell it back to you for two million dollars."

Fotheringay shook his head. "That kind of agreement is binding on me but not on you. You're a minor."

Jean said, "The sooner I get clear of Abercrombie the better. I'm not greedy. You can have your billion dollars. I merely want two million…Incidentally, how do you figure a billion? Webbard says the whole set-up is only worth a hundred million."

Lionel's mouth twisted in a wintry smile. "Webbard didn't include the holdings of the Abercrombie guests. Some very rich people are fat. The fatter they get, the less they like life on Earth."

"They could always move to another resort station."

Lionel shook his head. "It's not the same atmosphere. Abercrombie is Fatman's World. The one small spot in all the universe where a fat man is proud of his weight." There was a wistful overtone in his voice.

Jean said softly, "And you're lonesome for Abercrombie yourself."

Lionel smiled grimly. "Is that so strange?"

Jean shifted in her chair. "Now we'll go to a lawyer. I know a good one. Richard Mycroft. I want this deed drawn up without loopholes. Maybe I'll have to find myself a guardian, a trustee."

"You don't need a guardian."

Jean smiled complacently. "For a fact, I don't."

"You still haven't told me what this project consists of."

"I'll tell you when I have the deed. You don't lose a thing giving away property you don't own. And after you give it away, it's to my interest to help you get it."

Lionel rose to his feet. "It had better be good."

"It will be."

The fat woman came into the room. She was obviously an Earth girl, bewildered and delighted by Lionel's attentions. Looking at Jean her face became clouded with jealousy.

Out in the corridor Jean said wisely, "You get her up to Abercrombie, she'll be throwing you over for one of those fat rascals."

"Shut up!" said Lionel, in a voice like the whetting of a scythe.

>••<

The pilot of the supply barge said sullenly, "I don't know about this."

The pilot muttered churlishly, but made no further protest. Lionel buckled himself into the seat beside him. Jean, the horse-faced man named Hammond, two elderly men of professional aspect and uneasy manner settled themselves in the cargo hold.

The barge landed on the cargo deck, the handlers tugged it into its socket, the port sighed open.

"Come on," said Lionel. "Make it fast. Let's get it over with." He tapped Jean's shoulder. "You're first."

She led the way up the main core. Fat guests floated down past them, light and round as soap-bubbles, their faces masks of surprise at the sight of so many bone-people.

Up the core, along the vinculum into the Abercrombie private sphere. They passed the Pleasaunce, where Jean caught a glimpse of Mrs. Clara, fat as a blut-wurst, with the obsequious Webbard.

They passed Mrs. Blaiskell. "Why, Mr. Lionel!" she gasped. "Well, I never, I never!"

Lionel brushed past. Jean, looking over her shoulder into his face, felt a qualm. Something dark smouldered in his eyes. Triumph, malice, vindication, cruelty. Something not quite human. If nothing else, Jean was extremely human, and was wont to feel uneasy in the presence of out-world life…She felt uneasy now.

"Hurry," came Lionel's voice. "Hurry."

Past Mrs. Clara's chambers, to the door of Earl's bedroom. Jean pressed the button; the door slid open.

Earl stood before a mirror, tying a red and blue silk cravat around his bull-neck. He wore a suit of pearl-gray gabardine, cut very full and padded to make his body look round and soft. He saw Jean in the mirror, behind her the hard face of his brother Lionel. He whirled, lost his footing, drifted ineffectually into the air.

Lionel laughed. "Get him, Hammond. Bring him along."

Earl stormed and raved. He was the master here, everybody get out. He'd have them all jailed, killed. He'd kill them himself…

Hammond searched him for weapons, and the two professional-looking men stood uncomfortably in the background muttering to each other.

"Look here, Mr. Abercrombie," one of them said at last. "We can't be a party to violence…"

"Shut up," said Lionel. "You're here as witnesses, as medical men. You're being paid to look, that's all. If you don't like what you see, that's too bad." He motioned to Jean. "Get going."

Jean pushed herself to the study door. Earl called out sharply: "Get away from there, get away! That's private, that's my private study!"

Jean pushed herself to the furry two-legged creature. Here she waited.

Earl made some difficulty about coming through the door. Hammond manipulated his elbows; Earl belched up a hoarse screech, flung himself forward, panting like a winded chicken.

Lionel said, "Don't fool with Hammond, Earl. He likes hurting people."

The two witnesses muttered wrathfully. Lionel quelled them with a look.

Hammond seized Earl by the seat of the pants, raised him over his head, walked with magnetic shoes gripping the deck across the cluttered floor of the study, with Earl flailing and groping helplessly.

Jean fumbled in the fretwork over the panel into the annex. Earl screamed, "Keep your hands out of there! Oh, how you'll pay, how you'll pay for this, how you'll pay!" His voice hoarsened, he broke into sobs.

Hammond shook him, like a terrier shaking a rat.

Earl sobbed louder.

The sound grated on Jean's ears. She frowned, found the button, pushed. The panel flew open.

They all moved into the bright annex, Earl completely broken, sobbing and pleading.

"There it is," said Jean.

Lionel swung his gaze along the collection of monstrosities. The out-world things, the dragons, basilisks, griffins, the armored insects, the great-eyed serpents, the tangles of muscle, the coiled creatures of fang, brain, cartilage. And then there were the human creatures, no less grotesque. Lionel's eyes stopped at the fat man.

He looked at Earl, who had fallen numbly silent.

"Poor old Hugo," said Lionel. "You ought to be ashamed of yourself, Earl."

Earl made a sighing sound.

Lionel said, "But Hugo is dead...He's as dead as any of the other things. Right, Earl?" He looked at Jean. "Right?"

"I guess that's right," said Jean uneasily. She found no pleasure baiting Earl.

"Of course he's dead," panted Earl.

Jean went to the little key controlling the magnetic field.

Earl screamed, "You witch! You witch!"

Jean depressed the key. There was a musical hum, a hissing, a smell of ozone. A moment passed. There came a sigh of air. The cubicle opened with a sucking sound. Hugo drifted into the room.

He twitched his arms, gagged and retched, made a thin crying sound in his throat.

Lionel turned to his two witnesses. "Is this man alive?"

Hugo whispered feebly, pressed his elbows to his body, pulled up his atrophied little legs, tried to assume a foetal position.

Lionel asked the two men, "Is this man sane?"

They fidgeted. "That of course is hardly a matter we can determine off-hand." There was further mumbling about tests, cephalographs, reflexes.

Lionel waited a moment. Hugo was gurgling, crying like a baby. "Well— is he sane?"

The doctors said, "He's suffering from severe shock. The deep-freeze classically has the effect of disturbing the synapses—"

Lionel asked sardonically, "Is he in his right mind?"

"Well—no."

Lionel nodded. "In that case—you're looking at the new master of Abercrombie Station."

Earl protested, "You can't get away with that, Lionel! He's been insane a long time, and you've been off the station!"

Lionel grinned wolfishly. "Do you want to take the matter into Admiralty Court at Metropolis?"

Earl fell silent. Lionel looked at the doctors, who were whispering heatedly together.

"Talk to him," said Lionel. "Satisfy yourself whether he's in his right mind or not."

The doctors dutifully addressed Hugo, who made mewing sounds. They came to an uncomfortable but definite decision. "Clearly this man is not able to conduct his own affairs."

Earl pettishly wrenched himself from Hammond's grasp. "Let go of me."

"Better be careful," said Lionel. "I don't think Hammond likes you."

"I don't like Hammond," said Earl viciously. "I don't like anyone." His voice dropped in pitch. "I don't even like myself." He stood staring into the cubicle which Hugo had vacated.

Jean sensed a tide of recklessness rising in him. She opened her mouth to speak. But Earl had already started.

Time stood still. Earl seemed to move with bewildering slowness, but the others stood as if frozen in jelly.

Time turned on for Jean. "I'm getting out of here!" she gasped, knowing what the half-crazed Earl was about to do.

Earl ran down the line of his monsters, magnetic shoes slapping on the deck. As he ran, he flipped switches. When he finished he stood at the far end of the room. Behind him things came to life.

Hammond gathered himself, plunged after Jean. A black arm apparently groping at random caught hold of his leg. There was a dull cracking sound. Hammond bawled out in terror.

Jean started through the door. She jerked back, shrieking. Facing her was the eight-foot gorilla-thing with the French-poodle face. Somewhere along the line Earl had thrown a switch relieving it from magnetic catalepsy. The black eyes shone, the mouth dripped, the hands clenched and unclenched. Jean shrank back.

There was screaming bedlam. Jean pressed herself against the wall. A green flapping creature, coiling and uncoiling, twisted out into the study, smashing racks, screens, displays, sending books, minerals, papers, mechanisms, cases and cabinets floating and crashing. The gorilla-thing came after, one of its arms twisted and loose. A rolling flurry of webbed feet, scales, muscular tail and a human body followed—Hammond and a griffin from a world aptly named 'Pest-hole'.

Jean darted through the door, thought to hide in the alcove. Outside, on the deck, was Earl's space-boat. She shoved herself across to the port.

Jean crouched by the port, ready to slam it at any approach of danger…She sighed. All her hopes, plans, future had exploded. Death, debacle, catastrophe were hers instead.

She turned to the doctor. "Where's your partner?"

"Dead! Oh Lord, oh Lord, what can we do?"

Jean turned her head to look at him, lips curling in disgust. Then she saw him in a new, flattering, light. A disinterested witness. He looked like money. He could testify that for at least thirty seconds Lionel had been master of Abercrombie Station. That thirty seconds was enough to transfer title to her. Whether Hugo were sane or not didn't matter because Hugo had died thirty seconds before the metal frog with the knife-edged scissor-bill had fixed on Lionel's throat.

Best to make sure. "Listen," said Jean. "This may be important. Suppose you were to testify in court. Who died first, Hugo or Lionel?"

The doctor sat quiet a moment. "Why, Hugo! I saw his neck broken while Lionel was still alive."

"Are you sure?"

"Oh yes." He tried to pull himself together. "We must do something."

"Okay," said Jean. "What shall we do?"

"I don't know."

A brown face like a poodle-dog's, spotted red with blood, peered around the corner at them. Stealthily it pulled itself closer.

Mesmerized, Jean saw that now its arm had been twisted entirely off. It darted forward. Jean fell back, slammed the port. A heavy body thudded against the metal.

They were closed in Earl's space-boat. The man had fainted. Jean said, "Don't die on me, fellow. You're worth money…"

Faintly through the metal came crashing and thumping. Then came the muffled *spatttt* of proton guns.

The guns sounded with monotonous regularity. *Spatttt…spattt…spattt… spattt…spattt…*

Then there was utter silence.

Jean inched open the port. The alcove was empty. Across her vision drifted the broken body of the gorilla-thing.

Jean ventured into the alcove, looked out into the study. Thirty feet distant stood Webbard, planted like a pirate captain on the bridge of his ship. His face was white and wadded; pinched lines ran from his nose around his nearly invisible mouth. He carried two big proton guns; the orifices of both were white-hot.

He saw Jean; his eyes took on a glitter. "You! It's you that's caused all this, your sneaking and spying!"

He jerked up his proton guns.

"No!" cried Jean, "Its not my fault!"

Lionel's voice came weakly. "Put down those guns, Webbard." Clutching his throat he pushed himself into the study. "That's the new owner," he croaked sardonically. "You wouldn't want to murder your boss, would you?"

Webbard blinked in astonishment. "Mr. Lionel!"

"Yes," said Lionel. "Home again…And there's quite a mess to clean up, Webbard…"

Jean looked at the bank book. The figures burnt into the plastic, spread almost all the way across the tape.

"$2,000,000.00"

Mycroft puffed on his pipe, looked out the window. "There's a matter you should be considering," he said. "That's the investment of your money. You won't be able to do it by yourself; other parties will insist on dealing with a responsible entity—that is to say, a trustee or a guardian."

"I don't know much about these things," said Jean. "I—rather assumed that you'd take care of them."

Mycroft reached over, tapped the dottle out of his pipe.

"Don't you want to?" asked Jean.

Mycroft said with a compressed distant smile. "Yes, I want to…I'll be glad to administer a two million dollar estate. In effect, I'll become your legal guardian, until you're of age. We'll have to get a court order of appointment. The effect of the order will be to take control of the money out of your hands; we can include in the articles, however, a clause guaranteeing you the full income—which I assume is what you want. It should come to—oh, say fifty thousand a year after taxes."

"That suits me," said Jean listlessly. "I'm not too interested in anything right now…There seems to be something of a let-down."

Mycroft nodded. "I can see how that's possible."

Jean said, "I have the money. I've always wanted it, now I have it. And now—" she held out her hands, raised her eyebrows. "It's just a number in a bank book…Tomorrow morning I'll get up and say to myself, 'What shall I do today? Shall I buy a house? Shall I order a thousand dollars worth of clothes? Shall I start out on a two year tour of Argo Navis?' And the answer will come out, 'No, the hell with it all.'"

"What you need," said Mycroft, "are some friends, nice girls your own age."

Jean's mouth moved in rather a sickly smile. "I'm afraid we wouldn't have much in common…It's probably a good idea, but—it wouldn't work out." She sat passively in the chair, her wide mouth drooping.

Mycroft noticed that in repose it was a sweet generous mouth.

She said in a low voice, "I can't get out of my head the idea that somewhere in the universe I must have a mother and a father…"

Mycroft rubbed his chin. "People who'd abandon a baby in a saloon aren't worth thinking about, Jean."

"I know," she said in a dismal voice. "Oh Mr. Mycroft, I'm so damn lonely…" Jean was crying, her head buried in her arms.

Mycroft irresolutely put his hand on her shoulder, patted awkwardly.

After a moment she said, "You'll think I'm an awful fool."

"No," said Mycroft gruffly. "I think nothing of the kind. I wish that I…" He could not put it into words.

She pulled herself together, rose to her feet. "Enough of this…" She turned his head up, kissed his chin. "You're really very nice, Mr. Mycroft…But I don't want sympathy. I hate it. I'm used to looking out for myself."

Mycroft returned to his seat, loaded his pipe to keep his fingers busy. Jean picked up her little hand-bag. "Right now I've got a date with a couturier named André. He's going to dress me to an inch of my life. And then I'm going to—" She broke off. "I'd better not tell you. You'd be alarmed and shocked."

He cleared his throat. "I expect I would."

She nodded brightly. "So long." Then left his office.

He said, "I feel like going out and getting drunk…"

Ten minutes passed. His door opened. Jean looked in.

"Hello, Mr. Mycroft."

"Hello, Jean."

"I changed my mind. I thought it would be nicer if I took you out to dinner, and then maybe we could go to a show...Would you like that?"

"Very much," said Mycroft.

Afterword to "Abercrombie Station"

During these years [from 1937 at the University of California at Berkeley], when I found the time, I wrote science fiction. In my freshman year I wrote a long novelette, which I never submitted for publication, but which I later cannibalized.

During my sophomore year, since I was still an English major, I took a course in creative writing. The professor was George Hand: a tall, saturnine gentleman, stern and doctrinaire. Each week we were required to submit some item of creative writing, which he would comment upon and sometimes criticize. A fellow student in the class…submitted a pastiche concerning a prize fight. I, on the other hand, turned in a short science fiction story which I thought I would submit somewhere for publication, but which in the meantime I thought would serve as my weekly exercise in creative writing.

The class convened. George Hand entered the room, marched up to the podium and looked around the class. He gathered his energy, and spoke with almost painful deliberation. "This has been a remarkable week," he said, "and I have been impressed by the breadth and scope of the submissions. I should note that they range up and down the gamut of excellence. On the one hand, we have a pungent account by Mr. Fabun, which takes us to the front seats of a prize fight. His sentences are terse and alive. We can smell the sweat; we can feel the thud of the blows; we know the thrill of victory and the pathos of defeat. It is a memorable piece of work. On the other hand,"—and here Professor Hand rapped the top of the podium with his knuckles—"we have an almost incomprehensible example of what I believe is known as 'science fiction'."

The professor here allowed himself to show a small smile. "This sort of thing, perhaps unkindly, has been termed a semi-psychotic fugue from reality. I, of course, am not confident to make such a judgment." After class, I threw away the story, which I did not like very much anyway.

—Jack Vance

Three-Legged Joe

It might be well to make, in passing, a reference to old-time prospectors. Their experience has been gained through vast hardship and peril; no cause for wonder, then, that as a group they are secretive and solitary. It is hard to win their friendship; they are understandably contemptuous of academic training. Much of their lore will die with them and this is a pity, since locked in their minds is knowledge that might well save a thousand lives.

—Excerpt from Appendix II, Hade's Manual of Practical
Space Exploration and Mineral Survey.

John Milke and Oliver Paskell sauntered along Bang-out Row in Merlinville. Recent graduates of Highland Technical Institute, they walked with an assured and casual stride in order to convey an impression of hard-boiled competence. Old-timers on porches along the way stared, then turned and muttered briefly to each other.

John Milke was rubicund, energetic, positive; when he walked his cheeks and tidy little paunch jiggled. Oliver Paskell, who was dark, spare and slight, affected old-style spectacles and an underslung pipe. Paskell was noticeably less brisk than Milke. Where Milke swaggered, Paskell slouched; where Milke inspected the quiet gray men on the porches with a lordly air, Paskell watched from the corner of his eye.

Milke pointed. "Number 432, right there." He opened the gate and approached the porch with Paskell two steps behind.

A tall bony man sat watching them with eyes pale and hard as marbles.

Milke asked, "You're Abel Cooley?"

"That's me."

"I understand that you're one of the best outside men on the planet. We're going out on a prospect trip; we need a good all-around hand, and we'd like to hire you. You'd have to take care of chow, service space-suits, load samples, things like that."

Abel Cooley studied Milke briefly, then turned his pale eyes upon Paskell. Paskell looked away, out over the swells of naked granite that rolled six hundred miles west and south of Merlinville.

Cooley said in a mild voice, "Where you lads thinking to prospect?"

Milke blinked and frowned. It was his understanding that such questions were more or less taboo, though of course a man had a right to know where his job would take him. "In strict confidence," said Milke, "we're going out to Odfars."

"Odfars, eh?" Cooley's expression changed not at all. "What do you expect to find out there?"

"Well—Pillson's Almanac indicates a very high density. Which, as you may know, means heavy metal. Then the Deed Office shows neither claims nor workings on Odfars, so we thought we'd survey the territory before someone beat us to it."

Cooley nodded slowly. "So you're going out to Odfars...well, I tell you what to do. Get Three-legged Joe to wait on you. He'll make you a good hand."

"Three-legged Joe?" asked Milke in puzzlement. "Where do we find him?"

"He's out on Odfars now."

Paskell came closer. "How do we locate him on Odfars?"

Cooley smiled crookedly. "Don't worry about that. Leave it to Joe. He'll find you."

From the house came a dark-skinned man five feet tall and four feet wide. Cooley said, "James, these boys are going prospecting out on Odfars; they're looking for a flunky. Maybe you're interested?"

"Not just now, Abel."

"Maybe Three-legged Joe is the man to see."

"Can't beat Three-legged Joe."

Paskell drew Milke out to the street. "They're joking."

Milke said darkly, "No use trying to get work out of those old bums. They get by on their pensions; they don't want an honest job."

Paskell said thoughtfully, "Perhaps it's as well to go out by ourselves; it might be less trouble in the long run. These old-timers don't understand modern methods. Even if we found a man that satisfied us, we'd have to break him in on the Pinsley generator and the Hurd; he'd have the aerators out of adjustment before we'd been out twice."

Milke nodded. "There'll be more work for us, but I think you're right."

Paskell pointed. "There's the other place—Tom Hand's Chandlery."

Milke consulted a list. "I hope this doesn't turn out to be another wild goose chase; we need those extra filters."

Tom Hand's Chandlery occupied a large dirty building raised off the ground on four-foot stilts. Milke and Paskell climbed up on the loading platform. A scrawny near-bald man approached from out of the shadows. "What's the trouble, boys?"

Milke frowned at his list while Paskell stood aside puffing owlishly on his pipe. "If you'll take us to your technical superintendent," said Milke, "I think I can explain what we need."

The old man reached out two dirty fingers. "Lemme see what you want."

Milke fastidiously moved the list out of reach. "I think I'd better see someone in the technical department."

The old man said impatiently, "Son, out here we don't have departments, technical or otherwise. Lemme see what you want. If we got it, I'll know; if we don't, I'll know."

Milke handed over the list. The old man hissed through his teeth. "You want an ungodly amount of them filters."

"They keep burning out on us," said Milke. "I've diagnosed the trouble—an extra load on the circuit."

"Mmph, those things never burn out. You've probably been plugging them in backwise. This side here fits against the black thing-a-ma-jig; this side connects to your circuits. Is that how you had 'em?"

Milke cleared his throat. "Well—"

Paskell took the pipe out of his mouth. "No, as a matter of fact we had them in the other way."

The old man nodded. "I'll give you three. That's all you'll use in a lifetime. Now for this other stuff, we got to go around to the front."

He led them down a dark aisle, past racks crammed with nameless oddments, into a room split by a scarred wooden counter.

At a table near the door three men sat playing cards; nearby stood the dark thick man called James.

James called in a jocular baritone, "Give 'em a jug of acid for Three-legged Joe, Tom. These boys is going out to prospect Odfars."

"Odfars, eh?" Tom scrutinized Milke and Paskell with impersonal interest. "Don't know as I'd try it, boys. Three-legged Joe—"

Milke asked brusquely, "What do we owe you?"

Tom Hand scribbled out a bill, took Milke's money.

Paskell asked tentatively, "Who is this Three-legged Joe?…A joke? Or is there actually someone out there?"

Tom Hand bent over his cash box. The men at the table snapped cards along the green felt. James had his back turned.

Paskell put the pipe back in his mouth, sucked noisily.

On the way back, Milke said bitterly, "It's always been the same way; whenever these old-timers have a laugh on a stranger, they play it for all it's worth…"

"But who or what is Three-legged Joe?"

"Well," said Milke, "sooner or later, I suppose we'll find out."

Odfars ranked fourteenth in a scatter of dead worlds around Sigma Sculptoris, drifting in an orbit so wide that the sun showed like a medium-distant street lamp.

Paskell gingerly handled the controls, while Milke scanned the face of the planet with radar peaked to highest sensitivity. Milke pointed to a mirror-smooth surface winding like a fjord between axe-headed crags. "Look there, an ideal landing site—perfect!"

Paskell said doubtfully, "It looks like a chain of lakes."

"That's what it is—lakes of quicksilver." Milke turned Paskell a chiding glance. "It's absolute zero down there; it can't help but be solid, if that's what's on your mind."

"True," said Paskell. "But it has a peculiar soft look to it."

"If it's liquid," scoffed Milke, "I'll eat your hat."

"If it's liquid," said Paskell, "neither one of us will eat—ever again. Well—here goes."

The impact of landing substantiated Milke's position. He ran to the port, looked out. "Hmmph, can't see anything in this dark without booster goggles. In any event, we'll have a good level floor for our assay tent."

Paskell saw in his mind's eye a page from Hade's Manual: *"The assay tent is customarily a balloon of plastic film maintained by air pressure. Its use eliminates noxious, acrid or poisonous fumes inside the ship, formerly a source of great annoyance. Certain authorities advise a field survey before bringing out the tent; others maintain that erecting the tent first will facilitate examination of samples taken on the survey, and I generally favor the latter practice."*

Milke said off-handedly, "Some of the boys like to wait before they put up their bubble; others set it out first thing to give them a place to drop off their samples. I generally like to get it up and out of the way."

"Yes, yes," said Paskell. "Let's get it up."

In space-suits, with booster goggles over their eyes, they left the ship. Paskell looked across the quicksilver lake, up into the jutting rock—icy bright and black through the booster goggles. The lake gleamed like buffed nickel, terminating nearby in a long finger pointing up a defile. In the direction opposite it dropped off around the curve of the horizon.

Paskell said in a tone of dubious humor, "I don't see Three-legged Joe anywhere."

Milke's snort sounded loud in the earphones.

"He's supposed to know we're here."

Milke said crisply, "Let's get to work."

From an exterior locker they took the assay tent, carried it fifty feet across the quicksilver to the length of the air hose. Milke turned the valve; the tent swelled into a half-sphere fifteen feet in diameter.

Milke tested the lock with a deftness attained on lunar field trips. He squeezed the lock compartment against the tent, forcing the enclosed air into the tent through a flap valve; then entering the lock, he sealed the outside entry, opened the inside valve, letting the compartment fill with air, and entered the tent.

"Works fine," he told Paskell confidently. "Let's get the equipment."

From the locker they brought the knock-down bench, carried it inside through the lock. Milke brought out a rack of reagents and the pulverizer. Paskell carried out the furnace, then went into the ship for the spectroscope.

"That should be good for a while," said Milke. He shot a glance up at distant Sigma Sculptoris. "It's a six hour day here—about two hours of light left. Feel like taking a quick look around?"

"It might be a good idea." Paskell fingered the empty loop at his belt. "I think I'll get my gun."

Milke chuckled. "There's nothing alive here; it's a vacuum, absolute zero. You've let that talk of Three-legged Joe get you down."

"Quite right," said Paskell. "In any event, I'll feel better with my gun."

Milke followed him into the ship. "Might as well get in the habit of wearing the thing." He holstered his own gun.

They set out across the lake, past the tent, up the narrow finger of quicksilver, into the defile. "Strange stuff," said Paskell chipping a fragment from the cliff. "Looks like chalk—gray chalk."

"Can't be chalk," said Milke. "Chalk is sedimentary."

"Whatever it is," said Paskell, "it's still strange stuff, and it still looks like chalk."

The fissure widened, the cliffs fell away almost at once; another quicksilver lake spread before them. "Makes for easy walking," observed Milke. "Better than scrambling through the rocks."

Paskell eyed the mirror-like surface which wound like a glacier past alternating bluffs, and in a perceptible curve over the horizon. "It might easily be connected all the way around."

Milke motioned to him. "See that pink stone? Rhodochrosite. And look down at the end—somehow it's been fused and reduced, leaving the pure metal."

"Very encouraging," said Paskell.

"Encouraging?" boomed Milke. "Why it's downright wonderful! If we found nothing else but this one vein, we're made...perhaps it might even be economical to mine the quicksilver..."

Paskell glanced at the sun, "There's not much daylight left; perhaps—"

"Oh, just around the next bend," said Milke. "It's easy walking." He pointed ahead to a massive knob of shiny black material projecting from the crag. "Look at that knob of galena—interesting."

Paskell felt a throb and hum at his side. He looked down to the dial, stopped short, walked to the left, turned, walked back to the right. He looked up toward the knob of shiny black rock. "That's not galena, that's pitchblende."

"By Jove," breathed Milke reverently, "you're right! As big as the Margan-Annis strike...Oliver, my boy, we're made."

Paskell said with a puckered brow, "I can't understand why the planet hasn't been developed..." He glanced nervously up into the deep shadows, perceptibly lengthening. "I wonder—"

"Three-legged Joe?" Milke laughed. "Fairy-tale stuff." He looked at Paskell. "What's the matter?"

Paskell said in a husky whisper, "Feel the ground."

Milke stood stock-still.

Thud-bump. Thud-bump. Thud-bump.

The sun dropped behind a crag; even the boosters found no light in the sudden shade. "Come on," said Paskell. He turned, paced hurriedly back up the lake.

"Wait for me," said Milke breathlessly.

At the ridge of chalky rock which divided the two lakes, they paused, looked back. The ground felt solid, immobile under their feet.

"Strange," said Milke.

"Very strange," said Paskell.

They crossed the ridge; the hulk of their ship caught the last flat rays from Sigma Sculptoris.

Paskell came to a sudden halt. Milke stared at him, then followed his gaze. "Our assay tent!"

They ran forward to where the fabric lay in a crumpled heap. "There's been a hole cut in it," muttered Paskell.

"Three-legged Joe?" inquired Milke sarcastically. "More likely there's a leak."

Paskell kicked at the material, now stiff as sheet metal with the cold. "We'll have a devil of a time finding it."

"Oh not so bad. We'll pump in warm air—"

"And then?"

"Well, there's a leak. As soon as the air hits the vacuum the water vapor condenses. So we look for a little jet of steam."

Paskell said in a precise voice, "There's no leak."

"No? Then why—"

"We never turned on the heat. The air inside liquefied."

Milke turned away to look out over the lake. Paskell quietly plugged in the cord; power circulated through elements meshed into the tent fabric.

Milke turned back, slapping his gloves together. "That's about all we can do until the air thaws out…" He looked at Paskell, who again was standing as if listening. Irritably he asked, "What's the matter now?"

Paskell made a furtive motion toward the ground. Milke looked intently down.

Thud-bump. Thud-bump. Thud-bump. Thud-bump.

"Three-legged Joe," whispered Paskell.

Milke looked hurriedly in all directions. "There can't be anything out there." He turned. Paskell had disappeared.

"Oliver! Where are you?"

"I'm in the ship," came a calm voice.

Milke backed slowly toward the port. Night had come to Odfars; starlight shone on the quicksilver lake, intensified by the booster goggles to near the power of moonlight. Was that a black shadow standing in the defile? Milke hurriedly backed against the port.

It was locked. He pounded against the metal. "Hey, Oliver, open up!"

He looked over his shoulder. The black shape seemed to have moved forward.

Paskell came to the port, looked carefully out past Milke, threw back the bolts. Milke burst into the air-chamber, on into the ship. He took off his helmet. "What's the idea locking me out? Suppose that damn whatever it is was hot on my tail?"

Paskell said in a practical voice, "Well, we'd hardly want him inside the ship, would we?"

Milke roared, "If he got me first I wouldn't care whether he got into the ship or not." He jumped up into the central dome, played the searchlight around the lake. Paskell watched from the sideport. "See anything?"

"No," grumbled Milke. "I still don't believe there's anything out there. Let's eat dinner and get some sleep."

"Perhaps we should keep watch."

"What do we watch for? What good would it do if we saw something?"

Paskell shrugged. "We might be able to deal with it, if we knew what it was."

Milke said, "If there *is* anything out there—" he slapped the holster at his belt "—I'll know how to deal with it… A couple of bursts into its hide and we'll have to sift-screen for its pieces."

The ship vibrated; from the tail came a harsh sound. The floor jarred under their feet. Milke looked askance at Paskell, who puffed rather desperately at his pipe. Milke ran back to the searchlight. But the central dome interrupted the backward path of the beam and the tail was left in darkness.

"I can't see a thing," fretted Milke. He jumped down to the deck, looked indecisively at the after port.

The vibrations ceased. Milke squared his shoulders, pulled the helmet back over his head. Slowly Paskell followed suit.

"You bring a flashlight," said Milke. "I'll have my gun ready..."

They stepped into the air lock. Paskell gingerly thrust his arm out, aimed the light toward the tent. "Nothing there," grumbled Milke. He pushed past Paskell, stepped down to the ground. Paskell followed, played the light in a circle.

"Whatever it was, it's gone," grunted Milke. "It heard us coming—"

"Look," whispered Paskell.

It was no more than a zigzag of shadows, a moving mass.

Milke held out his arm; his gun spat pale blue sparks. Explosion—a great splash of orange light. "Got him!" cried Milke exultantly. "Dead center!"

Their eyes adjusted to the pallid illumination of the flashlight. Nothing but the glistening sheen of the quicksilver and—a rumpled tumbled mess where the assay tent had stood.

Milke said in an outrage too deep for vehemence, "He's ruined our gear—our tent!"

"Look out!" screamed Paskell. The flashlight took lunatic sweeps over the lake. Milke sent shot after shot at a tall shape; the explosions smote back on their suits; the orange glare blinded their eyes.

Thud-bump...Thud-bump... "Inside!" gasped Milke. "Inside, we can't hold him off..."

The outer port slammed. A breathless moment later the hull was jarred, scraped along the quicksilver. Milke and Paskell stood haunted and pale in the center of the deck.

Metal creaked at the stern under pressure or torsion. Milke's voice came high-pitched. "We're not built to take that kind of stuff—"

The ship lurched to the side. Paskell put his pipe in his pocket, grabbed a stanchion. Milke jumped up to the controls. "We'd better get out of here."

Paskell cleared his throat. "Wait, I think it's stopped."

The boat was quiet. Milke thought of the searchlight, flicked the switch. "Hah!"

"What is it?"

Milke stared out the port. He said slowly, "I really don't know. Something like a one-legged man on crutches...That's how he walks."

"Is he big?"

"Yes," said Milke. "Rather big…I think he's gone, through that fissure—" He came down to the deck, split open his space suit, climbed nervously out. "That was Three-legged Joe."

Paskell took a sudden seat on the bunk, reached for his pipe. "Quite an impressive fellow."

Milke laughed shortly. "I can certainly understand how he scared the bejabbers out of those old bindlestiffs."

"Yes," Paskell nodded earnestly. "I can too." He lit his pipe, puffed reflectively. "He can't be invulnerable…"

Milke dropped leadenly upon his own bunk. "We'll get him—somehow or other."

Paskell craned his neck out the port. "There'll be light in a few hours…I suppose we might as well sleep."

"Yes," said Milke. "If Three-legged Joe comes back, I imagine he'll let us know about it."

Sigma Sculptoris washed the quicksilver lake with the palest of lights. Milke and Paskell glumly examined the wreckage of the assay tent.

Milke's indignation brimmed over the restraints he had set upon himself. He clenched his fists inside the gloves, glared toward the defile. "I'd like to lay my hands on that three-legged devil…"

Paskell busied himself among the tatters of the tent. "Nothing but ribbons."

Milke said gloomily, "No use to think about mending it…" He watched Paskell curiously. "What are you looking for?"

"I wonder what possessed him to break into the tent."

"Sheer destructiveness."

Paskell said thoughtfully, "I notice one thing—" he paused.

"What?"

"All our reagents are gone."

Milke bent over the wreckage. "All of them?"

"All the acids. All the bases. He left distilled water, the salts…"

"Hm," said Milke. "What do you make of that?"

Paskell shrugged inside his suit. "It's suggestive."

"Of what, if I may ask?"

"I'm not sure." Paskell wandered out over the quicksilver, searching the surface. "He was about here when you shot at him?"

"Just about."

Paskell bent. "Look here." He held up a rough brownish-gray object the size of his thumb. "Here's a piece of Three-legged Joe."

Milke examined the fragment. "If this is all our weapons did to him—he's tough. This stuff is flexible!"

Paskell took back the fragment. "Let's take it in and run it through the works."

They returned into the ship. Paskell clamped the bit in a vise and after exasperating difficulty, succeeded in slicing free a brittle shaving. He forced it flat between a slide and a cover glass, examined it under the microscope. "Remarkable."

"Let's see." Milke applied his eye. "Hm···it's like a carpet—woven in three dimensions."

"Right. No matter which way you cut or tear, fibers mat up against you... now let's see what he's made of."

"You're the technician," said Milke.

Paskell looked up from the workbench an hour later. "It's a very complex silicon compound. The spectroscope shows silicon, lithium, fluorine, oxygen, iron, sulfur, selenium, but I can't begin to put a name to the stuff."

"Call it Joe-hide," Milke suggested.

Paskell blew into his pipe, looked solemnly down at the workbench . "I have a tentative theory about Joe's inner workings..."

"Well?"

"Obviously he needs energy to exist. His hide shows no radioactivity, so he must use chemical energy. At least I can't think of any other form of energy that he could be using."

Milke frowned. "Chemical energy? At absolute zero?"

"He's insulated. No telling how high his internal temperature goes ."

"What kind of chemical energy? There's no free oxygen, no fluorine, nothing..."

"Presumably he uses whatever he can get—anything that reacts to produce energy."

Milke pounded his fist. "We could bait him into a trap, with, say, a chunk of solid oxygen!"

"I should certainly think so. But what kind of trap?"

Milke scowled. "A dead-fall."

"Here on Odfars gravity is not too strong...we'd have to stack ten thousand cubic yards of rock to make an impression."

Milke paced up and down the room. "I've got it!"

"Well?" said Paskell mildly.

"Perhaps you could make a detonator that we could set off from the ship."

"Yes, that could be done."

"Here's what we'll do. We'll set out about twenty pounds of myradyne, with the detonator in the center. Joe will come past, tuck this bundle into whatever kind of stomach he's got. We wait till he gets a few hundred yards from the ship, then set it off."

Paskell pursed his lips. "If events proceeded along those lines, everything would be fine."

"Well, why shouldn't they? You claim that Joe eats—"

"Not 'claim'—'theorize'."

"—anything that produces energy. Well, the myradyne should look to him like ice cream and candy and cake all mixed up . It's nothing else *but* energy."

"It's a different kind of energy—the energy of instability. Perhaps he only digests energy of combination."

"You're quibbling," said Milke with disgust. "I say the idea's worth trying."

Paskell shrugged. "Get out your myradyne."

"How long will it take you to fix up a detonator?"

"Twenty minutes. I'll hook up a battery and a spare head-set to the cartridge..."

While Milke gingerly carried the packet of explosive across the lake, Paskell stood by the port watching. Milke surveyed the landscape with fine calculation, setting down the packet, moving it a few yards to the right, another few yards toward the defile. Finally satisfied, he looked back to Paskell for approval. Paskell signaled casually, and his hand fell against the detonation switch. He looked out toward Milke, hastily jumped into his suit, let himself through the port, ran across the lake.

Milke asked, "What's the trouble?"

Paskell said, "That remote detonator doesn't work. I'd better take a look at it."

Milke stared at him truculently. "How do you know it doesn't work?"

Paskell made a vague gesture, knelt beside the packet, unfolded the wrapping.

"You couldn't have just sensed it," Milke insisted.

"Well, as a matter of fact, my hand accidentally hit the switch, and it didn't go off—so I thought I'd better run out and see what was wrong."

Milke seemed to sink inside his suit. For a moment there was silence. "Ah," said Paskell. "Nothing very serious; I neglected to clip down the battery leads... now it's ready to go—"

"I'm going back to the ship," said Milke thickly.

Paskell glanced up toward Sigma Sculptoris. "Yes, there's only a few moments of daylight left…"

Inside the ship, without the booster goggles, night apparently had already come to the quicksilver lake.

Milke roused himself from his bunk where he had been quietly sitting, took his goggles, went up into the control blister. "Nothing in sight."

Paskell said mildly, "Maybe Joe won't be back."

Milke, with his back to Paskell, said nothing.

"Maybe he's been watching us all day," Paskell remarked.

Milke leaned forward. "There's something moving in the gulch…there goes the daylight. Blast it! Now I can't see anything…and the dome's in the way of the searchlight again."

In sudden inspiration Paskell said, "Use the radar!"

Milke ran to the screen, flipped some switches, set the key on Green, short range. Paskell swung around the antenna. "Hold it!" said Milke. "Right there!"

Paskell and Milke bent close to the screen. The plane of the lake, the bulk of the mountains, the gap were all clear. Three-legged Joe, much closer, was a blur. "Can't you adjust it finer?" demanded Paskell.

Milke ran to the workbench, came back with a screw-driver, set the Green adjustment to its limit. "How's that?"

"Turn off the lights. I feel like I'm in a peep-show."

"There, any better?"

"Yes, much better."

Milke came back to the screen. Three-legged Joe was a barrel surmounted by a keg. The legs were a blur; flickering wisps of light to either side of the trunk seemed to indicate arm-members.

"Look," sighed Milke. "He's stopping by the package."

The great trunk seemed to waver, collapse.

"He's reaching for it."

The shape once more reached its full height.

"He's stopped," said Paskell.

"He's eating the myradyne…"

Three-legged Joe came forward, and presently blurred out past the resolving power of the set.

The ship jerked tentatively. Milke and Paskell braced themselves. Nothing more. Silence. The radar screen was empty. Paskell swivelled the antenna. Nothing.

"He's gone," said Milke. "Where's the detonator switch?"

"Wait!" Paskell whispered. He turned on the lights. "Look!"

Milke jerked back. Pressed close to the port beside his face was a rough silvery brown-gray substance.

The port suddenly showed black. A flicker of movement passed the stern port.

"Off with the lights," hissed Milke. "Back to the radar."

A blur of golden light resolved into an ambling barrel and keg.

"Now," said Milke, "press the button! Quick! Before he gets out of range."

"Just a moment," said Paskell. "Suppose he's smarter than we think?"

"No time for theorizing now," cried Milke. "Where's the button?"

Paskell pushed him away stubbornly. "First, we'd better take a look around." He climbed into his space suit while Milke fumed and ranted.

Taking no heed, Paskell left the ship. Out the port Milke could see the glimmer of his head lamp.

The outside port sighed open, thudded shut. Paskell came back into the ship. Milke had his finger on the switch. Paskell, unable to talk through the helmet, banged his glove against the wall. In his other hand he held up a brown packet.

Milke's fingers fell nervously away.

Paskell split himself out of the suit. "I didn't think he'd like myradyne," he said in modest triumph. "The wrong kind of chemical energy. He left it beside the ship."

"Gad!" said Milke huskily. "Twice on the same day I'm blown to smithereens…"

Paskell carefully removed the detonator. "Every day we're learning more about Three-legged Joe."

Milke's voice was warm with emotion. "Every day we come closer to killing ourselves."

"Tomorrow," said Paskell, "we'll try again."

Over a cup of hot coffee Milke asked, "How do you mean, try again? So far as I can see, we're licked. Our guns are no good, he refuses to eat our explosives. Certainly nothing in the world could poison him."

"True." Paskell tamped black shag into his pipe. "The methods for killing human beings don't apply to Three-legged Joe."

"No wonder those old goats at Merlinville gave us the laugh."

Paskell puffed thoughtfully. "If we could concentrate enough heat on Joe, for a long enough time—"

"Nuts!" said Milke. "If we had an ocean we couldn't even drown him."

Paskell said through the cloud of smoke. "If we melted a puddle in the quicksilver and he fell in, and the quicksilver froze around him—"

"Impossible. Quicksilver at absolute zero is super-conductive. We'd have to heat half the planet."

"Super-conductive…Right. So it is." Paskell stared dreamily into the haze. "I wonder how far the quicksilver extends around the planet?"

"What difference does that make?"

"Maybe we'll electrocute Joe."

"Hah!" spat Milke. "With what? Our two thousand-watt generator?"

Paskell said, "First we'll have to check on the quicksilver."

"On foot? With Joe pounding along behind us, breathing down our necks?"

Paskell said carelessly, "I imagine we can move as fast as Joe."

"I'm not sure. Maybe he runs like a greyhound."

"We'll have our guns."

"Fat lot of good they'll do."

"Well—I suppose we could take up our ship and cruise around the planet. In fact it might be better…"

His companion had been completely absorbed in his theorizing when Milke called out in alarm, "You're setting down almost in that defile!"

"Good," said Paskell. "We want to have the ship as near to the gap as possible."

"I don't see why," Milke said petulantly. "In fact I don't understand what you're up to."

"We're planning to electrocute Three-legged Joe," said Paskell patiently. "We've been around the planet; we've established that the quicksilver is interconnected everywhere except at this fifty-foot saddle of gray chalk. We've got enough lead and copper aboard to bridge the gap with a fairly heavy cable—which we will do. We can melt a good connection into the quicksilver with thermite."

"So then?"

"While you're installing the cable, I'll be rigging up some kind of fancy induction coil to take power from our generator and build up watts in the round-planet circuit."

Milke stared incredulously at Paskell. "What good will that do?"

"You'll arrange the cable so that when Joe comes along the defile, he'll have to take hold of the cable to break it. As soon as he does, he'll get everything that we've been feeding into the circuit."

Milke shook his head. "It won't work."

Paskell puffed at his pipe. "And why not, pray?"

"Think of the hysteresis in all those miles of quicksilver—the inlets and bays and channels. There'll be a billion little whorls and eddies…"

"There's no energy lost," said Paskell. "There's no resistance, so there can't be any production of heat."

"There'll be field conflicts," insisted Milke.

"Only for a few hundredths of a second. After that the fields will necessarily enforce a flow pattern that minimizes the impedance."

Milke shook his head. "I hope you know what you're talking about… But—" he raised a finger "—we've got another problem."

"What's that?"

"The planet's natural magnetism. If we start current flowing around the planet, we're setting up artificial north and south poles. We'll be fighting the natural field."

Paskell blinked owlishly. "There is no natural field to this planet. I checked immediately."

Milke threw up his hands. "Go to it, Oliver. It's your party."

Milke and Paskell stood contemplating the defile, across which, at the height of their eyes, dangled a rude cable. Near the lake, the cable passed through a long box, from which came leads running to the generator inside the ship.

Paskell said solemnly, "There's a trillion amps running through the cable."

"A few more," said Milke, "it'll swell like a poisoned pup."

"There is a practical limit," admitted Paskell. "At absolute zero the resistance of super-conductive metals is infinitesimal, but still is greater than nothing. When the cable carries a load that generates heat faster than the heat radiates off, the temperature in the cable rises until it reaches the lower limit of super-conductivity."

"And then?"

Paskell flung up his arms. "No more cable."

Milke regarded his handiwork anxiously. "Perhaps we'd better check."

"How? We don't have a thermocouple aboard that sensitive."

Milke shrugged. "All we can do then is hope."

"Right. Hope that Joe comes down that pass before the cable goes." He looked up at the sun. "Still an hour or two of light."

Milke said doubtfully, "The set-up doesn't look very lethal. Suppose Joe grabs the cable and breaks it, and nothing happens—what then?"

"Something's got to happen. We're feeding a constant two thousand watts into that circuit. When Joe breaks the cable those watts have to go somewhere—they just don't evaporate. They keep on going—through Joe. And if Joe doesn't feel it, I'll personally go after him with a pocket-knife."

Milke turned Paskell a surprised glance: strong talk from modest Oliver Paskell.

Paskell was restlessly beating his hands together. "We're forgetting something."

Milke turned, looked toward the ship.

"Ah, yes," said Paskell.

Milke made a strange noise. His arm jerked up.

"The bait," said Paskell. "We want to set out some acid."

"Never mind the bait," rasped Milke. "We're the bait...Joe's behind us..."

Paskell sprang around. Three-legged Joe stood in front of the ship looking at them.

"Run," said Milke. "Up under the cable...And if it doesn't work—God help us..."

Three-legged Joe came forward, like a one-legged man on crutches.

Paskell stood frozen. "Run!" screamed Milke. He darted back, seized Paskell's arm.

Paskell broke into a shambling run.

"Faster," panted Milke. "He's gaining on us."

Paskell ran to the mountainside, tried to claw his way up the sheer rock.

"No, no!" yelled Milke. "Through the defile!"

Paskell turned, ducked under one of Joe's enormous arms, scuttled toward the defile.

Milke tackled him. "Under the cable—not through! *Under!*" He grabbed Paskell's legs, drew him under the cable. Three-legged Joe ambled casually after them.

Paskell rose to his feet, looked wildly around. "Easy," said Milke. "Easy..."

Cautiously they backed up the defile. Milke panted, "No use running now. If your contraption doesn't work, we might as well reconcile ourselves to death."

Paskell asked suddenly, "Did you turn on the generator?"

Milke froze. "The generator? Inside the ship? You mean the power out to the circuit?"

"Yes, the generator..."

"No, didn't you?"

"I don't remember!"

Milke said despairingly, "You'll know in a minute. Here comes Joe—"

Three-legged Joe paused by the cable. He walked forward. The cable touched his chest. He lifted up his arms. "Close your eyes," cried Paskell.

The sudden glare spattered darts of light through their eyelids.

"You turned on the generator, " said Milke.

Three-legged Joe lay forty feet distant, twitching feebly.

"He's not dead," muttered Paskell.

Milke stood looking down at the silver-gray hulk. "We can't cut him up. We can't tie him. We can't…"

Paskell ran to the ship. "Get out the grapples."

Returning from the Merlinville Deed Office, Milke and Paskell stepped into Tom Hand's Chandlery for a new tent and a replacement set of reagents.

Lounging at the table were Abel Cooley and his friend James. "Ah, here's the prospectors back from Odfars," said Cooley.

Tom Hand limped forward. His eyes were red, there was alcohol on his breath, and a series of black and blue bruises showed on one side of his face. "Well, young fellow," he said to Milke in a thick voice, "what'll it be?"

"First, we need a new assay tent."

From the table by the window came a chuckle. James called out in his jocular baritone, "Three-legged Joe maybe tried to bunk in with you?"

Milke made a noncommittal gesture; Paskell sucked at his pipe.

Tom Hand said, "Pick up your tent out on the loading platform. What else?"

"A set of assay reagents." Milke handed over a list.

Tom Hand looked at them from under his eyebrows. "You boys still going out prospecting?"

"Certainly. Why not?"

"I should think maybe you had a bellyful ."

Milke shrugged. "Odfars wasn't too bad. We never expected an easy life from prospecting. Joe gave us a pretty hard time, but we took care of him."

Hand leaned forward, red eyes blinking. "What's that?"

"We don't mind letting it out. We've got everything in sight sewed up and recorded ."

Abel Cooley said, "You took care of Joe, did you? Talk him to death maybe?"

"No. He's still alive. We've got him where he can't get away. A research team from the Institute is coming out to look him over."

James stepped forward. "You've got him where he can't get away? I've seen Joe break out of a net of two-inch cable like it was string. We blasted a mountain down on top of his cave. Twenty minutes later he pushes his way out… Now you tell me you've got him where he can't get away."

"Right," murmured Paskell. "Exactly right."

Milke turned to Tom Hand. "Give us about a hundred gallons of hydrogen peroxide, two hundred gallons of alcohol."

"We've got to keep Joe alive," Paskell told James .

Abel Cooley snorted. "Hogwash."

Tom Hand shrugged, turned away into the recesses of his shop.

James said, in an oil-smooth voice, "Suppose you break down and tell us just what you did to poor old Three-legged Joe."

"Why not?" said Paskell. "But I'm warning you—stay away from him."

"Never mind the jokes…I'm still listening."

"Well, first we electrocuted Joe. It stunned him."

"Yeah?"

"We couldn't kill him or tie him—so while he was still twitching, we threw grapples around his leg, hoisted him twenty miles out into space and gave him an orbit around Odfars. That's where he is now—alive and well and feeling rather foolish, I should imagine."

James pulled at his chin. He looked at Abel Cooley. "What do you think, Abel?" he asked.

Abel Cooley snorted, looked out the window.

James sat down by the table. "Yes," he said heavily, "Three-legged Joe *is* feeling rather foolish, I expect."

"About like the rest of you birds," came Tom Hand's voice from behind the shelves.

Afterword to "Three-Legged Joe"

Long, long ago, when I was afflicted with wanderlust—in fact even as a boy of twelve or fourteen—I longed to drift down the Danube in a *Faltboot* from Donaueschingen to the Black Sea. I consulted maps, books, although nothing ever came of this project. There is a phrase that sticks in my memory, even while its provenance eludes me: "Far-off places with sweet-sounding names". I had my own list of such names: Timbuktu, Kashmir, Bali, Tahiti, Vienna, Venice…Norma and I tried to touch in at these places over the years. The only one that we missed was Timbuktu…we were close on that, at Bamako, but wisdom prevailed, and Norma and I returned home before our money ran out.

As should now be apparent, much of my work was produced while Norma, John and I inhabited some agreeable location here and there about the world. I planned this system when I was still very young, before I had written anything, and by some freak of circumstance it worked out. Of course, an equal or greater amount of my writing was done at home—I have no way of measuring this.

—Jack Vance

DP!

An old woodcutter woman, hunting mushrooms up the north fork of the Kreuzberg, raised her eyes and saw the strangers. They came step by step through the ferns, arms extended, milk-blue eyes blank as clam shells. When they chanced into patches of sunlight, they cried out in hurt voices and clutched at their naked scalps, which were white as ivory, and netted with pale blue veins.

The old woman stood like a stump, the breath scraping in her throat. She stumbled back, almost falling at each step, her legs moving back to support her at the last critical instant. The strange people came to a wavering halt, peering through sunlight and dark-green shadow. The woman took an hysterical breath, turned, and put her gnarled old legs to flight.

A hundred yards downhill she broke out on a trail; here she found her voice. She ran, uttering cracked screams and hoarse cries, lurching from side to side. She ran till she came to a wayside shrine, where she flung herself into a heap to gasp out prayer and frantic supplication.

Two woodsmen, in leather breeches and rusty black coats, coming up the path from Tedratz, stared at her in curiosity and amusement. She struggled to her knees, pointed up the trail. "Fiends from the pit! Walking in all their evil; with my two eyes I've seen them!"

"Come now," the older woodsman said indulgently. "You've had a drop or two, and it's not reverent to talk so at a holy place."

"I saw them," bellowed the old woman. "Naked as eggs and white as lard; they came running at me waving their arms, crying out for my very soul!"

"They had horns and tails?" the younger man asked jocularly. "They prodded you with their forks, switched you with their whips?"

"Ach, you blackguards! You laugh, you mock; go up the slope, and see for yourself...Only five hundred meters, and then perhaps you'll mock!"

"Come along," said the first. "Perhaps someone's been plaguing the old woman; if so, we'll put him right."

They sauntered on, disappeared through the firs. The old woman rose to her feet, hobbled as rapidly as she could toward the village.

Five quiet minutes passed. She heard a clatter; the two woodsmen came running at breakneck speed down the path. "What now?" she quavered, but they pushed past her and ran shouting into Tedratz.

Half an hour later fifty men armed with rifles and shotguns stalked cautiously back up the trail, their dogs on leash. They passed the shrine; the dogs began to strain and growl.

"Up through here," whispered the older of the two woodsmen. They climbed the bank, threaded the firs, crossed sun-flooded meadows and balsam-scented shade.

From a rocky ravine, tinkling and chiming with a stream of glacier water, came the strange, sad voices.

The dogs snarled and moaned; the men edged forward, peered into the meadow. The strangers were clustered under an overhanging ledge, clawing feebly into the dirt.

"Horrible things!" hissed the foremost man, "Like great potato-bugs!" He aimed his gun, but another struck up the barrel. "Not yet! Don't waste good powder; let the dogs hunt them down. If fiends they be, their spite will find none of us!" The idea had merit; the dogs were loosed. They bounded forward, full of hate. The shadows boiled with fur and fangs and jerking white flesh.

One of the men jumped forward, his voice thick with rage. "Look, they've killed Tupp, my good old Tupp!" He raised his gun and fired, an act which became the signal for further shooting. And presently, all the strangers had been done to death, by one means or another.

Breathing hard, the men pulled off the dogs and stood looking down at the bodies. "A good job, whatever they are, man, beast, or fiend," said Johann Kirchner, the innkeeper. "But there's the point! What are they? When have such creatures been seen before?"

"Strange happenings for this earth; strange events for Austria!"

The men stared at the white tangle of bodies, none pushing too close, and now with the waning of urgency their mood became uneasy. Old Alois, the baker, crossed himself and, furtively examining the sky, muttered about the Apocalypse. Franz, the village atheist, had his reputation to maintain. "Demons," he asserted, "presumably would not succumb so easily to dog-bite and bullet; these must be refugees from the Russian zone, victims of torture and experimentation." Heinrich, the village Communist, angrily pointed out how much closer lay the big American lager near Innsbruck; this was the effect of Coca-Cola and comic books upon decent Austrians.

"Nonsense," snapped another. "Never an Austrian born of woman had such heads, such eyes, such skin. These things are something else. Salamanders!"

"Zombies," muttered another. "Corpses, raised from the dead."

Alois held up his hand. "Hist!"

Into the ravine came the pad and rustle of aimless steps, the forlorn cries of the troglodytes.

The men crouched back into the shadows; along the ridge appeared silhouettes, crooked, lumpy shapes feeling their way forward, recoiling from the shafts of sunlight.

Guns cracked and spat; once more the dogs were loosed. They bounded up the side of the ravine and disappeared.

Panting up the slope, the men came to the base of a great overhanging cliff, and here they stopped short. The base of the cliff was broken open. Vague pale-eyed shapes wadded the gap, swaying, shuddering, resisting, moving forward inch by inch, step by step.

"Dynamite!" cried the men. "Dynamite, gasoline, fire!"

These measures were never put into effect. The commandant of the French occupation garrison arrived with three platoons. He contemplated the fissure, the oyster-pale faces, the oyster-shell eyes and threw up his hands. He dictated a rapid message for the Innsbruck headquarters, then required the villagers to put away their guns and depart the scene.

The villagers sullenly retired; the French soldiers, brave in their sky-blue shorts, gingerly took up positions; and with a hasty enclosure of barbed wire and rails restrained the troglodytes to an area immediately in front of the fissure.

The April 18 edition of the *Innsbruck Kurier* included a skeptical paragraph: "A strange tribe of mountainside hermits, living in a Kreuzberg cave near Tedratz, was reported today. Local inhabitants profess the deepest mystification. The Tedratz constabulary, assisted by units of the French garrison, is investigating."

A rather less cautious account found its way into the channels of the wire services: "Innsbruck, April 19. A strange tribe has appeared from the recesses of the Kreuzberg near Innsbruck in the Tyrol. They are said to be hairless, blind, and to speak an incomprehensible language.

"According to unconfirmed reports, the troglodytes were attacked by terrified inhabitants of nearby Tedratz, and after bitter resistance were driven back into their caves.

"French occupation troops have sealed off the entire Kreuzertal. A spokesman for Colonel Courtin refuses either to confirm or deny that the troglodytes have appeared."

Bureau chiefs at the wire services looked long and carefully at the story. Why should French occupation troops interfere in what appeared on the face a purely civil disturbance? A secret colony of war criminals? Unlikely. What then? Mysterious race of troglodytes? Clearly hokum. What then? The story might develop, or it might go limp. In any case, on the late afternoon of April 19, a convoy of four cars started up the Kreuzertal, carrying reporters, photographers, and a member of the U.N. Minorities Commission, who by chance happened to be in Innsbruck.

The road to Tedratz wound among grassy meadows, story-book forests, in and out of little Alpine villages, with the massive snow-capped knob of the Kreuzberg gradually pushing higher into the sky.

At Tedratz, the party alighted and started up the now notorious trail, to be brought short almost at once at a barricade manned by French soldiers. Upon display of credentials the reporters and photographers were allowed to pass; the U.N. commissioner had nothing to show, and the NCO in charge of the barricade politely turned him back.

"But I am an official of the United Nations!" cried the outraged commissioner.

"That may well be," assented the NCO. "However, you are not a journalist, and my orders are uncompromising." And the angry commissioner was asked to wait in Tedratz until word would be taken to Colonel Courtin at the camp.

The commissioner seized on the word. "'Camp'? How is this? I thought there was only a cave, a hole in the mountainside?"

The NCO shrugged. "Monsieur le Commissionnaire is free to conjecture as he sees best."

A private was told off as a guide; the reporters and photographers started up the trail, with the long, yellow afternoon light slanting down through the firs.

It was a jocular group; repartee and wise cracks were freely exchanged. Presently the party became winded, as the trail was steep and they were all out of condition. They stopped by the wayside shrine to rest. "How much farther?" asked a photographer.

The soldier pointed through the firs toward a tall buttress of granite. "Only a little bit; then you shall see."

Once more they set out and almost immediately passed a platoon of soldiers stringing barbed wire from tree to tree.

"This will be the third extension," remarked their guide over his shoulder. "Every day they come pushing up out of the rock. It is—" he selected a word "—*formidable.*"

The jocularity and wise cracks died; the journalists peered through the firs, aware of the sudden coolness of the evening.

They came to the camp, and were taken to Colonel Courtin, a small man full of excitable motion. He swung his arm. "There, my friends, is what you came to see; look your fill, since it is through your eyes that the world must see."

For three minutes they stared, muttering to one another, while Courtin teetered on his toes.

"How many are there?" came an awed question.

"Twenty thousand by latest estimate, and they issue ever faster. All from that little hole." He jumped up on tiptoe, and pointed. "It is incredible; where do they fit? And still they come, like the objects a magician removes from his hat."

"But—do they eat?"

Courtin held out his hands. "Is it for me to ask? I furnish no food; I have none; my budget will not allow it. I am a man of compassion. If you will observe, I have hung the tarpaulins to prevent the sunlight."

"With that skin, they'd be pretty sensitive, eh?"

"Sensitive!" Courtin rolled up his eyes. "The sunlight burns them like fire."

"Funny that they're not more interested in what goes on."

"They are dazed, my friend. Dazed and blinded and completely confused."

"But—what *are* they?"

"That, my friend, is a question I am without resource to answer."

The journalists regained a measure of composure, and swept the enclosure with studiously impassive glances calculated to suggest, *we have seen so many strange sights that now nothing can surprise us.* "I suppose they're men," said one.

"But of course. What else?"

"What else indeed? But where do they come from? Lost Atlantis? The land of Oz?"

"Now then," said Colonel Courtin, "you make jokes. It is a serious business, my friends; where will it end?"

"That's the big question, Colonel. Whose baby is it?"

"I do not understand."

"Who takes responsibility for them? France?"

"No, no," cried Colonel Courtin. "You must not credit me with such a statement."

"Austria, then?"

Colonel Courtin shrugged. "The Austrians are a poor people. Perhaps—of course I speculate—your great country will once again share of its plenitude."

"Perhaps, perhaps not. The one man of the crowd who might have had something to say is down in Tedratz—the chap from the Minorities Commission."

❯•❮

The story pushed everything from the front pages, and grew bigger day by day. From the U.P. wire:

Innsbruck, April 23 (UP): The Kreuzberg miracle continues to confound the world. Today a record number of troglodytes pushed through the gap, bringing the total surface population up to forty-six thousand…

From the syndicated column, *Science Today* by Ralph Dunstaple, for April 28:

The scientific world seethes with the troglodyte controversy. According to the theory most frequently voiced, the trogs are descended from cavemen of the glacial eras, driven underground by the advancing wall of ice. Other conjectures, more or less scientific, refer to the lost tribes of Israel, the fourth dimension, Armageddon, and Nazi experiments.

Linguistic experts meanwhile report progress in their efforts to understand the language of the trogs. Dr. Allen K. Mendelson of the Princeton Institute of Advanced Research, spokesman for the group, classifies the trog speech as "one of the agglutinatives, with the slightest possible kinship to the Basque tongue— so faint as to be highly speculative, and it is only fair to say that there is considerable disagreement among us on this point. The trogs, incidentally, have no words for 'sun', 'moon', 'fight', 'bird', 'animal', and a host of other concepts we take for granted. 'Food' and 'fungus', however, are the same word.

From the *New York Herald Tribune:*
TROGS HUMAN, CLAIM SAVANTS; INTERBREEDING POSSIBLE
by Mollie Lemmon

Milan, April 30: Trogs are physiologically identical with surface humanity, and sexual intercourse between man and trog might well be fertile. Such was the opinion of a group of doctors and geneticists at an informal poll I conducted yesterday at the Milan Genetical Clinic, where a group of trogs are undergoing examination.

From *The Trog Story*, a daily syndicated feature by Harlan B. Temple, April 31:

"Today I saw the hundred thousandth trog push his way up out of the bowels of the Alps; everywhere in the world people are asking, where will it stop? I certainly have no answer. This tremendous migration, unparalleled since the days of Alaric the Goth, seems only just now shifting into high gear. Two new rifts have opened into the Kreuzberg; the trogs come shoving out in close ranks, faces blank as custard, and only God knows what is in their minds.

"The camps—there are now six, interconnected like knots on a rope—extend down the hillside and into the Kreuzertal. Tarpaulins over the treetops give the mountainside, seen from a distance, the look of a lawn with handkerchiefs spread out to dry.

"The food situation has improved considerably over the past three days, thanks to the efforts of the Red Cross, CARE, and FAO. The basic ration is a mush of rice, wheat, millet or other cereal, mixed with carrots, greens, dried eggs, and reinforced with vitamins; the trogs appear to thrive on it.

"I cannot say that the trogs are a noble, enlightened, or even ingratiating race. Their cultural level is abysmally low; they possess no tools, they wear neither clothing nor ornaments. To their credit it must be said that they are utterly inoffensive and mild; I have never witnessed a quarrel or indeed seen a trog exhibit anything but passive obedience.

"Still they rise in the hundreds and thousands. What brings them forth? Do they flee a subterranean Attila, some pandemonic Stalin? The linguists who have been studying the trog speech are close-mouthed, but I have it from a highly informed source that a report will be published within the next day or so..."

Report to the Assembly of the U.N., May 4, by V.G. Hendlemann, Coordinator for the Committee of Associated Anthropologists:

"I will state the tentative conclusions to which this committee has arrived. The processes and inductions which have led to these conclusions are outlined in the appendix to this report.

"Our preliminary survey of the troglodyte language has convinced a majority of us that the trogs are probably the descendants of a group of European cave-dwellers who either by choice or by necessity took up underground residence at least fifty thousand, at most two hundred thousand, years ago.

"The trog which we see today is a result of evolution and mutation, and represents adaptation to the special conditions under which the trogs have existed. He is quite definitely of the species *homo sapiens,* with a cranial capacity roughly identical to that of surface man.

"In our conversations with the trogs we have endeavored to ascertain the cause of the migration. Not one of the trogs makes himself completely clear on the subject, but we have been given to understand that the great caves which the race inhabited have been stricken by a volcanic convulsion and are being gradually filled with lava. If this be the case the trogs are seen to become literally 'displaced persons'.

"In their former home the trogs subsisted on fungus grown in shallow 'paddies', fertilized by their own wastes, finely pulverized coal, and warmed by volcanic heat.

"They have no grasp of 'time' as we understand the word. They have only the sparsest traditions of the past and are unable to conceive of a future further removed than two minutes. Since they exist in the present, they neither expect, hope, dread, nor otherwise take cognizance of what possibly may befall them.

"In spite of their deficiencies of cultural background, the trogs appear to have a not discreditable native intelligence. The committee agrees that a troglodyte child reared in ordinary surface surroundings, and given a typical education, might well become a valuable citizen, indistinguishable from any other human being except by his appearance."

Excerpt from a speech by Porfirio Hernandez, Mexican delegate to the U.N. Assembly, on May 17:

"...We have ignored this matter too long. Far from being a scientific curiosity or a freak, this is a very human problem, one of the biggest problems of our day and we must handle it as such. The trogs are pressing from the ground at an ever-increasing rate; the Kreuzertal, or Kreuzer Valley, is inundated with trogs as if by a flood. We have heard reports, we have deliberated, we have made solemn noises, but the fact remains that every one of us is sitting on his hands. These people—we must call them people—must be settled somewhere permanently; they must be made self-supporting. This hot iron must be grasped; we fail in our responsibilities otherwise..."

Excerpt from a speech, May 19, by Sir Lyandras Chandryasam, delegate from India:

"...My esteemed colleague from Mexico has used brave words; he exhibits a humanitarianism that is unquestionably praiseworthy. But he puts forward no positive program. May I ask how many trogs have come to the surface, thus to be cared for? Is not the latest figure somewhere short of a million? I would like to point out that in India alone five million people yearly die of malnutrition or preventable disease; but no one jumps up here in the assembly to cry for a crusade to help these unfortunate victims of nature. No, it is this strange race, with no claim upon anyone, which has contributed nothing to the civilization of the world, which now we feel has first call upon our hearts and purse-strings. I say, is not this a paradoxical circumstance..."

From a speech, May 20, by Dr. Karl Byrnisted, delegate from Iceland:

"...Sir Lyandras Chandryasam's emotion is understandable, but I would like to remind him that the streets of India swarm with millions upon millions of so-called sacred cattle and apes, who eat what and where they wish, very possibly the food to keep five million persons alive. The recurrent famines in India could be relieved, I believe, by a rationalistic dealing with these parasites, and by steps to make the new birth-control clinics popular, such as a tax on babies. In this way, the Indian government, by vigorous methods, has it within its power to cope with its terrible problem. These trogs, on the other hand, are completely unable to help themselves; they are like babies flung fresh into a world where even the genial sunlight kills them..."

From a speech, May 21, by Porfirio Hernandez, delegate from Mexico:

"I have been challenged to propose a positive program for dealing with the trogs...I feel that as an activating principle, each member of the U.N. agree to accept a number of trogs proportionate to its national wealth, resources, and density of population...Obviously the exact percentages will have to be thrashed out elsewhere...I hereby move the President of the Assembly appoint such a committee, and instruct them to prepare such a recommendation, said committee to report within two weeks."

(Motion defeated, 20 to 35)

The Trog Story, June 2, by Harlan B. Temple:

"No matter how many times I walk through Trog Valley, the former Kreuzertal, I never escape a feeling of the profoundest bewilderment and awe. The trogs number now well over a million; yesterday they chiseled open four new openings into the outside world, and they are pouring out at the rate of thousands every hour. And everywhere is heard the question, where will it stop? Suppose the earth is a honeycomb, a hive, with more trogs than surface men?

"Sooner or later our organization will break down; more trogs will come up than it is within our power to feed. Organization already has failed to some extent. All the trogs are getting at least one meal a day, but not enough clothes, not enough shelter is being provided. Every day hundreds die from sunburn. I understand that the Old-Clothes-for-Trogs drive has nowhere hit its quota. I find it hard to comprehend. Is there no feeling of concern or sympathy for these people merely because they do not look like so many chorus boys and screen starlets?"

From the *Christian Science Monitor:*
CONTROVERSIAL TROG BILL
PASSES U.N. ASSEMBLY
New York, June 4: By a 35 to 20 vote—exactly reversing its first tally on the measure—the U.N. Assembly yesterday accepted the motion of Mexico's Hernandez to set up a committee for the purpose of recommending a percentage-wise distribution of trogs among member states.

Tabulation of voting on the measure found the Soviet bloc lined up with the United States and the British Commonwealth in opposition to the measure—presumably the countries which would be awarded large numbers of the trogs.

Handbill passed out at rally of the Socialist Reich (Neo-Nazi) party at Bremen, West Germany, June 10:
A NEW THREAT
COMRADES! It took a war to clean Germany of the Jews; must we now submit to an invasion of troglodyte filth? All Germany cries *no!* All Germany cries, hold our borders firm against these cretin moles! Send them to Russia; send them to the Arctic wastes! Let them return to their burrows; let them perish! But guard the Fatherland; guard the sacred German Soil!

(Rally broken up by police, handbills seized.)

Letter to the *London Times*, June 18:
To the Editor:
I speak for a large number of my acquaintances when I say that the prospect of taking to ourselves a large colony of 'troglodytes' awakens in me no feeling of enthusiasm. Surely England has troubles more than enough of its own, without the added imposition of an unassimilable and non-productive minority to eat our already meager rations and raise our already sky-high taxes.

Yours, etc.,
Sir Clayman Winifred, Bart.
Lower Ditchley, Hants.

Letter to the *London Times*, June 21:
To the Editor:
Noting Sir Clayman Winifred's letter of June 18, I took a quick check-up of my friends and was dumbfounded to find how closely they hew to Sir Clayman's line. Surely this isn't our tradition, not to get under the load and help lift with everything we've got? The troglodytes are human beings, victims of a disaster we have no means of appreciating. They must be cared for, and if a qualified committee of experts sets us a quota, I say, let's bite the bullet and do our part.

The Ameriphobe section of our press takes great delight in baiting our cousins across the sea for the alleged denial of civil rights to the Negroes—which, may I add, is present in its most violent and virulent form in a country of the British Commonwealth: the Union of South Africa. What do these journalists say to evidences of the same unworthy emotion here in England?

Yours, etc.,
J.C.T. Harrodsmere
Tisley-on-Thames, Sussex.

Headline in the *New York Herald Tribune*, June 22:
FOUR NEW TROG CAMPS OPENED;
POPULATION AT TWO MILLION

Letter to the *London Times*, June 24:
To the Editor:

I read the letter of J.C.T. Harrodsmere in connection with the trog controversy with great interest. I think that in his praiseworthy efforts to have England do its bit, he is overlooking a very important fact: namely, we of England are a close-knit people, of clear clean vigorous blood, and admixture of any nature could only be for the worse. I know Mr. Harrodsmere will be quick to say, no admixture is intended. But mistakes occur, and as I understand a man-trog union to be theoretically fertile, in due course there would be a number of little half-breeds scampering like rats around our gutters, a bad show all around. There are countries where this type of mongrelization is accepted: the United States, for instance, boasts that it is the 'melting pot'. Why not send the trogs to the wide open spaces of the U.S. where there is room and to spare, and where they can 'melt' to their heart's content?

Yours, etc.,

Col. G.P. Barstaple (Ret.), Queens Own Hussars.

Mide Hill, Warwickshire.

Letter to the *London Times*, June 28:

To the Editor:

Contrasting the bank accounts, the general air of aliveness of mongrel U.S.A. and non-mongrel England, I say maybe it might do us good to trade off a few retired colonels for a few trogs extra to our quota. Here's to more and better mongrelization!

Yours, etc.,

(Miss) Elizabeth Darrow Brown

London, S.W.

The Trog Story, June 30, by Harlan B. Temple:

"Will it come as a surprise to my readers if I say the trog situation is getting out of hand? They are coming not slower but faster; every day we have more trogs and every day we have more at a greater rate than the day before. If the sentence sounds confused it only reflects my state of mind.

"Something has got to be done.

"Nothing is being done.

"The wrangling that is going on is a matter of public record. Each country is liberal with advice but with little else. Sweden says, send them to the center of Australia; Australia points to Greenland; Denmark would prefer the Ethiopian uplands; Ethiopia politely indicates Mexico; Mexico says, much more room in Arizona; and in Washington senators from below the Mason-Dixon Line threaten to filibuster from now till Kingdom Come rather than admit a single trog to the continental limits of the U.S. Thank the Lord for an efficient food administration! The U.N. and the world at large can be proud of the organization by which the trogs are being fed.

"Incidental Notes: trog babies are being born—over fifty yesterday."

From the *San Francisco Chronicle:*
REDS OFFER HAVEN TO TROGS
PROPOSAL STIRS WORLD
New York, July 3: Ivan Pudestov, the USSR's chief delegate to the U.N. Assembly, today blew the trog question wide open with a proposal to take complete responsibility for the trogs.

The offer startled the U.N. and took the world completely by surprise, since heretofore the Soviet delegation has held itself aloof from the bitter trog controversy, apparently in hopes that the free world would split itself apart on the problem…

Editorial in the *Milwaukee Journal*, July 5, headed "A Question of Integrity":
At first blush the Russian offer to take the trogs appears to ease our shoulders of a great weight. Here is exactly what we have been grasping for, a solution without sacrifice, a sop to our consciences, a convenient carpet to sweep our dirt under. The man in the street, and the responsible official, suddenly are telling each other that perhaps the Russians aren't so bad after all, that there's a great deal of room in Siberia, that the Russians and the trogs are both barbarians and really not so much different, that the trogs were probably Russians to begin with, etc.

Let's break the bubble of illusion, once and for all. We can't go on forever holding our Christian integrity in one hand and our inclinations in the other…Doesn't it seem an odd coincidence that while the Russians are desperately short of uranium miners at the murderous East German and Ural pits, the trogs, accustomed to life underground, might be expected to make a good labor force?…In effect, we would be turning over to Russia millions of slaves to be worked to death. We have rejected forced repatriation in West Europe and Korea, let's reject forced patriation and enslavement of the trogs.

Headline in the *New York Times*, July 20:
REDS BAN U.N. SUPERVISION OF TROG COMMUNITIES
SOVEREIGNTY ENDANGERED, SAYS PUDESTOV
ANGRILY WITHDRAWS TROG OFFER

Headline in the *New York Daily News*, July 26:
BELGIUM OFFERS CONGO FOR TROG HABITATION
ASKS FUNDS TO RECLAIM JUNGLE
U.N. GIVES QUALIFIED NOD

From *The Trog Story*, July 28, by Harlan B. Temple:
"Four million (give or take a hundred thousand) trogs now breathe surface air. The Kreuzertal camps now constitute one of the world's largest cities, ranking under New York, London, Tokyo. The formerly peaceful Tyrolean valley is now a vast array of tarpaulins, circus tents, Quonset huts, water tanks, and general disorder. Trog City doesn't smell too good either.

"Today might well mark the high tide in what the Austrians are calling 'the invasion from hell'. Trogs still push through a dozen gaps ten abreast, but the pressure doesn't seem so intense. Every once in a while a space appears in the ranks, where formerly they came packed like asparagus in crates. Another difference: the first trogs were meaty and fairly well nourished. These late arrivals are thin and ravenous. Whatever strange subterranean economy they practiced, it seems to have broken down completely..."

From *The Trog Story*, August 1, by Harlan B. Temple:
"Something horrible is going on under the surface of the earth. Trogs are staggering forth with raw stumps for arms, with great wounds..."

From *The Trog Story*, August 8, by Harlan B. Temple:

"Operation Exodus got underway today. One thousand trogs departed the Kreuzertal bound for their new home near Cabinda, at the mouth of the Congo River. Trucks and buses took them to Innsbruck, where they will board special trains to Venice and Trieste. Here ships supplied by the U.S. Maritime Commission will take them to their new home.

"As one thousand trogs departed Trog City, twenty thousand pushed up from their underground homeland, and camp officials are privately expressing concern over conditions. Trog City has expanded double, triple, ten times over the original estimates. The machinery of supply, sanitation and housing is breaking down. From now on, any attempts to remedy the situation are at best stopgaps, like adhesive tape on a rotten hose, when what is needed is a new hose or, rather, a four-inch pipe.

"Even to maintain equilibrium, thirty thousand trogs per day will have to be siphoned out of the Kreuzertal camps, an obvious impossibility under present budgets and efforts…"

From *Newsweek*, August 14:
Camp Hope, in the bush near Cabinda, last week took on the semblance of the Guadalcanal army base during World War II. There was the old familiar sense of massive confusion, the grind of bulldozers, sweating white, beet-red, brown and black skins, the raw earth dumped against primeval vegetation, bugs, salt tablets, Atabrine…

From the U.P. wire:
Cabinda, Belgian Congo, August 20 (UP): The first contingent of trogs landed last night under shelter of dark, and marched to temporary quarters, under the command of specially trained group captains.

Liaison officers state that the trogs are overjoyed at the prospect of a permanent home, and show an eagerness to get to work. According to present plans, they will till collective farms, and continuously clear the jungle for additional settlers.

On the other side of the ledger, it is rumored that the native tribesmen are showing unrest. Agitators, said to be Communist-inspired, are preying on the superstitious fears of a people themselves not far removed from savagery…

Headline in the *New York Times*, August 22:

CONGO WARRIORS RUN AMOK AT CAMP HOPE
KILL 800 TROG SETTLERS IN SINGLE HOUR
Military Law Established
Belgian Governor Protests
Says Congo Unsuitable

From the U.P. Wire:

Trieste, August 23 (UP): Three shiploads of trogs bound for Trogland in the Congo today marked a record number of embarkations. The total number of trogs to sail from European ports now stands at 24,965...

Cabinda, August 23 (UP): The warlike Matemba Confederation is practically in a state of revolt against further trog immigration, while Resident-General Bernard Cassou professes grave pessimism over eventualities.

Mont Blanc, August 24 (UP): Ten trogs today took up experimental residence in a ski-hut to see how well trogs can cope with the rigors of cold weather.

Announcement of this experiment goes to confirm a rumor that Denmark has offered Greenland to the trogs if it is found that they are able to survive Arctic conditions.

Cabinda, August 28 (UP): The Congo, home of witch-doctors, tribal dances, cannibalism and Tarzan, seethes with native unrest. Sullen anger smolders in the villages, riots are frequent and dozens of native workmen at Camp Hope have been killed or hospitalized.

Needless to say, the trogs, whose advent precipitated the crisis, are segregated far apart from contact with the natives, to avoid a repetition of the bloodbath of August 22...

Cabinda, August 29 (UP): Resident-General Bernard Cassou today refused to allow debarkation of trogs from four ships standing off Cabinda roadstead.

Mont Blanc, September 2 (UP): The veil of secrecy at the experimental trog home was lifted a significant crack this morning, when the bodies of two trogs were taken down to Chamonix via the ski-lift...

From *The Trog Story*, September 10, by Harlan B. Temple:
"It is one a.m.; I've just come down from Camp No. 4. The trog columns have dwindled to a straggle of old, crippled, diseased. The stench is frightful...

But why go on? Frankly, I'm heartsick. I wish I had never taken on this assignment. It's doing something terrible to my soul; my hair is literally turning gray. I pause a moment, the noise of my typewriter stops, I listen to the vast murmur through the Kreuzertal; despondency, futility, despair come at me in a wave. Most of us here at Trog City, I think, feel the same.

"There are now five or six million trogs in the camp; no one knows the exact count; no one even cares. The situation has passed that point. The flow has dwindled, one merciful dispensation—in fact, at Camp No. 4 you can hear the rumble of the lava rising into the trog caverns.

"Morale is going from bad to worse here at Trog City. Every day a dozen of the unpaid volunteers throw up their hands, and go home. I can't say as I blame them. Lord knows they've given the best they have, and no one backs them up. Everywhere in the world it's the same story, with everyone pointing at someone else. It's enough to make a man sick. In fact it has. I'm sick—desperately sick.

"But you don't read *The Trog Story* to hear me gripe. You want factual reporting. Very well, here it is. Big news today was that movement of trogs out of the camp to Trieste has been held up pending clarification of the Congo situation. Otherwise, everything's the same here—hunger, smell, careless trogs dying of sunburn..."

Headline in the *New York Times*, September 20:
TROG QUOTA PROBLEM RETURNED TO STUDY GROUP FOR ADJUSTMENT

From the U.P. Wire:

Cabinda, September 25 (UP): Eight ships, loaded with 9,462 trog refugees, still wait at anchor, as native chieftains reiterated their opposition to trog immigration...

Trog City, October 8 (UP): The trog migration is at its end. Yesterday for the first time no new trogs came up from below, leaving the estimated population of Trog City at six million.

New York, October 13 (UP): Deadlock still grips the Trog Resettlement Committee, with the original positions, for the most part, unchanged. Densely populated countries claim they have no room and no jobs; the underdeveloped states insist that they have not enough money to feed their own mouths. The U.S., with both room and money, already has serious minority headaches and doesn't want new ones...

Chamonix, France, October 18 (UP): The Trog Experimental Station closed its doors yesterday, with one survivor of the original ten trogs riding the ski-lift back down the slopes of Mont Blanc.

Dr. Sven Emeldson, director of the station, released the following statement: "Our work proves that the trogs, even if provided shelter adequate for a European, cannot stand the rigors of the North; they seem especially sensitive to pulmonary ailments..."

New York, October 26 (UP): After weeks of acrimony, a revised set of trog immigration quotas was released for action by the U.N. Assembly. Typical figures are: USA 31%, USSR 16%, Canada 8%, Australia 8%, France 6%, Mexico 6%.

New York, October 30 (UP): The USSR adamantly rejects the principle of U.N. checking of the trog resettlement areas inside the USSR...

New York, October 31 (UP): Senator Bullrod of Mississippi today promised to talk till his "lungs came out at the elbows" before he would allow the Trog Resettlement Bill to come to a vote before the Senate. An informal check revealed insufficient strength to impose cloture...

St. Arlberg, Austria, November 5 (UP): First snow of the season fell last night...

Trog City, November 10 (UP): Last night, frost lay a sparkling sheath across the valley...

Trog City, November 15 (UP): Trog sufferers from influenza have been isolated in a special section...

Buenos Aires, November 23 (UP): Dictator Peron today flatly refused to meet the Argentine quota of relief supplies to Trog City until some definite commitment has been made by the U.N....

Trog City, December 2 (UP): Influenza following the snow and rain of the last week has made a new onslaught on the trogs; camp authorities are desperately trying to cope with the epidemic...

Trog City, December 8 (UP): Two crematoriums, fired by fuel oil, are roaring full time in an effort to keep ahead of the mounting influenza casualties...

From *The Trog Story*, December 13, by Harlan B. Temple:
"This is it..."

From the U.P. Wire:

Los Angeles, December 14 (UP): The Christmas buying rush got under way early this year, in spite of unseasonably bad weather...

Trog City, December 15 (UP): A desperate appeal for penicillin, sulfa, blankets, kerosene heaters, and trained personnel was sounded today by Camp Commandant Howard Kerkovits. He admitted that disease among the trogs was completely out of control, beyond all human power to cope with...

From *The Trog Story*, December 23, by Harlan B. Temple:

"I don't know why I should be sitting here writing this, because—since there are no more trogs—there is no more trog story."

Afterword to "DP!"

Neither Norma nor I wished to explore the continent of Europe on two wheels, so we sold our bicycles, boarded a train, and departed England. We bypassed France and rode directly into Austria and debarked at Innsbruck. At this point we were ready to settle down for a time and produce some profitable words. This would establish the program we would subsequently follow in many future excursions. We would find some romantic spot, rent a house or apartment, and there work sometimes as long as two or three months turning out a novel or set of stories.

At Innsbruck, taking local advice, we boarded a strange little trolley which reminded us of the Toonerville Trolley, and rode fifteen miles south into the Alps to a picturesque mountain village, Fulpmes. There was nothing much here except the Hotel Lutz, a shop or two, and a few houses built in the traditional Tyrolean style of bare evergreen boards, so that the village smelled of fresh pine and fir. We adopted *en pension* accommodations at the Lutz and were accorded a room on the second floor with a balcony. I remember this balcony well; it became my habit to sit in the sunlight on it while I wrote. One day a bee stung me.

We remained at Fulpmes a month or so while I completed several novelettes and started *Vandals of the Void*, a boys' book commissioned by Winston Publishing.

—Jack Vance

Shape-Up

J arvis came down Riverview Way from the direction of the terminal ware-house, where he had passed an uncomfortable night. At the corner of Sion Novack Way he plugged his next-to-last copper into the *Pegasus Square Farm and Mining Bulletin* dispenser; taking the pink tissue envelope, he picked his way through the muck of the street to the Original Blue Man Cafe. He chose a table with precision and nicety, his back to a corner, the length of the street in his line of sight.

The waiter appeared, looked Jarvis up and down. Jarvis countered with a hard stare. "Hot anise, a viewer."

The waiter turned away. Jarvis relaxed, sat rubbing his sore hip and watch-ing the occasional dark shape hurrying against the mist. The streets were still dim; only one of the Procrustean suns had risen: no match for the fogs of Idle River.

The waiter returned with a dull metal pot and the viewer. Jarvis parted with his last coin, warmed his hands on the pot, notched in the film, and sipped the brew, giving his attention to the journal. Page after page flicked past: trifles of Earth news, cluster news, local news, topical discussions, practical mechanics. He found the classified advertisements, employment opportunities, skimmed down the listings. These were sparse enough: a well-digger wanted, glass puddlers, berry-pickers, creep-weed chasers. He bent forward; this was more to his interest:

Shape-up: Four travellers of top efficiency. Large profits for able workers; definite goals in sight. Only men of resource and willingness need apply. At 10 meridian see Belisarius at the Old Solar Inn.

Jarvis read the paragraph once more, translating the oblique phrases to more definite meanings. He looked at his watch: still three hours. He glanced at the street, at the waiter, sipped from the pot, and settled to a study of the *Farm and Mining Journal.*

Two hours later the second sun, a blue-white ball, rose at the head of Riverview Way, flaring through the mist; now the population of the town began to appear. Jarvis took quiet leave of the cafe and set off down Riverview Way in the sun.

Heat and the exercise loosened the throb in his hip; when he reached the river esplanade his walk was smooth. He turned to the right, past the Memorial Fountain, and there was the Old Solar Inn, looking across the water to the gray marble bluffs.

Jarvis inspected it with care. It looked expensive but not elaborate, exuding dignity rather than elegance. He felt less skeptical; Bulletin notices occasionally promised more than they fulfilled; a man could not be too careful.

He approached the inn. The entrance was a massive wooden door with a stained glass window, where laughing Old Sol shot a golden ray upon green and blue Earth. The door swung open; Jarvis entered, bent to the wicket.

"Yes, sir?" asked the clerk.

"Mr. Belisarius," said Jarvis.

The clerk inspected Jarvis with much the expression of the waiter at the cafe. With the faintest of shrugs, he said, "Suite B—down the lower hall."

Jarvis crossed the lobby. As he entered the hall he heard the outer door open; a huge blond man in green suede came into the inn, paused like Jarvis by the wicket. Jarvis continued along the hall. The door to Suite B was ajar; Jarvis pushed it open, entered.

He stood in a large room panelled with dark green sea-tree, furnished simply—a tawny rug, chairs and couches around the walls, an elaborate chandelier decorated with glowing spangles—so elaborate, indeed, that Jarvis suspected a system of spy-cells. In itself this meant nothing; in fact, it might be construed as commendable caution.

Five others were waiting: men of various ages, size, skin-color. Only one aspect did they have in common; a way of seeming to look to all sides at once. Jarvis took a seat, sat back; a moment later the big blond man in green suede entered. He looked around the room, glanced at the chandelier, took a seat. A stringy gray-haired man with corrugated brown skin and a sly reckless smile said, "Omar Gildig! What are you here for, Gildig?"

The big blond man's eyes became blank for an instant; then he said, "For motives much like your own, Tixon."

The old man jerked his head back, blinked. "You mistake me; my name is Pardee, Captain Pardee."

"As you say, Captain."

There was silence in the room; then Tixon, or Pardee, nervously crossed to where Gildig sat and spoke in low tones. Gildig nodded like a placid lion.

Other men entered; each glanced around the room, at the chandelier, then took seats. Presently the room held twenty or more.

Other conversations arose. Jarvis found himself next to a small sturdy man with a round moon-face, a bulbous little paunch, a hooked little nose and dark owlish eyes. He seemed disposed to speak, and Jarvis made such comments as seemed judicious. "A cold night, last, for those of us to see the red sun set."

Jarvis assented.

"A lucky planet to win free from, this," continued the round man. "I've been watching the Bulletin for three weeks now; if I don't join Belisarius—why, by the juice of Jonah, I'll take a workaway job on a packet."

Jarvis asked, "Who is this Belisarius?"

The round man opened his eyes wide. "Belisarius? It's well-known—he's Belson!"

"Belson?" Jarvis could not hold the surprised note out of his voice; the bruise on his hip began to jar and thud. "Belson?"

The round man had turned away his head, but was staring over the bridge of his little beak-nose. "Belson is an effective traveller, much respected."

"So I understand," said Jarvis.

"Rumor comes that he has suffered reverses—notably one such, two months gone, on the swamps of Fenn."

"How goes the rumor?" asked Jarvis.

"There is large talk, small fact," the round man replied gracefully. "And have you ever speculated on the concentration of talent in so small a one room? There is yourself. And my own humble talents—there is Omar Gildig—brawn like a Beshauer bull, a brain of guile. Over there is young Hancock McManus, an effective worker, and there—he who styles himself Lachesis, a metaphor. And I'll wager in all our aggregate pockets there's not twenty Juillard crowns!"

"Certainly not in mine," admitted Jarvis.

"This is our life," said the round man. "We live at the full—each minute an entity to be squeezed of its maximum; our moneys, our crowns, our credits—they buy us great sweetness, but they are soon gone. Then Belisarius hints of brave goals, and we come, like moths to a flame!"

"I wonder," mused Jarvis.

"What's your wonder?"

"Belisarius surely has trusted lieutenants…When he calls for travellers through the Farm Bulletin—there always is the chance of Authority participation."

"Perhaps they are unaware of the convention, the code."

"More likely not."

The round man shook his head, sighed. "A brave agent would come to the Old Solar Inn on this day!"

"There are such men."

"But they will not come to the shape-ups—and do you know why not?"

"Why not then?"

"Suppose they do—suppose they trap six men—a dozen."

"A dozen less to cope with."

"But the next time a shape-up is called, the travellers will prove themselves by the Test Supreme."

"And this is?" inquired Jarvis easily, though he knew quite well.

The round man explained with zest. "Each party kills in the presence of an umpire. The Authority will not risk the resumption of such tests; and so they allow the travellers to meet and foregather in peace." The round man peered at Jarvis. "This can hardly be new information?"

"I have heard talk," said Jarvis.

The round man said, "Caution is admirable when not carried to an excess."

Jarvis laughed, showing his long sharp teeth. "Why not use an excess of caution, when it costs nothing?"

"Why not?" assented the round man, and said no more to Jarvis.

A few moments later the inner door opened; an old man, slight, crotchety, in tight black trousers and vest, peered out. His eyes were mild, his face was long, waxy, melancholy; his voice was suitably grave. "Your attention, if you please."

"By Crokus," muttered the round man, "Belson has hired undertakers to staff his conferences!"

The old man in black spoke on. "I will summon you one at a time, in the order of your arrival. You will be given certain tests, you will submit to certain interrogations...Anyone who finds the prospect over-intimate may leave at this moment."

He waited. No one rose to depart, although scowls appeared, and Omar Gildig said, "Reasonable queries are resented by no one. If I find the interrogation too searching—then I shall protest."

The old man nodded, "Very well, as you wish. First then—you, Paul Pulliam."

A slim elegant man in wine-colored jacket and tight trousers rose to his feet, entered the inner room.

"So that is Paul Pulliam," breathed the round man. "I have wondered six years, ever since the Myknosis affair."

"Who is that old man—the undertaker?" asked Jarvis.

"I have no idea."

"In fact," asked Jarvis, "Who is Belson? What is Belson's look?"

"In truth," said the round man, "I know no more to that."

The second man was called, then the third, the fourth, then: "Gilbert Jarvis!"

Jarvis rose to his feet, thinking: how in thunder do they know *my first name?* He passed through into an anteroom, whose only furnishing was a scale. The old man in black said, "If you please, I wish to learn your weight."

Jarvis stepped on the scale; the dial glowed with the figure 163, which the old man recorded in a book. "Very well, now—I will prick your ear—"

Jarvis grabbed the instrument; the old man squawked, "Here, here, here!"

Jarvis inspected the bit of glass and metal, gave it back with a wolfish grin. "I am a man of caution; I'll have no drugs pumped into my ear."

"No, no," protested the old man, "I need but a drop to learn your blood characteristics."

"Why is this important?" asked Jarvis cynically. "It's been my experience that if a man bleeds, why so much the worse, but let him bleed till either he stops or he runs dry."

"Belisarius is a considerate master."

"I want no master," said Jarvis.

"Mentor, then—a considerate mentor."

"I think for myself."

"Devil drag me deathways!" exclaimed the old man, "you are a ticklish man to please." He put the drop from Jarvis' ear into an analyzer, peered at the dials. "Type O...Index 96...Granuli B...Very good, Gilbert Jarvis, very good indeed!"

"Humph," said Jarvis, "is that all the test Belisarius gives a man—his weight, his blood?"

"No, no," said the old man earnestly, "these are but the preliminaries; but allow me to congratulate you, you are so far entirely suitable. Now—come with me and wait; in an hour we will have our lunch, and then discuss the remainder of the problem."

Of the original applicants only eight remained after the preliminary elimination. Jarvis noticed that all of the eight approximated his own weight, with the exception of Omar Gildig, who weighed two hundred fifty or more.

The old man in black summoned them to lunch; the eight filed into a round green dining-saloon; they took places at a round green table. The old man gave a signal and wine and appetizers appeared in the service slots. He put on an air of heartiness. "Let us forget the background of our presence here," he said. "Let us enjoy the good food and such fellowship as we may bring to the occasion."

Omar Gildig snorted, a vast grimace that pulled his nose down over his mouth. "Who cares about fellowship? We want to know that which concerns us. What is this affair that Belson plans for?"

The old man shook his head smilingly. "There are still eight of you—and Belisarius needs but four."

"Then get on with your tests; there are better things to be doing than jumping through these jackanape hoops."

"There have been no hoops so far," said the old man gently. "Bear with me only an hour longer; none of you eight will go without your recompense, of one kind or another."

Jarvis looked from face to face. Gildig; sly reckless old Tixon—or Captain Pardee, as he called himself; the round owlish man; a blond smiling youth like a girl in men's gear; two quiet nondescripts; a tall pencil-thin black, who might have been dumb for any word he spoke.

Food was served: small steaks of a local venison, a small platter of toasted pods with sauce of herbs and minced mussels. In fact, so small were the portions that Jarvis found his appetite merely whetted.

Next came glasses of frozen red punch, then came braised crescents of white flesh, each with a bright red nubbin at both ends, swimming in a pungent sauce.

Jarvis smiled to himself and glanced around the table. Gildig had fallen to with gusto, as had the thin dark-skinned man; one or two of the others were eating with more caution. Jarvis thought, I won't be caught quite so easily, and toyed with the food; and he saw from the corner of his eye that Tixon, the blond youth and the round man were likewise abstaining.

Their host looked around the table with a pained expression. "The dish, I see, is not popular."

The round man said plaintively, "Surely it's uncommon poor manners to poison us with the Fenn swamp-shrimp."

Gildig spat out a mouthful. "Poison!"

"Peace, Conrad, peace," said the old man, grinning. "These are not what you think them." He reached out a fork, speared one of the objects from the plate of Conrad, the round man, and ate it. "You see, you are mistaken. Perhaps these resemble the Fenn swamp-shrimp—but they are not."

Gildig looked suspiciously at his plate. "And what did you think they were?" he asked Conrad.

Conrad picked up one of the morsels, looked at it narrowly. "On Fenn when a man wants to put another man in his power for a day or a week, he seeks these—or shrimp like these—from the swamps. The toxic principle is in these red sacs." He pushed his plate away. "Swamp-shrimp or not, they still dull my appetite."

"We'll remove them," said the old man. "To the next dish, by all means—a bake of capons, as I recall."

The meal progressed; the old man produced no more wine—"because," he explained, "we have a test of skill approaching us; it's necessary that you have all faculties with you."

"A complicated system of filling out a roster," muttered Gildig.

The old man shrugged. "I act for Belisarius."

"Belson, you mean."

"Call him any name you wish."

Conrad, the round man, said thoughtfully, "Belson is not an easy master."

The old man looked surprised. "Does not Belson—as you call him—bring you large profits?"

"Belson allows no man's interference—and Belson never forgets a wrong."

The old man laughed a mournful chuckle. "That makes him an easy man to serve. Obey him, do him no wrongs—and you will never fear his anger."

Conrad shrugged, Gildig smiled. Jarvis sat watchfully. There was more to the business than filling out a roster, more than a profit to be achieved.

"Now," said the old man, "if you please, one at a time, through this door. Omar Gildig, I'll have you first."

The seven remained at the table, watching uneasily from the corners of their eyes. Conrad and Tixon—or Captain Pardee—spoke lightly; the blond youth joined their talk; then a thud caused them all to look up, the talk to stop short. After a pause, the conversation continued rather lamely.

The old man appeared. "Now you, Captain Pardee."

Captain Pardee—or Tixon—left the room. The six remaining listened; there were no further sounds.

The old man next summoned the blond youth, then Conrad, then one of the nondescripts, then the tall black man, the other nondescript, and finally returned to where Jarvis sat alone.

"My apologies, Gilbert Jarvis—but I think we are effecting a satisfactory elimination. If you will come this way…"

Jarvis entered a long dim room.

The old man said, "This, as I have intimated, is a test of skill, agility, resource. I presume you carry your favorite weapons with you?"

Jarvis grinned. "Naturally."

"Notice," said the old man, "the screen at the far end of this room. Imagine behind two armed and alert men who are your enemies, who are not yet aware of your presence." He paused; watched Jarvis, who grinned his humorless smile.

"Well then, are you imagining the situation?"

Jarvis listened; did he hear breathing? There was the feel of stealth in the room, of mounting strain, expectancy.

"Are you imagining?" asked the old man. "They will kill you if they find you…They will kill you…"

A sound, a rush—not from the end of the room—but at the side—a hurtling dark shape. The old man ducked; Jarvis jumped back, whipped out his weapon, a Parnassian sliver-spit…The dark shape thumped with three internal explosions.

"Excellent," said the old man. "You have good reactions, Gilbert Jarvis—and with a sliver-spit too. Are they not difficult weapons?"

"Not to a man who knows their use; then they are most effective."

"An interesting diversity of opinion," said the old man. "Gildig, for instance, used a collapsible club. Where he had it hidden, I have no idea—a miracle of swiftness. Conrad was almost as adept with the shoot-blade as you are with the sliver-spit, and Noel, the blond youngster—he preferred a dammel-ray."

"Bulky," said Jarvis. "Bulky and delicate, with limited capacity."

"I agree," said the old man. "But each man to his own methods."

"It puzzles me," said Jarvis. "Where does he carry the weapon? I noticed none of the bulk of a dammel-ray on his person."

"He had it adjusted well," said the old man cryptically. "This way, if you please."

They returned to the original waiting room. Instead of the original twenty men, there were now but four: Gildig, old Tixon, the blond young Noel, and Conrad, the round man with the owlish face. Jarvis looked Noel over critically to see where he carried his weapon, but it was nowhere in evidence, though his clothes were pink, yellow and black weave, skin-tight.

The old man seemed in the best of spirits; his mournful jowls quivered and twitched. "Now, gentlemen, now—we come to the end of the elimination. Five men, when we need but four. One man must be dispensed with; can anyone propose a means to this end?"

The five men stiffened, looked sideways around with a guarded wariness, as the same idea suggested itself to each mind.

"Well," said the old man, "it would be one way out of the impasse, but there might be several simultaneous eliminations, and it would put Belisarius to considerable trouble."

No one spoke.

The old man mused, "I think I can resolve the quandary. Let us assume that all of us are hired by Belisarius."

"I assume nothing," growled Gildig. "Either I'm hired, or I'm not! If I'm hired I want a retainer."

"Very well," said the old man. "You all are, then, hired by Belisarius."

"By Belson."

"Yes—by Belson. Here—" he distributed five envelopes "—here is earnest-money. A thousand crowns. Now, each and all of you are Belson's men. You understand what this entails?"

"It entails loyalty," intoned Tixon, looking with satisfaction into the envelope.

"Complete, mindless, unswerving loyalty," echoed the old man. "What's that?" he asked to Gildig's grumble.

Gildig said, "He doesn't leave a man a mind of his own."

"When he serves Belson, a man needs his mind only to serve. Before, and after, he is as free as air. During his employment, he must be Belson's man, an extension of Belson's mind. The rewards are great—but the punishments are certain."

Gildig grunted with resignation. "What next, then?"

"Now—we seek to eliminate the one superfluous man. I think now we can do it." He looked around the faces. "Gildig—Tixon—"

"Captain Pardee, call me—that's my name!"

"—Conrad—Noel—and Gilbert Jarvis."

"Well," said Conrad shortly, "get on with it."

"The theory of the situation," said the old man didactically, "is that now we are all Belson's loyal followers. Suppose we find a traitor to Belson, an enemy—what do we do then?"

"Kill him!" said Tixon.

"Exactly."

Gildig leaned forward, and the bulging muscles sent planes of soft light moving down his green suede jacket. "How can there be traitors when we are just hired?"

The old man looked mournfully at his pale fingers. "Actually, gentlemen, the situation goes rather deeper than one might suppose. This unwanted fifth man—the man to be eliminated—he happens to be one who has violated Belson's trust. The disposal of this man," he said sternly, "will provide an object lesson for the remaining four."

"Well," said Noel easily, "shall we proceed? Who is the betrayer?"

"Ah," said the old man, "we have gathered today to learn this very fact."

"Do you mean to say," snapped Conrad, "that this entire rigmarole is not to our benefit, but only yours?"

"No, no!" protested the old man. "The four who are selected will have employment—if I may say, employment on the instant. But let me explain; the background is this: at a lonesome camp, on the marshes of Fenn, Belson had stored a treasure—a rare treasure! Here he left three men to guard. Two were known to Belson, the third was a new recruit, an unknown from somewhere across the universe.

"When the dawn was breaking this new man rose, killed the two men, took the treasure across the marsh to the port city Momart, and there sold it. Belson's loyal lieutenant—myself—was on the planet. I made haste to investigate. I found tracks in the marsh. I established that the treasure had been sold.

I learned that passage had been bought—and followed. Now, gentlemen," and the old man sat back, "we are all persons of discernment. We live for the pleasurable moment. We gain money, we spend money, at a rather predictable rate. Knowing the value of Belson's treasure, I was able to calculate just when the traitor would feel the pinch of poverty. At this time I baited the trap; I published the advertisement; the trap is sprung. Is that not clever? Admit it now!"

And he glanced from face to face.

Jarvis eased his body around in the chair to provide swifter scope for movement, and also to ease his hip, which now throbbed painfully.

"Go on," said Gildig, likewise glaring from face to face.

"I now exercised my science. I cut turves from the swamp, those which held the tracks, the crushed reeds, the compressed moss. At the laboratory, I found that a hundred and sixty pounds pressure, more or less, might make such tracks. Weight—" he leaned forward to confide "—formed the basis of the first elimination. Each of you was weighed, you will recall, and you that are here—with the exception of Omar Gildig—fulfill the requirement."

Noel asked lightly, "Why was Gildig included?"

"Is it not clear?" asked the old man. "He can not be the traitor, but he makes an effective sergeant-at-arms."

"In other words," said Conrad dryly, "the traitor is either Tixon—I mean Captain Pardee, Noel, Jarvis or myself."

"Exactly," said the old man mournfully. "Our problem is reducing the four to one—and then, reducing the one to nothing. For this purpose we have our zealous sergeant-at-arms here—Omar Gildig."

"Pleased to oblige," said Gildig, now relaxed, almost sleepy.

The old man slid back a panel, drew with chalk on a board.

"We make a chart—so:"

	Weight	Food	Blood	Weapon
Captain Pardee				
Noel				
Conrad				
Jarvis				

and as he spoke he wrote the figures beside each name: "Captain Pardee: 162; Noel: 155; Conrad: 166; and Jarvis: 163. Next—each of you four were familiar with the Fenn swamp-shrimp, indicating familiarity with the Fenn swamps. So—a check beside each of your names." He paused to look around. "Are you attending, Gildig?"

"At your service."

"Next," said the old man, "there was blood on the ground, indicating a wound. It was not the blood of the two slain men—nor blood from the treasure. Therefore it must be blood from the traitor; and today I have taken blood from each of the four. I leave this column blank. Next—to the weapons. The men were killed, very neatly, very abruptly—with a Parnassian sliver. Tixon uses a JAR-gun; Noel, dammel-ray; Conrad, a shoot-blade—and Jarvis, a sliver-spit. So—an X beside the name of Jarvis!"

Jarvis began drawing himself up. "Easy," said Gildig. "I'm watching you, Jarvis."

Jarvis relaxed, smiling a wolfish grin.

The old man, watching him from the corner of his eye, said, "This, of course, is hardly conclusive. So to the blood. In the blood are body-cells. The cells contain nuclei, with genes—and each man's genes are distinctive. So now with the blood—"

Jarvis, still smiling, spoke. "You find it to be mine?"

"Exactly."

"Old man—you lie. I have no wound on my body."

"Wounds heal fast, Jarvis."

"Old man—you fail as Belson's trusted servant."

"Eh? And how?"

"Through stupidity. Perhaps worse."

"Yes? And precisely?"

"The tracks...In the laboratory you compressed turves of the swamp. You found you needed weight of one hundred and sixty pounds to achieve the effect of the Fenn prints."

"Yes. Exactly."

"Fenn's gravity is six-tenths Earth standard. The compression of one-sixty pounds on Fenn is better achieved by a man of two hundred and forty or two-fifty pounds—such as Gildig."

Gildig half-raised. "Do you dare to accuse me?"

"Are you guilty?"

"No."

"You can't prove it."

"I don't need to prove it! Those tracks might be made by a lighter man carrying the treasure. How much was the weight?"

"A light silken treasure," said the old man. "No more than a hundred pounds."

Tixon drew back to a corner. "Jarvis is guilty!"

Noel threw open his gay coat, to disclose an astonishing contrivance: a gun muzzle protruding from his chest, a weapon surprisingly fitted into his body. Now Jarvis knew where Noel carried his dammel-ray.

Noel laughed. "Jarvis—the traitor!"

"No," said Jarvis, "you're wrong. I am the only loyal servant of Belson's in the room. If Belson were near, I would tell him about it."

The old man said quickly, "We've heard enough of his wriggling. Kill him, Gildig."

Gildig stretched his arm; from under his wrist, out his sleeve shot a tube of metal three feet long, already swinging to the pull of Gildig's wrist. Jarvis sprang back, the tube struck him on the bruised hip; he shot the sliver-spit. Gildig's hand was gone—exploded.

"Kill, kill," sang the old man, dodging back.

The door opened; a sedate handsome man came in. "I am Belson."

"The traitor, Belson," cried the old man. "Jarvis, the traitor!"

"No, no," said Jarvis. "I can tell you better."

"Speak, Jarvis—your last moment!"

"I was on Fenn, yes! I was the new recruit, yes! It was my blood, yes!…But traitor, no! I was the man left for dead when the traitor went."

"And who is this traitor?"

"Who was on Fenn? Who was quick to raise the cry for Jarvis? Who knew of the treasure?"

"Pah!" said the old man, as Belson's mild glance swung toward him.

"Who just now spoke of the sun rising at the hour of the deed?"

"A mistake!"

"A mistake, indeed!"

"Yes, Finch," said Belson to the old man, "how did you know so closely the hour of the theft?"

"An estimate, a guess, an intelligent deduction."

Belson turned to Gildig, who had been standing stupidly clutching the stump of his arm. "Go, Gildig; get yourself a new hand at the clinic. Give them the name Belisarius."

"Yes, sir." Gildig tottered out.

"You, Noel," said Belson, "Book you a passage to Achernar; go to Pasatiempo, await word at the Auberge Bacchanal."

"Yes, Belson." Noel departed.

"Tixon—"

"Captain Pardee is my name, Belson."

"—I have no need for you now, but I will keep your well-known abilities in mind."

"Thank you sir, good-day." Tixon departed.

"Conrad, I have a parcel to be travelled to the city Sudanapolis on Earth; await me at Suite RS above."

"Very good, Belson." Conrad wheeled, marched out the door.

"Jarvis."

"Yes, Belson."

"I will speak to you further today. Await me in the lobby."

"Very well." Jarvis turned, started from the room. He heard Belson say quietly to the old man, "And now, Finch, as for you—" and then further words and sounds were cut off by the closing of the door.

Afterword to "Shape-Up"

This time it was Tahiti that beckoned.

Preparations were made; and one day in 1965 we set off [and] arrived at the Faaa's International Airport, three miles southwest of Papeete, and for the first day or so put up in a rather run-down hotel. A few days later we came upon a house for rent in the district known as Paea, near the beach about twelve miles east of Papeete…We settled in, set up housekeeping, and began to churn out fiction. These were absolutely idyllic circumstances. Along the driveway were pineapple bushes, although I don't think we ever harvested any pineapple. In the back yard was a lime tree full of fruit, in the front a custard apple tree, which dropped custard apples on the roof of our house, which always made a thunderous bang. For supplies unavailable at the Chinese grocery, Norma rode the bus into Papeete and then back, which was no great ordeal…

We received news of an unfortunate occurrence back in New York. One of Scott Meredith's associates sold one of my stories to Frederick Pohl, who was currently editor of *Galaxy* magazine, but then unwittingly sold the same story to another publication. This meant that Fred Pohl could not use the story and there was all hell to pay. Scott Meredith fired the guilty associate, but no one made any move to reimburse me, so I simply gritted my teeth and sat down to write another story for Fred. This became *The Last Castle*, which turned out to be a pretty good story.

—Jack Vance

Sjambak

Howard Frayberg, Production Director of *Know Your Universe!*, was a man of sudden unpredictable moods; and Sam Catlin, the show's Continuity Editor, had learned to expect the worst.

"Sam," said Frayberg, "regarding the show last night…" He paused to seek the proper words, and Catlin relaxed. Frayberg's frame of mind was merely critical. "Sam, we're in a rut. What's worse, the show's dull!"

Sam Catlin shrugged, not committing himself.

"*Seaweed Processors of Alphard IX*—who cares about seaweed?"

"It's factual stuff," said Sam, defensive but not wanting to go too far out on a limb. "We bring 'em everything—color, fact, romance, sight, sound, smell… Next week, it's the Ball Expedition to the Mixtup Mountains on Gropus."

Frayberg leaned forward. "Sam, we're working the wrong slant on this stuff…We've got to loosen up, sock 'em! Shift our ground! Give 'em the old human angle—glamor, mystery, thrills!"

Sam Catlin curled his lips. "I got just what you want."

"Yeah? Show me."

Catlin reached into his waste basket. "I filed this just ten minutes ago…" He smoothed out the pages. "'Sequence idea, by Wilbur Murphy. Investigate "Horseman of Space", the man who rides up to meet incoming spaceships'."

Frayberg tilted his head to the side. "Rides up on a *horse?*"

"That's what Wilbur Murphy says."

"How far up?"

"Does it make any difference?"

"No—I guess not."

"Well, for your information, it's up ten thousand, twenty thousand miles. He waves to the pilot, takes off his hat to the passengers, then rides back down."

"And where does all this take place?"

"On—on—" Catlin frowned. "I can write it, but I can't pronounce it." He printed on his scratch-screen: CIRGAMESÇ.

"Sirgamesk," read Frayberg.

Catlin shook his head. "That's what it looks like—but those consonants are all aspirated gutturals. It's more like 'Hrrghameshgrrh'."

"Where did Murphy get this tip?"

"I didn't bother to ask."

"Well," mused Frayberg, "we could always do a show on strange superstitions. Is Murphy around?"

"He's explaining his expense account to Shifkin."

"Get him in here; let's talk to him."

Wilbur Murphy had a blond crew-cut, a broad freckled nose, and a serious sidelong squint. He looked from his crumpled sequence idea to Catlin and Frayberg. "Didn't like it, eh?"

"We thought the emphasis should be a little different," explained Catlin. "Instead of 'The Space Horseman', we'd give it the working title, 'Odd Superstitions of Hrrghameshgrrh'."

"Oh, hell!" said Frayberg. "Call it Sirgamesk."

"Anyway," said Catlin, "that's the angle."

"But it's not superstition," said Murphy.

"Oh, come, Wilbur..."

"I got this for sheer sober-sided fact. A man rides a horse up to meet the incoming ships!"

"Where did you get this wild fable?"

"My brother-in-law is purser on the *Celestial Traveller*. At Riker's Planet they make connection with the feeder line out of Cirgamesç."

"Wait a minute," said Catlin. "How did you pronounce that?"

"Cirgamesç. The steward on the shuttle-ship gave out this story, and my brother-in-law passed it along to me."

"Somebody's pulling somebody's leg."

"My brother-in-law wasn't, and the steward was cold sober."

"They've been eating *bhang*. Sirgamesk is a Javanese planet, isn't it?"

"Javanese, Arab, Malay."

"Then they took a *bhang* supply with them, and *hashish, chat,* and a few other sociable herbs."

"Well, this horseman isn't any drug-dream."

"No? What is it?"

"So far as I know it's a man on a horse."

"Ten thousand miles up? In a vacuum?"

"Exactly."

"No space-suit?"

"That's the story."

Catlin and Frayberg looked at each other.

"Well, Wilbur," Catlin began.

Frayberg interrupted. "What we can use, Wilbur, is a sequence on Sirgamesk superstition. Emphasis on voodoo or witchcraft—naked girls dancing—stuff with roots in Earth, but now typically Sirgamesk. Lots of color. Secret rite stuff…"

"Not much room on Cirgamesç for secret rites."

"It's a big planet, isn't it?"

"Not quite as big as Mars. There's no atmosphere. The settlers live in mountain valleys, with airtight lids over 'em."

Catlin flipped the pages of *Thumbnail Sketches of the Inhabited Worlds*. "Says here there's ancient ruins millions of years old. When the atmosphere went, the population went with it."

Frayberg became animated. "There's lots of material out there! Go get it, Wilbur! Life! Sex! Excitement! Mystery!"

"Okay," said Wilbur Murphy.

"But lay off this horseman-in-space. There *is* a limit to public credulity, and don't you let anyone tell you different."

Cirgamesç hung outside the port, twenty thousand miles ahead. The steward leaned over Wilbur Murphy's shoulder and pointed a long brown finger. "It was right out there, sir. He came riding up—"

"What kind of a man was it? Strange looking?"

"No. He was Cirgameski."

"Oh. You saw him with your own eyes, eh?"

The steward bowed, and his loose white mantle fell forward. "Exactly, sir."

"No helmet, no space-suit?"

"He wore a short Singhalût vest and pantaloons and a yellow Hadrasi hat. No more."

"And the horse?"

"Ah, the horse! There's a different matter."

"Different how?"

"I can't describe the horse. I was intent on the man."

"Did you recognize him?"

"By the brow of Lord Allah, it's well not to look too closely when such matters occur."

"Then—you *did* recognize him!"

"I must be at my task, sir."

Murphy frowned in vexation at the steward's retreating back, then bent over his camera to check the tape-feed. If anything appeared now, and his eyes could see it, the two-hundred million audience of *Know Your Universe!* could see it with him.

When he looked up, Murphy made a frantic grab for the stanchion, then relaxed. Cirgameşç had taken the Great Twitch. It was an illusion, a psychological quirk. One instant the planet lay ahead; then a man winked or turned away, and when he looked back, 'ahead' had become 'below'; the planet had swung an astonishing ninety degrees across the sky, and they were *falling!*

Murphy leaned against the stanchion. "'The Great Twitch'," he muttered to himself, "I'd like to get that on two hundred million screens!"

Several hours passed. Cirgameşç grew. The Sampan Range rose up like a dark scab; the valley sultanates of Singhalût, Hadra, New Batavia, and Boeng-Bohôt showed like glistening chicken-tracks; the Great Rift Colony of Sundaman stretched down through the foothills like the trail of a slug.

A loudspeaker voice rattled the ship. "Attention passengers for Singhalût and other points on Cirgameşç! Kindly prepare your luggage for disembarkation. Customs at Singhalût are extremely thorough. Passengers are warned to take no weapons, drugs or explosives ashore. This is important!"

The warning turned out to be an understatement. Murphy was plied with questions. He suffered search of an intimate nature. He was three-dimensionally X-rayed with a range of frequencies calculated to excite fluorescence in whatever object he might have secreted in his stomach, in a hollow bone, or under a layer of flesh.

His luggage was explored with similar minute attention, and Murphy rescued his cameras with difficulty. "What're you so damn anxious about? I don't have drugs; I don't have contraband..."

"It's guns, your Excellency. Guns, weapons, explosives..."

"I don't have any guns."

"But these objects here?"

"They're cameras. They record pictures and sounds and smells."

The inspector seized the cases with a glittering smile of triumph. "They resemble no cameras of my experience; I fear I shall have to impound..."

A young man in loose white pantaloons, a pink vest, pale green cravat and a complex black turban strolled up. The inspector made a swift obeisance, with arms spread wide. "Excellency."

The young man raised two fingers. "You may find it possible to spare Mr. Murphy any unnecessary formality."

"As your Excellency recommends…" The inspector nimbly repacked Murphy's belongings, while the young man looked on benignly.

Murphy covertly inspected his face. The skin was smooth, the color of the rising moon; the eyes were narrow, dark, superficially placid. The effect was of silken punctilio with hot ruby blood close beneath.

Satisfied with the inspector's zeal, he turned to Murphy. "Allow me to introduce myself, Tuan Murphy. I am Ali-Tomás, of the House of Singhalût, and my father the Sultan begs you to accept our poor hospitality."

"Why, thank you," said Murphy. "This is a very pleasant surprise."

"If you will allow me to conduct you…" He turned to the inspector. "Mr. Murphy's luggage to the palace."

Murphy accompanied Ali-Tomás into the outside light, fitting his own quick step to the prince's feline saunter. This is coming it pretty soft, he said to himself. I'll have a magnificent suite, with bowls of fruit and gin pahits, not to mention two or three silken girls with skin like rich cream bringing me towels in the shower…Well, well, well, it's not so bad working for *Know Your Universe!* after all! I suppose I ought to unlimber my camera…

Prince Ali-Tomás watched him with interest. "And what is the audience of *Know Your Universe!?*"

"We call 'em 'participants'."

"Expressive. And how many participants do you serve?"

"Oh, the Bowdler Index rises and falls. We've got about two hundred million screens, with five hundred million participants."

"Fascinating! And tell me—how do you record smells?"

Murphy displayed the odor recorder on the side of the camera, with its gelatinous track which fixed the molecular design.

"And the odors recreated—they are like the originals?"

"Pretty close. Never exact, but none of the participants knows the difference. Sometimes the synthetic odor is an improvement."

"Astounding!" murmured the prince.

"And sometimes…Well, Carson Tenlake went out to get the myrrh-blossoms on Venus. It was a hot day—as days usually are on Venus—and a long climb. When the show was run off, there was more smell of Carson than of flowers."

Prince Ali-Tomás laughed politely. "We turn through here."

They came out into a compound paved with red, green and white tiles. Beneath the valley roof was a sinuous trough, full of haze and warmth and golden light. As far in either direction as the eye could reach, the hillsides were terraced, barred in various shades of green. Spattering the valley floor were tall canvas pavilions, tents, booths, shelters.

"Naturally," said Prince Ali-Tomás, "we hope that you and your participants will enjoy Singhalût. It is a truism that, in order to import, we must export; we wish to encourage a pleasurable response to the 'Made in Singhalût' tag on our *batiks*, carvings, lacquers."

They rolled quietly across the square in a surface-car displaying the House emblem. Murphy rested against deep, cool cushions. "Your inspectors are pretty careful about weapons."

Ali-Tomás smiled complacently. "Our existence is ordered and peaceful. You may be familiar with the concept of *adak?*"

"I don't think so."

"A word, an idea from old Earth. Every living act is ordered by ritual. But our heritage is passionate—and when unyielding *adak* stands in the way of an irresistible emotion, there is turbulence, sometimes even killing ."

"An *amok*."

"Exactly. It is as well that the *amok* has no weapons other than his knife. Otherwise he would kill twenty where now he kills one."

The car rolled along a narrow avenue, scattering pedestrians to either side like the bow of a boat spreading foam. The men wore loose white pantaloons and a short open vest; the women wore only the pantaloons.

"Handsome set of people," remarked Murphy.

Ali-Tomás again smiled complacently. "I'm sure Singhalût will present an inspiring and beautiful spectacle for your program."

Murphy remembered the keynote to Howard Frayberg's instructions: *"Excitement! Sex! Mystery!"* Frayberg cared little for inspiration or beauty. "I imagine," he said casually, "that you celebrate a number of interesting festivals? Colorful dancing? Unique customs?"

Ali-Tomás shook his head. "To the contrary. We left our superstitions and ancestor-worship back on Earth. We are quiet Mohammedans and indulge in very little festivity. Perhaps here is the reason for *amoks* and sjambaks."

"Sjambaks?"

"We are not proud of them. You will hear sly rumor, and it is better that I arm you beforehand with truth ."

"What is a sjambak?"

"They are bandits, flouters of authority. I will show you one presently."

"I heard," said Murphy, "of a man riding a horse up to meet the spaceships. What would account for a story like that?"

"It can have no possible basis," said Prince Ali-Tomás. "We have no horses on Cirgamesç. None whatever."

"But…"

"The veriest idle talk. Such nonsense will have no interest for your intelligent participants."

The car rolled into a square a hundred yards on a side, lined with luxuriant banana palms. Opposite was an enormous pavilion of gold and violet silk, with a dozen peaked gables casting various changing sheens. In the center of the square a twenty-foot pole supported a cage about two feet wide, three feet long, and four feet high.

Inside this cage crouched a naked man.

The car rolled past. Prince Ali-Tomás waved an idle hand. The caged man glared down from bloodshot eyes. "That," said Ali-Tomás, "is a sjambak. As you see," a faint note of apology entered his voice, "we attempt to discourage them."

"What's that metal object on his chest?"

"The mark of his trade. By that you may know all sjambak. In these unsettled times only we of the House may cover our chests—all others must show themselves and declare themselves true Singhalûsi."

Murphy said tentatively, "I must come back here and photograph that cage."

Ali-Tomás smilingly shook his head. "I will show you our farms, our vines and orchards. Your participants will enjoy these; they have no interest in the dolor of an ignoble sjambak."

"Well," said Murphy, "our aim is a well-rounded production. We want to show the farmers at work, the members of the great House at their responsibilities, as well as the deserved fate of wrongdoers."

"Exactly. For every sjambak there are ten thousand industrious Singhalûsi. It follows then that only one ten-thousandth part of your film should be devoted to this infamous minority."

"About three-tenths of a second, eh?"

"No more than they deserve."

"You don't know my Production Director. His name is Howard Frayberg, and…"

Howard Frayberg was deep in conference with Sam Catlin, under the influence of what Catlin called his philosophic kick. It was the phase which Catlin feared most.

"Sam," said Frayberg, "do you know the danger of this business?"

"Ulcers," Catlin replied promptly.

Frayberg shook his head. "We've got an occupational disease to fight— progressive mental myopia."

"Speak for yourself," said Catlin.

"Consider. We sit in this office. We think we know what kind of show we want. We send out our staff to get it. We're signing the checks, so back it comes the way we asked for it. We look at it, hear it, smell it—and pretty soon we believe it: our version of the universe, full-blown from our brains like Minerva stepping out of Zeus. You see what I mean?"

"I understand the words."

"We've got our own picture of what's going on. We ask for it, we get it. It builds up and up—and finally we're like mice in a trap built of our own ideas. We cannibalize our own brains."

"Nobody'll ever accuse you of being stingy with a metaphor."

"Sam, let's have the truth. How many times have you been off Earth?"

"I went to Mars once. And I spent a couple of weeks at Aristillus Resort on the Moon."

Frayberg leaned back in his chair as if shocked. "And we're supposed to be a couple of learned planetologists!"

Catlin made a grumbling noise in his throat. "I haven't been around the zodiac, so what? You sneezed a few minutes ago and I said *gesundheit*, but I don't have any doctor's degree."

"There comes a time in a man's life," said Frayberg, "when he wants to take stock, get a new perspective."

"Relax, Howard, relax."

"In our case it means taking out our preconceived ideas, looking at them, checking our illusions against reality."

"Are you serious about this?"

"Another thing," said Frayberg, "I want to check up a little. Shifkin says the expense accounts are frightful. But he can't fight it. When Keeler says he paid ten munits for a loaf of bread on Nekkar IV, who's gonna call him on it?"

"Hell, let him eat bread! That's cheaper than making a safari around the cluster, spot-checking the super-markets."

Frayberg paid no heed. He touched a button; a three-foot sphere full of glistening motes appeared. Earth was at the center, with thin red lines, the scheduled spaceship routes, radiating out in all directions.

"Let's see what kind of circle we can make," said Frayberg. "Gower's here at Canopus, Keeler's over here at Blue Moon, Wilbur Murphy's at Sirgamesk…"

"Don't forget," muttered Catlin, "we got a show to put on."

"We've got material for a year," scoffed Frayberg. "Get hold of Space-Lines. We'll start with Sirgamesk, and see what Wilbur Murphy's up to."

❖•❖

Wilbur Murphy was being presented to the Sultan of Singhalût by the Prince Ali-Tomás. The Sultan, a small mild man of seventy, sat cross-legged on an enormous pink and green air-cushion. "Be at your ease, Mr. Murphy. We dispense with as much protocol here as practicable." The Sultan had a dry clipped voice and the air of a rather harassed corporation executive. "I understand you represent Earth-Central Home Screen Network?"

"I'm a staff photographer for the *Know Your Universe!* show."

"We export a great deal to Earth," mused the Sultan, "but not as much as we'd like. We're very pleased with your interest in us, and naturally we want to help you in every way possible. Tomorrow the Keeper of the Archives will present a series of charts analyzing our economy. Ali-Tomás shall personally conduct you through the fish-hatcheries. We want you to know we're doing a great job out here in Singhalût."

"I'm sure you are," said Murphy uncomfortably. "However, that isn't quite the stuff I want."

"No? Just where do your desires lie?"

Ali-Tomás said delicately, "Mr. Murphy took a rather profound interest in the sjambak displayed in the square."

"Oh. And you explained that these renegades could hold no interest for serious students of our planet?"

Murphy started to explain that clustered around two hundred million screens tuned to *Know Your Universe!* were four or five hundred million participants, the greater part of them neither serious nor students. The Sultan cut in decisively. "I will now impart something truly interesting. We Singhalûsi are making preparations to reclaim four more valleys, with an added area of six hundred thousand acres! I shall put my physiographic models at your disposal; you may use them to the fullest extent!"

"I'll be pleased for the opportunity," declared Murphy. "But tomorrow I'd like to prowl around the valley, meet your people, observe their customs, religious rites, courtships, funerals..."

The Sultan pulled a sour face. "We are ditch-water dull. Festivals are celebrated quietly in the home; there is small religious fervor; courtships are consummated by family contract. I fear you will find little sensational material here in Singhalût."

"You have no temple dances?" asked Murphy. "No fire-walkers, snake-charmers—voodoo?"

The Sultan smiled patronizingly. "We came out here to Cirgamesç to escape the ancient superstitions. Our lives are calm, orderly. Even the *amoks* have practically disappeared."

"But the sjambaks—"

"Negligible."

"Well," said Murphy, "I'd like to visit some of these ancient cities."

"I advise against it," declared the Sultan. "They are shards, weathered stone. There are no inscriptions, no art. There is no stimulation in dead stone. Now. Tomorrow I will hear a report on hybrid soybean plantings in the Upper Kam District. You will want to be present."

Murphy's suite matched or even excelled his expectation. He had four rooms and a private garden enclosed by a thicket of bamboo. His bathroom walls were slabs of glossy actinolite, inlaid with cinnabar, jade, galena, pyrite and blue malachite, in representations of fantastic birds. His bedroom was a tent thirty feet high. Two walls were dark green fabric; a third was golden rust; the fourth opened upon the private garden.

Murphy's bed was a pink and yellow creation ten feet square, soft as cobweb, smelling of rose sandalwood. Carved black lacquer tubs held fruit; two dozen wines, liquors, syrups, essences flowed at a touch from as many ebony spigots.

The garden centered on a pool of cool water, very pleasant in the hothouse climate of Singhalût. The only shortcoming was the lack of the lovely young servitors Murphy had envisioned. He took it upon himself to repair this lack, and in a shady wine-house behind the palace, called the Barangipan, he made the acquaintance of a girl-musician named Soek Panjoebang. He found her enticing tones of quavering sweetness from the *gamelan*, an instrument well-loved in Old Bali. Soek Panjoebang had the delicate features and transparent skin of Sumatra, the supple long limbs of Arabia and in a pair of wide and golden eyes a heritage from somewhere in Celtic Europe. Murphy bought her a goblet of frozen shavings, each a different perfume, while he himself drank white rice-beer. Soek Panjoebang displayed an intense interest in the ways of Earth, and Murphy found it hard to guide the conversation. "Weelbrrr," she said. "Such a funny name, Weelbrrr. Do you think I could play the *gamelan* in the great cities, the great palaces of Earth?"

"Sure. There's no law against *gamelans.*"

"You talk so funny, Weelbrrr. I like to hear you talk."

"I suppose you get kinda bored here in Singhalût?"

She shrugged. "Life is pleasant, but it concerns with little things. We have no great adventures. We grow flowers, we play the *gamelan*." She eyed him archly sidelong. "We love...We sleep..."

Murphy grinned. "You run *amok*."

"No, no, no. That is no more."

"Not since the sjambaks, eh?"

"The sjambaks are bad. But better than *amok*. When a man feels the knot forming around his chest, he no longer takes his kris and runs down the street—he becomes sjambak."

This was getting interesting. "Where does he go? What does he do?"

"He robs."

"Who does he rob? What does he do with his loot?"

She leaned toward him. "It is not well to talk of them."

"Why not?"

"The Sultan does not wish it. Everywhere are listeners. When one talks sjambak, the Sultan's ears rise, like the points on a cat."

"Suppose they do—what's the difference? I've got a legitimate interest. I saw one of them in that cage out there. That's torture. I want to know about it."

"He is very bad. He opened the monorail car and the air rushed out. Forty-two Singhalûsi and Hadrasi bloated and blew up."

"And what happened to the sjambak?"

"He took all the gold and money and jewels and ran away."

"Ran where?"

"Out across Great Pharasang Plain. But he was a fool. He came back to Singhalût for his wife; he was caught and set up for all people to look at, so they might tell each other, 'thus it is for sjambaks'."

"Where do the sjambaks hide out?"

"Oh," she looked vaguely around the room, "out on the plains. In the mountains."

"They must have some shelter—an air-dome."

"No. The Sultan would send out his patrol-boat and destroy them. They roam quietly. They hide among the rocks and tend their oxygen stills. Sometimes they visit the old cities."

"I wonder," said Murphy, staring into his beer, "could it be sjambaks who ride horses up to meet the spaceships?"

Soek Panjoebang knit her black eyebrows, as if preoccupied.

"That's what brought me out here," Murphy went on. "This story of a man riding a horse out in space."

"Ridiculous; we have no horses in Cirgamesç."

"All right, the steward won't swear to the horse. Suppose the man was up there on foot or riding a bicycle. But the steward recognized the man."

"Who was this man, pray?"

"The steward clammed up...The name would have been just noise to me, anyway."

"*I* might recognize the name..."

"Ask him yourself. The ship's still out at the field."

She shook her head slowly, holding her golden eyes on his face. "I do not care to attract the attention of either steward, sjambak—or Sultan."

Murphy said impatiently. "In any event, it's not who—but *how*. How does the man breathe? Vacuum sucks a man's lungs up out of his mouth, bursts his stomach, his ears..."

"We have excellent doctors," said Soek Panjoebang shuddering, "but alas! I am not one of them."

Murphy looked at her sharply. Her voice held the plangent sweetness of her instrument, with additional overtones of mockery. "There must be some kind of invisible dome around him, holding in air," said Murphy.

"And what if there is?"

"It's something new, and if it is, I want to find out about it."

Soek smiled languidly. "You are so typical an old-lander—worried, frowning, dynamic. You should relax, cultivate *napaû,* enjoy life as we do here in Singhalût."

"What's *napaû?*"

"It's our philosophy, where we find meaning and life and beauty in every aspect of the world."

"That sjambak in the cage could do with a little less *napaû* right now."

"No doubt he is unhappy," she agreed.

"Unhappy! He's being tortured!"

"He broke the Sultan's law. His life is no longer his own. It belongs to Singhalût. If the Sultan wishes to use it to warn other wrong-doers, the fact that the man suffers is of small interest."

"If they all wear that metal ornament, how can they hope to hide out?" He glanced at her own bare bosom.

"They appear by night—slip through the streets like ghosts..." She looked in turn at Murphy's loose shirt. "You will notice persons brushing up against you, feeling you," she laid her hand along his breast, "and when this happens you will know they are agents of the Sultan, because only strangers and the House may wear shirts. But now, let me sing to you—a song from the Old Land, old Java. You will not understand the tongue, but no other words so join the voice of the *gamelan.*"

"This is the gravy-train," said Murphy. "Instead of a garden suite with a private pool, I usually sleep in a bubble-tent, with nothing to eat but condensed food."

Soek Panjoebang flung the water out of her sleek black hair. "Perhaps, Weelbrrr, you will regret leaving Cirgamesç?"

"Well," he looked up to the transparent roof, barely visible where the sunlight collected and refracted, "I don't particularly like being shut up like a bird in an aviary…Mildly claustrophobic, I guess."

After breakfast, drinking thick coffee from tiny silver cups, Murphy looked long and reflectively at Soek Panjoebang.

"What are you thinking, Weelbrrr?"

Murphy drained his coffee. "I'm thinking that I'd better be getting to work."

"And what do you do?"

"First I'm going to shoot the palace, and you sitting here in the garden playing your *gamelan*."

"But Weelbrrr—not *me!*"

"You're a part of the universe, rather an interesting part. Then I'll take the square…"

"And the sjambak?"

A quiet voice spoke from behind. "A visitor, Tuan Murphy."

Murphy turned his head. "Bring him in." He looked back to Soek Panjoebang. She was on her feet.

"It is necessary that I go."

"When will I see you?"

"Tonight—at the Barangipan."

The quiet voice said, "Mr. Rube Trimmer, Tuan."

Trimmer was small and middle-aged, with thin shoulders and a paunch. He carried himself with a hell-raising swagger, left over from a time twenty years gone. His skin had the waxy look of lost floridity, his tuft of white hair was coarse and thin, his eyelids hung in the off-side droop that amateur physiognomists like to associate with guile.

"I'm Resident Director of the Import-Export Bank," said Trimmer. "Heard you were here and thought I'd pay my respects."

"I suppose you don't see many strangers."

"Not too many—there's nothing much to bring 'em. Cirgamesç isn't a comfortable tourist planet. Too confined, shut in. A man with a sensitive psyche goes nuts pretty easy here."

"Yeah," said Murphy. "I was thinking the same thing this morning. That dome begins to give a man the willies. How do the natives stand it? Or do they?"

Trimmer pulled out a cigar case. Murphy refused the offer.

"Local tobacco," said Trimmer. "Very good." He lit up thoughtfully. "Well, you might say that the Cirgameski are schizophrenic. They've got the docile Javanese blood, plus the Arabian èlan. The Javanese part is on top, but every once in a while you see a flash of arrogance...You never know. I've been out here nine years and I'm still a stranger." He puffed on his cigar, studied Murphy with his careful eyes. "You work for *Know Your Universe!,* I hear."

"Yeah. I'm one of the leg men."

"Must be a great job."

"A man sees a lot of the galaxy, and he runs into queer tales, like this sjambak stuff."

Trimmer nodded without surprise. "My advice to you, Murphy, is lay off the sjambaks. They're not healthy around here."

Murphy was startled by the bluntness. "What's the big mystery about these sjambaks?"

Trimmer looked around the room. "This place is bugged."

"I found two pick-ups and plugged 'em," said Murphy.

Trimmer laughed. "Those were just plants. They hide 'em where a man might just barely spot 'em. You can't catch the real ones. They're woven into the cloth—pressure-sensitive wires."

Murphy looked critically at the cloth walls.

"Don't let it worry you," said Trimmer. "They listen more out of habit than anything else. If you're fussy we'll go for a walk."

The road led past the palace into the country. Murphy and Trimmer sauntered along a placid river, overgrown with lily pads, swarming with large white ducks.

"This sjambak business," said Murphy. "Everybody talks around it. You can't pin anybody down."

"Including me," said Trimmer. "I'm more or less privileged around here. The Sultan finances his reclamation through the bank, on the basis of my reports. But there's more to Singhalût than the Sultan."

"Namely?"

Trimmer waved his cigar waggishly. "Now we're getting in where I don't like to talk. I'll give you a hint. Prince Ali thinks roofing-in more valleys is a waste of money, when there's Hadra and New Batavia and Sundaman so close."

"You mean—armed conquest?"

Trimmer laughed. "You said it, not me."

"They can't carry on much of a war—unless the soldiers commute by monorail."

"Maybe Prince Ali thinks he's got the answer."

"Sjambaks?"

"I didn't say it," said Trimmer blandly.

Murphy grinned. After a moment he said, "I picked up with a girl named Soek Panjoebang who plays the *gamelan*. I suppose she's working for either the Sultan or Prince Ali. Do you know which?"

Trimmer's eyes sparkled. He shook his head. "Might be either one. There's a way to find out."

"Yeah?"

"Get her off where you're sure there's no spy-cells. Tell her two things— one for Ali, the other for the Sultan. Whichever one reacts you know you've got her tagged."

"For instance?"

"Well, for instance she learns that you can rig up a hypnotic ray from a flashlight battery, a piece of bamboo, and a few lengths of wire. That'll get Ali in an awful sweat. He can't get weapons. None at all. And for the Sultan," Trimmer was warming up to his intrigue, chewing on his cigar with gusto, "tell her you're on to a catalyst that turns clay into aluminum and oxygen in the presence of sunlight. The Sultan would sell his right leg for something like that. He tries hard for Singhalût and Cirgamesç."

"And Ali?"

Trimmer hesitated. "I never said what I'm gonna say. Don't forget—I never said it."

"Okay, you never said it."

"Ever hear of a *jehad?*"

"Mohammedan holy wars."

"Believe it or not, Ali wants a *jehad.*"

"Sounds kinda fantastic."

"Sure it's fantastic. Don't forget, I never said anything about it. But suppose someone—strictly unofficial, of course—let the idea percolate around the Peace Office back home."

"Ah," said Murphy. "That's why you came to see me."

Trimmer turned a look of injured innocence. "Now, Murphy, you're a little unfair. I'm a friendly guy. Of course I don't like to see the bank lose what we've got tied up in the Sultan."

"Why don't you send in a report yourself?"

"I have! But when they hear the same thing from you, a *Know Your Universe!* man, they might make a move."

Murphy nodded.

"Well, we understand each other," said Trimmer heartily, "and everything's clear."

"Not entirely. How's Ali going to launch a *jehad* when he doesn't have any weapons, no warships, no supplies?"

"Now," said Trimmer, "we're getting into the realm of supposition." He paused, looked behind him. A farmer pushing a rotary tiller bowed politely, trundled ahead. Behind was a young man in a black turban, gold earrings, a black and red vest, white pantaloons, black curl-toed slippers. He bowed, started past. Trimmer held up his hand. "Don't waste your time up there; we're going back in a few minutes."

"Thank you, Tuan."

"Who are you reporting to? The Sultan or Prince Ali?"

"The Tuan is sure to pierce the veil of my evasions. I shall not dissemble. I am the Sultan's man."

Trimmer nodded. "Now, if you'll kindly remove to about a hundred yards, where your whisper pick-up won't work."

"By your leave, I go." He retreated without haste.

"He's almost certainly working for Ali," said Trimmer.

"Not a very subtle lie."

"Oh yes—third level. He figured I'd take it second level."

"How's that again?"

"Naturally I wouldn't believe him. He knew I knew that he knew it. So when he said 'Sultan', I'd think he wouldn't lie simply, but that he'd lie double—that he actually was working for the Sultan."

Murphy laughed. "Suppose he told you a fourth level lie?"

"It starts to be a toss-up pretty soon," Trimmer admitted. "I don't think he gives me credit for that much subtlety…What are you doing the rest of the day?"

"Taking footage. Do you know where I can find some picturesque rites? Mystical dances, human sacrifice? I've got to work up some glamor and exotic lore."

"There's this sjambak in the cage. That's about as close to the medieval as you'll find anywhere in Earth Commonwealth."

"Speaking of sjambaks…"

"No time," said Trimmer. "Got to get back. Drop in at my office—right down the square from the palace."

Murphy returned to his suite. The shadowy figure of his room servant said, "His Highness the Sultan desires the Tuan's attendance in the Cascade Garden."

"Thank you," said Murphy. "As soon as I load my camera."

The Cascade Room was an open patio in front of an artificial waterfall. The Sultan was pacing back and forth, wearing dusty khaki puttees, brown plastic boots, a yellow polo shirt. He carried a twig which he used as a riding crop, slapping his boots as he walked. He turned his head as Murphy appeared, pointed his twig at a wicker bench.

"I pray you sit down, Mr. Murphy." He paced once up and back. "How is your suite? You find it to your liking?"

"Very much so."

"Excellent," said the Sultan. "You do me honor with your presence."

Murphy waited patiently.

"I understand that you had a visitor this morning," said the Sultan.

"Yes. Mr. Trimmer."

"May I inquire the nature of the conversation?"

"It was of a personal nature," said Murphy, rather more shortly than he meant.

The Sultan nodded wistfully. "A Singhalûsi would have wasted an hour telling me half-truths—distorted enough to confuse, but not sufficiently inaccurate to anger me if I had a spy-cell on him all the time."

Murphy grinned. "A Singhalûsi has to live here the rest of his life."

A servant wheeled a frosted cabinet before them, placed goblets under two spigots, withdrew. The Sultan cleared his throat. "Trimmer is an excellent fellow, but unbelievably loquacious."

Murphy drew himself two inches of chilled rosy-pale liquor. The Sultan slapped his boots with the twig. "Undoubtedly he confided all my private business to you, or at least as much as I have allowed him to learn."

"Well—he spoke of your hope to increase the compass of Singhalût."

"That, my friend, is no hope; it's absolute necessity. Our population density is fifteen hundred to the square mile. We must expand or smother. There'll be too little food to eat, too little oxygen to breathe."

Murphy suddenly came to life. "I could make that idea the theme of my feature! Singhalût Dilemma: Expand or Perish!"

"No, that would be inadvisable, inapplicable."

Murphy was not convinced. "It sounds like a natural."

The Sultan smiled. "I'll impart an item of confidential information—although Trimmer no doubt has preceded me with it." He gave his boots an irritated whack. "To expand I need funds. Funds are best secured in an atmosphere of calm and confidence. The implication of emergency would be disastrous to my aims."

"Well," said Murphy, "I see your position."

The Sultan glanced at Murphy sidelong. "Anticipating your cooperation, my Minister of Propaganda has arranged an hour's program, stressing our progressive social attitude, our prosperity and financial prospects..."

"But, Sultan..."

"Well?"

"I can't allow your Minister of Propaganda to use me and *Know Your Universe!* as a kind of investment brochure."

The Sultan nodded wearily. "I expected you to take that attitude...Well—what do you yourself have in mind?"

"I've been looking for something to tie to," said Murphy. "I think it's going to be the dramatic contrast between the ruined cities and the new domed valleys. How the Earth settlers succeeded where the ancient people failed to meet the challenge of the dissipating atmosphere."

"Well," the Sultan said grudgingly, "that's not too bad."

"Today I want to take some shots of the palace, the dome, the city, the paddies, groves, orchards, farms. Tomorrow I'm taking a trip out to one of the ruins."

"I see," said the Sultan. "Then you won't need my charts and statistics?"

"Well, Sultan, I could film the stuff your Propaganda Minister cooked up, and I could take it back to Earth. Howard Frayberg or Sam Catlin would tear into it, rip it apart, lard in some head-hunting, a little cannibalism and temple prostitution, and you'd never know you were watching Singhalût. You'd scream with horror, and I'd be fired."

"In that case," said the Sultan, "I will leave you to the dictates of your conscience."

Howard Frayberg looked around the gray landscape of Riker's Planet, gazed out over the roaring black Mogador Ocean. "Sam, I think there's a story out there."

Sam Catlin shivered inside his electrically heated glass overcoat. "Out on that ocean? It's full of man-eating plesiosaurs—horrible things forty feet long."

"Suppose we worked something out on the line of Moby Dick? *The White Monster of the Mogador Ocean.* We'd set sail in a catamaran—"

"Us?"

"No," said Frayberg impatiently. "Of course not us. Two or three of the staff. They'd sail out there, look over these gray and red monsters, maybe fake a fight or two, but all the time they're after the legendary white one. How's it sound?"

"I don't think we pay our men enough money."

"Wilbur Murphy might do it. He's willing to look for a man riding a horse up to meet his spaceships."

"He might draw the line at a white plesiosaur riding up to meet his catamaran."

Frayberg turned away. "Somebody's got to have ideas around here..."

"We'd better head back to the space-port," said Catlin. "We got two hours to make the Sirgamesk shuttle."

Wilbur Murphy sat in the Barangipan, watching marionettes performing to xylophone, castanet, gong and *gamelan*. The drama had its roots in proto-historic Mohenjō-Darō. It had filtered down through ancient India, medieval Burma, Malaya, across the Straits of Malacca to Sumatra and Java; from modern Java across space to Cirgamesç, five thousand years of time, two hundred light-years of space. Somewhere along the route it had met and assimilated modern technology. Magnetic beams controlled arms, legs and bodies, guided the poses and posturings. The manipulator's face, by agency of clip, wire, radio control and minuscule selsyn, projected his scowl, smile, sneer or grimace to the peaked little face he controlled. The language was that of Old Java, which perhaps a third of the spectators understood. This portion did not include Murphy, and when the performance ended he was no wiser than at the start.

Soek Panjoebang slipped into the seat beside Murphy. She wore musician's garb: a sarong of brown, blue, and black *batik*, and a fantastic headdress of tiny silver bells. She greeted him with enthusiasm.

"Weelbrrr! I saw you watching..."

"It was very interesting."

"Ah, yes." She sighed. "Weelbrrr, you take me with you back to Earth? You make me a great picturama star, please, Weelbrrr?"

"Well, I don't know about that."

"I behave very well, Weelbrrr." She nuzzled his shoulder, looked soulfully up with her shiny yellow-hazel eyes. Murphy nearly forgot the experiment he intended to perform.

"What did you do today, Weelbrrr? You look at all the pretty girls?"

"Nope. I ran footage. Got the palace, climbed the ridge up to the condensation vanes. I never knew there was so much water in the air till I saw the stream pouring off those vanes! And *hot!*"

"We have much sunlight; it makes the rice grow."

"The Sultan ought to put some of that excess light to work. There's a secret process…Well, I'd better not say."

"Oh come, Weelbrrr! Tell me your secrets!"

"It's not much of a secret. Just a catalyst that separates clay into aluminum and oxygen when sunlight shines on it."

Soek's eyebrows rose, poised in place like a seagull riding the wind. "Weelbrrr! I did not know you for a man of learning!"

"Oh, you thought I was just a bum, eh? Good enough to make picturama stars out of *gamelan* players, but no special genius…"

"No, no, Weelbrrr."

"I know lots of tricks. I can take a flashlight battery, a piece of copper foil, a few transistors and bamboo tube and turn out a paralyzer gun that'll stop a man cold in his tracks. And you know how much it costs?"

"No, Weelbrrr. How much?"

"Ten cents. It wears out after two or three months, but what's the difference? I make 'em as a hobby—turn out two or three an hour."

"Weelbrrr! You're a man of marvels! Hello! We will drink!"

And Murphy settled back in the wicker chair, sipping his rice beer.

"Today," said Murphy, "I get into a space-suit, and ride out to the ruins in the plain. Ghatamipol, I think they're called. Like to come?"

"No, Weelbrrr." Soek Panjoebang looked off into the garden, her hands busy tucking a flower into her hair. A few minutes later she said, "Why must you waste your time among the rocks? There are better things to do and see. And it might well be—dangerous." She murmured the last word offhandedly.

"Danger? From the sjambaks?"

"Yes, perhaps."

"The Sultan's giving me a guard. Twenty men with crossbows."

"The sjambaks carry shields."

"Why should they risk their lives attacking me?"

Soek Panjoebang shrugged. After a moment she rose to her feet. "Goodbye, Weelbrrr."

"Goodbye? Isn't this rather abrupt? Won't I see you tonight?"

"If so be Allah's will."

Murphy looked after the lithe swaying figure. She paused, plucked a yellow flower, looked over her shoulder. Her eyes, yellow as the flower, lucent as water-jewels, held his. Her face was utterly expressionless. She turned, tossed away the flower with a jaunty gesture, and continued, her shoulders swinging.

Murphy breathed deeply. She might have made picturama at that…

One hour later he met his escort at the valley gate. They were dressed in space-suits for the plains, twenty men with sullen faces. The trip to Ghatamipol clearly was not to their liking. Murphy climbed into his own suit, checked the oxygen pressure gauge, the seal at his collar. "All ready, boys?"

No one spoke. The silence drew out. The gatekeeper, on hand to let the party out, snickered. "They're all ready, Tuan."

"Well," said Murphy, "let's go then."

Outside the gate Murphy made a second check of his equipment. No leaks in his suit. Inside pressure: 14.6. Outside pressure: zero. His twenty guards morosely inspected their crossbows and slim swords.

The white ruins of Ghatamipol lay five miles across Pharasang Plain. The horizon was clear, the sun was high, the sky was black.

Murphy's radio hummed. Someone said sharply, "Look! There it goes!" He wheeled around; his guards had halted, and were pointing. He saw a fleet something vanishing into the distance.

"Let's go," said Murphy. "There's nothing out there."

"Sjambak."

"Well, there's only one of them."

"Where one walks, others follow."

"That's why the twenty of you are here."

"It is madness! Challenging the sjambaks!"

"What is gained?" another argued.

"I'll be the judge of that," said Murphy, and set off along the plain. The warriors reluctantly followed, muttering to each other over their radio intercoms.

The eroded city walls rose above them, occupied more and more of the sky. The platoon leader said in an angry voice, "We have gone far enough."

"You're under my orders," said Murphy. "We're going through the gate." He punched the button on his camera and passed under the monstrous portal.

The city was frailer stuff than the wall, and had succumbed to the thin storms which had raged a million years after the passing of life. Murphy marvelled at the scope of the ruins. Virgin archaeological territory! No telling what a few weeks digging might turn up. Murphy considered his expense account. Shifkin was the obstacle.

There'd be tremendous prestige and publicity for *Know Your Universe!* if Murphy uncovered a tomb, a library, works of art. The Sultan would gladly provide diggers. They were a sturdy enough people; they could make quite a showing in a week, if they were able to put aside their superstitions, fears and dreads.

Murphy sized one of them up from the corner of his eye. He sat on a sunny slab of rock, and if he felt uneasy he concealed it quite successfully. In fact, thought Murphy, he appeared completely relaxed. Maybe the problem of securing diggers was a minor one after all...

And here was an odd sidelight on the Singhalûsi character. Once clear of the valley the man openly wore his shirt, a fine loose garment of electric blue, in defiance of the Sultan's edict. Of course out here he might be cold...

Murphy felt his own skin crawling. How could he be cold? How could he be alive? Where was his space-suit? He lounged on the rock, grinning sardonically at Murphy. He wore heavy sandals, a black turban, loose breeches, the blue shirt. Nothing more.

Where were the others?

Murphy turned a feverish glance over his shoulder. A good three miles distant, bounding and leaping toward Singhalût, were twenty desperate figures. They all wore space-suits. This man here...A sjambak? A wizard? A hallucination?

The creature rose to his feet, strode springily toward Murphy. He carried a crossbow and a sword, like those of Murphy's fleet-footed guards. But he wore no space-suit. Could there be breathable traces of an atmosphere? Murphy glanced at his gauge. Outside pressure: zero.

Two other men appeared, moving with long elastic steps. Their eyes were bright, their faces flushed. They came up to Murphy, took his arm. They were solid, corporeal. They had no invisible force fields around their heads.

Murphy jerked his arm free. "Let go of me, damn it!" But they certainly couldn't hear him through the vacuum.

He glanced over his shoulder. The first man held his naked blade a foot or two behind Murphy's bulging space-suit. Murphy made no further resistance. He punched the button on his camera to automatic. It would now run for several hours, recording one hundred pictures per second, a thousand to the inch.

The sjambaks led Murphy two hundred yards to a metal door. They opened it, pushed Murphy inside, banged it shut. Murphy felt the vibration through his shoes, heard a gradually waxing hum. His gauge showed an outside pressure of 5, 10, 12, 14, 14.5. An inner door opened. Hands pulled Murphy in, unclamped his dome.

"Just what's going on here?" demanded Murphy angrily.

Prince Ali-Tomás pointed to a table. Murphy saw a flashlight battery, aluminum foil, wire, a transistor kit, metal tubing, tools, a few other odds and ends.

"There it is," said Prince Ali-Tomás. "Get to work. Let's see one of these paralysis weapons you boast of."

"Just like that, eh?"

"Just like that."

"What do you want 'em for?"

"Does it matter?"

"I'd like to know." Murphy was conscious of his camera, recording sight, sound, odor.

"I lead an army," said Ali-Tomás, "but they march without weapons. Give me weapons! I will carry the word to Hadra, to New Batavia, to Sundaman, to Boeng-Bohôt!"

"How? Why?"

"It is enough that I will it. Again, I beg of you..." He indicated the table.

Murphy laughed. "I've got myself in a fine mess. Suppose I don't make this weapon for you?"

"You'll remain until you do, under increasingly difficult conditions."

"I'll be here a long time."

"If such is the case," said Ali-Tomás, "we must make our arrangements for your care on a long-term basis."

Ali made a gesture. Hands seized Murphy's shoulders. A respirator was held to his nostrils. He thought of his camera, and he could have laughed. Mystery! Excitement! Thrills! Dramatic sequence for *Know Your Universe!* Staff-man murdered by fanatics! The crime recorded on his own camera! See the blood, hear his death-rattle, smell the poison!

The vapor choked him. *What a break! What a sequence!*

"Sirgamesk," said Howard Frayberg, "bigger and brighter every minute."

"It must've been just about in here," said Catlin, "that Wilbur's horseback rider appeared."

"That's right! Steward!"

"Yes, sir?"

"We're about twenty thousand miles out, aren't we?"

"About fifteen thousand, sir."

"Sidereal Cavalry! What an idea! I wonder how Wilbur's making out on his superstition angle?"

Sam Catlin, watching out the window, said in a tight voice, "Why not ask him yourself?"

"Eh?"

"Ask him for yourself! There he is—outside, riding some kind of critter..."

"It's a ghost," whispered Frayberg. "A man without a spacesuit...There's no such thing!"

"He sees us...Look..."

Murphy was staring at them, and his surprise seemed equal to their own. He waved his hand. Catlin gingerly waved back.

Said Frayberg, "That's not a horse he's riding. It's a combination ram-jet and kiddie car with stirrups!"

"He's coming aboard the ship," said Catlin. "That's the entrance port down there..."

Wilbur Murphy sat in the captain's stateroom, taking careful breaths of air.

"How are you now?" asked Frayberg.

"Fine. A little sore in the lungs."

"I shouldn't wonder," the ship's doctor growled. "I never saw anything like it."

"How does it feel out there, Wilbur?" Catlin asked.

"It feels awful lonesome and empty. And the breath seeping up out of your lungs, never going in—that's a funny feeling. And you miss the air blowing on your skin. I never realized it before. Air feels like—like silk, like whipped cream—it's got texture..."

"But aren't you cold? Space is supposed to be absolute zero!"

"Space is nothing. It's not hot and it's not cold. When you're in the sunlight you get warm. It's better in the shade. You don't lose any heat by air convection, but radiation and sweat evaporation keep you comfortably cool."

"I still can't understand it," said Frayberg. "This Prince Ali, he's a kind of a rebel, eh?"

"I don't blame him in a way. A normal man living under those domes has to let off steam somehow. Prince Ali decided to go out crusading. I think he would have made it too—at least on Cirgamesç."

"Certainly there are many more men inside the domes..."

"When it comes to fighting," said Murphy, "a sjambak can lick twenty men in spacesuits. A little nick doesn't hurt him, but a little nick bursts open a spacesuit, and the man inside comes apart."

"Well," said the Captain. "I imagine the Peace Office will send out a team to put things in order now."

Catlin asked, "What happened when you woke up from the chloroform?"

"Well, nothing very much. I felt this attachment on my chest, but didn't think much about it. Still kinda woozy. I was halfway through decompression. They keep a man there eight hours, drop pressure on him two pounds an hour, nice and slow so he don't get the bends."

"Was this the same place they took you, when you met Ali?"

"Yeah, that was their decompression chamber. They had to make a sjambak out of me; there wasn't anywhere else they could keep me. Well, pretty soon my head cleared, and I saw this apparatus stuck to my chest." He poked at the mechanism on the table. "I saw the oxygen tank, I saw the blood running through the plastic pipes—blue from me to that carburetor arrangement, red on the way back in—and I figured out the whole arrangement. Carbon dioxide still exhales up through your lungs, but the vein back to the left auricle is routed through the carburetor and supercharged with oxygen. A man doesn't need to breathe. The carburetor flushes his blood with oxygen, the decompression tank adjusts him to the lack of air-pressure. There's only one thing to look out for; that's not to touch anything with your naked flesh. If it's in the sunshine it's blazing hot; if it's in the shade it's cold enough to cut. Otherwise you're free as a bird."

"But—how did you get away?"

"I saw those little rocket-bikes, and began figuring. I couldn't go back to Singhalût; I'd be lynched on sight as a sjambak. I couldn't fly to another planet—the bikes don't carry enough fuel.

"I knew when the ship would be coming in, so I figured I'd fly up to meet it. I told the guard I was going outside a minute, and I got on one of the rocket-bikes. There was nothing much to it."

"Well," said Frayberg, "it's a great feature, Wilbur—a great film! Maybe we can stretch it into two hours."

"There's one thing bothering me," said Catlin. "Who did the steward see up here the first time?"

Murphy shrugged. "It might have been somebody up here skylarking. A little too much oxygen and you start cutting all kinds of capers. Or it might have been someone who decided he had enough crusading.

"There's a sjambak in a cage, right in the middle of Singhalût. Prince Ali walks past; they look at each other eye to eye. Ali smiles a little and walks on. Suppose this sjambak tried to escape to the ship. He's taken aboard, turned over to the Sultan and the Sultan makes an example of him…"

"What'll the Sultan do to Ali?"

Murphy shook his head. "If I were Ali I'd disappear."

A loudspeaker turned on. "Attention all passengers. We have just passed through quarantine. Passengers may now disembark. Important: no weapons or explosives allowed on Singhalût!"

"This is where I came in," said Murphy.

Afterword to "Sjambak"

My grandfather's law office was situated on the ninth floor of the Balboa building on Market Street in San Francisco, and I visited him often. In the outer office was a typewriter, and when I was eight or nine years old I sat at this typewriter and set out to write cowboy stories. I made this attempt a few times but never got much farther than two or three pages. I don't remember much about these stories, but I was here dipping my toe into what was to be my future career.

When I was about sixteen or seventeen, I was impelled to write some very silly stories describing the adventures of a group of teenagers at a seaside resort. These also have been consigned to the farthest precincts of oblivion.

I have already mentioned...that I wrote a science fiction story for my Creative English course at the university, and that the professor reviewed it in such sardonic terms that, had I been sensitive, my career would have gone glimmering. Fortunately I did not take his remarks to heart.

A few years later, some friends of mine started a science fiction society in Berkeley, which they called *The Chowder and Marching Science Fiction Society of Berkeley*. I wrote them a little story called "Seven Exits from Bocz", which they published in their magazine.

Eventually I decided to become a professional writer: I started writing stories for sale. The first of these were gadget stories, dealing with some recondite aspect of science. I sold most of them, but I don't look back on them with any pride. For a fact they were rather boring to write, and after the first few I abandoned this formula.

I then decided that my *métier* was novels, which I began to produce. The first of these I called *Clarges*, though it was published as *To Live Forever*, a title I detest.

The longer I wrote, the more I liked the results. I discovered that if I wrote to please and amuse myself, instead of editors and publishers, the books turned out better. Looking back, I am especially fond of my *Cadwal* sequence, and the latter two books of the *Durdane* set, *Emphyrio*, and more recently *Night Lamp*, *Ports of Call* and *Lurulu*. There are others I like as well: the so-called *Demon Princes* books, and of course the *Cugel* stories, *Rhialto the Marvellous* and the *Lyonesse* cycle.

Among the characters I've conceived, I also have my favorites: Navarth, the Mad Poet (*Demon Princes*); Baron Bodissey (*Demon Princes*), who wrote the encyclopedic tautology *Life*; also Henry Belt from "Sail 25". Among the ladies I like Wayness (*Cadwal*), and Madouc (*Lyonesse*).

—Jack Vance

The Absent-Minded Professor

I stood in the dark in front of the observatory, watching the quick fiery meteor trails streaking down from Perseus. My plans were completed. I had been meticulous, systematic.

The night was remarkable: clear and limpid…a perfect night for what we had arranged, the cosmos and I. And here came Dr. Patcher—old "Dog" Patcher, as the students called him—the lights of his staid sedan sniffing out the road up the hill. I looked at my watch: ten-fifteen. The old rascal was late, probably had spent an extra three minutes shining his high-top shoes, or punctiliously brushing the coarse white plume of his hair.

The car nosed up over the hill, the head-lights sent scurrying yellow shapes and shadows past my feet. I heard the motor thankfully gasp and die, and, after a sedate moment, the slam of the door, then the *crush-crush* of Dr. Patcher's feet across the gravel. He seemed surprised to see me standing in the doorway, and looked at me sharply as much as to say, "Nothing better to do, Sisley?"

"Good evening, Dr. Patcher," I said smoothly. "It's a lovely night. The Perseids are showing very well…Ah! There's one now." I pointed at one of the instant white meteor streaks.

Dr. Patcher shook his head with that mulish nicety which has infuriated me since I first laid eyes on him. "Sorry, Sisley, I can't waste a moment of this wonderful seeing." He pushed past me, remarking over his shoulder, "I hope that everything is in order."

I remained silent. I could hardly say "no"; if I said "yes", he would pry and poke until he found something—anything—at which he could raise his eyebrows: a smudge of oil, the roof opening not precisely symmetrical to the telescope, a cigarette butt on the floor. Anything. Then I would hear a snort of disparagement; a quick gleam of a glance would flick in my direction; the deficiency would be ostentatiously remedied. And at last he would get busy with his work—if work it could be called. Myself, I considered it trivial, a piddling waste of time, a repetition of what better men at better instruments had already accomplished. Dr. Patcher was seeking novae. He would not be satisfied until a nova bore his name—"Patcher's Nova". And night after night, when the seeing was best, Dr. Patcher had crowded me away from the telescope, I who had research that was significant and important. Tonight I would show Dr. Patcher a nova indeed.

He was inside now, rustling and probing; tonight he would find nothing a millimeter out of place. I was wrong. "Oh, Sisley," came his voice, "are you busy?"

I hurried inside. Patcher was standing by the senior faculty closet with his old tweed coat already carefully arranged on a hanger. Instantly I knew his complaint. Patcher affected a white laboratory coat, which he called his "duster". About twice a month the janitor, in cleaning out the senior faculty closet, would remove the duster and replace it in the junior closet—whether as an act of crafty malice or sheer wool-gathering I had never made up my mind. In any event the ritual ran its course as usual. "Have you seen my duster, Sisley? It's not in the clothes closet where it should be."

It was on the tip of my tongue to retort, "Dr. Patcher, I am a professor of astronomy, not your valet." To which he would make the carping correction: "*Assistant* professor, my dear Sisley," thus enraging me. But tonight of all nights a state of normality must be assured, since what was to happen would be so curious and unique that only a framework of absolute humdrum routine would make the circumstances convincing.

So I swallowed my temper and, opening the junior closet, handed Patcher his duster. "Well, well," said Patcher as usual, "what on earth is it doing in there?"

"I suppose the janitor has been careless."

"We'll have to bring him up short," said Patcher. "One place where carelessness can never be tolerated is an observatory."

"I agree whole-heartedly," I said, as indeed I did. I am a systematic man, with every aspect of my life conducted along lines of the most rigorous efficiency.

Buttoning his duster, Dr. Patcher looked me up and down. "You seem restless tonight, Sisley."

"I? Certainly not. Perhaps a little tired, a little fatigued. I was prospecting up Mount Tinsley today and found several excellent specimens of sphalerite." Perhaps I should mention that my hobby is mineralogy, that I am an assiduous "rock-hound", and devote a good deal of time to my collection of rocks, minerals and crystals.

Dr. Patcher shook his head a little. "I personally could not afford to dilute my energy to such an extent. I feel that every ounce of attention belongs to my work."

This was a provocative misstatement. Dr. Patcher was an ardent horticulturalist and had gone so far as to plant a border of roses around the observatory.

"Well, well," I said, perhaps a trifle heavily, "I suppose each of us must go his own way." I glanced at my watch. Twenty-five minutes. "I'll leave the place in your hands, Doctor. If the visibility is good I'll be here about three—"

"I'm afraid I'll be using the instrument," said Patcher. "This is a perfect night in spite of the breeze—"

I thought: it is a perfect night *because* of the breeze.

"—I can't afford to waste a minute."

I nodded. "Very well; you can telephone me if you change your mind."

He looked at me queerly; I seldom showed such good grace. "Good-night, Sisley."

"Good-night, Dr. Patcher. Perhaps I'll watch the Perseids for a bit."

He made no reply. I went outside, strolled around the observatory, re-entered. I cried, "Dr. Patcher, Dr. Patcher!"

"Yes, yes, what is it?"

"Most extraordinary! Of course I'm no gardener, but I've never seen anything like it before, a luminescent rose!"

"What's that?"

"One of the rose bushes seems to be bearing luminescent blossoms."

"Oh, nonsense," muttered Patcher. "It's a trick of vision."

"A remarkable illusion, if so."

"Never heard of such a thing," said Patcher. "I can't see how it's possible. Where is this 'luminescent rose-bush'?"

"It's right around here," I said. "I could hardly believe my eyes." I led him a few feet around the observatory, to where the bed of roses rustled and swayed in the breeze. "Just in there."

Dr. Patcher spoke the last words of his existence on earth. "I don't see any—"

I hurried to my car, which I had parked headed down-slope. I started the motor, roared down the hill as fast as the road and my excellent reflexes allowed. Three days ago I had timed myself: six minutes from the observatory to the outskirts of town. Tonight I made it in five.

Slowing to my usual pace, I rounded the last turn and pulled into Sam's Service Station, stopping the car at a spot which I had calculated to a nicety several weeks earlier. And now I had a stroke of rather good luck. Pulled up in the inside lane was a white police car, with a trooper leaning against the fender.

"Hello, Mr. Sisley," said Sam. "How's all the stars in their courses tonight?"

At any other time I might have treated the pleasantry to the cool rejoinder it deserved. Sam, a burly young man with a perpetual smut on his nose, was a typical layman, in a total fog concerning the exacting and important work that we do at the observatory. Tonight, however, I welcomed his remark. "The stars are about as usual, Sam, but if you keep your eyes open, you'll see any number of shooting stars tonight."

"Honest to Pete?" Sam glanced politely around the sky.

"Yes." I looked at my watch. "Astronomers call them the Perseids. Every year about this time we run into a meteoric shower which seems to come from the constellation of Perseus—right up there. A little later in the year come the Leonids, from Leo."

Sam shook his head admiringly. "My mother's nuts on that stuff, but I didn't know she got it from you guys." He turned to the trooper. "How about that? All the time I thought these guys up at the observatory was—well, kinda passing the time, but now Professor Sisley tells me that they put out these Sign of the Zodiac books—you know, don't-invest-money-with-a-blonde-woman-today stuff. Real practical dope."

The trooper said, "What do you know? I always figured that stuff for so much hogwash."

"Of course it is," I said heatedly. "All foolishness. I said that was the constellation Leo up there, not the 'sign of Leo'!" I checked the time. About thirty seconds. "I'll have five gallons of ethyl, Sam."

"Right," said Sam. "Can you back up a bit? Wait! I guess the hose will reach…" He stood facing the direction I wished him to face.

Glare lit the sky; a flaming gout of white fire plunged down from the heavens, followed an instant later by a flat orange smear of light.

"Heavens to Betsy," cried Sam, standing with his mouth open and the hose in his hand, "what was that?"

"A meteor," I said. "A shooting star."

"That was a humdinger," the trooper said. "You don't see many that close!"

Out of the sky came a sharp report, an explosion.

Sam shook his head and numbly valved gas into the tank. "Looked like that one struck ground right up close to the observatory too."

"Yes," I said, "it certainly did. I think I'll telephone Dr. Patcher and ask if he noticed it."

"Notice it!" said Sam. "He's lucky if he got out of the way!"

I went into the station, dropped a dime into the box, called the observatory.

"Sorry," the operator said a moment later. "There's no reply."

I returned outside. "He doesn't answer. He's probably up in the cage and can't be bothered."

"Cantankerous old devil," said Sam. "But then—excuse me, Professor—all you astronomers act a little bit odd, one way or another. I don't mean screwy or anything like that—but just, well, odd. Absent-minded like."

"Ha, ha," I said. "That's where you're mistaken. I imagine that very few people are as methodical and systematic as I am."

Sam shrugged. "I can't argue with you, Doc."

I got into my car and drove through town toward the University; I parked in front of the Faculty Club, walked into the lounge, and ordered a pot of tea.

John Dalrymple of the English Department joined me. "I say, Sisley, something in your line—saw a whacking great fire-ball a moment or two ago. Lit up the entire sky, marvellous thing."

"Yes, I saw it at the service station. It apparently struck ground somewhere up near the observatory. This is the time of year for them, you know."

Dalrymple rubbed his chin. "Seems to me I see 'em all the time."

"Oh indeed! But these are the Perseids, a special belt of meteorites, or perhaps, a small comet traversing a regular orbit. The earth, entering this orbit, collides with the rocks and pebbles that make up the comet. When we watch, it seems as if the meteors are coming from the constellation of Perseus—hence we call them Perseids."

Dalrymple rose to his feet. "Well put, old man, awfully interesting and all that, but I've got something to say to Benjamin. See you again."

"Good evening, Dalrymple."

I read a magazine, played a game of chess with Hodges of the Economics Department, and discovered it was twelve-thirty. I rose to my feet. "Excuse me; Dr. Patcher's alone at the observatory. I think I'll call and find out how long he's going to be."

I called the observatory once more, and was told, "Sorry, sir, no answer."

"He's probably up in the cage," I told Hodges. "If he gets busy, he refuses to move."

"Rather crusty old bird, isn't he?"

"Not the easiest person in the world to work with. No doubt but what he has his good points. Well, good-night, Hodges; thanks for the game. I think I'll snooze a bit in one of the chairs before heading up the hill. I'm due at three or thereabouts."

At two o'clock Jake the night janitor aroused me. "Everybody's gone home, sir, and the heat's been turned off. Don't know as you'd want to catch your death of cold sitting here."

"No, by all means. Thank you, Jake." I looked at my watch. "I must be off to work."

"You and me," said Jake, "we keep strange hours."

"The best time of the day is night," I said. "By day, of course, I mean the sidereal day."

"Oh, I understand you, sir. I'm used to hearing all manner of strange talk, and I understand lots better than some of 'em think."

"I'm sure you do, Jake."

"The things I've heard, Mr. Sisley."

"Yes, interesting indeed. Well, good-night, Jake. I must be off to work."

"Getcher coat, Mr. Sisley?"

"Thank you, Jake."

The night was glorious beyond description. Stars, stars, stars—magnificent flowers of heaven, spurting pips of various lights down from their appointed places. I know the night skies as I know my face; I know all the lore, the fable, the mystery. I know where to expect Arcturus, in one corner of the Great Diamond, with Denebola to the side, Spica below, Cor Caroli above. I know Argo Navis and the Northern Cross, sometimes called Cygnus, and the little rocking-horse of Lyra, with Vega at the head. I know how to sight down the three stars in Aquila, with Altair at the center, to find Fomalhaut, when it comes peering briefly over the southern horizon. I know the Lair of the Howling Dog, with Vindemiatrix close by; I can find Algol the demon star and Mira the Wonderful on the spine of Cetus the whale. I know Orion and his upraised arm, with the river Eridanus winding across twenty million light-years of desolation. Ah, the stars! Poetry the poor day-dweller never dreams of! Poetry in the star names: Alpheta, Achernar, Alpheratz; Canopus, Antares, Markab; Sirius, Rigel, Bellatrix; Aldebaran, Betelgeuse, Fomalhaut; Alphard, Spica, Procyon; Deneb Kaitos, Alpha Centauri: rolling magnificent sounds, each king of a myriad worlds. And now, with old Dog Patcher gone to his reward, the heavens were mine, to explore at my leisure; possibly with the help of young Katkus, who would be promoted to my place, when I became head of the department.

I drove up the familiar road, winding among aromatic eucalyptus, and breasted over the edge of the parking area.

The observatory was as I had left it, with Patcher's shiny old sedan pressed close to the wall, much more lonesome and pathetic than ever Patcher's body would look.

But I must not cry out the alarm too quickly; first I had one or two matters to take care of.

I found my flashlight and walked out on the slope behind the observatory. I knew approximately where to look and exactly what I was looking for—and there it was: a bit of cardboard, a scrap of red paper, a length of stick.

Everything was proceeding as I had planned, and after all, why should it not? It is very easy to kill a man, so I find. I merely had chosen one of many ways, perhaps a trifle more elaborate than necessary, but it seemed such a fitting end for old Dog Patcher. I could have arranged for his car to have left the road; there would have been precedent in the death of Professor Harlow T. Kane, Patcher's predecessor as Senior Astronomer, who had lost his life in just such a manner... So the thoughts ran through my head as I burned the stick and cardboard and paper, and scattered the ashes.

I returned to the observatory, sauntered inside, looked over the big reflector with a sense of proprietorship...About time now for the alarm.

I wandered outside, turned my flashlight on the body. Everything just so. I ran back in, telephoned the sheriff's office, since the observatory is outside city limits. "Sheriff?"

A sleepy voice grumbled, "What in Sam Hill's the idea, waking me up this time of night?"

"This is Professor Sisley up at the observatory. Something terrible has happened! I've just discovered the body of Dr. Patcher!"

The sheriff was a fat and amiable man, much more concerned with his take from slot machines and poker rooms than the prevention of crime. He arrived at the observatory with a doctor. They stood looking down at the body, the sheriff holding a flashlight, neither one showing zest or enthusiasm.

"Looks like he's been beaned with a rock," said the sheriff. "Find out how long he's been dead, will you, Doc?"

He turned to me. "Just what happened, Professor?"

"It looks to me," I said, "as if he's been struck by a meteorite."

"A meteorite, hey?" He pulled at his chin doubtfully. "Ain't that a little far-fetched? One chance in a thousand, you might say?"

"I can't be sure, naturally. You'll have to get an expert to check on that piece of metal or rock, whatever it is."

The sheriff was still rubbing his chin.

"When I left him at about ten-thirty, he said he was going to watch the meteors—we're passing through the Perseids, you know—and shortly after— I was in town by then at Sam's Service Station—we saw a very large shooting star, meteor, fire-ball, whatever you want to call it, come down from the sky. Sam saw it, the state trooper saw it—"

"Yeah," said the sheriff, "I saw it myself. Monstrous thing..." He bent over Dr. Patcher's dead body. "You think this might be a meteorite, hey?"

"I certainly couldn't say at a glance, but Professor Doheny of the Geology Department could tell you in jig-time."

"Humph," said the sheriff. To the doctor, "Any idea when he died, Doc?"

"Oh, roughly five or six hours ago."

"Humph. That's ten-thirty to eleven-thirty…That meteor came down at, let's see—"

"At exactly twelve minutes to eleven."

"Well, well," said the sheriff, looking at me with mild speculation. After this, I told myself, I would volunteer no more information. But no matter, no harm done.

"I suppose," said the sheriff, "we'd better wait till it's light, and then we can look around a little bit more."

"If you will come into the observatory," I said, "I'll brew up a pot of coffee. This night air is a trifle brisk."

Dawn came; the sheriff called his office; an ambulance climbed the hill. I was asked a few more questions, photographs were taken, and the body was moved.

Newspapers from coast to coast featured accounts of the "freak accident". The "man bites dog" angle was played up heavily; the astronomer who made a career of hunting down "comets" had got a taste of his own medicine. Of course a meteor is by no means a comet, and Dr. Patcher was uninterested in comets, but in the general hullabaloo no one cared very much, and I suppose that insofar as the public is concerned it is all one and the same.

The president of the University telephoned his sympathy. "You'll take Patcher's place, of course; I hope you won't refuse out of any misplaced feelings of delicacy. I've approached young Katkus, and he'll move up to your previous place."

"Thank you, sir," said I, "I'll do my best. With your encouragement and the help of young Katkus I'll see that Patcher's work goes on; indeed, I think it would be a fitting memorial if the first nova we found we named for poor old Patcher."

"Excellent," said the president. "I'll put through your appointment at once."

So events went their course. I cleaned Patcher's notes and books out of the study and moved my own in. Young Katkus made his appearance, and I was pleased by the modest manner in which he accepted his good fortune.

A week passed and the sheriff called at my apartment. "Come in, sheriff, come in. Glad to see you. Here—" I moved some journals "—have a chair."

"Thanks, thanks very much." He eased his fat little body gingerly into the seat.

I had not quite finished my breakfast. "Will you have a cup of coffee?"

He hesitated. "No, think I'd better not. Not today."

"What's on your mind, sheriff?"

He put his hands on his knees. "Well, Professor, it's that Patcher accident. I'd like to talk it over with you."

"Why certainly, if you wish…but I thought that was all water under the bridge."

"Well—not entirely. We've been lying low, you might say. Maybe it's an accident—and again, maybe it's not."

· I said with great interest, "What do you mean, sheriff? Surely…?"

As I have mentioned, the sheriff is a mild man, and looks more like an insurance salesman than a law-enforcement officer. But at the moment a rather dogged and unpleasant expression stiffened his features.

"I've been doing a bit of investigating, and a bit of thinking. And I've got to admit I'm puzzled."

"How so?"

"Well, there's no question but what Dr. Patcher was killed with a meteorite. That chunk of rock was a funny kind of nickel—iron mixture, and showed a peculiar set of marks under the microscope. Professor Doheny said meteorite it was, and no doubt about it."

"Oh?" I said, sipping my coffee.

"There's no question but what a streak of fire was seen shooting down out of the sky at about the time Dr. Patcher was killed."

"Yes, I believe so. In fact, I saw it myself. Quite an impressive phenomenon."

"I thought at first that a meteorite would be hot, and I wondered why Patcher's hair wasn't singed, but I find that when a meteor comes down, only a little bit of the surface heats up and glows off, but the rest stays icy-cold."

"Right," I said cordially. "Exactly right."

"But let's suppose," said the sheriff, looking at me sidewise with an expression I can only call crafty, "let's suppose that someone wanted to kill poor old Dr. Patcher—"

I shook my head doubtfully. "Far-fetched."

"—and wanted to fake the murder so that it looked like an accident, how would he go about it?"

"But—who would want to do away with Patcher?"

The sheriff laughed uneasily. "That's what's got us stumped. There's no one with a speck of motive—except, possibly, yourself."

"Ridiculous."

"Of course, of course. But we were just—"

"Why should I want to kill Dr. Patcher?"

"I hear," said the sheriff, watching me sidelong, "that he was a hard man to get along with."

"Not when you understood his foibles."

"I hear that you and he had a few bust-ups over the work up at the observatory?"

"Now that," I said with feeling, "is pure taradiddle. Naturally, we had our differences. I felt, as many of my colleagues did, that Patcher was entering upon his dotage, and it shows in the rather trivial nature of the work he was doing."

"Exactly what was the work, Professor? In words of one syllable?"

"Well," and I laughed, "he was actually going over the sky with a fine-tooth comb, looking for novae, and I'll admit that occasionally it was a vexation, when I had important work to do—"

"Er, what is your work, Professor?"

"I am conducting a statistical count of the Cepheid variables in the Great Nebula of Andromeda."

"Ah, I see," said the sheriff. "Pretty tough job, sounds like."

"The work is progressing now, of course. But certainly you don't think—you can't assume—"

The sheriff waved his hand. "We don't assume anything. We just, well, call it figure a little."

"How could I, how could anyone, control what might literally be called a bolt from the blue?"

"Ah, now we're getting down to brass tacks. How could you, indeed? I admit I racked my brains, and I think I've got it puzzled out."

"My dear sheriff, are you accusing—"

"No, no, sit still. We're just talking things over. I was telling you how you could—if you wanted, mind you, *if* you wanted—fake a meteor."

"Well," I asked in fine scorn, "how could I fake a meteor?"

"You'd need something to make a good streak of light. You'd need something to get it up there. You'd need a way of setting it off at the right time."

"And?"

"Well, the first could be a good strong old-fashioned sky-rocket."

"Why—theoretically, I suppose so. But—"

"I thought of all kinds of things," said the sheriff. "Airplanes, balloons, birds—everything except flying fish. The answer has to be one thing: a kite. A big box kite."

"I admire your ingenuity, sheriff. But—"

"Then you'd need some way to send this thing off, and aim it right. Now I may be all wet on this—but I imagine that you had the rocket fixed with a couple of wire loops over the string, so that it would follow the string to the ground."

"Sheriff, I—"

"Now as for setting it off—why that's a simple matter. I could probably rig up something of the sort myself. A wrist-watch with the glass off, a flashlight battery, a contact stuck on the dial, insulated from the rest of the watch, so that when the minute hand met it, the circuit would open. Then you'd use magnesium floss and magnesium tape to start the fuse of your rocket, and that's practically the whole of it."

"My dear sheriff," I said with all my dignity, "if I were guilty of such a pernicious offense, how in the world would I dispose of the kite?"

"Well," said the sheriff, scratching his chin, "I hadn't thought of that. I suppose you could haul it down and burn it, together with the string."

I was taken aback. Actually, I hadn't thought of anything so simple. The kite I had blown up with half a stick of dynamite, fused to explode after the rocket had started down; the string I had soaked in a solution of potassium chlorate; it had burned to dust like a train of gunpowder. "Humph. Well, if you are accusing me of this crime you have conceived—"

"No, no, no!" cried the sheriff. "I'm not accusing anybody. We're just sitting here chewing this thing over. But I admit I am wondering why you bought all that kite-string from Fuller's Hardware about three weeks ago."

I stared at him indignantly. "Kite-string? Nonsense. I bought that string at the request of Dr. Patcher himself, with which to tie up his sweet peas, and if you check at his home they'll tell you the same story."

The sheriff nodded. "I see. Well, just a point I'm glad to have cleared up. I understand you're an amateur rock-hunter?"

"That's perfectly true," I said. "I have a small but not unrepresentative collection."

"Any meteorites in the bunch?" the sheriff asked carelessly.

Just as carelessly I replied, "Why I believe so. One or two."

"I wonder if I could see them."

"Certainly, if you wish. I keep my collection out here, in the back rooms. I'm very methodical about all this; I don't let the rocks intrude into the astronomy, or vice versa."

"That's how hobbies should be," said the sheriff.

We went out upon the back-porch, which I have converted to a display room. On all sides are chests of narrow drawers, glass-topped tables where my choicest pieces are on view, geological charts, and the like. At the far end is my little laboratory, with my reagents, scales, and furnace. Midway is the file cabinet where I have indexed and catalogued each piece in my collection.

The sheriff glanced with an unconvincing show of interest along the trays and shelves. "Now, let's see them meteorites."

Although I knew their whereabouts to the inch, I made a move of indecision. "I'll have to check in the catalogue; I'm afraid it's slipped my mind."

I pulled open the filing cabinet, flipped the dividers to M. "Meteorites—RG-17. Ah yes, right on here, sheriff. Case R, tray G, space 17. As you see, I'm nothing if not systematic…"

"What's the matter?" asked the sheriff.

I suppose I was staring at the sheet of paper. It read:

RG-17-A—Meteorite—Nickel—iron
Weight—171 grams
Origin—Burnt Rock Ranch, Arizona

RG-17-B—Meteorite—Granitic stone
Weight—216 grams
Origin—Kelsey, Nevada

RG-17-C—Meteorite—Nickel—iron
Weight—1,842 grams
Origin—Kilgore, Mojave Desert

Meticulously, systematically, I had typed in red against RG-17-C: *Removed from collection, August 9.* Three days before Dr. Patcher had been killed by a meteorite weighing 1,842 grams.

"What's the matter?" asked the sheriff. "Not feeling so good?"

"The meteorites," I croaked, "are over here."

"Let's see that sheet of paper."

"No—it's just a memorandum."

"Sure—but I want to see it."

"I'll show you the meteorites."

"Show me that paper."

"Do you want to see the meteorites or don't you?"

"I want to see that paper."

"Go to blazes."

"Professor Sisley—"

I went to the tray, pulled it open. "The meteorites. Look at them!"

The sheriff stepped over, bent his head. "Hm. Yeah. Just rocks." He cocked an eye at the sheet of paper I gripped in my hand. "Are you going to show me that paper or not?"

"No. It's got nothing to do with this business. It's a record of where I obtained these rocks. They're valuable, and I promised not to reveal the source."

"Well, well." The sheriff turned away. I walked quickly to the toilet, locked the door, quickly tore the paper to shreds, flushed it down the drain.

"There," I said, emerging, "the paper is gone. If it was evidence, it's gone too."

The sheriff shook his head a little mournfully. "I should have known better than to come calling so friendly-like. I should have had a gun and a search-warrant and my two big deputies. But now—" he paused, chewed thoughtfully at something inside his mouth.

"Well," I asked impatiently, "are you going to arrest me or not?"

"Arrest you? No, Professor Sisley. We know what we know, you and I, but how will we get a jury to see it? You claim a meteorite killed Dr. Patcher, and a thousand people saw a meteor head toward him. I'll say, Professor Sisley was mad at Dr. Patcher; Professor Sisley could have whopped Dr. Patcher with a rock, then fired his sky-rocket down from a kite. You'll say, prove it. And I'll say, Professor Sisley flushed a piece of paper down the toilet. And then the judge will bang his gavel a couple of times and that's all there is to it. No, Professor, I'm not going to arrest you. My job wouldn't be worth a plugged nickel. But I'll tell you what I'm going to do—just like I told Doc Patcher when the head man before him died so sudden."

"Well, go ahead, say it! What are you going to do?"

"It's really not a great lot," the sheriff said modestly. "I'm just going to let events take their course."

"I can't say as I understand your meaning."

But the sheriff had gone. I blew my nose, mopped my brow, and considered the file which had so nearly betrayed me. Even at this juncture, I took a measure of satisfaction in the fact that it was system and method which had come so close to undoing me, and not the absent-mindedness which an ignorant public ascribes to men of learning.

I am senior astronomer at the observatory. My work is progressing. I have control of the telescope. I have the vastness of the universe under my finger-tips.

Young Katkus is developing well, although he currently displays a particularly irritating waywardness and independence. The young idiot thinks he is hot on the track of an undiscovered planet beyond Pluto, and if I gave him his head, he'd waste every minute of good seeing peering back and forth along the ecliptic. He sulks now and again, but he'll have to wait his chance, as I did, as Dr. Patcher did before me, and, presumably, Dr. Kane before him.

Dr. Kane—I have not thought of him since the day his car went out of control and took him over the cliff. I must learn who preceded him as senior astronomer. A telephone call to Nolbert at Administration Hall will do the trick…I find that Dr. Kane succeeded a Professor Maddox, who drowned when a boat he and Dr. Kane were paddling capsized on Lake Niblis. Nolbert says the tragedy weighed on Dr. Kane to the day of his death, which came as an equally violent shock to the department. He had been computing the magnetic orientation of globular clusters, a profoundly interesting topic, although it was no secret that Dr. Patcher considered the work fruitless and didactic. It is sometimes tempting to speculate—but no, they all are decently in their graves, and I have more serious demands upon my attention. Such as Katkus, who comes demanding the telescope at the very moment when air and sky are at their best. I tell him quite decisively that off-trail investigations such as his must be conducted when the telescope is otherwise idle. He goes off sulking. I can feel no deep concern for his hurt feelings; he must learn to fit himself to the schedule of research as mapped out by the senior astronomer.

I saw the sheriff today; he nodded quite politely. I wonder what he meant, letting events take their course? Cryptic and not comfortable; it has put me quite out of sorts. Perhaps, after all, I was overly sharp with Katkus. He is sitting at his desk, pretending to check the new plates into the glossary, watching me from the corner of his eye.

I wonder what is passing through his mind.

Afterword to "The Absent-Minded Professor" (aka "First Star I See Tonight")

[After] I read a book by Sir James Jeans, *The Universe Around Us*, I became involved with a new preoccupation: namely, identifying the stars. I obtained star charts. I would take a flashlight, cover it over with a red bandana, lie out in the sand a few hundred feet from the house, stare up into the sky and trace out the constellations. In due course I learned all the constellations and all the first magnitude stars, and many of the second magnitude stars. I find it hard to convey how much pleasure this pursuit gave me. The stars all became familiar, friends almost, and I rejoiced when, in the middle of the summer, Fomalhaut would appear over the southern horizon. Even now, as I write this, I can envision how the skies looked, aglow with those wonderful stars: Arcturus, Vega, Betelgeuse, Antares, Sirius, Achernar, Algol, Polaris…

Aboard another tanker…the *Verendrye*, I obtained some luminous tape and, for no particular reason, created a star chart on the overhead of our forecastle, with the major constellations, the first and second magnitude stars picked out accurately. The captain, learning of this enterprise, came down to the forecastle, lay down on his back, looked up and marveled at this unprecedented creation. At the end of the voyage, he gave me a glossy photograph of the ship signed with his name and best regards. I still have this photograph and am naturally very proud of it.

Background for "First Star" was assimilated during my association with Palomar astronomer Robert Richardson ("Philip Latham"), during the time we both wrote *Captain Video* scripts for television. There are dark and sinister aspects to the astronomer's life of which the public is unaware; this story, so I am told, prompts astronomers to nod in grim corroboration and look over their shoulders.

—Jack Vance

When the Five Moons Rise

Seguilo could not have gone far; there was no place for him to go. Once Perrin had searched the lighthouse and the lonesome acre of rock, there were no other possibilities—only the sky and the ocean.

Seguilo was neither inside the lighthouse nor was he outside.

Perrin went out into the night, squinted up against the five moons. Seguilo was not to be seen on top of the lighthouse.

Seguilo had disappeared.

Perrin looked indecisively over the flowing brine of Maurnilam Var. Had Seguilo slipped on the damp rock and fallen into the sea, he certainly would have called out…The five moons blinked, dazzled, glinted along the surface; Seguilo might even now be floating unseen a hundred yards distant.

Perrin shouted across the dark water: "Seguilo!"

He turned, once more looked up the face of the lighthouse. Around the horizon whirled the twin shafts of red and white light, guiding the barges crossing from South Continent to Spacetown, warning them off Isel Rock.

Perrin walked quickly toward the lighthouse; Seguilo was no doubt asleep in his bunk or in the bathroom.

Perrin went to the top chamber, circled the lumenifer, climbed down the stairs. "Seguilo!"

No answer. The lighthouse returned a metallic vibrating echo.

Seguilo was not in his room, in the bathroom, in the commissary, or in the storeroom. Where else could a man go?

Perrin looked out the door. The five moons cast confusing shadows. He saw a gray blot—"Seguilo!" He ran outside. "Where have you been?"

Seguilo straightened to his full height, a thin man with a wise doleful face. He turned his head; the wind blew his words past Perrin's ears.

Sudden enlightenment came to Perrin. "You must have been under the generator!" The only place he could have been.

Seguilo had come closer. "Yes…I was under the generator." He paused uncertainly by the door, stood looking up at the moons, which this evening had risen all bunched together. Puzzlement creased Perrin's forehead. Why should Seguilo crawl under the generator? "Are you—well?"

"Yes. Perfectly well."

Perrin stepped closer and in the light of the five moons, Ista, Bista, Liad, Miad and Poidel, scrutinized Seguilo sharply. His eyes were dull and noncommittal; he seemed to carry himself stiffly. "Have you hurt yourself? Come over to the steps and sit down."

"Very well." Seguilo ambled across the rock, sat down on the steps.

"You're certain you're all right?"

"Certain."

After a moment Perrin said, "Just before you—went under the generator, you were about to tell me something you said was important."

Seguilo nodded slowly. "That's true."

"What was it?"

Seguilo stared dumbly up into the sky. There was nothing to be heard but the wash of the sea, hissing and rushing where the rock shelved under.

"Well?" asked Perrin finally. Seguilo hesitated.

"You said that when five moons rose together in the sky, it was not wise to believe anything."

"Ah," nodded Seguilo, "so I did."

"What did you mean?"

"I'm not sure."

"Why is not believing anything important?"

"I don't know."

Perrin rose abruptly to his feet. Seguilo normally was crisp, dryly emphatic. "Are you sure you're all right?"

"Right as rain."

That was more like Seguilo. "Maybe a drink of whiskey would fix you up."

"Sounds like a good idea."

Perrin knew where Seguilo kept his private store. "You sit here, I'll get you a shot."

"Yes, I'll sit here."

Perrin hurried inside the lighthouse, clambered the two flights of stairs to the commissary. Seguilo might remain seated or he might not; something in his posture, in the rapt gaze out to sea, suggested that he might not. Perrin found the bottle and a glass, ran back down the steps. Somehow he knew that Seguilo would be gone.

Seguilo was gone. He was not on the steps, nowhere on the windy acre of Isel Rock. It was impossible that he had passed Perrin on the stairs. He might have slipped into the engine room and crawled under the generator once more.

Perrin flung open the door, switched on the lights, stooped, peered under the housing. Nothing.

A greasy film of dust, uniform, unmarred, indicated that no one had ever been there.

Where was Seguilo?

Perrin went up to the top-most part of the lighthouse, carefully searched every nook and cranny down to the outside entrance. No Seguilo.

Perrin walked out on the rock. Bare and empty; no Seguilo.

Seguilo was gone. The dark water of Maurnilam Var sighed and flowed across the shelf.

Perrin opened his mouth to shout across the moon-dazzled swells, but somehow it did not seem right to shout. He went back to the lighthouse, seated himself before the radio transceiver.

Uncertainly he touched the dials; the instrument had been Seguilo's responsibility. Seguilo had built it himself, from parts salvaged from a pair of old instruments.

Perrin tentatively flipped a switch. The screen sputtered into light, the speaker hummed and buzzed. Perrin made hasty adjustments. The screen streaked with darts of blue light, a spatter of quick, red blots. Fuzzy, dim, a face looked forth from the screen. Perrin recognized a junior clerk in the Commission office at Spacetown. He spoke urgently. "This is Harold Perrin, at Isel Rock Lighthouse; send out a relief ship."

The face in the screen looked at him as through thick pebble-glass. A faint voice, overlaid by sputtering and crackling, said, "Adjust your tuning...I can't hear you..."

Perrin raised his voice. "Can you hear me now?"

The face in the screen wavered and faded.

Perrin yelled, "This is Isel Rock Lighthouse! Send out a relief ship! Do you hear? There's been an accident!"

"...signals not coming in. Make out a report, send..." the voice sputtered away.

Cursing furiously under his breath, Perrin twisted knobs, flipped switches. He pounded the set with his fist. The screen flashed bright orange, went dead.

Perrin ran behind, worked an anguished five minutes, to no avail. No light, no sound.

Perrin slowly rose to his feet. Through the window he glimpsed the five moons racing for the west. "When the five moons rise together," Seguilo had said, "it's not wise to believe anything." Seguilo was gone. He had been gone once before and come back; maybe he would come back again. Perrin grimaced, shuddered. It would be best now if Seguilo stayed away. He ran down to the outer door, barred and bolted it. Hard on Seguilo, if he came wandering back...Perrin leaned a moment with his back to the door, listening. Then he went to the generator room, looked under the generator. Nothing. He shut the door, climbed the steps.

Nothing in the commissary, the storeroom, the bathroom, the bedrooms. No one in the light-room. No one on the roof.

No one in the lighthouse but Perrin.

He returned to the commissary, brewed a pot of coffee, sat half an hour listening to the sigh of water across the shelf, then went to his bunk.

Passing Seguilo's room he looked in. The bunk was empty.

When at last he rose in the morning, his mouth was dry, his muscles like bundles of withes, his eyes hot from long staring up at the ceiling. He rinsed his face with cold water and, going to the window, searched the horizon. A curtain of dingy overcast hung halfway up the east; blue-green Magda shone through like an ancient coin covered with verdigris. Over the water oily skeins of blue-green light formed and joined and broke and melted…Out along the south horizon Perrin spied a pair of black barges riding the Trade Current to Spacetown. After a few moments they disappeared into the overcast.

Perrin threw the master switch; above him came the fluttering hum of the lumenifer slowing and dimming.

He descended the stairs, with stiff fingers unbolted the door, flung it wide. The wind blew past his ears, smelling of Maurnilam Var. The tide was low; Isel Rock rose out of the water like a saddle. He walked gingerly to the water's edge. Blue-green Magda broke clear of the overcast; the light struck under the water. Leaning precariously over the shelf, Perrin looked down, past shadows and ledges and grottos, down into the gloom…Movement of some kind; Perrin strained to see. His foot slipped, he almost fell.

Perrin returned to the lighthouse, worked a disconsolate three hours at the transceiver, finally deciding that some vital component had been destroyed.

He opened a lunch unit, pulled a chair to the window, sat gazing across the ocean. Eleven weeks to the relief ship. Isel Rock had been lonely enough with Seguilo.

Blue-green Magda sank in the west. A sulfur overcast drifted up to meet it. Sunset brought a few minutes of sad glory to the sky: jade-colored stain with violet streakings. Perrin started the twin shafts of red and white on their nocturnal sweep, went to stand by the window.

The tide was rising, the water surged over the shelf with a heavy sound. Up from the west floated a moon: Ista, Bista, Liad, Miad, or Poidel? A native would know at a glance. Up they came, one after the other, five balls blue as old ice.

"It's not wise to believe…" What had Seguilo meant? Perrin tried to think back. Seguilo had said, "It's not often, very rare, in fact, that the five moons bunch up—but when they do, then there're high tides." He had hesitated, glancing out at the shelf. "When the five moons rise together," said Seguilo, "it's not wise to believe anything."

Perrin had gazed at him with forehead creased in puzzlement. Seguilo was an old hand, who knew the fables and lore, which he brought forth from time to time. Perrin had never known quite what to expect from Seguilo; he had the trait indispensable to a lighthouse-tender—taciturnity. The transceiver had been his hobby; in Perrin's ignorant hands, the instrument had destroyed itself. What the lighthouse needed, thought Perrin, was one of the new transceivers with self-contained power unit, master control, the new organic screen, soft and elastic, like a great eye...A sudden rain squall blanketed half the sky; the five moons hurtled toward the cloud bank. The tide surged high over the shelf, almost over a gray mass. Perrin eyed it with interest; what could it be?...About the size of a transceiver, about the same shape. Of course, it could not possibly *be* a transceiver; yet, what a wonderful thing if it were...He squinted, strained his eyes. There, surely, that was the milk-colored screen; those black spots were dials. He sprang to his feet, ran down the stairs, out the door, across the rock... It was irrational; why should a transceiver appear just when he wanted it, as if in answer to his prayer? Of course it might be part of a cargo lost overboard...

Sure enough, the mechanism was bolted to a raft of Manasco logs, and evidently had floated up on the shelf on the high tide.

Perrin, unable to credit his good fortune, crouched beside the gray case. Brand new, with red seals across the master switch.

It was too heavy to carry. Perrin tore off the seals, threw on the power: here was a set he understood. The screen glowed bright.

Perrin dialed to the Commission band. The interior of an office appeared and facing out was, not the officious subordinate, but Superintendent Raymond Flint himself. Nothing could be better.

"Superintendent," cried out Perrin, "this is Isel Rock Lighthouse, Harold Perrin speaking."

"Oh, yes," said Superintendent Flint. "How are you, Perrin? What's the trouble?"

"My partner, Andy Seguilo, disappeared—vanished into nowhere; I'm alone out here."

Superintendent Flint looked shocked. "Disappeared? What happened? Did he fall into the ocean?"

"I don't know. He just disappeared. It happened last night—"

"You should have called in before," said Flint reprovingly. "I would have sent out a rescue copter to search for him."

"I tried to call," Perrin explained, "but I couldn't get the regular transceiver to work. It burnt up on me...I thought I was marooned here."

Superintendent Flint raised his eyebrows in mild curiosity. "Just what are you using now?"

Perrin stammered, "It's a brand new instrument...floated up out of the sea. Probably was lost from a barge."

Flint nodded. "Those bargemen are a careless lot—don't seem to understand what good equipment costs...Well, you sit tight. I'll order a plane out in the morning with a relief crew. You'll be assigned to duty along the Floral Coast. How does that suit you?"

"Very well, sir," said Perrin. "Very well indeed. I can't think of anything I'd like better...Isel Rock is beginning to get on my nerves."

"When the five moons rise, it's not wise to believe anything," said Superintendent Flint in a sepulchral voice.

The screen went dead.

Perrin lifted his hand, slowly turned off the power. A drop of rain fell on his face. He glanced skyward. The squall was almost on him. He tugged at the transceiver, although well aware that it was too heavy to move. In the storeroom was a tarpaulin that would protect the transceiver until morning. The relief crew could help him move it inside.

He ran back to the lighthouse, found the tarpaulin, hurried back outside. Where was the transceiver?...Ah—there. He ran through the pelting drops, wrapped the tarpaulin around the box, lashed it into place, ran back to the lighthouse. He barred the door, and whistling, opened a canned dinner unit.

The rain spun and slashed at the lighthouse. The twin shafts of white and red swept wildly around the sky. Perrin climbed into his bunk, lay warm and drowsy...Seguilo's disappearance was a terrible thing; it would leave a scar on his mind. But it was over and done with. Put it behind him; look to the future. The Floral Coast...

In the morning the sky was bare and clean. Maurnilam Var spread mirror-quiet as far as the eye could reach. Isel Rock lay naked to the sunlight. Looking out the window, Perrin saw a rumpled heap—the tarpaulin, the lashings. The transceiver, the Manasco raft had disappeared utterly.

Perrin sat in the doorway. The sun climbed the sky. A dozen times he jumped to his feet, listening for the sound of engines. But no relief plane appeared.

The sun reached the zenith, verged westward. A barge drifted by, a mile from the rock. Perrin ran out on the shelf, shouting, waving his arms.

The lank, red bargemen sprawled on the cargo stared curiously, made no move. The barge dwindled into the east.

Perrin returned to the doorstep, sat with his head in his hands. Chills and fever ran along his skin. There would be no relief plane. On Isel Rock he would remain, day in, day out, for eleven weeks.

Listlessly he climbed the steps to the commissary. There was no lack of food, he would never starve. But could he bear the solitude, the uncertainty? Seguilo going, coming, going…The unsubstantial transceiver…Who was responsible for these cruel jokes? The five moons rising together—was there some connection?

He found an almanac, carried it to the table. At the top of each page five white circles on a black strip represented the moons. A week ago they strung out at random. Four days ago Liad, the slowest, and Poidel, the fastest, were thirty degrees apart, with Ista, Bista, and Miad between. Two nights ago the peripheries almost touched; last night they were even closer. Tonight Poidel would bulge slightly out in front of Ista, tomorrow night Liad would lag behind Bista…But between the five moons and Seguilo's disappearance—where was the connection?

Gloomily, Perrin ate his dinner. Magda settled into Maurnilam Var without display, a dull dusk settled over Isel Rock, water rose and sighed across the shelf.

Perrin turned on the light, barred the door. There would be no more hoping, no more wishing—no more believing. In eleven weeks the relief ship would convey him back to Spacetown; in the meantime he must make the best of the situation.

Through the window he saw the blue glow in the east, watched Poidel, Ista, Bista, Liad, and Miad climb the sky. The tide came with the moons. Maurnilam Var was still calm, and each moon laid a separate path of reflection along the water.

Perrin looked up into the sky, around the horizon. A beautiful, lonesome sight. With Seguilo he sometimes had felt lonely, but never isolation such as this. Eleven weeks of solitude…If he could select a companion…Perrin let his mind wander.

Into the moonlight a slim figure came walking, wearing tan breeches and a short-sleeved white sports shirt.

Perrin stared, unable to move. The figure walked up to the door, rapped. The muffled sound came up the staircase. "Hello, anybody home?" It was a clear girl's voice.

Perrin swung open the window, called hoarsely, "Go away!"

She moved back, turned up her face, and the moonlight fell upon her features. Perrin's voice died in his throat. He felt his heart beating wildly.

"Go away?" she said in a soft puzzled voice. "I've no place to go."

"Who are you?" he asked. His voice sounded strange to his own ears—desperate, hopeful. After all, she was possible—even though almost impossibly beautiful…She might have flown out from Spacetown. "How did you get here?"

She gestured at Maurnilam Var. "My plane went down about three miles out. I came over on the life raft."

Perrin looked along the water's edge. The outline of a life raft was barely visible.

The girl called up, "Are you going to let me in?"

Perrin stumbled downstairs. He halted at the door, one hand on the bolts, and the blood rushed in his ears.

An impatient tapping jarred his hand. "I'm freezing to death out here."

Perrin let the door swing back. She stood facing him, half-smiling. "You're a very cautious lighthouse-tender—or perhaps a woman-hater?"

Perrin searched her face, her eyes, the expression of her mouth. "Are you... real?"

She laughed, not at all offended. "Of course I'm real." She held out her hand. "Touch me." Perrin stared at her—the essence of night-flowers, soft silk, hot blood, sweetness, delightful fire. "Touch me," she repeated softly.

Perrin moved back uncertainly, and she came forward, into the lighthouse. "Can you call the shore?"

"No...my transceiver is out of order."

She turned him a quick firefly look. "When is your next relief boat?"

"Eleven weeks."

"Eleven weeks!" she sighed a soft shallow sigh.

Perrin moved back another half-step. "How did you know I was alone?"

She seemed confused. "I didn't know...Aren't lighthouse-keepers always alone?"

"No."

She came a step closer. "You don't seem pleased to see me. Are you...a hermit?"

"No," said Perrin in a husky voice. "Quite the reverse...But I can't quite get used to you. You're a miracle. Too good to be true. Just now I was wishing for someone...exactly like you. Exactly."

"And here I am."

Perrin moved uneasily. "What's your name?"

He knew what she would say before she spoke. "Sue."

"Sue what?" He tried to hold his mind vacant.

"Oh...just Sue. Isn't that enough?"

Perrin felt the skin of his face tighten. "Where is your home?"

She looked vaguely over her shoulder. Perrin held his mind blank, but the word came through.

"Hell."

Perrin's breath came hard and sharp.

"And what is Hell like?"

"It is...cold and dark."

Perrin stepped back. "Go away. Go away." His vision blurred; her face melted as if tears had come across his eyes.

"Where will I go?"

"Back where you came from."

"But—" forlornly "—there is nowhere but Maurnilam Var. And up here—" She stopped short, took a swift step forward, stood looking up into his face. He could feel the warmth of her body. "Are you afraid of me?"

Perrin wrenched his eyes from her face. "You're not real. You're something which takes the shape of my thoughts. Perhaps you killed Seguilo...I don't know what you are. But you're not real."

"Not real? Of course I'm real. Touch me. Feel my arm." Perrin backed away. She said passionately, "Here, a knife. If you are of a mind, cut me; you will see blood. Cut deeper...you will find bone."

"What would happen," said Perrin, "if I drove the knife into your heart?"

She said nothing, staring at him with big eyes.

"Why do you come here?" cried Perrin. She looked away, back toward the water.

"It's magic...darkness..." The words were a mumbled confusion; Perrin suddenly realized that the same words were in his own mind. Had she merely parrotted his thoughts during the entire conversation? "Then comes a slow pull," she said. "I drift, I crave the air, the moons bring me up...I do anything to hold my place in the air..."

"Speak your own words," said Perrin harshly. "I know you're not real—but where is Seguilo?"

"Seguilo?" She reached a hand behind her head, touched her hair, smiled sleepily at Perrin. Real or not, Perrin's pulse thudded in his ears. Real or not...

"I'm no dream," she said. "I'm real..." She came slowly toward Perrin, feeling his thoughts, face arch, ready.

Perrin said in a strangled gasp, "No, no. Go away. *Go away!*"

She stopped short, looked at him through eyes suddenly opaque. "Very well. I will go now—"

"Now! Forever!"

"—but perhaps you will call me back..."

She walked slowly through the door. Perrin ran to the window, watched the slim shape blur into the moonlight. She went to the edge of the shelf; here she paused. Perrin felt a sudden intolerable pang; what was he casting away? Real or not, she was what he wanted her to be; she was identical to reality...He leaned forward to call, "Come back...whatever you are..." He restrained himself. When he looked again she was gone...Why was she gone? Perrin pondered, looking across the moonlit sea. He had wanted her, but he no longer believed in her. He had believed in the shape called Seguilo; he had believed in the transceiver—and both had slavishly obeyed his expectations. So had the girl, and he had sent her away…Rightly, too, he told himself regretfully. Who knows what she might become when his back was turned…

When dawn finally came, it brought a new curtain of overcast. Blue-green Magda glimmered dull and sultry as a moldy orange. The water shone like oil…Movement in the west—a Panapa chieftain's private barge, walking across the horizon like a water-spider. Perrin vaulted the stairs to the light-room, swung the lumenifer full at the barge, dispatched an erratic series of flashes.

The barge moved on, jointed oars swinging rhythmically in and out of the water. A torn banner of fog drifted across the water. The barge became a dark, jerking shape, disappeared.

Perrin went to Seguilo's old transceiver, sat looking at it. He jumped to his feet, pulled the chassis out of the case, disassembled the entire circuit.

He saw scorched metal, wires fused into droplets, cracked ceramic. He pushed the tangle into a corner, went to stand by the window.

The sun was at the zenith, the sky was the color of green grapes. The sea heaved sluggishly, great amorphous swells rising and falling without apparent direction. Now was low tide; the shelf shouldered high up, the black rock showing naked and strange. The sea palpitated, up, down, up, down, sucking noisily at bits of sea-wrack.

Perrin descended the stairs. On his way down he looked in at the bathroom mirror, and his face stared back at him, pale, wide-eyed, cheeks hollow and lusterless. Perrin continued down the stairs, stepped out into the sunlight.

Carefully he walked out on the shelf, looked in a kind of fascination down over the edge. The heave of the swells distorted his vision; he could see little more than shadows and shifting fingers of light.

Step by step he wandered along the shelf. The sun leaned to the west. Perrin retreated up the rock.

At the lighthouse he seated himself in the doorway. Tonight the door remained barred. No inducement could persuade him to open up; the most entrancing visions would beseech him in vain. His thoughts went to Seguilo. What had Seguilo believed; what being had he fabricated out of his morbid fancy with the power and malice to drag him away?…It seemed that every man was victim to his own imaginings. Isel Rock was not the place for a fanciful man when the five moons rose together.

Tonight he would bar the door, he would bed himself down and sleep, secure both in the barrier of welded metal and his own unconsciousness.

The sun sank in a bank of heavy vapor. North, east, south flushed with violet; the west glowed lime and dark green, dulling quickly through tones of brown. Perrin entered the lighthouse, bolted the door, set the twin shafts of red and white circling the horizon.

He opened a dinner unit, ate listlessly. Outside was dark night, emptiness to all the horizons. As the tide rose, the water hissed and moaned across the shelf.

Perrin lay in his bed, but sleep was far away. Through the window came an electric glow, then up rose the five moons, shining through a high overcast as if wrapped in blue gauze.

Perrin heaved fitfully. There was nothing to fear, he was safe in the lighthouse. No human hands could force the door; it would take the strength of a mastodon, the talons of a rock choundril, the ferocity of a Maldene land-shark…

He elbowed himself up on his bunk…A sound from outside? He peered through the window, heart in his mouth. A tall shape, indistinct. As he watched, it slouched toward the lighthouse—as he knew it would.

"No, no," cried Perrin softly. He flung himself into his bunk, covered his head in the blankets. "It's only what I think up myself, it's not real…Go away," he whispered fiercely. "Go away." He listened. It must be near the door now. It would be lifting a heavy arm, the talons would glint in the moonlight.

"No, no," cried Perrin. "There's nothing there…" He held up his head and listened.

A rattle, a rasp at the door. A thud as a great mass tested the lock.

"Go away!" screamed Perrin. "You're not real!"

The door groaned, the bolts sagged.

Perrin stood at the head of the stairs, breathing heavily through his mouth. The door would slam back in another instant. He knew what he would see: a black shape tall and round as a pole, with eyes like coach-lamps. Perrin even knew the last sound his ears would hear—a terrible grinding discord…

The top bolt snapped, the door reeled. A huge black arm shoved inside. Perrin saw the talons gleam as the fingers reached for the bolt.

His eyes flickered around the lighthouse for a weapon…Only a wrench, a tableknife.

The bottom bolt shattered, the door twisted. Perrin stood staring, his mind congealed. A thought rose up from some hidden survival-node. Here, Perrin thought, was the single chance.

He ran back into his room. Behind him the door clattered, he heard heavy steps. He looked around the room. His shoe.

Thud! Up the stairs, and the lighthouse vibrated. Perrin's fancy explored the horrible, he knew what he would hear. And so came a voice—harsh, empty, but like another voice which had been sweet. "I told you I'd be back."

Thud—thud—up the stairs. Perrin took the shoe by the toe, swung, struck the side of his head.

Perrin recovered consciousness. He stumbled to the wall, supported himself. Presently he groped to his bunk, sat down.

Outside there was still dark night. Grunting, he looked out the window into the sky. The five moons hung far down in the west. Already Poidel ranged ahead, while Liad trailed behind.

Tomorrow night the five moons would rise apart.

Tomorrow night there would be no high tides, sucking and tremulous along the shelf.

Tomorrow night the moons would call up no yearning shapes from the streaming dark.

Eleven weeks to relief. Perrin gingerly felt the side of his head...Quite a respectable lump.

Afterword to "When the Five Moons Rise"

Norma was strongly supportive of my writing from the start, and we began to work together as a team. I cannot emphasize enough how hard Norma worked over the course of my career—certainly as hard as I have, if not more. In these early days, however, the writing wasn't enough to support us, and I continued to work day jobs...

My work was accomplished partly when I was at home and partly while I was traveling. At home, I always wrote longhand using four or five different fountain pens, each filled with a different color of ink. As I wrote and paused to think about something, I would begin doodling, making pretty designs on the page; then I would become absorbed with these designs, which I colored with the various inks. Most of this artwork, I regret to say, I later discarded. I think back with nostalgia about my fountain pens and colored inks.

While traveling, of course, I used only one fountain pen and plain black or blue ink. We carried with us a portable typewriter, and Norma would type my first draft, which I would edit; then she would type a second draft, to which I would make a few further emendations; at last she would type a final draft to be sent forth to my agent.

—Jack Vance

The Devil on Salvation Bluff

A few minutes before noon the sun took a lurch south and set.

Sister Mary tore the solar helmet from her fair head and threw it at the settee—a display that surprised and troubled her husband, Brother Raymond.

He clasped her quivering shoulders. "Now, dear, easy does it. A blow-up can't help us at all."

Tears were rolling down Sister Mary's cheeks. "As soon as we start from the house the sun drops out of sight! It happens every time!"

"Well—we know what patience is. There'll be another soon."

"It may be an hour! Or ten hours! And we've got our jobs to do!"

Brother Raymond went to the window, pulled aside the starched lace curtains, peered into the dusk. "We could start now, and get up the hill before night."

"'Night'?" cried Sister Mary. "What do you call this?"

Brother Raymond said stiffly, "I mean night by the Clock. *Real* night."

"The Clock..." Sister Mary sighed, sank into a chair. "If it weren't for the Clock we'd all be lunatics."

Brother Raymond, at the window, looked up toward Salvation Bluff, where the great clock bulked unseen. Mary joined him; they stood gazing through the dark. Presently Mary sighed. "I'm sorry, dear. But I get so upset."

Raymond patted her shoulder. "It's no joke living on Glory."

Mary shook her head decisively. "I shouldn't let myself go. There's the Colony to think of. Pioneers can't be weaklings."

They stood close, drawing comfort from each other.

"Look!" said Raymond. He pointed. "A fire, and up in Old Fleetville!"

In perplexity they watched the far spark.

"They're all supposed to be down in New Town," muttered Sister Mary. "Unless it's some kind of ceremony...The salt we gave them..."

Raymond, smiling sourly, spoke a fundamental postulate of life on Glory. "You can't tell anything about the Flits. They're liable to do most anything."

Mary uttered a truth even more fundamental. "*Anything* is liable to do anything."

"The Flits most liable of all...They've even taken to dying without our comfort and help!"

"We've done our best," said Mary. "It's not our fault!"—almost as if she feared that it was.

"No one could possibly blame us."

"Except the Inspector…The Flits were thriving before the Colony came."

"We haven't bothered them; we haven't encroached, or molested, or interfered. In fact we've knocked ourselves out to help them. And for thanks they tear down our fences and break open the canal and throw mud on our fresh paint!"

Sister Mary said in a low voice, "Sometimes I hate the Flits…Sometimes I hate Glory. Sometimes I hate the whole Colony."

Brother Raymond drew her close, patted the fair hair that she kept in a neat bun. "You'll feel better when one of the suns comes up. Shall we start?"

"It's dark," said Mary dubiously. "Glory is bad enough in the daytime."

Raymond shot his jaw forward, glanced up toward the Clock. "It *is* daytime. The Clock says it's daytime. That's Reality; we've got to cling to it! It's our link with truth and sanity!"

"Very well," said Mary, "we'll go."

Raymond kissed her cheek. "You're very brave, dear. You're a credit to the Colony."

Mary shook her head. "No, dear. I'm no better or braver than any of the others. We came out here to found homes and live the Truth. We knew there'd be hard work. So much depends on everybody; there's no room for weakness."

Raymond kissed her again, although she laughingly protested and turned her head. "I still think you're brave—and very sweet."

"Get the light," said Mary. "Get several lights. One never knows how long these—these insufferable darknesses will last."

They set off up the road, walking because in the Colony private power vehicles were considered a social evil. Ahead, unseen in the darkness, rose the Grand Montagne, the preserve of the Flits. They could feel the harsh bulk of the crags, just as behind them they could feel the neat fields, the fences, the roads of the Colony. They crossed the canal, which led the meandering river into a mesh of irrigation ditches. Raymond shone his light into the concrete bed. They stood looking in a silence more eloquent than curses.

"It's dry! They've broken the banks again."

"Why?" asked Mary. "*Why?* They don't use the river water!"

Raymond shrugged. "I guess they just don't like canals. Well," he sighed, "all we can do is the best we know how."

The road wound back and forth up the slope. They passed the lichen-covered hulk of a star-ship which five hundred years ago had crashed on Glory. "It seems impossible," said Mary. "The Flits were once men and women just like us."

"Not like *us*, dear," Raymond corrected gently.

Sister Mary shuddered. "The Flits and their goats! Sometimes it's hard to tell them apart."

A few minutes later Raymond fell into a mudhole, a bed of slime, with enough water-seep to make it sucking and dangerous. Floundering, panting, with Mary's desperate help, he regained solid ground, and stood shivering—angry, cold, wet.

"That blasted thing wasn't there yesterday!" He scraped slime from his face, his clothes. "It's these miserable things that makes life so trying."

"We'll get the better of it, dear." And she said fiercely: "We'll fight it, subdue it! Somehow we'll bring order to Glory!"

While they debated whether or not to proceed, Red Robundus belled up over the northwest horizon, and they were able to take stock of the situation. Brother Raymond's khaki puttees and his white shirt of course were filthy. Sister Mary's outfit was hardly cleaner.

Raymond said dejectedly, "I ought to go back to the bungalow for a change."

"Raymond—do we have time?"

"I'll look like a fool going up to the Flits like this."

"They'll never notice."

"How can they help?" snapped Raymond.

"We haven't time," said Mary decisively. "The Inspector's due any day, and the Flits are dying like flies. They'll say it's our fault—and that's the end of Gospel Colony." After a pause she said carefully, "Not that we wouldn't help the Flits in any event."

"I still think I'd make a better impression in clean clothes," said Raymond dubiously.

"Pooh! A fig they care for clean clothes, the ridiculous way they scamper around."

"I suppose you're right."

A small yellow-green sun appeared over the southwest horizon. "Here comes Urban...If it isn't dark as pitch we get three or four suns at once!"

"Sunlight makes the crops grow," Mary told him sweetly.

They climbed half an hour, then, stopping to catch their breath, turned to look across the valley to the colony they loved so well. Seventy-two thousand souls on a checkerboard green plain, rows of neat white houses, painted and scrubbed, with snowy curtains behind glistening glass; lawns and flower gardens full of tulips; vegetable gardens full of cabbages, kale and squash.

Raymond looked up at the sky. "It's going to rain."

Mary asked, "How do you know?"

"Remember the drenching we had last time Urban and Robundus were both in the west?"

Mary shook her head. "That doesn't mean anything."

"Something's got to mean something. That's the law of our universe—the basis for all our thinking!"

A gust of wind howled down from the ridges, carrying great curls and feathers of dust. They swirled with complicated colors, films, shades, in the opposing lights of yellow-green Urban and Red Robundus.

"There's your rain," shouted Mary over the roar of the wind. Raymond pressed on up the road. Presently the wind died.

Mary said, "I believe in rain or anything else on Glory when I see it."

"We don't have enough facts," insisted Raymond. "There's nothing magic in unpredictability."

"It's just—unpredictable." She looked back along the face of the Grand Montagne. "Thank God for the Clock—something that's dependable."

The road wandered up the hill, through stands of horny spile, banks of gray scrub and purple thorn. Sometimes there was no road; then they had to cast ahead like surveyors; sometimes the road stopped at a bank or at a blank wall, continuing on a level ten feet above or below. These were minor inconveniences which they overcame as a matter of course. Only when Robundus drifted south and Urban ducked north did they become anxious.

"It wouldn't be conceivable that a sun should set at seven in the evening," said Mary. "That would be too normal, too matter-of-fact."

At seven-fifteen both suns set. There would be ten minutes of magnificent sunset, another fifteen minutes of twilight, then night of indeterminate extent.

They missed the sunset because of an earthquake. A tumble of stones came pelting across the road; they took refuge under a jut of granite while boulders clattered into the road and spun on down the mountainside.

The shower of rocks passed, except for pebbles bouncing down as an afterthought. "Is that all?" Mary asked in a husky whisper.

"Sounds like it."

"I'm thirsty."

Raymond handed her the canteen; she drank.

"How much further to Fleetville?"

"Old Fleetville or New Town?"

"I don't care," she said wearily. "Either one."

Raymond hesitated. "As a matter of fact, I don't know the distance to either."

"Well, we can't stay here all night."

"It's day coming up," said Raymond as the white dwarf Maude began to silver the sky to the northeast.

"It's night," Mary declared in quiet desperation. "The Clock says it's night; I don't care if every sun in the galaxy is shining, including Home Sun. As long as the Clock says it's night, it's night!"

"We can see the road anyway…New Town is just over this ridge; I recognize that big spile. It was here last time I came."

Of the two, Raymond was the more surprised to find New Town where he placed it. They trudged into the village. "Things are awful quiet."

There were three dozen huts, built of concrete and good clear glass, each with filtered water, a shower, wash-tub and toilet. To suit Flit prejudices the roofs were thatched with thorn, and there were no interior partitions. The huts were all empty.

Mary looked into a hut. "Mmmph—horrid!" She puckered her nose at Raymond. "The smell!"

The windows of the second hut were innocent of glass. Raymond's face was grim and angry. "I packed that glass up here on my blistered back! And that's how they thank us."

"I don't care whether they thank us or not," said Mary. "I'm worried about the Inspector. He'll blame us for—" she gestured "—this filth. After all it's supposed to be our responsibility."

Seething with indignation Raymond surveyed the village. He recalled the day New Town had been completed—a model village, thirty-six spotless huts, hardly inferior to the bungalows of the Colony. Arch-Deacon Burnette had voiced the blessing; the volunteer workers knelt to pray in the central compound. Fifty or sixty Flits had come down from the ridges to watch—a wide-eyed ragged bunch: the men all gristle and unkempt hair; the women sly, plump and disposed to promiscuity, or so the colonists believed.

After the invocation Arch-Deacon Burnette had presented the chief of the tribe a large key of gilded plywood. "In your custody, Chief—the future and welfare of your people! Guard it—cherish it!"

The chief stood almost seven feet tall; he was lean as a pike, his profile cut in and out, sharp and hard as a turtle's. He wore greasy black rags and carried a long staff, upholstered with goat-hide. Alone in the tribe he spoke the language of the colonists, with a good accent that always came as a shock. "They are no concern of mine," he said in a casual, hoarse voice. "They do as they like. That's the best way."

Arch-Deacon Burnette had encountered this attitude before. A large-minded man, he felt no indignation, but rather sought to argue away what he considered an irrational attitude. "Don't you want to be civilized? Don't you want to worship God, to live clean, healthy lives?"

"No."

The Arch-Deacon grinned. "Well, we'll help anyway, as much as we can. We can teach you to read, to cipher; we can cure your disease. Of course you must keep clean and you must adopt regular habits—because that's what civilization means."

The chief grunted. "You don't even know how to herd goats."

"We are not missionaries," Arch-Deacon Burnette continued, "but when you choose to learn the Truth, we'll be ready to help you."

"Mmph-mmph—where do you profit by this?"

The Arch-Deacon smiled. "We don't. You are fellow-humans; we are bound to help you."

The chief turned, called to the tribe; they fled up the rocks pell-mell, climbing like desperate wraiths, hair waving, goat-skins flapping.

"What's this? What's this?" cried the Arch-Deacon. "Come back here," he called to the chief, who was on his way to join the tribe.

The chief called down from a crag. "You are all crazy people."

"No, no," exclaimed the Arch-Deacon, and it was a magnificent scene, stark as a stage-set: the white-haired Arch-Deacon calling up to the wild chief with his wild tribe behind him; a saint commanding satyrs, all in the shifting light of three suns.

Somehow he coaxed the chief back down to New Town. Old Fleetville lay half a mile farther up, in a saddle funnelling all the winds and clouds of the Grand Montagne, until even the goats clung with difficulty to the rocks. It was cold, dank, dreary. The Arch-Deacon hammered home each of Old Fleetville's drawbacks. The chief insisted he preferred it to New Town.

Fifty pounds of salt made the difference, with the Arch-Deacon compromising his principles over the use of bribes. About sixty of the tribe moved into the new huts with an air of amused detachment, as if the Arch-Deacon had asked them to play a foolish game.

The Arch-Deacon called another blessing upon the village; the colonists knelt; the Flits watched curiously from the doors and windows of their new homes. Another twenty or thirty bounded down from the crags with a herd of goats which they quartered in the little chapel. Arch-Deacon Burnette's smile became fixed and painful, but to his credit he did nothing to interfere.

After a while the colonists filed back down into the valley. They had done the best they could, but they were not sure exactly what it was they had done.

Two months later New Town was deserted. Brother Raymond and Sister Mary Dunton walked through the village; and the huts showed dark windows and gaping doorways.

"Where have they gone?" asked Mary in a hushed voice.

"They're all mad," said Raymond. "Stark staring mad." He went to the chapel, pushed his head through the door. His knuckles shone suddenly white where they gripped the door frame.

"What's the trouble?" Mary asked anxiously.

Raymond held her back. "Corpses...There's—ten, twelve, maybe fifteen bodies in there."

"Raymond!" They looked at each other. "How? Why?"

Raymond shook his head. With one mind they turned, looked up the hill toward Old Fleetville.

"I guess it's up to us to find out."

"But this is—is such a nice place," Mary burst out. "They're—they're *beasts!* They should *love* it here!" She turned away, looked out over the valley, so that Raymond wouldn't see her tears. New Town had meant so much to her; with her own hands she had white-washed rocks and laid neat borders around each of the huts. The borders had been kicked askew, and her feelings were hurt. "Let the Flits live as they like, dirty, shiftless creatures. They're irresponsible," she told Raymond, "just completely *irresponsible!*"

Raymond nodded. "Let's go on up, Mary; we have our duty."

Mary wiped her eyes. "I suppose they're God's creatures, but I can't see why they should be." She glanced at Raymond. "And don't tell me about God moving in a mysterious way."

"Okay," said Raymond. They started to clamber up over the rocks, up toward Old Fleetville. The valley became smaller and smaller below. Maude swung up to the zenith and seemed to hang there.

They paused for breath. Mary mopped her brow. "Am I crazy, or is Maude getting larger?"

Raymond looked. "Maybe it is swelling a little."

"It's either a nova or we're falling into it!"

"I suppose anything could happen in this system," sighed Raymond. "If there's any regularity in Glory's orbit it's defied analysis."

"We might very easily fall into one of the suns," said Mary thoughtfully.

Raymond shrugged. "The system's been milling around for quite a few million years. That's our best guarantee."

"Our only guarantee." She clenched her fists. "If there were only some certainty somewhere—something you could look at and say, this is immutable, this is changeless, this is something you can count on. But there's nothing! It's enough to drive a person crazy!"

Raymond put on a glassy smile. "Don't, dear. The Colony's got too much trouble like that already."

Mary sobered instantly. "Sorry...I'm sorry, Raymond. Truly."

"It's got me worried," said Raymond. "I was talking to Director Birch at the Rest Home yesterday."

"How many now?"

"Almost three thousand. More coming in every day." He sighed. "There's something about Glory that grinds at a person's nerves—no question about it."

Mary took a deep breath, pressed Raymond's hand. "We'll fight it, darling, and beat it! Things will fall into routine; we'll straighten everything out."

Raymond bowed his head. "With the Lord's help."

"There goes Maude," said Mary. "We'd better get up to Old Fleetville while there's still light."

A few minutes later they met a dozen goats, herded by as many scraggly children. Some wore rags; some wore goat-skin clothes; others ran around naked, and the wind blew on their washboard ribs.

On the other side of the trail they met another herd of goats—perhaps a hundred, with one urchin in attendance.

"That's the Flit way," said Raymond, "twelve kids herd twelve goats and one kid herds a hundred."

"They're surely victims of some mental disease...Is insanity hereditary?"

"That's a moot point...I can smell Old Fleetville."

Maude left the sky at an angle which promised a long twilight. With aching legs Raymond and Mary plodded up into the village. Behind came the goats and the children, mingled without discrimination.

Mary said in a disgusted voice, "They leave New Town—pretty, clean New Town—to move up into this filth."

"Don't step on that goat!" Raymond guided her past the gnawed carcass which lay on the trail. Mary bit her lip.

They found the chief sitting on a rock, staring into the air. He greeted them with neither surprise nor pleasure. A group of children were building a pyre of brush and dry spile.

"What's going on?" asked Raymond with forced cheer. "A feast? A dance?"

"Four men, two women. They go crazy, they die. We burn them."

Mary looked at the pyre. "I didn't know you cremated your dead."

"This time we burn them." He reached out, touched Mary's glossy golden hair. "You be my wife for a while."

Mary stepped back, and said in a quivering voice, "No, thanks. I'm married to Raymond."

"All the time?"

"All the time."

The chief shook his head. "You are crazy. Pretty soon you die."

Raymond said sternly, "Why did you break the canal? Ten times we've fixed it; ten times the Flits came down in the dark and pulled down the banks."

The chief deliberated. "The canal is crazy."

"It's not crazy. It helps irrigate, helps the farmers."

"It goes too much the same."

"You mean, it's straight?"

"Straight? Straight? What word is that?"

"In *one* line—in one direction."

The chief rocked back and forth. "Look—mountain. Straight?"

"No, of course not."

"Sun—straight?"

"Look here—"

"My leg." The chief extended his left leg, knobby and covered with hair. "Straight?"

"No," sighed Raymond. "Your leg is not straight."

"Then why make canal straight? Crazy." He sat back. The topic was disposed of. "Why do you come?"

"Well," said Raymond. "Too many Flits die. We want to help you."

"That's all right. It's not me, not you."

"We don't want you to die. Why don't you live in New Town?"

"Flits get crazy, jump off the rocks." He rose to his feet. "Come along, there's food."

Mastering their repugnance, Raymond and Mary nibbled on bits of grilled goat. Without ceremony, four bodies were tossed into the fire. Some of the Flits began to dance.

Mary nudged Raymond. "You can understand a culture by the pattern of its dances. Watch."

Raymond watched. "I don't see any pattern. Some take a couple hops, sit down; others run in circles; some just flap their arms."

Mary whispered, "They're all crazy. Crazy as sandpipers."

Raymond nodded. "I believe you."

Rain began to fall. Red Robundus burnt the eastern sky but never troubled to come up. The rain became hail. Mary and Raymond went into a hut. Several men and women joined them, and with nothing better to do, noisily began loveplay.

Mary whispered in agony. "They're going to do it right in front of us! They don't have any shame!"

Raymond said grimly, "I'm not going out in that rain. They can do anything they want."

Mary cuffed one of the men who sought to remove her shirt; he jumped back. "Just like dogs!" she gasped.

"No repressions there," said Raymond apathetically. "Repressions mean psychoses."

"Then I'm psychotic," sniffed Mary, "because I have repressions!"

"I have too."

The hail stopped; the wind blew the clouds through the notch; the sky was clear. Raymond and Mary left the hut with relief.

The pyre was drenched; four charred bodies lay in the ashes; no one heeded them.

Raymond said thoughtfully, "It's on the tip of my tongue—the verge of my mind…"

"What?"

"The solution to this whole Flit mess."

"Well?"

"It's something like this: The Flits are crazy, irrational, irresponsible."

"Agreed."

"The Inspector's coming. We've got to demonstrate that the Colony poses no threat to the aborigines—the Flits, in this case."

"We can't force the Flits to improve their living standards."

"No. But if we could make them sane; if we could even make a start against their mass psychosis…"

Mary looked rather numb. "It sounds like a terrible job."

Raymond shook his head. "Use rigorous thinking, dear. It's a real problem: a group of aborigines too psychotic to keep themselves alive. But we've *got* to keep them alive. The solution: remove the psychoses."

"You make it sound sensible, but how in heaven's name shall we begin?"

The chief came spindle-legged down from the rocks, chewing at a bit of goat-intestine. "We've got to begin with the chief," said Raymond.

"That's like belling the cat."

"Salt," said Raymond. "He'd skin his grandmother for salt."

Raymond approached the chief, who seemed surprised to find him still in the village. Mary watched from the background.

Raymond argued; the chief looked first shocked, then sullen. Raymond expounded, expostulated. He made his telling point: salt—as much as the chief could carry back up the hill. The chief stared down at Raymond from his seven feet, threw up his hands, walked away, sat down on a rock, chewed at the length of gut.

Raymond rejoined Mary. "He's coming."

Director Birch used his heartiest manner toward the chief. "We're honored! It's not often we have visitors so distinguished. We'll have you right in no time!"

The chief had been scratching aimless curves in the ground with his staff. He asked Raymond mildly, "When do I get the salt?"

"Pretty soon now. First you've got to go with Director Birch."

"Come along," said Director Birch. "We'll have a nice ride."

The chief turned and strode off toward the Grand Montagne. "No, no!" cried Raymond. "Come back here!" The chief lengthened his stride.

Raymond ran forward, tackled the knobby knees. The chief fell like a loose sack of garden tools. Director Birch administered a shot of sedative, and presently the shambling, dull-eyed chief was secure inside the ambulance.

Brother Raymond and Sister Mary watched the ambulance trundle down the road. Thick dust roiled up, hung in the green sunlight. The shadows seemed tinged with bluish-purple.

Mary said in a trembling voice, "I do so hope we're doing the right thing… The poor chief looked so—*pathetic*. Like one of his own goats trussed up for slaughter."

Raymond said, "We can only do what we think best, dear."

"But *is* it the best?"

The ambulance had disappeared; the dust had settled. Over the Grand Montagne lightning flickered from a black-and-green thunderhead. Faro shone like a cat's-eye at the zenith. The Clock—the staunch Clock, the good, sane Clock—said twelve noon.

"The best," said Mary thoughtfully. "A relative word…"

Raymond said, "If we clear up the Flit psychoses—if we can teach them clean, orderly lives—surely it's for the best." And he added after a moment, "Certainly it's best for the Colony."

Mary sighed. "I suppose so. But the chief looked so stricken."

"We'll go see him tomorrow," said Raymond. "Right now, sleep!"

When Raymond and Mary awoke, a pink glow seeped through the drawn shades: Robundus, possibly with Maude. "Look at the clock," yawned Mary. "Is it day or night?"

Raymond raised up on his elbow. Their clock was built into the wall, a replica of the Clock on Salvation Bluff, and guided by radio pulses from the central movement. "It's six in the afternoon—ten after."

They rose and dressed in their neat puttees and white shirts. They ate in the meticulous kitchenette, then Raymond telephoned the Rest Home.

Director Birch's voice came crisp from the sound box. "God help you, Brother Raymond."

"God help you, Director. How's the chief?"

Director Birch hesitated. "We've had to keep him under sedation. He's got pretty deep-seated troubles."

"Can you help him? It's important."

"All we can do is try. We'll have a go at him tonight."

"Perhaps we'd better be there," said Mary.

"If you like…Eight o'clock?"

"Good."

The Rest Home was a long, low building on the outskirts of Glory City. New wings had recently been added; a set of temporary barracks could also be seen to the rear.

Director Birch greeted them with a harassed expression.

"We're so pressed for room and time; is this Flit so terribly important?"

Raymond gave him assurance that the chief's sanity was a matter of grave concern for everyone.

Director Birch threw up his hands. "Colonists are clamoring for therapy. They'll have to wait, I suppose."

Mary asked soberly, "There's still—the trouble?"

"The Home was built with five hundred beds," said Director Birch. "We've got thirty-six hundred patients now; not to mention the eighteen hundred colonists we've evacuated back to Earth."

"Surely things are getting better?" asked Raymond. "The Colony's over the hump; there's no need for anxiety."

"Anxiety doesn't seem to be the trouble."

"What *is* the trouble?"

"New environment, I suppose. We're Earth-type people; the surroundings are strange."

"But they're not really!" argued Mary. "We've made this place the exact replica of an Earth community. One of the nicer sort. There are Earth houses and Earth flowers and Earth trees."

"Where is the chief?" asked Brother Raymond.

"Well—right now, in the maximum-security ward."

"Is he violent?"

"Not unfriendly. He just wants to get out. Destructive! I've never seen anything like it!"

"Have you any ideas—even preliminary?"

Director Birch shook his head grimly. "We're still trying to classify him. Look." He handed Raymond a report. "That's his zone survey."

"Intelligence zero." Raymond looked up. "I *know* he's not that stupid."

"You'd hardly think so. It's a vague referent, actually. We can't use the usual tests on him—thematic perception and the like; they're weighted for our own cultural background. But these tests here—" he tapped the report "—they're basic; we use them on animals—fitting pegs into holes; matching up colors; detecting discordant patterns; threading mazes."

"And the chief?"

Director Birch sadly shook his head. "If it were possible to have a negative score, he'd have it."

"How so?"

"Well, for instance, instead of matching a small round peg into a small round hole, first he broke the star-shaped peg and forced it in sideways, and then he broke the board."

"But why?"

Mary said, "Let's go see him."

"He's safe, isn't he?" Raymond asked Birch.

"Oh, entirely."

The chief was confined in a pleasant room exactly ten feet on a side. He had a white bed, white sheets, gray coverlet. The ceiling was restful green, the floor was quiet gray.

"My!" said Mary brightly, "you've been busy!"

"Yes," said Director Birch between clenched teeth. "He's been busy."

The bedclothes were shredded, the bed lay on its side in the middle of the room, the walls were befouled. The chief sat on the doubled mattress.

Director Birch said sternly, "Why do you make this mess? It's really not clever, you know!"

"You keep me here," spat the chief. "I fix the way I like it. In your house you fix the way *you* like." He looked at Raymond and Mary. "How much longer?"

"In just a little while," said Mary. "We're trying to help you."

"Crazy talk, everybody crazy." The chief was losing his good accent; his words rasped with fricatives and glottals. "Why you bring me here?"

"It'll be just for a day or two," said Mary soothingly, "then you get salt—lots of it."

"Day—that's while the sun is up."

"No," said Brother Raymond. "See this thing?" He pointed to the clock in the wall. "When this hand goes around twice—that's a day."

The chief smiled cynically.

"We guide our lives by this," said Raymond. "It helps us."

"Just like the big Clock on Salvation Bluff," said Mary.

"Big Devil," the chief said earnestly. "You good people; you all crazy. Come to Fleetville. I help you; lots of good goat. We throw rocks down at Big Devil."

"No," said Mary quietly, "that would never do. Now you try your best to do what the doctor says. This mess for instance—it's very bad."

The chief took his head in his hands. "You let me go. You keep salt; I go home."

"Come," said Director Birch kindly. "We won't hurt you." He looked at the clock. "It's time for your first therapy."

Two orderlies were required to conduct the chief to the laboratory. He was placed in a padded chair, and his arms and legs were constricted so that he might not harm himself. He set up a terrible, hoarse cry. "The Devil, the Big Devil—it comes down to look at my life…"

Director Birch said to the orderly, "Cover over the wall clock; it disturbs the patient."

"Just lie still," said Mary. "We're trying to help you—you and your whole tribe."

The orderly administered a shot of D-beta hypnidine. The chief relaxed, his eyes open, vacant, his skinny chest heaving.

Director Birch said in a low tone to Mary and Raymond, "He's now entirely suggestible—so be very quiet; don't make a sound."

Mary and Raymond eased themselves into chairs at the side of the room.

"Hello, Chief," said Director Birch.

"Hello."

"Are you comfortable?"

"Too much shine—too much white."

The orderly dimmed the lights.

"Better?"

"That's better."

"Do you have any troubles?"

"Goats hurt their feet, stay up in the hills. Crazy people down the valley; they won't go away."

"How do you mean 'crazy'?"

The chief was silent. Director Birch said in a whisper to Mary and Raymond, "By analyzing his concept of sanity we get a clue to his own derangement."

The chief lay quiet. Director Birch said in his soothing voice, "Suppose you tell us about your own life."

The chief spoke readily. "Ah, that's good. I'm chief. I understand all talks; nobody else knows about things."

"A good life, eh?"

"Sure, everything good." He spoke on, in disjointed phrases, in words sometimes unintelligible, but the picture of his life came clear. "Everything go easy—no bother, no trouble—everything good. When it rain, fire feels good. When suns shine hot, then wind blow, feels good. Lots of goats, everybody eat."

"Don't you have troubles, worries?"

"Sure. Crazy people live in valley. They make town: New Town. No good. Straight—straight—straight. No good. Crazy. That's bad. We get lots of salt, but we leave New Town, run up hill to old place."

"You don't like the people in the valley?"

"They good people, they all crazy. Big Devil bring them to valley. Big Devil watch all time. Pretty soon all go tick-tick-tick—like Big Devil."

Director Birch turned to Raymond and Mary, his face in a puzzled frown. "This isn't going so good. He's too assured, too forthright."

Raymond said guardedly, "Can you cure him?"

"Before I can cure a psychosis," said Director Birch, "I have to locate it. So far I don't seem to be even warm."

"It's not sane to die off like flies," whispered Mary. "And that's what the Flits are doing."

The Director returned to the chief. "Why do your people die, Chief? Why do they die in New Town?"

The chief said in a hoarse voice, "They look down. No pretty scenery. Crazy cut-up. No river. Straight water. It hurts the eyes; we open canal, make good river…Huts all same. Go crazy looking at all same. People go crazy; we kill 'em."

Director Birch said, "I think that's all we'd better do just now till we study the case a little more closely."

"Yes," said Brother Raymond in a troubled voice. "We've got to think this over."

They left the Rest Home through the main reception hall. The benches bulged with applicants for admission and their relatives, with custodian officers and persons in their care. Outside the sky was wadded with overcast. Sallow light indicated Urban somewhere in the sky. Rain spattered in the dust, big, syrupy drops.

Brother Raymond and Sister Mary waited for the bus at the curve of the traffic circle.

"There's something wrong," said Brother Raymond in a bleak voice. "Something very very wrong."

"And I'm not so sure it isn't in us." Sister Mary looked around the landscape, across the young orchards, up Sarah Gulvin Avenue into the center of Glory City.

"A strange planet is always a battle," said Brother Raymond. "We've got to bear faith, trust in God—and fight!"

Mary clutched his arm. He turned. "What's the trouble?"

"I saw—or thought I saw—someone running through the bushes."

Raymond craned his neck. "I don't see anybody."

"I thought it looked like the chief."

"Your imagination, dear."

They boarded the bus, and presently were secure in their white-walled, flower-gardened home.

The communicator sounded. It was Director Birch. His voice was troubled. "I don't want to worry you, but the chief got loose. He's off the premises—where we don't know."

Mary said under her breath, "I knew, I knew!"

Raymond said soberly, "You don't think there's any danger?"

"No. His pattern isn't violent. But I'd lock my door anyway."

"Thanks for calling, Director."

"Not at all, Brother Raymond."

There was a moment's silence. "What now?" asked Mary.

"I'll lock the doors, and then we'll get a good night's sleep."

Sometime in the night Mary woke up with a start. Brother Raymond rolled over on his side. "What's the trouble?"

"I don't know," said Mary. "What time is it?"

Raymond consulted the wall clock. "Five minutes to one."

Sister Mary lay still.

"Did you hear something?" Raymond asked.

"No. I just had a—twinge. Something's wrong, Raymond!"

He pulled her close, cradled her fair head in the hollow of his neck. "All we can do is our best, dear, and pray that it's God's will."

They fell into a fitful doze, tossing and turning. Raymond got up to go to the bathroom. Outside was night—a dark sky except for a rosy glow at the north horizon. Red Robundus wandered somewhere below.

Raymond shuffled sleepily back to bed.

"What's the time, dear?" came Mary's voice.

Raymond peered at the clock. "Five minutes to one."

He got into bed. Mary's body was rigid. "Did you say—five minutes to one?"

"Why yes," said Raymond. A few seconds later he climbed out of bed, went into the kitchen. "It says five minutes to one in here, too. I'll call the Clock and have them send out a pulse."

He went to the communicator, pressed buttons. No response.

"They don't answer."

Mary was at his elbow. "Try again."

Raymond pressed out the number. "That's strange."

"Call Information," said Mary.

Raymond pressed for Information. Before he could frame a question, a crisp voice said, "The Great Clock is momentarily out of order. Please have patience. The Great Clock is out of order."

Raymond thought he recognized the voice. He punched the visual button. The voice said, "God keep you, Brother Raymond."

"God keep you, Brother Ramsdell…What in the world has gone wrong?"

"It's one of your protégés, Raymond. One of the Flits—raving mad. He rolled boulders down on the Clock."

"Did he—did he—"

"He started a landslide. We don't have any more Clock."

Inspector Coble found no one to meet him at the Glory City space-port. He peered up and down the tarmac; he was alone. A scrap of paper blew across the far end of the field; nothing else moved.

Odd, thought Inspector Coble. A committee had always been on hand to welcome him, with a program that was flattering but rather wearing. First to the Arch-Deacon's bungalow for a banquet, cheerful speeches and progress reports, then services in the central chapel, and finally a punctilious escort to the foot of the Grand Montagne.

Excellent people, by Inspector Coble's lights, but too painfully honest and fanatical to be interesting.

He left instructions with the two men who crewed the official ship, and set off on foot toward Glory City. Red Robundus was high, but sinking toward the east; he looked toward Salvation Bluff to check local time. A clump of smoky lace-veils blocked his view.

Inspector Coble, striding briskly along the road, suddenly jerked to a halt. He raised his head as if testing the air, looked about him in a complete circle. He frowned, moved slowly on.

The colonists had been making changes, he thought. Exactly what and how, he could not instantly determine: the fence there—a section had been torn out. Weeds were prospering in the ditch beside the road. Examining the ditch, he sensed movement in the harp-grass behind, the sound of young voices. Curiosity aroused, Coble jumped the ditch, parted the harp-grass.

A boy and girl of sixteen or so were wading in a shallow pond; the girl held three limp water-flowers, the boy was kissing her. They turned up startled faces; Inspector Coble withdrew.

Back on the road he looked up and down. Where in thunder was everybody? The fields—empty. Nobody working. Inspector Coble shrugged, continued.

He passed the Rest Home, and looked at it curiously. It seemed considerably larger than he remembered it: a pair of wings, some temporary barracks had been added. He noticed that the gravel of the driveway was hardly as neat as it might be. The ambulance drawn up to the side was dusty. The place looked vaguely run down. The inspector for the second time stopped dead in his tracks. Music? From the Rest Home?

He turned down the driveway, approached. The music grew louder. Inspector Coble slowly pushed through the front door. In the reception hall were eight or ten people—they wore bizarre costumes: feathers, fronds of dyed grass, fantastic necklaces of glass and metal. The music sounded loud from the auditorium, a kind of wild jig.

"Inspector!" cried a pretty woman with fair hair. "Inspector Coble! You've arrived!"

Inspector Coble peered into her face. She wore a kind of patchwork jacket sewn with small iron bells. "It's—it's Sister Mary Dunton, isn't it?"

"Of course! You've arrived at a wonderful time! We're having a carnival ball—costumes and everything!"

Brother Raymond clapped the inspector heartily on the back. "Glad to see you, old man! Have some cider—it's the early press."

Inspector Coble backed away. "No, no thanks." He cleared his throat. "I'll be off on my rounds…and perhaps drop in on you later."

Inspector Coble proceeded to the Grand Montagne. He noted that a number of the bungalows had been painted bright shades of green, blue, yellow; that fences in many cases had been pulled down, that gardens looked rather rank and wild.

He climbed the road to Old Fleetville, where he interviewed the chief. The Flits apparently were not being exploited, suborned, cheated, sickened, enslaved, forcibly proselyted or systematically irritated. The chief seemed in a good humor.

"I kill the Big Devil," he told Inspector Coble. "Things go better now."

Inspector Coble planned to slip quietly to the space-port and depart, but Brother Raymond Dunton hailed him as he passed their bungalow.

"Had your breakfast, Inspector?"

"Dinner, darling!" came Sister Mary's voice from within. "Urban just went down."

"But Maude just came up."

"Bacon and eggs anyway, Inspector!"

The inspector was tired; he smelled hot coffee. "Thanks," he said, "don't mind if I do."

After the bacon and eggs, over the second cup of coffee, the inspector said cautiously, "You're looking well, you two."

Sister Mary looked especially pretty with her fair hair loose.

"Never felt better," said Brother Raymond. "It's a matter of rhythm, Inspector."

The inspector blinked. "Rhythm, eh?"

"More precisely," said Sister Mary, "a lack of rhythm."

"It all started," said Brother Raymond, "when we lost our Clock."

Inspector Coble gradually pieced out the story. Three weeks later, back at Surge City he put it in his own words to Inspector Keefer.

"They'd been wasting half their energies holding onto—well, call it a false reality. They were all afraid of the new planet. They pretended it was Earth—tried to whip it, beat it, and just plain hypnotize it into being Earth. Naturally they were licked before they started. Glory is about as completely random a world as you could find. The poor devils were trying to impose Earth rhythm and Earth routine upon this magnificent disorder; this monumental chaos!"

"No wonder they all went nuts."

Inspector Coble nodded. "At first, after the Clock went out, they thought they were goners. Committed their souls to God and just about gave up. A couple of days passed, I guess—and to their surprise they found they were still alive. In fact, even enjoying life. Sleeping when it got dark, working when the sun shone."

"Sounds like a good place to retire," said Inspector Keefer. "How's the fishing out there on Glory?"

"Not so good. But the goat-herding is great!"

Afterword to "The Devil on Salvation Bluff"

Who has been influential upon my development as a writer? Who indeed? I don't know. To name some names, I admire C. L. Moore from the old *Weird Tales* magazine. As a boy I was quite affected by the prose of Clark Ashton Smith. I revere P. G. Wodehouse. I also admire the works of Jeffery Farnol, who wrote splendid adventure books but who is today unknown except to connoisseurs of swashbuckler fiction. There are perhaps others—Edgar Rice Burroughs and his wonderful Barsoomian atmosphere; Lord Dunsany and his delicate fairylands; Baum's *Oz* books, which regrettably are of less and less interest to today's children.

—Jack Vance

Where Hesperus Falls

My servants will not allow me to kill myself. I have sought self-extinction by every method, from throat-cutting to the intricate routines of Yoga, but so far they have thwarted my most ingenious efforts.

I grow ever more annoyed. What is more personal, more truly one's own, than a man's own life? It is his basic possession, to retain or relinquish as he sees fit. If they continue to frustrate me, someone other than myself will suffer. I guarantee this.

My name is Henry Revere. My appearance is not remarkable, my intelligence is hardly noteworthy, and my emotions run evenly. I live in a house of synthetic shell, decorated with wood and jade, and surrounded by a pleasant garden. The view to one side is the ocean, the other, a valley sprinkled with houses similar to my own. I am by no means a prisoner, although my servants supervise me with the most minute care. Their first concern is to prevent my suicide, just as mine is to achieve it.

It is a game in which they have all the advantages—a detailed knowledge of my psychology, corridors behind the walls from which they can observe me, and a host of technical devices. They are men of my own race, in fact my own blood. But they are immeasurably more subtle than I.

My latest attempt was clever enough—although I had tried it before without success. I bit deeply into my tongue and thought to infect the cut with a pinch of garden loam. The servants either noticed me placing the soil in my mouth or observed the tension of my jaw.

They acted without warning. I stood on the terrace, hoping the soreness in my mouth might go undetected. Then, without conscious hiatus, I found myself reclining on a pallet, the dirt removed, the wound healed. They had used a thought-damping ray to anaesthetize me, and their sure medical techniques, aided by my almost invulnerable constitution, defeated the scheme.

As usual, I concealed my annoyance and went to my study. This is a room I have designed to my own taste, as far as possible from the complex curvilinear style which expresses the spirit of the age.

Almost immediately the person in charge of the household entered the room. I call him Dr. Jones because I cannot pronounce his name. He is taller than I, slender and fine-boned. His features are small, beautifully shaped, except for his chin which to my mind is too sharp and long, although I understand that such a chin is a contemporary criterion of beauty. His eyes are very large, slightly protuberant; his skin is clean of hair, by reason both of the racial tendency toward hairlessness, and the depilation which every baby undergoes upon birth.

Dr. Jones' clothes are vastly fanciful. He wears a body mantle of green film and a dozen vari-colored disks which spin slowly around his body like an axis. The symbolism of these disks, with their various colors, patterns, and directions of spin, are discussed in a chapter of my *History of Man*—so I will not be discursive here. The disks serve also as gravity deflectors, and are used commonly in personal flight.

Dr. Jones made me a polite salute, and seated himself upon an invisible cushion of anti-gravity. He spoke in the contemporary speech, which I could understand well enough, but whose nasal trills, gutturals, sibilants and indescribable fricatives, I could never articulate.

"Well, Henry Revere, how goes it?" he asked.

In my pidgin-speech I made a non-committal reply.

"I understand," said Dr. Jones, "that once again you undertook to deprive us of your company."

I nodded. "As usual I failed," I said.

Dr. Jones smiled slightly. The race had evolved away from laughter, which, as I understand, originated in the cave-man's bellow of relief at the successful clubbing of an adversary.

"You are self-centered," Dr. Jones told me. "You consider only your own pleasure."

"My life is my own. If I want to end it, you do great wrong in stopping me."

Dr. Jones shook his head. "But you are not your own property. You are the ward of the race. How much better if you accepted this fact!"

"I can't agree," I told him.

"It is necessary that you so adjust yourself." He studied me ruminatively. "You are something over ninety-six thousand years old. In my tenure at this house you have attempted suicide no less than a hundred times. No method has been either too crude or too painstaking."

He paused to watch me but I said nothing. He spoke no more than the truth, and for this reason I was allowed no object sharp enough to cut, long enough to strangle, noxious enough to poison, heavy enough to crush—even if I could have escaped surveillance long enough to use any deadly weapon.

I was ninety-six thousand, two hundred and thirty-two years old, and life long ago had lost that freshness and anticipation which makes it enjoyable. I found existence not so much unpleasant, as a bore. Events repeated themselves with a deadening familiarity. It was like watching a rather dull drama for the thousandth time: the boredom becomes almost tangible and nothing seems more desirable than oblivion.

Ninety-six thousand, two hundred and two years ago, as a student of biochemistry, I had offered myself as a guinea pig for certain tests involving glands and connective tissue. An incalculable error had distorted the experiment, with my immortality as the perverse result. To this day I appear not an hour older than my age at the time of the experiment, when I was so terribly young.

Needless to say, I suffered tragedy as my parents, my friends, my wife, and finally my children grew old and died, while I remained a young man. So it has been. I have seen untold generations come and go; faces flit before me like snowflakes as I sit here. Nations have risen and fallen, empires extended, collapsed, forgotten. Heroes have lived and died; seas drained, deserts irrigated, glaciers melted, mountains levelled. Almost a hundred thousand years I have persisted, for the most part effacing myself, studying humanity. My great work has been the *History of Man.*

Although I have lived unchanging, across the years the race evolved. Men and women grew taller, and more slender. Every century saw features more refined, brains larger, more flexible. As a result, I, Henry Revere, *homo sapiens* of the twentieth century, today am a freakish survival, somewhat more advanced than the Neanderthal, but essentially a precursor to the true Man of today.

I am a living fossil, a curio among curios, a public ward, a creature denied the option of life or death. This was what Dr. Jones had come to explain to me, as if I were a retarded child. He was as kindly as he knows how, but unusually emphatic. Presently he departed and I was left to myself, in whatever privacy the scrutiny of a half a dozen pairs of eyes allows.

It is harder to kill one's self than one might imagine. I have considered the matter carefully, examining every object within my control for lethal potentialities. But my servants are preternaturally careful. Nothing in this house could so much as bruise me. And when I leave the house, as I am privileged to do, gravity deflectors allow me no profit from high places, and in this exquisitely organized civilization there are no dangerous vehicles or heavy machinery in which I could mangle myself.

In the final analysis I am flung upon my own resources. I have an idea. Tonight I shall take a firm grasp on my head and try to break my neck...

Dr. Jones came as always, and inspected me with his usual reproach. "Henry Revere, you trouble us all with your discontent. Why can't you reconcile yourself to life as you have always known it?"

"Because I am bored! I have experienced everything. There is no more possibility of novelty or surprise! I feel so sure of events that I could predict the future!"

He was rather more serious than usual. "You are our guest. You must realize that our only concern is to ensure your safety."

"But I don't want safety! Quite the reverse!"

Dr. Jones ignored me. "You must make up your mind to cooperate. Otherwise—" he paused significantly "—we will be forced into a course of action that will detract from the dignity of us all."

"Nothing could detract any further from my dignity," I replied bitterly. "I am hardly better than an animal in a zoo."

"That is neither your fault nor ours. We all must fulfill our existences to the optimum. Today your function is to serve as vinculum with the past."

He departed. I was left to my thoughts. The threats had been veiled but were all too clear. I was to desist from further attempts upon my life or suffer additional restraint.

I went out on the terrace, and stood looking across the ocean, where the sun was setting into a bed of golden clouds. I was beset by a dejection so vast that I felt stifled. Completely weary of a world to which I had become alien, I was yet denied freedom to take my leave. Everywhere I looked were avenues to death: the deep ocean, the heights of the palisade, the glitter of energy in the city. Death was a privilege, a bounty, a prize, and it was denied to me.

I returned to my study and leafed through some old maps. The house was silent—as if I were alone. I knew differently. Silent feet moved behind the walls, which were transparent to the eyes above these feet, but opaque to mine. Gauzy webs of artificial nerve tissue watched me from various parts of the room. I had only to make a sudden gesture to bring an anaesthetic beam snapping at me.

I sighed, slumped into my chair. I saw with the utmost clarity that never could I kill myself by my own instrumentality. Must I then submit to an intolerable existence? I sat looking bleakly at the nacreous wall behind which eyes noted my every act.

No, I would never submit. I must seek some means outside myself, a force of destruction to strike without warning: a lightning bolt, an avalanche, an earthquake.

Such natural cataclysms, however, were completely beyond my power to ordain or even predict.

I considered radioactivity. If by some pretext I could expose myself to a sufficient number of roentgens…

I sat back in my chair, suddenly excited. In the early days atomic wastes were sometimes buried, sometimes blended with concrete and dropped into the ocean. If only I were able to—but no. Dr. Jones would hardly allow me to dig in the desert or dive in the ocean, even if the radioactivity were not yet vitiated.

Some other disaster must be found in which I could serve the role of a casualty. If, for instance, I had foreknowledge of some great meteor, and where it would strike...

The idea awoke an almost forgotten association. I sat up in my chair. Then, conscious that knowledgeable minds speculated upon my every expression, I once again slumped forlornly.

Behind the passive mask of my face, my mind was racing, recalling ancient events. The time was too far past, the circumstances obscured. But details could be found in my great *History of Man*.

I must by all means avoid suspicion. I yawned, feigned acute ennui. Then with an air of surly petulance, I secured the box of numbered rods which was my index. I dropped one of them into the viewer, focused on the molecule-wide items of information.

Someone might be observing me. I rambled here and there, consulting articles and essays totally unrelated to my idea: *The Origin and Greatest Development of the Dithyramb; The Kalmuk Tyrants; New Camelot, 18119 A.D.; Oestheotics; The Caves of Phrygia; The Exploration of Mars; The Launching of the Satellites.* I undertook no more than a glance at this last; it would not be wise to show any more than a flicker of interest. But what I read corroborated the inkling which had tickled the back of my mind.

The date was during the twentieth century, during what would have been my normal lifetime.

The article read in part:

Today HESPERUS, *last of the unmanned satellites, was launched into orbit around Earth. This great machine will swing above the equator at a height of a thousand miles, where atmospheric resistance is so scant as to be negligible. Not quite negligible, of course; it is estimated that in something less than a hundred thousand years* HESPERUS *will lose enough momentum to return to Earth.*

Let us hope that no citizen of that future age suffers injury when HESPERUS *falls.*

I grunted and muttered. A fatuous sentiment! Let us hope that one person, at the very least, suffers injury. Injury enough to erase him from life!

I continued to glance through the monumental work which had occupied so much of my time. I listened to aquaclave music from the old Poly-Pacific Empire; read a few pages from *The Revolt of the Manitobans*. Then, yawning and simulating hunger, I called for my evening meal.

Tomorrow I must locate more exact information, and brush up on orbital mathematics.

⇒••⇐

The *Hesperus* will drop into the Pacific Ocean at Latitude 0° 0' 0.0" ± 0.1", Longitude 141° 12' 36.9" ± 0.2", at 2 hours 22 minutes 18 seconds after standard noon on January 13 of next year. It will strike with a velocity of approximately one thousand miles an hour, and I hope to be on hand to absorb a certain percentage of its inertia.

I have been occupied seven months establishing these figures. Considering the necessary precautions, the dissimulation, the delicacy of the calculations, seven months is a short time to accomplish as much as I have. I see no reason why my calculations should not be accurate. The basic data were recorded to the necessary refinement and there have been no variables or fluctuations to cause error.

I have considered light pressure, hysteresis, meteoric dust; I have reckoned the calendar reforms which have occurred over the years; I have allowed for any possible Einsteinian, Gambade, or Kolbinski perturbation. What is there left to disturb the *Hesperus?* Its orbit lies in the equatorial plane, south of spaceship channels; to all intents and purposes it has been forgotten.

The last mention of the *Hesperus* occurs about eleven thousand years after it was launched. I find a note to the effect that its orbital position and velocity were in exact accordance with theoretical values. I believe I can be certain that the *Hesperus* will fall on schedule.

The most cheerful aspect to the entire affair is that no one is aware of the impending disaster but myself.

The date is *January 9.* To every side long blue swells are rolling, rippled with cat's-paws. Above are blue skies and dazzling white clouds. The yacht slides quietly south-west in the general direction of the Marquesas Islands.

Dr. Jones had no enthusiasm for this cruise. At first he tried to dissuade me from what he considered a whim but I insisted, reminding him that I was theoretically a free man, and he made no further difficulty.

The yacht is graceful, swift, and seems as fragile as a moth. But when we cut through the long swells there is no shudder or vibration—only a gentle elastic heave. If I had hoped to lose myself overboard, I would have suffered disappointment. I am shepherded as carefully as in my own house. But for the first time in many years I am relaxed and happy. Dr. Jones notices and approves.

The weather is beautiful—the water so blue, the sun so bright, the air so fresh that I almost feel a qualm at leaving this life. Still, now is my chance and I must seize it. I regret that Dr. Jones and the crew must die with me. Still—what do they lose? Very little. A few short years. This is the risk they assume when they guard me. If I could allow them survival I would do so—but there is no such possibility.

I have requested and have been granted nominal command of the yacht.

That is to say, I plot the course, I set the speed. Dr. Jones looks on with indulgent amusement, pleased that I interest myself in matters outside myself.

January 12. Tomorrow is my last day of life. We passed through a series of rain squalls this morning, but the horizon ahead is clear. I expect good weather tomorrow.

I have throttled down to Dead-Slow, as we are only a few hundred miles from our destination.

January 13. I am tense, active, charged with vitality and awareness. Every part of me tingles. On this day of my death it is good to be alive. And why? Because of anticipation, eagerness, hope.

I am trying to mask my euphoria. Dr. Jones is extremely sensitive; I would not care to start his mind working at this late date.

The time is noon. I keep my appointment with *Hesperus* in two hours and twenty-two minutes. The yacht is coasting easily over the water. Our position, as recorded by a pin-point of light on the chart, is only a few miles from our final position. At this present rate we will arrive in about two hours and fifteen minutes. Then I will halt the yacht and wait…

The yacht is motionless on the ocean. Our position is exactly at Latitude 0° 0' 0.0", Longitude 141° 12' 36.9". The degree of error represents no more than a yard or two. This graceful yacht with the unpronounceable name sits directly on the bull's-eye. There is only five minutes to wait.

Dr. Jones comes into the cabin. He inspects me curiously. "You seem very keyed up, Henry Revere."

"Yes, I feel keyed up, stimulated. This cruise is affording me much pleasure."

"Excellent!" He walks to the chart, glances at it. "Why are we halted?"

"I took it into mind to drift quietly. Are you impatient?"

Time passes—minutes, seconds. I watch the chronometer. Dr. Jones follows my glance. He frowns in sudden recollection, goes to the telescreen. "Excuse me; something I would like to watch. You might be interested."

The screen depicts an arid waste. "The Kalahari Desert," Dr. Jones tells me. "Watch."

I glance at the chronometer. Ten seconds—they tick off. Five—four—three—two—one. A great whistling sound, a roar, a crash, an explosion! It comes from the telescreen. The yacht rides on a calm sea.

"There went Hesperus," said Dr. Jones. "Right on schedule!"

He looks at me, where I have sagged against a bulkhead. His eyes narrow, he looks at the chronometer, at the chart, at the telescreen, back to me. "Ah, I understand you now! All of us you would have killed!"

"Yes," I mutter, "all of us."

"Aha! You savage!"

I pay him no heed. "Where could I have miscalculated? I considered every-thing. Loss of entropic mass, lunar attractions—I know the orbit of *Hesperus* as I know my hand. How did it shift, and so far?"

Dr. Jones' eyes shine with a baleful light. "You know the orbit of *Hesperus* then?"

"Yes. I considered every aspect."

"And you believe it shifted?"

"It must have. It was launched into an equatorial orbit; it falls into the Kalahari."

"There are two bodies to be considered."

"Two?"

"*Hesperus* and Earth."

"Earth is constant...Unchangeable." I say this last word slowly, as the terrible knowledge comes.

And Dr. Jones, for the first time in my memory, laughs, an unpleasant harsh sound. "Constant—unchangeable. Except for libration of the poles. *Hesperus* is the constant. Earth shifts below."

"Yes! What a fool I am!"

"An insensate murdering fool! I see you cannot be trusted!"

I charge him. I strike him once in the face before the anaesthetic beam hits me.

Afterword to "Where Hesperus Falls"

Words, words, words are the enemy of a writer. I take great pleasure in simplifying language and sentences whenever I can. If I've started something, I write through to the end of the paragraph or section, then go back and prune out whole sentences. I'm pleased if I reach the end having deleted thirty sentences, making the thing tighter without losing any of the impact.

Of course, I keep having to go back to make sure that I have the right words and no repetition. Norma catches a lot of this, and it's a great deal of work. I liked it much better in the old days when I could still see and could assimilate a whole page at a time like other writers do.

You mustn't try too hard to produce effects either. They have to come kind of quietly, sneaking up on you out of the action and feeling. When you want to describe something that's flamboyant, weird and strange, anything a little bit outrageous, wicked or nasty, you don't do it by exposition, which can become long-winded and tiresome. You have one of your characters describe it to somebody else. Instead of writing that a man is an evil beast, without a redeeming quality, you have a girl come in out of the cold with her clothes torn and say: 'I met this fellow, Steve, and he did such and such. That man is a beast. Do you know what he did to Henrietta? He pulled all her hair out.' I'm exaggerating, but this is almost a trade secret: not having the exposition come from the writer, but rather from the mouths of the characters themselves.

So cut those words out. Sometimes you can combine the adjective and the noun into a single notion. Instead of saying there was a horse colored all kinds of different colors, you say a palomino came down the road.

—Jack Vance

The Phantom Milkman

I've had all I can stand. I've got to get out, away from the walls, the glass, the white stone, the black asphalt. All of a sudden I see the city for the terrible place that it is. Lights burn my eyes, voices crawl on my skin like sticky insects, and I notice that the people look like insects too. Burly brown beetles, wispy mosquito-men in tight black trousers, sour sow-bug women, mantids and scorpions, fat little dung-beetles, wasp-girls gliding with poisonous nicety, children like loathsome little flies…This isn't a pleasant thought; I must not think of people so; the picture could linger to bother me. I think I'm a hundred times more sensitive than anyone else in the world, and I'm given to very strange fancies. I could list some that would startle you, and it's just as well that I don't. But I do have this frantic urge to flee the city; it's settled. I'm going.

I consult my maps—there's the Andes, the Atlas, the Altai; Mt. Godwin-Austin, Mt. Kilimanjaro; Stromboli and Etna. I compare Siberia above Baikal Nor with the Pacific between Antofagasta and Easter Island. Arabia is hot; Greenland is cold. Tristan da Cunha is very remote; Bouvet even more so. There's Timbuktu, Zanzibar, Bali, the Great Australian Bight.

I am definitely leaving the city. I have found a cabin in Maple Valley, four miles west of Sunbury. It stands a hundred feet back from Maple Valley Road, under two tall trees. It has three rooms and a porch, a fireplace, a good roof, a good well and windmill.

Mrs. Lipscomb is skeptical, even a little shocked. "A good-looking girl like you shouldn't go off by yourself; time to hide away when you're old and nobody wants you." She predicts hair-raising adventures, but I don't care. I was married to Poole for six weeks; nothing could happen that would be any worse.

I'm in my new house. There's lots of work ahead of me: scrubbing, chopping wood. I'll probably bulge with muscles before the winter's over.

My cats are delighted. They are Homer and Moses. Homer is yellow; Moses is black and white. Which reminds me: milk. I saw a Sunbury Dairy delivery truck on the highway. I'll write them an order now.

> Sunbury Dairy   November 14
> Sunbury
> Dear Sirs:
> Please leave me a quart of milk three times a week on whatever days are convenient. Please bill me.
>
> Isabel Durbrow
> RFD Route 2, Box 82
> Sunbury

My mailbox is battered and dusty; one day I'll paint it: red, white and blue, to cheer the mailman. He delivers at ten in the morning, in an old blue panel truck.

When I mail the letter, I see that there's already one in the box. It's for me—forwarded from the city by Mrs. Lipscomb. I take it slowly. I don't want it; I recognize the handwriting: it's from Poole, the dark-visaged brute I woke up from childhood to find myself married to. I tear it in pieces; I'm not even curious. I'm still young and very pretty, but right now there's no one I want, Poole least of all. I shall wear blue jeans and write by the fireplace all winter; and in the spring, who knows?

During the night the wind comes up; the windmill cries from the cold. I lie in bed, with Homer and Moses at my feet. The coals in the fireplace flicker...Tomorrow I'll write Mrs. Lipscomb; by no means must she give Poole my address.

I have written the letter. I run down the slope to the mailbox. It's a glorious late autumn day. The wind is crisp, the hills are like an ocean of gold with scarlet and yellow trees for surf.

I pull open the mailbox...Now, this is odd! My letter to Sunbury Dairy—gone. Perhaps the carrier came early? But it's only nine o'clock. I put in the letter to Mrs. Lipscomb and look all around...Nothing. Who would want my letter? My cats stand with tails erect, looking keenly up the road, first in one direction, then the other, like surveyors planning a new highway. Well, come kittens, you'll drink canned milk today.

At ten o'clock the carrier passes, driving his dusty blue panel truck. He did not come early. That means—someone took my letter.

It's all clear; I understand everything. I'm really rather angry. This morning I found milk on my porch—a quart, bottled by the Maple Valley Dairy. They have no right to go through my mailbox; they thought I'd never notice…I won't use the milk; it can sit and go sour; I'll report them to the Sunbury Dairy and the post office besides…

I've worked quite hard. I'm not really an athletic woman, much as I'd like to be. The pile of wood that I've chopped and sawed is quite disproportionate to the time I've spent. Homer and Moses help me not at all. They sit on the logs, wind in and out underfoot. It's time for their noon meal. I'll give them canned milk, which they detest.

On investigation I see that there's not even canned milk; the only milk in the house is that of the Maple Valley Dairy…Well, I'll use it, if only for a month.

I pour milk into a bowl; the cats strop their ribs on my shins.

I guess they're not hungry. Homer takes five or six laps, then draws back, making a waggish face. Moses glances up to see if I'm joking. I know my cats very well; to some extent I can understand their language. It's not all in the 'meows' and 'maroos'; there's the slope of the whiskers and set of the ear. Naturally they understand each other better than I do, but I generally get the gist.

Neither one likes his milk.

"Very well," I say severely, "you're not going to waste good milk; you won't get any more."

They saunter across the room and sit down. Perhaps the milk is sour; if so, that's the last straw. I smell the milk, and very nice milk it smells: like hay and pasturage. Surely this isn't pasteurized milk! And I look at the cap. It says: "Maple Valley Dairy. Fresh milk. Sweet and clean, from careless cows."

I presume that 'careless' is understood in the sense of 'free from care', rather than 'slovenly'.

Well, careless cows or not, Homer and Moses have turned up their noses. What a wonderful poem I could write, in the Edwardian manner.

Homer and Moses have turned up their noses;
They're quite disappointed with tea.
Their scones are like stones, the fish is all bones;
The milk that they've tasted, it's certainly wasted,
But they're getting no other from me.

They'll just learn to like fresh milk or do without, ungrateful little scamps.

I have been scrubbing floors and white-washing the kitchen. No more chopping and sawing. I've ordered wood from the farmer down the road. The cabin is looking very cheerful. I have curtains at the windows, books on the mantel, sprays of autumn leaves in a big blue bottle I found in the shed.

Speaking of bottles: tomorrow morning the milk is delivered. I must put out the bottle.

Homer and Moses still won't drink Maple Valley Dairy milk…They look at me so wistfully when I pour it out, I suppose I'll have to give in and get something else. It's lovely milk; I'd drink it myself if I liked milk.

Today I drove into Sunbury, and just for a test I brought home a bottle of Sunbury Dairy Milk. Now we'll see…I fill a bowl. Homer and Moses are wondering almost audibly if this is the same distasteful stuff I've been serving the last week. I put down the bowl; they fall to with such gusto that milk splashes on to their whiskers and drips all over the floor. That settles it. Tonight I'll put a note in the bottle, stopping delivery from Maple Valley Dairy.

I don't understand it! I wrote very clearly. "Please deliver no more milk." Lo and behold, the driver has the gall to leave me two bottles. I certainly won't pay for it. The ineffable, unutterable nerve of the man!

Sunbury Dairy doesn't deliver up Maple Valley. I'll just buy milk with my groceries. And tonight I'll write a firm note to Maple Valley Dairy.

November 21

Dear Sirs:

Leave no more milk! I don't want it. My cats won't drink it. Here is fifty cents for the two bottles I have used.

Isabel Durbrow

I am perplexed and angry. The insolence of the people is incredible. They took the two bottles back, then left me another. And a note. It's on rough gray paper, and it reads:

"You asked for it; you are going to get it."

The note has a rather unpleasant ring to it. It certainly couldn't be a threat...I don't think I like these people...They must deliver very early; I've never heard so much as a step.

The farmer down the road is delivering my wood. I say to him, "Mr. Gable, this Maple Valley Dairy, they have a very odd way of doing business."

"Maple Valley Dairy?" Mr. Gable looks blank. "I don't think I know them."

"Oh," I ask him, "don't you buy their milk?"

"I've got four cows of my own to milk."

"Maple Valley Dairy must be further up the road."

"I hardly think so," says Mr. Gable. "I've never heard of them."

I show him the bottle; he looks surprised, and shrugs.

Many of these country people don't travel more than a mile or two from home the whole of their lives.

Tomorrow is milk day; I believe I'll get up early and tell the driver just what I think of the situation.

It is six o'clock; very gray and cold. The milk is already on the porch. What time do they deliver, in Heaven's name?

Tomorrow is milk day again. This time I'll get up at four o'clock and wait till he arrives.

The alarm goes off. It startles me. The room is still dark. I'm warm and drowsy. For a moment I can't remember why I should get up...The milk, the insufferable Maple Valley Dairy. Perhaps I'll let it go till next time...I hear a thump on the porch. There he is now! I jump up, struggle into a bathrobe, run across the room.

I open the door. The milk is on the porch. I don't see the milkman. I don't see the truck. I don't hear anything. How could he get away so fast? It's incredible. I find this whole matter very disturbing.

To make matters worse there's another letter from Poole in the mail. This one I read, and am sorry that I bothered. He is planning to fight the divorce. He wants to come back and live with me. He explains at great length the effect I have on him; it's conceited and parts are rather disgusting. Where have I disappeared to? He's sick of this stalling around. The letter is typical of Poole, the miserable soul in the large flamboyant body. I was never a person to him; I was an ornamental vessel into which he could spend his passion—a lump of therapic clay he could knead and pound and twist. He is a very ugly man; I was his wife all of six weeks...I'd hate to have him find me out here. But Mrs. Lipscomb won't tell...

Farmer Gable brought me another load of wood. He says he smells winter in the air. I suppose it'll snow before long. Then won't the fire feel good!

The alarm goes off. Three-thirty. I'm going to catch that milkman if it's the last thing I do.

I crawl out on the cold floor. Homer and Moses wonder what the hell's going on. I find my slippers, my bathrobe. I go to the porch.

No milk yet. Good. I'm in time. So I wait. The east is only tinged with gray; a pale moon shines on the porch. The hill across the road is tarnished silver, the trees black.

I wait...It is four o'clock. The moon is setting.

I wait...It is four-thirty.

Then five.

No milkman.

I am cold and stiff. My joints ache. I cross the room and light a fire in the wood stove. I see Homer looking at the door. I run to the window. The milk is in its usual place.

There is something very wrong here. I look up the valley, down the valley. The sky is wide and dreary. The trees stand on top of the hills like people looking out to sea. I can't believe that anyone is playing a joke on me…Today I'll go looking for the Maple Valley Dairy.

I haven't found it. I've driven the valley one end to the other. No one's heard of it.

I stopped the Sunbury Dairy delivery truck. He never heard of it.

The telephone book doesn't list it.

No one knows them at the post office…Or the police station…Or the feed store.

It would almost seem that there is no Maple Valley Dairy. Except for the milk that they leave on my porch three times a week.

I can't think of anything to do—except ignore them…It's interesting if it weren't so frightening…I won't move; I won't return to the city…

Tonight it's snowing. The flakes drift past the window, the fire roars up the flue. I've made myself a wonderful hot buttered rum. Homer and Moses sit purring. It's very cozy—except I keep looking at the window, wondering what's watching me.

Tomorrow there'll be more milk. They can't be doing this for nothing! Could it be that—no…For a moment I felt a throb. Poole. He's cruel enough, and he's subtle enough, but I don't see how he could have done it.

I'm lying awake. It's early morning. I don't think the milk has come; I've heard nothing.

It's stopped snowing; there's a wonderful hush outside.

A faint thud. The milk. I'm out of bed, but I'm terribly frightened. I force myself to the window. I've no idea what I'll see.

The milk is there; the bottle shining, white…Nothing else. I turn away. Back to bed. Homer and Moses look bored.

I swing back in sudden excitement; my flashlight, where is it? There'll be tracks.

I open the door. The snow is an even blanket everywhere—shimmering, glimmering, pale and clear. No tracks…Not a mark!

If I have any sense I'll leave Maple Valley, I'll never come back…
Around the neck of the bottle hangs a printed form.
I reach out into the cold.

> Dear Customer:
> Does our service satisfy you?
> Have you any complaints?
> Can we leave you any other commodities?
> Just let us know; we will deliver and you will be billed.

I write on the card:

> My cats don't like your milk and I don't like you. The only thing I want
> you to leave is your footprints. No more milk! I won't pay for it!
> Isabel Durbrow

I can't get my car started; the battery's dead. It's snowing again. I'll wait till it stops, then hike up to Gable's for a push.

It's still snowing. Tomorrow the milk. I've asked for his footprints. Tomorrow morning…

I haven't slept. I'm still awake, listening. There are noises off in the woods, and windmill creaks and groans, a dismal sound.

Three o'clock. Homer and Moses jump down to the floor—two soft thuds. They pad back and forth, then jump back up on the bed. They're restless tonight. Homer is telling Moses, "I don't like this at all. We never saw stuff like this going on in the city."

Moses agrees without reservation.

I lie quiet, huddled under the blankets, listening. The snow crunches a little. Homer and Moses turn to look.

A thud. I am out of bed; I run to the door.

The milk.

I run out in my slippers.

The footprints.

There are two of them in the snow just under the milk bottle. Two footprints, the mark of two feet. Bare feet!

I yell. "You cowards! You miserable sneaks! I'm not afraid of you!"

I am though. It's easy to yell when you know that no one will answer…But I'm not sure…Suppose they do?

There is a note on the bottle. It reads:

"You ordered milk; you'll be billed. You ordered footprints; you'll be billed. On the first of the month all accounts are due and payable."

I sit in the chair by the fire.

I don't know what to do. I'm terribly scared. I don't dare to look at the window for fear of seeing a face. I don't dare to wander up into the woods.

I know I should leave. But I hate to let anyone or anything drive me away. Someone must be playing a joke on me…But they're not…I wonder how they expect me to pay; in what coin?…What is the value of a footprint? Of six quarts of goblin milk the cats won't drink? Today is the 30th of November.

Tomorrow is the first.

At ten o'clock the mailman drives past. I run down and beg him to help me start my car. It takes only a minute; the motor catches at once.

I drive into Sunbury and put in a long distance call, to Howard Mansfield. He's a young engineer I knew before I was married. I tell him everything in a rush. He is interested but he takes the practical viewpoint. He says he'll come tomorrow and check the situation. I think he's more interested in checking me. I don't mind; he'll behave himself if I tell him to. I do want someone here the next time the milk comes…Which should be the morning of the day after tomorrow.

It's clear and cool. I've recharged the battery; I've bought groceries; I drive home. The fire in the stove has gone down; I build it up and make a fire in the fireplace.

I fry two lamb chops and make a salad. I feed Homer and Moses and eat my dinner.

Now it's very quiet. The cold makes small creaking noises outside; about ten o'clock the wind starts to come up. I'm tired, but I'm too nervous to go to sleep. These are the last hours of November 30th, they're running out…

I hear a soft sound outside, a tap at the door. The knob turns, but the door is bolted. For some reason I look at the clock. Eleven-thirty. Not yet the first. Howard has arrived?

I slowly go to the door. I wish I had a gun.

"Who's there?" My voice sounds strange.

"It's me." I recognize the voice.

"Go away."

"Open up. Or I'll bust in."

"Go away." I'm suddenly very frightened. It's so dark and far away; how could he have found me? Mrs. Lipscomb? Or through Howard?

"I'm coming in, Isabel. Open up, or I'll tear a hole in the wall!"

"I'll shoot you..."

He laughs. "You wouldn't shoot me...I'm your husband."

The door creaks as he puts his shoulder to it. The screws pull out of old wood; the bolt snaps loose, the door bursts open.

He poses for a moment, half-smiling. He has very black hair, a sharp thin nose, pale skin. His cheeks are red with the cold. He has the look of a decadent young Roman senator, and I know he's capable of anything queer and cruel.

"Hello, honey. I've come to take you back."

I know I'm in for a long hard pull. Telling him to get out, to go away, is a waste of breath.

"Shut the door." I go back to the fire. I won't give him the satisfaction of seeing that I'm frightened.

He comes slowly across the room. Homer and Moses crouch on the bed hoping he won't notice them.

"You're pretty well hid out."

"I'm not hiding." And I wonder if after all he's behind the Maple Valley Dairy. It must be.

"Have you come to collect for the milk, Poole?" I try to speak softly, as if I've known all the time.

He looks at me half-smiling. I see he's puzzled. He pretends that he understands. "Yeah. I've been missing my cream."

I sit looking at him, trying to convey my contempt. He wants me to fear him. He knows I don't love him. Fear or love—one suits him as well as the other. Indifference he won't take.

His mouth starts to droop. It looks as if he's thinking wistful thoughts, but I know he is becoming angry.

I don't want him angry. I say, "It's almost my bed-time, Poole."

He nods. "That's a good idea."

I say nothing.

He swings a chair around, straddles it with his arms along the back, his chin on his arms. The firelight glows on his face.

"You're pretty cool, Isabel."

"I've no reason to be otherwise."

"You're my wife."

"No."

He jumps up, grabs my wrists, looks down into my eyes. He's playing with me. We both know what he's planning; he advances to it by easy stages.

"Poole," I say in a cool voice, "you make me sick."

He slaps my face. Not hard. Just enough to indicate that he's the master. I stare at him; I don't intend to lose control. He can kill me; I won't show fear, nothing but contempt.

He reads my mind, he takes it as a challenge; his lips droop softly. He drops my arms, sits down, grins at me. Whatever he felt when he came here, now it's hate. Because I see through his poses, past his good looks, his black, white and rose beauty.

"The way I see it," says Poole, "you're up here playing around with two or three other men."

I blush; I can't help it. "Think what you like."

"Maybe it's just one man."

"If he finds you here—he'll give you a beating."

He looks at me interestedly; then laughs, stretches his magnificent arms, writhes his shoulder muscles. He is proud of his physique.

"It's a good bluff, Isabel. But knowing you, your virginal mind…"

The clock strikes twelve. Someone taps at the door. Poole jerks around, looks at the door, then at me.

I jump to my feet. I look at the door.

"Who's that?"

"I—really don't—know." I'm not sure. But it's twelve o'clock; it's December first. Who else could it be? "It's—it's the milkman." I start for the door—slowly. Of course I don't intend to open it.

"Milkman, eh? At midnight?" He jumps up, catches my arm. "Come to collect the milk bill, I suppose."

"That's quite right." My voice sounds weird and dry.

"Maybe he'd like to collect from me."

"I'll take care of him, Poole." I try to pull away, knowing that whatever I seem to want he won't allow. "Let me go."

"I'll pay your milk bill…After all, dear," he says silkily, "I'm your husband."

He shoves me across the room, goes to the door. I bury my face in my arms.

The door swings wide. "So you're the milkman," he says. His voice trails away. I hear a sudden gasp. I don't look.

Poole is paying the milk bill.

The door creaks slowly shut. A quick shuffle of steps on the porch, a crunching of snow.

After a while I get up, prop a chair under the door knob, build up the fire. I sit looking at the flames. I don't go near the window.

The cold yellow dawn-sun is shining through the window. The room is cold. I build a roaring fire, put on the coffee, look around the cabin. I've put in lots of work, but I don't have much to pack. Howard is coming today. He can help me.

The sun shines bright through the window. At last—I open the door, step out on the porch. The sun is dazzling on the snow. I wonder where Poole is. There's a shuffle of prints around the door, but away from the porch the snow is pure and clean. His convertible sits in the road.

A milk bill is stuck in a bottle and it's marked, "Paid in full."

I go inside the house, where I drink coffee, pet Homer and Moses, and try to stop my hands from shaking.

Afterword to "The Phantom Milkman"

"The Phantom Milkman" derives from a rainy evening and several batches of rum punch in an old farm-house behind Kenwood, California, where the Vances and the Frank Herberts had taken up residence prior to departure for Mexico. Someone—or something—had delivered a quart of milk to the doorstep that morning. All day Norma and Beverly had been attempting to resolve the mystery, without success. We discussed the affair long into the night, and at last decided that in the absence of trained and experienced investigators, it might be foolhardy to proceed further...

Leaving Kenwood we drove south through California, across the border, down the west coast of Mexico, turned eastward to Guadalajara, then thirty miles further to Lake Chapala, which at that time had lost most of its water and was mainly mud flats. Here in Chapala we rented a very pleasant house a block or two from the main beer garden, which was always a source of amusement and entertainment, because musicians rolled through the place every night.

We set up our writers' workshop. We had an arrangement that when we hoisted a white flag, silence must descend upon the house, and nothing must occur that might disturb the writers, a system which worked out fairly well.

Life proceeded productively for a month or two. I don't know what Frank was writing; I wrote some short stories and started work on a novel which I called *Clarges* but which was ultimately published under the name *To Live Forever*, a title I detest. However, our income was less than our output, and in fact was nonexistent. Finally we were forced to terminate the writers' workshop and return to the States.

—Jack Vance

Dodkin's Job

The Theory of Organized Society—as developed by Kinch, Kolbig, Penton and others—yields such a wealth of significant information, such manifold intricacies and portentous projections, that occasionally it is well to consider the deceptively simple premise—here stated by Kolbig:

> When self-willed micro-units combine to form and sustain a durable macro-unit, certain freedoms of action are curtailed.
> This is the basic process of Organization.
> The more numerous and erratic the micro-units, the more complex must be the structure and function of the macro-unit—hence the more pervasive and restricting the details of Organization.

—from Leslie Penton, *First Principles of Organization*

In general the population of the City had become forgetful of curtailed freedoms, as a snake no longer remembers the legs of his forebears. Somewhere someone has stated, "When the discrepancy between the theory and practice of a culture is very great, this indicates that the culture is undergoing rapid change." By such a test the culture of the City was stable, if not static. The population ordered their lives by schedule, classification and precedent, satisfied with the bland rewards of Organization.

But in the healthiest tissue bacteria exist, and the most negligible impurity flaws a critical crystallization. Luke Grogatch was forty, thin and angular, dour of forehead, sardonic of mouth and eyebrow, with a sidewise twist to his head as if he suffered from earache. He was too astute to profess Nonconformity, too perverse to strive for improved status, too pessimistic, captious, sarcastic and outspoken to keep the jobs to which he found himself assigned. Each new reclassification depressed his status, each new job he disliked with increasing fervor.

Finally, rated as *Flunky/Class D/Unskilled,* Luke was dispatched to the District 8892 Sewer Maintenance Department and from there ordered out as night-shift swamper on Tunnel Gang No. 3's rotary drilling machine.

Reporting for work, Luke presented himself to the gang foreman, Fedor Miskitman, a big buffalo-faced man with flaxen hair and placid blue eyes. Miskitman produced a shovel and took Luke to a position close up behind the drilling machine's cutting head. Here, said Miskitman, was Luke's station. Luke would be required to keep the tunnel floor clean of loose rock and gravel. When the tunnel broke through into an old sewer, there would be scale and that detritus known as 'wet waste' to remove. Luke must keep the dust trap clean and in optimum adjustment. During the breaks he must lubricate those bearings isolated from the automatic lubrication system, and replace broken teeth on the cutting head as necessary.

Luke inquired if this was the extent of his duties, his voice strong with an irony the guileless Fedor Miskitman failed to notice.

"That is all," said Miskitman. He handed Luke the shovel. "Mostly it is the trash. The floor must be clean."

Luke suggested a modification of the hopper jaws which would tend to eliminate the spill of broken rock; in fact, argued Luke, why bother at all? Let the rock lay where it fell. The concrete lining of the tunnel would mask so trivial a scatter of gravel. Miskitman dismissed the suggestion out of hand: the rock must be removed. Luke asked why, and Miskitman told him, "That is the way the job is done."

Luke made a rude noise under his breath. He tested the shovel, and shook his head in dissatisfaction. The handle was too long, the blade too short. He reported this fact to Miskitman, who merely glanced at his watch and signaled the drill operator. The machine whined into revolution, and with an ear-splitting roar made contact with the rock. Miskitman departed, and Luke went to work.

During the shift he found that if he worked in a half-crouch most of the hot dust-laden exhaust would pass over his head. Changing a cutting tooth during the first rest period he burned a blister on his left thumb. At the end of the shift a single consideration deterred Luke from declaring himself unqualified: he would be declassified from *Flunky/Class D/Unskilled* to *Junior Executive,* with a corresponding cut in expense account. Such a declassification would take him to the very bottom of the Status List, and could not be countenanced; his present expense account was barely adequate, comprising nutrition at a Type RP Victualing Service, sleeping space in a Sublevel 22 dormitory, and sixteen Special Coupons per month. He took Class 14 Erotic Processing, and was allowed twelve hours per month at his Recreation Club, with optional use of barbells, table-tennis equipment, two miniature bowling alleys, and any of the six telescreens tuned permanently to Band H.

Luke often daydreamed of a more sumptuous life: AAA nutrition, a suite of rooms for his exclusive use, Special Coupons by the bale, Class 7 Erotic Processing, or even Class 6, or 5: despite Luke's contempt for the High Echelon he had no quarrel with High Echelon perquisites. And always as a bitter coda to the daydreams came the conviction that he might have enjoyed these good things in all reality. He had watched his fellows jockeying; he knew all the tricks and techniques: the beavering, the gregarization, the smutting, knuckling and subuculation...

"I'd rather be Class D Flunky," sneered Luke to himself.

Occasionally a measure of doubt would seep into Luke's mind. Perhaps he merely lacked the courage to compete, to come to grips with the world! And the seep of doubt would become a trickle of self-contempt. A Nonconformist, that's what he was—and lacked the courage to admit it!

Then Luke's obstinacy would reassert itself. Why admit to Nonconformity when it meant a trip to the Disorganized House? A fool's trick—and Luke was no fool. Perhaps he was a Nonconformist in all reality; again perhaps not—he had never really made up his mind. He presumed that he was suspected; occasionally he intercepted queer side-glances and significant jerks of the head among his fellow workers. Let them leer. They could prove nothing.

But now...he was Luke Grogatch, Class D Flunky, separated by a single status from the nonclassified sediment of criminals, idiots, children and proved Nonconformists. Luke Grogatch, who had dreamed such dreams of the High Echelon, of pride and independence! Instead—Luke Grogatch, Class D Flunky. Taking orders from a hay-headed lunk, working with semiskilled laborers with status almost as low as his own: Luke Grogatch, flunky.

Seven weeks passed. Luke's dislike for his job became a mordant passion. The work was arduous, hot, repellent. Fedor Miskitman turned an uncomprehending gaze on Luke's most rancorous grimaces, grunted and shrugged at Luke's suggestions and arguments. This was the way things were done—his manner implied—always had been done, and always would be done.

Fedor Miskitman received a daily policy directive from the works superintendent which he read to the crew during the first rest break of the shift. These directives generally dealt with such matters as work norms, team spirit and cooperation; pleas for a finer polish on the concrete; warnings against off-shift indulgence which might dull enthusiasm and decrease work efficiency. Luke usually paid small heed, until one day Fedor Miskitman, pulling out the familiar yellow sheet, read in his stolid voice:

PUBLIC WORKS DEPARTMENT, PUBLIC UTILITIES DIVISION AGENCY OF SANITARY WORKS, DISTRICT 8892 SEWAGE DISPOSAL SECTION

Bureau of Sewer Construction and Maintenance
Office of Procurement

Policy Directive:	6511 Series BV96
Order Code:	GZP—AAR—REG
Reference:	G98—7542
Date Code:	BT—EQ—LLT
Authorized:	LL8—P-SC 8892
Checked:	48
Counterchecked:	92C

From:	Lavester Limon, Manager, Office of Procurement
Through:	All construction and maintenance offices
To:	All construction and maintenance superintendents
Attention:	All job foremen

Subject:	Tool longevity, the promotion thereof
Instant of Application:	Immediate
Duration of Relevance:	Permanent
Substance:	At beginning of each shift all hand-tools shall be checked out of District 8892 Sewer Maintenance Warehouse. At close of each shift all hand-tools shall be carefully cleaned and returned to District 8892 Sewer Maintenance Warehouse.

Directive reviewed and transmitted:Butry Keghorn, General Superintendent of Construction, Bureau of Sewer Construction

Clyde Kaddo, Superintendent of Sewer Maintenance

❯❯·❮❮

As Fedor Miskitman read the 'Substance' section, Luke expelled his breath in an incredulous snort. Miskitman finished, folded the sheet with careful movements of his thick fingers, looked at his watch. "That is the directive. We are twenty-five seconds over time; we must get back to work."

"Just a minute," said Luke. "One or two things about that directive I want explained."

Miskitman turned his mild gaze upon Luke. "You did not understand it?"

"Not altogether. Who does it apply to?"

"It is an order for the entire gang."

"What do they mean 'hand-tools'?"

"These are tools which are held in the hands."

"Does that mean a shovel?"

"A shovel?" Miskitman shrugged his burly shoulders. "A shovel is a hand-tool."

Luke asked in a voice of hushed wonder: "They want me to polish my shovel, carry it four miles to the warehouse, then pick it up tomorrow and carry it back here?"

Miskitman unfolded the directive, held it at arm's length, read with moving lips. "That is the order." He refolded the paper, returned it to his pocket.

Luke again feigned astonishment. "Certainly there's a mistake."

"A mistake?" Miskitman was puzzled. "Why should there be a mistake?"

"They can't be serious," said Luke. "It's not only ridiculous, it's peculiar."

"I do not know," said Miskitman incuriously. "To work. We are late one minute and a half."

"I assume that all this cleaning and transportation is done on Organization time," Luke suggested.

Miskitman unfolded the directive, held it at arm's length, read. "It does not say so. Our quota is not different." He folded the directive, put it in his pocket.

Luke spat on the rock floor. "I'll bring my own shovel. Let 'em carry around their own precious hand-tools."

Miskitman scratched his chin, once more re-read the directive. He shook his head dubiously. "The order says that all hand-tools must be cleaned and taken to the warehouse. It does not say who owns the tools."

Luke could hardly speak for exasperation. "You know what I think of that directive?"

Fedor Miskitman paid him no heed. "To work. We are over time."

"If I was general superintendent—" Luke began, but Miskitman rumbled roughly. "We do not earn perquisites by talking. To work. We are late."

The rotary cutter started up; seventy-two teeth snarled into gray-brown sandstone. Hopper jaws swallowed the chunks, passing them down an epiglottis into a feeder gut which evacuated far down the tunnel into lift-buckets.

Stray chips rained upon the tunnel floor, which Luke Grogatch must scrape up and return into the hopper. Behind Luke two reinforcement men flung steel hoops into place, flash-welding them to longitudinal bars with quick pinches of the fingers, contact-plates in their gauntlets discharging the requisite gout of energy. Behind came the concrete-spray man, mix hissing out of his revolving spider, followed by two finishers, nervous men working with furious energy, stroking the concrete into a glossy polish. Fedor Miskitman marched back and forth, testing the reinforcement, gauging the thickness of the concrete, making frequent progress checks on the chart to the rear of the rotary cutter, where an electronic device traced the course of the tunnel, guiding it through the system of conduits, ducts, passages, pipes, tubes for water, air, gas, steam, transportation, freight and communication which knit the City into an Organized unit.

The night shift ended at four o'clock in the morning. Miskitman made careful entries in his log; the concrete-spray man blew out his nozzles; the reinforcement workers removed their gauntlets, power packs and insulating garments. Luke Grogatch straightened, rubbed his sore back, stood glowering at the shovel. He felt Miskitman's ox-calm scrutiny. If he threw the shovel to the side of the tunnel as usual and marched off about his business, he would be guilty of Disorganized Conduct. The penalty, as Luke knew well, was declassification. Luke stared at the shovel, fuming with humiliation. Conform, or be declassified. Submit—or become a Junior Executive.

Luke heaved a deep sigh. The shovel was clean enough; one or two swipes with a rag would remove the dust. But there was the ride by crowded man-belt to the warehouse, the queue at the window, the check-in, the added distance to his dormitory. Tomorrow the process must be repeated. Why the necessity for this added effort? Luke knew well enough. An obscure functionary somewhere along the chain of bureaus and commissions had been at a loss for a means to display his diligence. What better method than concern for valuable City property? Consequently the absurd directive, filtering down to Fedor Miskitman and ultimately Luke Grogatch, the victim. What joy to meet this obscure functionary face to face, to tweak his sniveling nose, to kick his craven rump along the corridors of his own office.

Fedor Miskitman's voice disturbed his reverie. "Clean your shovel. It is the end of the shift."

Luke made token resistance. "The shovel is clean," he growled. "This is the most absurd antic I've ever been coerced into. If only I—"

Fedor Miskitman, in a voice as calm and unhurried as a deep river, said, "If you do not like the policy, you should put a petition in the Suggestion Box. That is the privilege of all. Until the policy is changed you must conform. That is the way we live. That is Organization, and we are Organized men."

"Let me see that directive," Luke barked. "I'll get it changed. I'll cram it down somebody's throat. I'll—"

"You must wait until it is logged. Then you may have it; it is useless to me."

"I'll wait," said Luke between clenched teeth.

With method and deliberation Fedor Miskitman made a final check of the job: inspecting machinery, the teeth of the cutter-head, the nozzles of the spider, the discharge belt. He went to his little desk at the rear of the rotary drill, noted progress, signed expense-account vouchers, finally registered the policy directive on mini-film. Then with a ponderous sweep of his arm, he tendered the yellow sheet to Luke. "What will you do with it?"

"I'll find who formed this idiotic policy. I'll tell him what I think of it and what I think of him, to boot."

Miskitman shook his head in disapproval. "That is not the way such things should be done."

"How would you do it?" asked Luke with a wolfish grin.

Miskitman considered, pursing his lips, perking his bristling eyebrows. At last with great simplicity of manner he said, "I would not do it."

Luke threw up his hands, set off down the tunnel. Miskitman's voice boomed against his back. "You must take the shovel!"

Luke halted. Slowly he faced about, glared back at the hulking figure of the foreman. Obey the policy directive, or be declassified. With slow steps, a hanging head and averted eyes, he retraced his path. Snatching the shovel, he stalked back down the tunnel. His bony shoulder blades were exposed and sensitive, and Fedor Miskitman's mild blue gaze, following him, seemed to scrape the nerves of his back.

Ahead the tunnel extended, a glossy pale sinus, dwindling back along the distance they had bored. Through some odd trick of refraction alternate bright and dark rings circled the tube, confusing the eye, creating a hypnotic semblance of two-dimensionality. Luke shuffled drearily into this illusory bull's-eye, dazed with shame and helplessness, the shovel a load of despair. Had he come to this—Luke Grogatch, previously so arrogant in his cynicism and barely concealed Nonconformity? Must he cringe at last, submit slavishly to witless regulations?…If only he were a few places farther up the list! Drearily he pictured the fine incredulous shock with which he would have greeted the policy directive, the sardonic nonchalance with which he would have let the shovel fall from his limp hands…Too late, too late! Now he must toe the mark, must carry his shovel dutifully to the warehouse. In a spasm of rage he flung the blameless implement clattering down the tunnel ahead of him. Nothing he could do! Nowhere to turn! No way to strike back! Organization: smooth and relentless; Organization, massive and inert, tolerant of the submissive, serenely cruel to the unbeliever...Luke came to his shovel and whispering an obscenity snatched it up and half-ran down the pallid tunnel.

He climbed through a manhole, emerged upon the deck of the 1123rd Avenue Hub, where he was instantly absorbed in the crowds trampling between the man-belts, which radiated like spokes, and the various escalators. Clasping the shovel to his chest, Luke struggled aboard the Fontego Man-belt and rushed south, in a direction opposite to that of his dormitory. He rode ten minutes to Astoria Hub, dropped a dozen levels on the Grimesby College Escalator, crossed a gloomy dank area smelling of old rock to a local feeder-belt which carried him to the District 8892 Sewer Maintenance Warehouse.

Luke found the warehouse brightly lit, and the center of considerable activity, with several hundred men coming and going. Those coming, like Luke, carried tools; those going went empty-handed.

Luke joined the line which had formed in front of the tool storeroom. Fifty or sixty men preceded him, a drab centipede of arms, shoulders, heads, legs, the tools projecting to either side. The centipede moved slowly, the men exchanging badinage and quips.

Observing their patience, Luke's normal irascibility asserted itself. Look at them, he thought, standing like sheep, jumping to attention at the rustle of an unfolding directive. Did they inquire the reason for the order? Did they question the necessity for their inconvenience? No! The louts stood chuckling and chatting, accepting the directive as one of life's incalculable vicissitudes, something elemental and arbitrary, like the changing of the seasons...And he, Luke Grogatch, was he better or worse? The question burned in Luke's throat like the aftertaste of vomit.

Still, better or worse, where was his choice? Conform or declassify. A poor choice. There was always the recourse of the Suggestion Box, as Fedor Miskitman, perhaps in bland jest, had pointed out. Luke growled in disgust. Weeks later he might receive a printed form with one statement of a multiple-choice list checked off by some clerical flunky or junior executive: "The situation described by your petition is already under study by responsible officials. Thank you for your interest." Or "The situation described by your petition is temporary and may shortly be altered. Thank you for your interest." Or "The situation described by your petition is the product of established policy and is not subject to change. Thank you for your interest."

A novel thought occurred to Luke: he might exert himself and reclassify *up* the list...As soon as the idea arrived he dismissed it. In the first place he was close to middle age; too many young men were pushing up past him. Even if he could goad himself into the competition...

The line moved slowly forward. Behind Luke a plump little man sagged under the weight of a Velstro inchskip. A forelock of light brown floss dangled into his moony face; his mouth was puckered into a rosebud of concentration; his eyes were absurdly serious. He wore a rather dapper pink and brown overall with orange ankle-boots and a blue beret with the three orange pom-poms affected by the Velstro technicians.

Between shabby sour-mouthed Luke and this short moony man in the dandy's coveralls existed so basic a difference that an immediate mutual dislike was inevitable. The short man's prominent hazel eyes rested on Luke's shovel, traveled thoughtfully over Luke's dirt-stained trousers and jacket. He turned his eyes to the side.

"Come a long way?" Luke asked maliciously.

"Not far," said the moon-faced man.

"Worked overtime, eh?" Luke winked. "A bit of quiet beavering, nothing like it—or so I'm told."

"We finished the job," said the plump man with dignity. "Beavering doesn't enter into it. Why spend half tomorrow's shift on five minutes work we could do tonight?"

"I know a reason," said Luke wisely. "To do your fellow man a good one in the eye."

The moon-faced man twisted his mouth in a quick uncertain smile, then decided that the remark was not humorous. "That's not my way of working," he said stiffly.

"That thing must be heavy," said Luke, noting how the plump little arms struggled and readjusted to the irregular contours of the tool.

"Yes," came the reply. "It is heavy."

"An hour and a half," intoned Luke. "That's how long it's taking me to park this shovel. Just because somebody up the list has a nightmare. And we poor hoodlums at the bottom suffer."

"I'm not at the bottom of the list. I'm a Technical Tool Operator."

"No difference," said Luke. "The hour and a half is the same. Just for somebody's silly notion."

"It's not really so silly," said the moon-faced man. "I fancy there is a good reason for the policy."

Luke shook the handle of the shovel. "And so I have to carry this back and forth along the man-belt three hours a day?"

The little man pursed his lips. "The author of the directive undoubtedly knows his business very well. Otherwise he'd not hold his classification."

"Just who is this unsung hero?" sneered Luke. "I'd like to meet him. I'd like to learn why he wants me to waste three hours a day."

The short man now regarded Luke as he might an insect in his victual ration. "You talk like a Nonconformist. Excuse me if I seem offensive."

"Why apologize for something you can't help?" asked Luke and turned his back.

He flung his shovel to the clerk behind the wicket and received a check. Elaborately Luke turned to the moon-faced man, tucked the check into his breast pocket. "You keep this; you'll be using that shovel before I will."

He stalked proudly out of the warehouse. A grand gesture, but—he hesitated before stepping on the man-belt—was it sensible? The moony technical tool operator in the pink and brown coveralls came out of the warehouse behind him, turned him a queer glance, and hurried away.

Luke looked back into the warehouse. If he returned now he could set things right and tomorrow there'd be no trouble. If he stormed off to his dormitory, it meant another declassification. Luke Grogatch, Junior Executive... Luke reached into his jumper, took out the policy directive he had acquired from Fedor Miskitman: a bit of yellow paper, printed with a few lines of type, a trivial thing in itself—but it symbolized the Organization: massive force in irresistible operation. Nervously Luke plucked at the paper and looked back into the warehouse. The tool operator had called him a Nonconformist; Luke's mouth squirmed in a brief weary grimace. It wasn't true. Luke was not a Nonconformist; Luke was nothing in particular. And he needed his bed, his nutrition ticket, his meager expense account. Luke groaned quietly—almost a whisper. The end of the road. He had gone as far as he could go; had he ever thought he could defeat the Organization? Maybe he was wrong and everyone else was right. Possible, thought Luke without conviction. Miskitman seemed content enough; the technical tool operator seemed not only content but complacent. Luke leaned against the warehouse wall, eyes burning and moist with self-pity. Nonconformist. Misfit. What was he going to do?

He curled his lip spitefully, stepped forward onto the man-belt. Devil take them all! They could declassify him; he'd become a junior executive and laugh!

In subdued spirits Luke rode back to the Grimesby Hub. Here, about to board the escalator, he stopped short, blinking and rubbing his long sallow chin, considering still another aspect to the matter. It seemed to offer a chance of—but no. Hardly likely...and yet, why not? Once again he examined the directive. Lavester Limon, Manager of the District Office of Procurement, presumably had issued the policy; Lavester Limon could rescind it. If Luke could so persuade Limon, his troubles, while not dissipated, at least would be lessened. He could report shovel-less to his job; he could return sardonic grin for bland hidden grin with Fedor Miskitman. He might even go to the trouble of locating the moon-faced little technical tool operator with the inchskip...

Luke sighed. Why continue this futile daydream? First Lavester Limon must be induced to rescind the directive—and what were the odds of this?... Perhaps not astronomical after all, mused Luke as he rode the man-belt back to his dormitory. The directive clearly was impractical. It worked an inconvenience on many people, while accomplishing very little. If Lavester Limon could be persuaded of this, if he could be shown that his own prestige and reputation were suffering, he might agree to recall the ridiculous directive.

Luke arrived at his dormitory shortly after seven. He went immediately to the communication booth, called the District 8892 Office of Procurement. Lavester Limon, he was told, would be arriving at eight-thirty.

Luke made a careful toilet, and after due consideration invested four Special Coupons in a fresh set of fibers: a tight black jacket and blue trousers of somewhat martial cut, of considerably better quality than his usual costume. Surveying himself in the washroom mirror, Luke felt that he cut not so poor a figure.

He took his morning quota of nutrition at a nearby Type RP Victualing Service, then ascended to Sublevel 14 and rode the man-belt to District 8892 Bureau of Sewer Construction and Maintenance.

A pert office girl, dark hair pulled forward over her face in the modish 'Robber Baron' style, conducted Luke into Lavester Limon's office. At the door she glanced demurely backward, and Luke was glad that he had invested in new clothes. Responding to the stimulus, he threw back his shoulders, marched confidently into Lavester Limon's office.

Lavester Limon, sitting at his desk, bumped briefly to his feet in courteous acknowledgement—an amiable-seeming man of middle stature, golden-brown hair brushed carefully across a freckled and sun-tanned bald spot; golden-brown eyes, round and easy; a golden-brown lounge jacket and trousers of fine golden-brown corduroy. He waved his arm to a chair. "Won't you sit down, Mr. Grogatch?"

In the presence of so much cordiality Luke relaxed his truculence, and even felt a burgeoning of hope. Limon seemed a decent sort; perhaps the directive was, after all, an administrative error.

Limon raised his golden-brown eyebrows inquiringly.

Luke wasted no time on preliminaries. He brought forth the directive. "My business concerns this, Mr. Limon: a policy which you seem to have formulated."

Limon took the directive, read, nodded. "Yes, that's my policy. Something wrong?"

Luke felt surprise and a pang of premonition: surely so reasonable-seeming a man must instantly perceive the folly of the directive!

"It's simply not a workable policy," said Luke earnestly. "In fact, Mr. Limon, it's completely unreasonable!"

Lavester Limon seemed not at all offended. "Well, well! And why do you say that? Incidentally, Mr. Grogatch, you're..." Again the golden-brown eyebrows arched inquiringly.

"I'm a flunky, Class D, on a tunnel gang," said Luke. "Today it took me an hour and a half to check my shovel. Tomorrow, there'll be another hour and a half checking the shovel out. All on my own time. I don't think that's reasonable."

Lavester Limon reread the directive, pursed his lips, nodded his head once or twice. He spoke into his desk phone. "Miss Rab, I'd like to see—" he consulted the directive's reference number "—Item 7542, File G98." To Luke he said in rather an absent voice: "Sometimes these things become a trifle complicated..."

"But can you change the policy?" Luke burst out. "Do you agree that it's unreasonable?"

Limon cocked his head to the side, made a doubtful grimace. "We'll see what's on the reference. If my memory serves me..." His voice faded away.

Twenty seconds passed. Limon tapped his fingers on his desk. A soft chime sounded. Limon touched a button; his desk-screen exhibited the item he had requested: another policy directive similar in form to the first.

PUBLIC WORKS DEPARTMENT, PUBLIC UTILITIES DIVISION
AGENCY OF SANITARY WORKS, DISTRICT 8892
SEWAGE DISPOSAL SECTION

Director's Office

Policy Directive:	2888 Series BQ008
Order Code:	GZP—AAR—REF
Reference:	OR9—123
Date Code:	BR—EQ—LLT
Authorized:	JR D-SDS
Checked:	AC
Counterchecked:	CX McD

From:	Judiath Ripp, Director
Through:	
To:	Lavester Limon, Manager, Office of Procurement
Attention:	

Subject:	Economies of operation
Instant of Application:	Immediate
Duration of Relevance:	Permanent
Substance:	Your monthly quota of supplies for disbursement Type A, B, D, F, H is hereby reduced 2.2%. It is suggested that you advise affected personnel of this reduction, and take steps to insure most stringent economies. It has been noticed that department use of supplies Type D in particular is in excess of calculated norm.
Suggestion:	Greater care by individual users of tools, including warehouse storage at night.

"Type D supplies," said Lavester Limon wryly, "are hand-tools. Old Ripp wants stringent economies. I merely pass along the word. That's the story behind 6511." He returned the directive in question to Luke, leaned back in his seat. "I can see how you're exercised, but—" he raised his hands in a careless, almost flippant gesture "—that's the way the Organization works."

Luke sat rigid with disappointment. "Then you won't revoke the directive?"

"My dear fellow! How can I?"

Luke made an attempt at reckless nonchalance. "Well, there's always room for me among the junior executives. I told them where to put their shovel."

"Mmmf. Rash. Sorry I can't help." Limon surveyed Luke curiously, and his lips curved in a faint grin. "Why don't you tackle old Ripp?"

Luke squinted sidewise in suspicion. "What good will that do?"

"You never know," said Limon breezily. "Suppose lightning strikes—suppose he rescinds his directive? I can't agitate with him myself; I'd get in trouble— but there's no reason why you can't." He turned Luke a quick knowing smile, and Luke understood that Lavester Limon's amiability, while genuine, served as a useful camouflage for self-interest and artful playing of the angles.

Luke rose abruptly to his feet. He played cat's-paw for no one, and he opened his mouth to tell Lavester Limon as much. In that instant a recollection crossed his mind: the scene in the warehouse, where he had contemptuously tossed the check for his shovel to the technical tool operator. Always Luke had been prone to the grand gesture, the reckless commitment which left him no scope for retreat. When would he learn self-control? In a subdued voice Luke asked, "Who is this Ripp again?"

"Judiath Ripp, Director of the Sewage Disposal Section. You may have difficulty getting in to see him; he's a troublesome old brute. Wait, I'll find out if he's at his office."

He made inquiries into his desk phone. Information returned to the effect that Judiath Ripp had just arrived at the Section office on Sublevel 3, under Bramblebury Park.

Limon gave Luke tactical advice. "He's choleric, something of a barker. Here's the secret: pay no attention to him. He respects firmness. Pound the table. Roar back at him. If you pussyfoot he'll sling you out. Give him tit for tat and he'll listen."

Luke looked hard at Lavester Limon, well aware that the twinkle in the golden-brown eyes was malicious glee. He said, "I'd like a copy of that directive, so he'll know what I'm talking about."

Limon sobered instantly. Luke could read his mind: *Will Ripp hold it against me if I send up this crackpot? It's worth the chance.* "Sure," said Limon. "Pick it up from the girl."

Luke ascended to Sublevel 3 and walked through the pleasant tri-level arcade below Bramblebury Park. He passed the tall glass-walled fish tank open to the sky and illuminated by sunlight, boarded the local man-belt, and after a ride of two or three minutes alighted in front of the District 8892 Agency of Sanitary Works.

The Sewage Disposal Section occupied a rather pretentious suite off a small courtyard garden. Luke walked along a passage tiled with blue, gray and green mosaic, entered a white room furnished in pale gray and pink. A long mural of cleverly twisted gold, black and white tubing decorated one wall; another was swathed in heavy green leaves growing from a chest-high planter. At a desk sat the receptionist, a plump pouty blonde girl with a simulated bone through her nose and a shark's-tooth necklace dangling around her neck. She wore her hair tied up over her head like a sheaf of wheat, and an amusing black and brown primitive symbol decorated her forehead.

Luke explained that he wished a few words with Mr. Judiath Ripp, Director of the Section.

Perhaps from uneasiness, Luke spoke brusquely. The girl blinked in surprise, examined him curiously. After a moment's hesitation the girl shook her head doubtfully. "Won't someone else do? Mr. Ripp's day is tightly scheduled. What did you want to see him about?"

Luke, attempting a persuasive smile, achieved a leer of sinister significance. The girl was frankly startled.

"Perhaps you'll tell Mr. Ripp I'm here," said Luke. "One of his policy directives...well, there have been irregularities, or rather a misapplication—"

"Irregularities?" The girl seemed to hear only the single word. She gazed at Luke with new eyes, observing the crisp new black and blue garments with their quasi-military cut. Some sort of inspector? "I'll call Mr. Ripp," she said nervously. "Your name, sir, and status?"

"Luke Grogatch. My status—" Luke smiled once more, and the girl averted her eyes. "It's not important."

"I'll call Mr. Ripp, sir. One moment, if you please." She swung around, murmured anxiously into her screen, looked at Luke and spoke again. A thin voice rasped a reply. The girl swung back around, nodded at Luke. "Mr. Ripp can spare a few minutes. The first door, please."

Luke walked with stiff shoulders into a tall wood-paneled room, one wall of which displayed green-glowing tanks of darting red and yellow fish. At the desk sat Judiath Ripp, a tall heavy man, himself resembling a large fish. His head was narrow, pale as mackerel, and rested backward-tilting on his shoulders. He had no perceptible chin; the neck ran up to his carplike mouth. Pale eyes stared at Luke over small round nostrils; a low brush of hair thrust up from the rear of his head like dry grass over a sand dune. Luke remembered Lavester Limon's verbal depiction of Ripp: "choleric". Hardly appropriate. Had Limon a grudge against Ripp? Was he using Luke as an instrument of mischievous revenge? Luke suspected as much; he felt uncomfortable and awkward.

Judiath Ripp surveyed him with cold unblinking eyes. "What can I do for you, Mr. Grogatch? My secretary tells me you are an investigator of some sort."

Luke considered the situation, his narrow black eyes fixed on Ripp's face. He told the exact truth. "For several weeks I have been working in the capacity of a Class D Flunky on a tunnel gang."

"What the devil do you investigate on a tunnel gang?" Ripp asked in chilly amusement.

Luke made a slight gesture, signifying much or nothing, as one might choose to take it. "Last night the foreman of this gang received a policy directive issued by Lavester Limon of the Office of Procurement. For sheer imbecility this policy caps any of my experience."

"If it's Limon's doing, I can well believe it," said Ripp between his teeth.

"I sought him out in his office. He refused to accept responsibility and referred me to you."

Ripp sat a trifle straighter in his chair. "What policy is this?"

Luke passed the two directives across the desk. Ripp read slowly, then reluctantly returned the directives. "I fail to see exactly—" He paused. "I should say, these directives merely reflect instructions received by me which I have implemented. Where is the difficulty?"

"Let me cite my personal experience," said Luke. "This morning—as I say, in my temporary capacity as a flunky—I carried a shovel from tunnel head to warehouse and checked it. The operation required an hour and a half. If I were working steadily on a job of this sort, I'd be quite demoralized."

Ripp appeared untroubled. "I can only refer you to my superiors." He spoke aside into his desk phone. "Please transmit File OR9, Item 123." He turned back to Luke. "I can't take responsibility, either for the directive or for revoking it. May I ask what sort of investigation takes you down into the tunnels? And to whom you report?"

At a loss for words at once evasive and convincing, Luke conveyed an attitude of contemptuous silence.

Judiath Ripp contracted the skin around his blank round eyes in a frown. "As I consider this matter I become increasingly puzzled. Why is this subject a matter for investigation? Just who—"

From a slot appeared the directive Ripp had requested. He glanced at it, tossed it to Luke. "You'll see that this relieves me totally of responsibility," he said curtly.

The directive was the standard form:

PUBLIC WORKS DEPARTMENT, PUBLIC UTILITIES DIVISION

Office of
The Commissioner of Public Utilities

Policy Directive:	449 Series UA-14-G2
Order Code:	GZP—AAR—REF
Reference:	TQ9—1422
Date Code:	BP—EQ—LLT
Authorized:	PU-PUD-Org.
Checked:	G. Evan
Counterchecked:	Hernon Klanech
From:	Parris deVicker, Commissioner of Public Utilities
Through:	All District Agencies of Sanitary Works
To:	All Department Heads
Attention:	
Subject:	The urgent need for sharp and immediate economies in the use of equipment and consumption of supplies.
Instant of Application:	Immediate

Duration of Relevance: Permanent

Substance: All department heads are instructed to initiate, effect
                        and enforce rigid economies in the employment of sup-
                        plies and equipment, especially those items comprised
                        of or manufactured from alloy metals or requiring the
                        functional consumption of same, in those areas in
                        which official authority is exercised. A decrement of 2%
                        will be considered minimal. Status augmentation will
                        in some measure be affected by economies achieved.

Directive reviewed and transmitted: Lee Jon Smith, District Agent of
                                           Sanitary Works 8892

Luke rose to his feet, concerned now only to depart from the office as
quickly as possible. He indicated the directive. "This is a copy?"

"Yes."

"I'll take it, if I may." He included it with the previous two.

Judiath Ripp watched with a faint but definite suspicion. "I fail to understand
whom you represent."

"Sometimes the less one knows the better," said Luke.

The suspicion faded from Judiath Ripp's piscine face. Only a person secure
in his status could afford to use language of this sort to a member of the low
High Echelon. He nodded slightly. "Is that all you require?"

"No," said Luke, "but it's all I can get here."

He turned toward the door, feeling the rake of Ripp's eyes on his back.

Ripp's voice cut at him suddenly and sharply. "Just a moment."

Luke slowly turned.

"Who are you? Let me see your credentials."

Luke laughed coarsely. "I don't have any."

Judiath Ripp rose to his feet, stood towering with knuckles pressed on the
desk. Suddenly Luke saw that, after all, Judiath Ripp *was* choleric. His face,
mackerel-pale, became suffused with salmon-pink. "Identify yourself," he said
throatily, "before I call the watchman."

"Certainly," said Luke. "I have nothing to hide. I am Luke Grogatch. I
work as Class D Flunky on Tunnel Gang No. 3 out of the Bureau of Sewer
Construction and Maintenance."

"What are you doing here, misrepresenting yourself, wasting my time?"

"Where did I misrepresent myself?" demanded Luke in a contentious
voice. "I came here to find out why I had to carry my shovel to the warehouse
this morning. It cost me an hour and a half. It doesn't make sense. You've been

ordered to economize two percent, so I spend three hours a day carrying a shovel back and forth."

Judiath Ripp stared at Luke for ten seconds, then abruptly sat down. "You're a Class D Flunky?"

"That's right."

"Hmm. You've been to the Office of Procurement. The manager sent you here?"

"No. He gave me a copy of his directive, just as you did."

The salmon-pink flush had died from Ripp's flat cheeks. The carplike mouth twitched in infinitesimal amusement. "No harm in that, certainly. What do you hope to achieve?"

"I don't want to carry that blasted shovel back and forth. I'd like you to issue orders to that effect."

Judiath Ripp spread his pale mouth in a cold drooping smile. "Bring me a policy directive to that effect from Parris deVicker and I'll be glad to oblige you. Now—"

"Will you make an appointment for me?"

"An appointment?" Ripp was puzzled. "With whom?"

"With the Commissioner of Public Utilities."

"Pffah." Ripp waved his hand in cold dismissal. "Get out."

Luke stood in the blue-mosaic entry seething with hate for Ripp, Limon, Miskitman and every intervening functionary. If he were only Chairman of the Board for a brief two hours—went the oft-repeated daydream—how they'd quick-step! In his mind's eye he saw Judiath Ripp shoveling wads of 'wet waste' with a leaden shovel while a rotary driller, twice as noisy and twice as violent, blew back gales of hot dust and rock chips across his neck. Lavester Limon would be forced to change the smoking teeth of the drill with a small and rusty monkey wrench, while Fedor Miskitman, before and after the shift, carried shovel, monkey wrench and all the worn teeth to and from the warehouse.

Luke stood moping in the passage for five minutes, then escalated to the surface, which at this point, by virtue of Bramblebury Park, could clearly be distinguishable as the surface and not just another level among co-equal levels. He walked slowly along the gravel paths, ignoring the open sky for the immediacy of his problems. He faced a dead end. There was no further scope of action. Judiath Ripp mockingly had suggested that he consult the Commissioner of Public Utilities. Even if by some improbable circumstance he secured an appointment with the Commissioner, what good would ensue? Why should the Commissioner revoke a policy directive of such evident importance? Unless he could be persuaded—by some instrumentality Luke was unable to define or even imagine—to issue a special directive exempting Luke from the provision of the policy...

Luke chuckled hollowly, a noise which alarmed the pigeons strutting along the walk. Now what? Back to the dormitory. His dormitory privileges included twelve hours use of his cot per day, and he was not extracting full value from his expense account unless he made use of it. But Luke had no desire for sleep. As he glanced up at the perspective of the towers surrounding the park he felt a melancholy exhilaration. The sky, the wonderful clear open sky, blue and brilliant! Luke shivered, for the sun here was hidden by the Morgenthau Moonspike, and the air was brisk.

Luke crossed the park, thinking to sit where a band of hazy sunlight slashed down between the towers. The benches were crowded with blinking old men and women, but Luke presently found a seat. He sat looking up into the sky, enjoying the mild natural sun-warmth. How seldom did he see the sun! In his youth he had frequently set forth on long cross-city hikes, rambling high along the skyways, with space to right and left, the clouds near enough for intimate inspection, the sunlight sparkling and stinging his skin. Gradually the hikes had spread apart, coming at ever longer intervals, and now he could hardly remember when last he'd tramped the wind-lanes. What dreams he had had in those early days, what exuberant visions! Obstacles seemed trivial; he had seen himself clawing up the list, winning a good expense account, the choicest of perquisites, unnumbered Special Coupons! He had planned a private air-car, unrestricted nutrition, an apartment far above the surface, high and remote...Dreams. Luke had been victimized by his tongue, his quick temper, his obstinacy. At heart, he was no Nonconformist—no, cried Luke, never! Luke had been born of tycoon stock, and through influence, a word here, a hint there, had been launched into the Organization on a high status. But circumstances and Luke's chronic truculence had driven him into opposition with established ways, and down the Status List he had gone: through professional scholarships, technical trainee appointments, craft apprenticeships, all the varieties of semiskills and machine operation. Now he was Luke Grogatch, flunky, unskilled, Class D, facing the final declassification. But still too vain to carry a shovel. No: Luke corrected himself. His vanity was not at stake. Vanity he had discarded long ago, along with his youthful dreams. All he had left was pride, his right to use the word "I" in connection with himself. If he submitted to Policy Directive 6511 he relinquished this right; he combined with the masses of the

Organization as a spatter of foam falls back and is absorbed into the ocean…
Luke jerked nervously to his feet. He wasted time sitting here. Judiath Ripp,
with conger-like malice, had suggested a directive from the Commissioner
of Public Utilities. Very well, Luke would obtain that directive and fling it
down under Ripp's pale round nostrils.

How?

Luke rubbed his chin dubiously. He walked to a communication booth,
checked the directory. As he had surmised, the Commission of Public Utilities
was housed in the Organization Central Tower, in Silverado, District 3666,
ninety miles to the north.

Luke stood in the watery sunlight, hoping for inspiration. The aged idlers,
huddling on the benches like winterbound sparrows, watched him incuriously.
Once again Luke was obscurely pleased with his purchase of new clothes. A
fine figure he cut, he assured himself.

How? wondered Luke. How to gain an appointment with the Commissioner? How to persuade him to change his views?

No inkling of a solution presented itself.

He looked at his watch: still only middle morning. Ample time to visit
Organization Central and return in time to report for duty…Luke grimaced
wanly. Was his resolution so feeble, then? Was he, after all, to slink back into
the tunnel tonight carrying the hated shovel? Luke shook his head slowly. He
did not know.

At the Bramblebury Interchange Luke boarded an express highline north-
bound for Silverado Station. With a hiss and a whine, the shining metal worm
darted forward, sliding up to Level 13, flashing north at great speed, in and
out of the sunlight, through tunnels, across inter-tower chasms, with far below
the nervous seethe of the City. Four times the express sighed to a halt: at IBM
University, at Braemar, at Great Northern Junction, and finally, thirty minutes
out of Bramblebury, at Silverado Central. Luke disembarked; the express slid
away through the towers, lithe as an eel through waterweed.

Luke entered the tenth-level foyer of the Central Tower, a vast cave of
marble and bronze. Throngs of men and women thrust past him: grim striding
tycoons, stamped with the look of destiny, High Echelon personnel, their assistants, the assistants to their assistants, functionaries on down the list, all dutifully wearing high-status garments, the lesser folk hoping to be mistaken for
their superiors. All hurried, tense-faced and abrupt, partly from habit, partly
because only a person of low status had no need to hurry. Luke thrust and

elbowed with the best of them, and made his way to the central kiosk where he consulted a directory.

Parris deVicker, Commissioner of Public Utilities, had his office on Level 59. Luke passed him by and located the Secretary of Public Affairs, Mr. Sewell Sepp, on Level 81. No more underlings, thought Luke. This time I'm going to the top. If anyone can resolve this matter, it's Sewell Sepp.

He put himself aboard the lift and emerged into the lobby of the Department of Public Affairs—a splendid place, glittering with disciplined color and ornament after that mock-antique décor known as Second Institutional. The walls were of polished milk glass inset with medallions of shifting kaleidoscopic flashes. The floor was diapered in blue and white sparkle-stone. A dozen bronze statues dominated the room, massive figures symbolizing the basic public services: communication, transport, education, water, energy and sanitation. Luke skirted the pedestals, crossed to the reception counter, where ten young women in handsome brown and black uniforms stood with military precision, each to her six feet of counter top. Luke selected one of these girls, who curved her lips in an automatic empty smile. "Yes sir?"

"I want to see Mr. Sepp," said Luke brazenly.

The girl's smile remained frozen while she looked at him with startled eyes. "Mr. who?"

"Sewell Sepp, the Secretary of Public Affairs."

The girl asked gently, "Do you have an appointment, sir?"

"No."

"It's impossible, sir."

Luke nodded sourly. "Then I'll see Commissioner Parris deVicker."

"Do you have an appointment to see Mr. deVicker?"

"No, I'm afraid not."

The girl shook her head with a trace of amusement. "Sir, you can't just walk in on these people. They're extremely busy. Everyone must have an appointment."

"Oh come now," said Luke. "Surely it's conceivable that—"

"Definitely not, sir."

"Then," said Luke, "I'll make an appointment. I'd like to see Mr. Sepp some time today, if possible."

The girl lost interest in Luke. She resumed her manner of impersonal courtesy. "I'll call the office of Mr. Sepp's appointment secretary."

She spoke into a mesh, turned back to Luke. "No appointments are open this month, sir. Will you speak to someone else? Some under-official?"

"No," said Luke. He gripped the edge of the counter for a moment, started to turn away, then asked, "Who authorizes these appointments?"

"The secretary's first aide, who screens the list of applications."

"I'll speak to the first aide, then."

The girl sighed. "You need an appointment, sir."

"I need an appointment to make an appointment?"

"Yes, sir."

"Do I need an appointment to make an appointment for an appointment?"

"No, sir. Just walk right in."

"Where?"

"Suite 42, inside the rotunda, sir."

Luke passed through twelve-foot crystal doors, walked down a short hall. Scurrying patterns of color followed him like shadows along both the walls, grotesque cubistic shapes parodying the motion of his body: a whimsy which surprised Luke and might have pleased him under less critical circumstances.

He passed through another pair of crystal portals into the rotunda. Six levels above, a domed ceiling depicted scenes of legend in stained glass. Behind a ring of leather couches doors gave into surrounding offices; one of these doors, directly across from the entrance, bore the words:

Offices of the Secretary
Department of Public Affairs

On the couches half a hundred men and women waited, with varying degrees of patience. The careful disdain with which they surveyed each other suggested that their status was high; the frequency with which they consulted their watches conveyed the impression that they were momentarily on the point of departure.

A mellow voice sounded over a loudspeaker: "Mr. Artur Coff, please, to the Office of the Secretary." A plump gentleman threw down the periodical he had fretfully been examining, jumped to his feet. He crossed to the bronze and black glass door, passed through.

Luke watched him enviously, then turned aside through an arch marked *Suite 42*. An usher in a brown and black uniform stepped forward; Luke stated his business and was conducted into a small cubicle.

A young man behind a metal desk peered intently at him. "Sit down, please." He motioned to a chair. "Your name?"

"Luke Grogatch."

"Ah, Mr. Grogatch. May I inquire your business?"

"I have something to say to the Secretary of Public Affairs."

"Regarding what subject?"

"A personal matter."

"I'm sorry, Mr. Grogatch. The Secretary is more than busy. He's swamped with important Organization business. But if you'll explain the situation to me, I'll recommend you to an appropriate member of the staff."

"That won't help," said Luke. "I want to consult the Secretary in relation to a recently issued policy directive."

"Issued by the Secretary?"

"Yes."

"You wish to object to this directive?"

Luke grudgingly admitted as much.

"There are appropriate channels for this process," said the aide decisively. "If you will fill out this form—not here, but in the rotunda—drop it into the Suggestion Box to the right of the door as you go out—"

In sudden fury Luke wadded up the form, flung it down on the desk. "Surely he has five minutes free—"

"I'm afraid not, Mr. Grogatch," the aide said in a voice of ice. "If you will look through the rotunda you will see a number of very important people who have waited, some of them for months, for five minutes with the Secretary. If you wish to fill out an application, stating your business in detail, I will see that it receives due consideration."

Luke stalked out of the cubicle. The aide watched him go with a bleak smile of dislike. The man obviously had Nonconformist tendencies, he thought... probably should be watched.

Luke stood in the rotunda, muttering, "What now? What now? What now?" in a half-mesmerized undertone. He stared around the rotunda, at the pompous High Echelon folk, arrogantly consulting their watches and tapping their feet. "Mr. Jepper Prinn!" called the mellow voice over the loudspeaker. "The Office of the Secretary, if you please." Luke watched Jepper Prinn walk to the bronze and black glass portal.

Luke slumped into a chair, scratched his long nose, looked cautiously around the rotunda. Nearby sat a big, bull-necked man with a red face, protruding lips, a shock of rank blond hair—a tycoon, judging from his air of absolute authority.

Luke rose and went to a desk placed for the convenience of those waiting. He took several sheets of paper with the Tower letterhead, unobtrusively circled the rotunda to the entrance into Suite 42. The bull-necked tycoon paid him no heed.

Luke girded himself, closing his collar, adjusting the set of his jacket. He took a deep breath, then, when the florid man glanced in his direction, came forward officiously. He looked briskly around the circle of couches, consulting his papers; then catching the eye of the tycoon, frowned, squinted, walked forward.

"Your name, sir?" asked Luke in an official voice.

"I'm Hardin Arthur," rasped the tycoon. "Why?"

Luke nodded, consulted his paper. "The time of your appointment?"

"Eleven-ten. What of it?"

"The Secretary would like to know if you can conveniently lunch with him at one-thirty?"

Arthur considered. "I suppose it's possible," he grumbled. "I'll have to rearrange some other business…An inconvenience—but I can do it, yes."

"Excellent," said Luke. "At lunch the Secretary feels that he can discuss your business more informally and at greater length than at eleven-ten, when he can only allow you seven minutes."

"Seven minutes!" rumbled Arthur indignantly. "I can hardly spread my plans out in seven minutes."

"Yes sir," said Luke. "The Secretary realizes this, and suggests that you lunch with him."

Arthur petulantly hauled himself to his feet. "Very well. Lunch at one-thirty, correct?"

"Correct, sir. If you will walk directly into the Secretary's office at that time."

Arthur departed the rotunda, and Luke settled into the seat Arthur had vacated.

Time passed very slowly. At ten minutes after eleven the mellow voice called out, "Mr. Hardin Arthur, please. To the Office of the Secretary."

Luke rose to his feet, stalked with great dignity across the rotunda and through the bronze and black glass door.

Behind a long black desk sat the Secretary, a rather undistinguished man with gray hair and snapping gray eyes. He raised his eyebrows as Luke came forward: Luke evidently did not fit his preconception of Hardin Arthur.

The Secretary spoke. "Sit down, Mr. Arthur. I may as well tell you bluntly and frankly that we think your scheme is impractical. By 'we' I mean myself and the Board of Policy Evaluation—who of course have referred to the Files. First, the costs are excessive. Second, there's no guarantee that you can phase your program into that of our other tycoons. Third, the Board of Policy Evaluation tells me that Files doubts whether we'll need that much new capacity."

"Ah," Luke nodded wisely. "I see. Well, no matter. It's not important."

"Not important?" The Secretary sat up in his chair, stared at Luke in wonder. "I'm surprised to hear you say so."

Luke made an airy gesture. "Forget it. Life's too short to worry about these things. Actually there's another matter I want to discuss with you."

"Ah?"

"It may seem trivial, but the implications are large. A former employee called the matter to my attention. He's now a flunky on one of the sewer maintenance tunnel gangs, an excellent chap. Here's the situation. Some idiotic jack-in-office has issued a directive which forces this man to carry a shovel back and forth to the warehouse every day, before and after work. I've taken the trouble to follow up the matter and the chain leads here." He displayed his three policy directives.

Frowningly the Secretary glanced through them. "These all seem perfectly regular. What do you want me to do?"

"Issue a directive clarifying the policy. After all, we can't have these poor devils working three hours overtime for tomfoolishness."

"Tomfoolishness?" The Secretary was displeased. "Hardly that, Mr. Arthur. The economy directive came to me from the Board of Directors, from the Chairman himself, and if—"

"Don't mistake me," said Luke hastily. "I've no quarrel with economy; I merely want the policy applied sensibly. Checking a shovel into the warehouse—where's the economy in that?"

"Multiply that shovel by a million, Mr. Arthur," said the Secretary coldly.

"Very well, multiply it," argued Luke. "We have a million shovels. How many of these million shovels are conserved by this order? Two or three a year?"

The Secretary shrugged. "Obviously in a general directive of this sort, inequalities occur. So far as I'm concerned, I issued the directive because I was instructed to do so. If you want it changed you'll have to consult the Chairman of the Board."

"Very well. Can you arrange an appointment for me?"

"Let's settle the matter even sooner," said the Secretary. "Right now. We'll talk to him across the screen, although, as you say, it seems a trivial matter…"

"Demoralization of the working force isn't trivial, Secretary Sepp."

The Secretary shrugged, touched a button, spoke into a mesh. "The Chairman of the Board, if he's not occupied."

The screen glowed. The Chairman of the Board of Directors looked out at them. He sat in a lounge chair on the deck of his penthouse at the pinnacle of the tower. In one hand he held a glass of pale effervescent liquid; beyond him opened sunlight and blue air and a wide glimpse of the miraculous City.

"Good morning, Sepp," said the Chairman cordially, and nodded toward Luke. "Good morning to you, sir."

"Chairman, Mr. Arthur here is protesting the economy directive you sent down a few days ago. He claims that strict application is causing hardship among the labor force: demoralization, actually. Something to do with shovels."

The Chairman considered. "Economy directive? I hardly recall the exact case."

Secretary Sepp described the directive, citing code and reference numbers, explaining the provisions, and the Chairman nodded in recollection. "Yes, the metal-shortage thing. Afraid I can't help you, Sepp, or you, Mr. Arthur. Policy Evaluation sent it up. Apparently we're running short of minerals; what else can we do? Cinch in the old belts, eh? Hard on all of us. What's this about shovels?"

"It's the whole matter," cried Luke in sudden shrillness, evoking startled glances from Secretary and Chairman. "Carrying a shovel back and forth to the warehouse three hours a day! It's not economy, it's a disorganized farce!"

"Come now, Mr. Arthur," the Chairman chided humorously. "So long as you're not carrying the shovel yourself why the excitement? It works the very devil with one's digestion. Until Policy Evaluation changes its collective mind—as it often does—then we've got to string along. Can't go counter to Policy Evaluation, you know. They're the people with the facts and figures."

"Neither here nor there," mumbled Luke. "Carrying a shovel three hours—"

"Perhaps a bit of bother for the men concerned," said the Chairman with a hint of impatience, "but they've got to see the thing from the long view. Sepp, perhaps you'll lunch with me? A marvelous day, lazy weather."

"Thank you, Mr. Chairman. I'll be pleased indeed."

"Excellent. At one or one-thirty, whenever convenient for you."

The screen went blank. Secretary Sepp rose to his feet. "There it is, Mr. Arthur. I can't do any more."

"Very well, Mr. Secretary," said Luke in a hollow voice.

"Sorry I can't be of more help in the other matter, but as I say—"

"It's inconsequential."

Luke turned, left the elegant office, passed through the bronze and black glass doors into the rotunda. Through the arch into Suite 42 he saw a large bull-necked man, tomato-red in the face, hunched forward across a counter. Luke stepped forward smartly, leaving the rotunda just as the authentic Mr. Arthur and the aide came forth, deep in agitated conversation.

Luke stopped by the information desk. "Where is the Policy Evaluation Board?"

"Level 29, sir, this building."

In Policy Evaluation on Level 29 Luke talked with a silk-mustached young man, courtly and elegant, with the status classification *Plan Coordinator*. "Certainly!" exclaimed the young man in response to Luke's question. "Authoritative information is the basis of authoritative organization. Material from Files is collated, digested in the Bureau of Abstracts and sent up to us. We shape it and present it to the Board of Directors in the form of a daily précis."

Luke expressed interest in the Bureau of Abstracts, and the young man quickly became bored. "Grubbers among the statistics, barely able to compose an intelligible sentence. If it weren't for us—" His eyebrows, silken as his mustache, hinted of the disasters which in the absence of Policy Evaluation would overtake the Organization. "They work in a suite down on the Sixth Level."

Luke descended to the Bureau of Abstracts, and found no difficulty gaining admission to the general office. In contrast to the rather nebulous intellectualism of Policy Evaluation, the Bureau of Abstracts seemed workaday and matter-of-fact. A middle-aged woman, cheerfully fat, inquired Luke's business, and when Luke professed himself a journalist, conducted him about the premises. They went from the main lobby, walled in antique cream-colored plaster with gold scrollwork, past the small fusty cubicles, where clerks sat at projection-desks scanning ribbons of words, extracting idea-sequences, emending, excising, condensing, cross-referring, finally producing the abstract to be submitted to Policy Evaluation. Luke's fat and cheerful guide brewed them a pot of tea; she asked questions which Luke answered in general terms, straining his voice and pursing his mouth in the effort to seem agreeable and hearty. He himself asked questions. "I'm interested in a set of statistics on the scarcity of metals, or ores, or something similar which recently went up to Policy Evaluation. Would you know anything about this?"

"Heavens no," the woman responded. "There's just too much material coming in—the business of the entire Organization."

"Where does this material come from? Who sends it to you?"

The woman made a humorous little grimace of distaste. "From Files, down on Sublevel 12. I can't tell you much, because we don't associate with the personnel. They're low status: clerks and the like. Sheer automatons."

Luke expressed an interest in the source of the Bureau of Abstracts' information. The woman shrugged, as if to say, everyone to his own taste. "I'll call down to the Chief File Clerk; I know him, very slightly."

The Chief File Clerk, Mr. Sidd Boatridge, was self-important and brusque, as if aware of the low esteem in which he was held by the Bureau of Abstracts. He dismissed Luke's questions with a stony face of indifference. "I really have no idea, sir. We file, index, and cross-index material into the Information Bank, but concern ourselves very little with outgoing data. My duties in fact are mainly administrative. I'll call in one of the under-clerks; he can tell you more than I can."

The under-clerk who answered Boatridge's summons was a short turnip-faced man with matted red hair. "Take Mr. Grogatch into the outer office," said the Chief File Clerk testily. "He wants to ask you a few questions."

In the outer office, out of the Chief File Clerk's hearing, the under-clerk became rather surly and pompous, as if he had divined the level of Luke's status. He referred to himself as a "line-tender" rather than a "file clerk", the latter apparently being a classification of lesser prestige. His "line-tending" consisted of sitting beside a panel which glowed and blinked with a thousand orange and green lights. "The orange lights indicate information going down into the Bank," said the file clerk. "The green lights show where somebody up-level is drawing information out—generally at the Bureau of Abstracts."

Luke observed the orange and green flickers for a moment. "What information is being transmitted now?"

"Couldn't say," the file clerk grunted. "It's all coded. Down in the old office we had a monitoring machine and never used it. Too much else to do."

Luke considered. The file clerk showed signs of restiveness. Luke's mind worked hurriedly. He asked, "So—as I understand it—you file information, but have nothing further to do with it?"

"We file it and code it. Whoever wants information puts a program into the works and the information goes out to him. We never see it, unless we went and looked in the old monitoring machine."

"Which is still down at your old office?"

The file clerk nodded. "They call it the staging chamber now. Nothing there but input and output pipes, the monitor, and the custodian."

"Where is the staging chamber?"

"Way down the levels, behind the Bank. Too low for me to work. I got more ambition." For emphasis he spat on the floor.

"A custodian is there, you say?"

"An old junior executive named Dodkin. He's been there a hundred years."

Luke dropped thirty levels aboard an express lift, then rode the down escalator another six levels to Sublevel 48. He emerged on a dingy landing, a low-perquisite nutrition hall to one side, a lift-attendants dormitory to the other. The air carried the familiar reek of the deep underground, a compound of dank concrete, phenol, mercaptans, a discreet but pervasive human smell. Luke realized with bitter amusement that he had returned to familiar territory.

Following instructions grudgingly detailed by the under-file clerk, Luke stepped aboard a chattering man-belt labeled '902—Tanks'. Presently he came to a brightly-lit landing marked by a black and yellow sign: *Information Tanks: Technical Station.* Inside the door a number of mechanics sat on stools, dangling their legs, lounging, chaffering.

Luke changed to a side-belt, even more dilapidated, almost in a state of disrepair. At the second junction—this unmarked—he left the man-belt, turned down a narrow passage toward a far yellow bulb. The passage was silent, almost sinister in its disassociation from the life of the City.

Below the single yellow bulb a dented metal door was daubed with a sign:

Information Tanks: Staging Chamber
No Admittance

Luke tested the door and found it locked. He rapped and waited.

Silence shrouded the passage, broken only by a faint sound from the distant man-belt.

Luke rapped again, and now from within came a shuffle of movement. The door slid back, a pale placid eye looked forth. A rather weak voice inquired, "Yes sir?"

Luke attempted a manner of easy authority. "You're Dodkin the custodian?"

"Yes, sir, I'm Dodkin."

"Open up, please, I'd like to come in."

The pale eye blinked in mild wonder. "This is only the staging room, sir. There's nothing here to see. The storage complexes are around to the front; if you'll go back to the junction—"

Luke broke into the flow of words. "I've just come down from Files; it's you I want to see."

The pale eye blinked once more; the door slid open. Luke entered the long narrow concrete-floored staging room. Conduits dropped from the ceiling by the thousands, bent, twisted and looped, entered the wall, each conduit labeled with a dangling metal tag. At one end of the room was a grimy cot where Dodkin apparently slept; at the other end was a long black desk: the monitoring machine? Dodkin himself was small and stooped, but moved nimbly in spite of his evident age. His white hair was stained but well brushed; his gaze, weak and watery, was without guile, and fixed on Luke with an astronomer's detachment. He opened his mouth, and words quavered forth in spate, with Luke vainly seeking to interrupt.

"Not often do visitors come from above. Is something wrong?"

"No, nothing wrong."

"They should tell me if aught isn't correct, or perhaps there's been new policies of which I haven't been notified."

"Nothing like that, Mr. Dodkin. I'm just a visitor—"

"I don't move out as much as I used to, but last week I—"

Luke pretended to listen while Dodkin maundered on in obbligato to Luke's bitter thoughts. The continuity of directives leading from Fedor Miskitman to Lavester Limon to Judiath Ripp, by-passing Parris deVicker to Sewell Sepp and the Chairman of the Board, then returning down the classifications, down the levels through the Policy Evaluation Board, the Bureau of Abstracts, the File Clerk's Office—the continuity had finally ended; the thread he had traced with such forlorn hope seemed about to lose itself. Well, Luke told himself, he had accepted Miskitman's challenge; he had failed, and now was faced with his original choice. Submit, carry the wretched shovel back and forth to the warehouse, or defy the order, throw down his shovel, assert himself as a free-willed man, and be declassified, to become a junior executive like old Dodkin—who, sucking and wheezing, still rambled on in compulsive loquacity.

"...something incorrect, I'd never know, because who ever tells me? From year end to year end I'm quiet down here and there's no one to relieve me, and I only get to the up-side rarely, once a fortnight or so, but then once you've seen the sky, does it ever change? And the sun, the marvel of it, but once you've seen a marvel—"

Luke drew a deep breath. "I'm investigating an item of information which reached the File Clerk's Office. I wonder if you can help me."

Dodkin blinked his pale eyes. "What item is this, sir? Naturally I'll be glad to help in any way, even though—"

"The item dealt with economy in the use of metals and metal tools."

Dodkin nodded. "I remember the item perfectly."

It was Luke's turn to stare. "You *remember* this item?"

"Certainly. It was, if I may say so, one of my little interpolations. A personal observation which I included among the other material."

"Would you be kind enough to explain?"

Dodkin would be only too pleased to explain. "Last week I had occasion to visit an old friend over by Claxton Abbey, a fine Conformist, well adapted and cooperative, even if, alas, like myself, a junior executive. Of course, I mean no disrespect to good Davy Evans, like myself about ready for the pension—though little enough they allow nowadays..."

"The interpolation?"

"Yes, indeed. On my way home along the man-belt—on Sublevel 32, as I recall—I saw a workman of some sort—perhaps an electrical technician—toss several tools into a crevice on his way off-shift. I thought, now there's a slovenly act—disgraceful! Suppose the man forgot where he had hidden his tools? They'd be lost! Our reserves of raw metallic ore are very low—that's common knowledge—and every year the ocean water becomes weaker and more dilute. That man had no regard for the future of Organization. We should cherish our natural resources, do you not agree, sir?"

"I agree, naturally. But—"

"In any event, I returned here and added a memorandum to that effect into the material which goes up to the Assistant File Clerk. I thought that perhaps he'd be impressed and say a word to someone with influence—perhaps the Head File Clerk. In any event, there's the tale of my interpolation. Naturally I attempted to give it weight by citing the inevitable diminution of our natural resources."

"I see," said Luke. "And do you frequently include interpolations into the day's information?"

"Occasionally," said Dodkin, "and sometimes, I'm glad to say, people more important than I share my views. Only three weeks ago I was delayed several minutes on my way between Claxton Abbey and Kittsville on Sublevel 30. I made a note of it, and last week I noticed that construction has commenced on a new eight-lane man-belt between the two points, a really magnificent and modern undertaking. A month ago I noticed a shameless group of girls daubed like savages with cosmetic. What a waste! I told myself, what vanity and folly! I hinted as much in a little message to the Under-File Clerk. I seem to be just one of the many with these views, for two days later a general order discouraging these petty vanities was issued by the Secretary of Education."

"Interesting," Luke muttered. "Interesting indeed. How do you include these 'interpolations' into the information?"

Dodkin hobbled nimbly to the monitoring machine, beckoned. "The output from the tanks comes through here. I print a bit on the typewriter and tuck it in where the Under-Clerk will see it."

"Admirable," sighed Luke. "A man with your intelligence should have ranked higher in the Status List."

Dodkin shook his placid old head. "I don't have the ambition nor the ability. I'm fit for just this simple job, and only barely. I'd take my pension tomorrow, only the Chief File Clerk asked me to stay on a bit until he could find a man to take my place. No one seems to like the quiet down here."

"Perhaps you'll have your pension sooner than you think," said Luke.

✻•✻

Luke strolled along the glossy tube, ringed with alternate pale and dark refractions like a bull's-eye. Ahead was motion, the glint of metal, the mutter of voices. The entire crew of Tunnel Gang No. 3 stood idle and restless.

Fedor Miskitman waved his arm with uncharacteristic vehemence. "Grogatch! At your post! You've held up the entire crew!" His heavy face was suffused with pink. "Four minutes already we're behind schedule."

Luke strolled closer.

"Hurry!" bellowed Miskitman. "What do you think this is, a blasted promenade?"

If anything Luke slackened his pace. Fedor Miskitman lowered his big bull-head, staring balefully. Luke halted in front of him.

"Where's your shovel?" Fedor Miskitman asked.

"I don't know," said Luke. "I'm here on the job. It's up to you to provide tools."

Fedor Miskitman stared unbelievingly. "Didn't you take it to the warehouse?"

"Yes," said Luke. "I took it there. If you want it, go get it."

Fedor Miskitman opened his mouth. He roared, "Get off the job!"

"Just as you like," said Luke. "You're the foreman."

"Don't come back!" bellowed Miskitman. "I'll report you before the day is out. You won't gain status from me, I tell you that!"

"'Status'?" Luke laughed. "Go ahead. Cut me down to junior executive. Do you think I care? No. And I'll tell you why. There's going to be a change or two made. When things seem different to you, think of me."

Luke Grogatch, Junior Executive, said good-by to the retiring custodian of the staging chamber. "Don't thank me, not at all," said Luke. "I'm here by my own doing. In fact—well, never mind all that. Go up-side, sit in the sun, enjoy the air."

Finally Dodkin, in mingled joy and sorrow, hobbled for the last time down the musty passageway to the chattering man-belt.

Luke was alone in the staging chamber. Around his ears hummed the near-inaudible rush of information. From behind the wall came the sense of a million relays clicking, twitching, meshing; of cylinders and trace-tubes and memory-lanes whirring with activity. At the monitoring machine the output streamed forth on a reel of yellow tape. Nearby rested the typewriter.

Luke seated himself. His first interpolation...what should it be? Freedom for the Nonconformists? Tunnel-gang foremen to carry tools for the entire crew? A higher expense account for junior executives?

Luke rose to his feet and scratched his chin. Power...to be subtly applied. How should he use it? To secure rich perquisites for himself? Yes, of course, this he would accomplish, by devious means. And then—what? Luke thought of the billions of men and women living and working in the Organization. He looked at the typewriter. He could shape their lives, change their thoughts, disorganize the Organization. Was this wise? Or right? Or even amusing?

Luke sighed. In his mind's eye he saw himself standing on a high terrace overlooking the city. Luke Grogatch, Chairman of the Board. Not impossible, quite feasible. A little at a time, the correct interpolations...Luke Grogatch, Chairman of the Board. Yes. This for a starter. But it was necessary to move cautiously, with great delicacy...

Luke seated himself at the typewriter and began to pick out his first interpolation.

Afterword to "Dodkin's Job"

After my eyes went, my life became much simplified. Our travels became a thing of the past, apart from the occasional junket to a convention. I continued to write, although since longhand was obviously no longer possible, I learned to use a word processor. John modified computers with special keyboards I could feel my way around, and with what little eyesight I had left I could make out words on the monitor if they were big enough—enlarged to about ten words per screen! Eventually, however, I became totally blind and had to rely on the computer's voice synthesizer to read back what I had written. I wrote most of *Lyonesse* this way, and everything after that—*Cadwal, Night Lamp, Ports of Call* and *Lurulu*. I have no way of knowing for certain, but I may well be the only writer who bypassed the typewriter completely, going straight from longhand to computer! Still, the computer was never a perfect solution for me and writing became an increasingly laborious process as the last ray of my eyesight went glimmering. I never considered dictating my novels to tape...After *Lurulu* I retired from writing fiction. Finishing *Lurulu*—which I like to call my "swansong"—was like going through triage...That guy who wrote all that junk for so many years—he seems like another person!

—Jack Vance